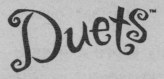

Duets™

Two brand-new stories in every volume... twice a month!

Duets Vol. #59

What could be better than *one* sexy hero who wants like heck to avoid marriage? How about *two?* Talented mother-and-daughter writing team Jennifer Drew is back with a hilarious Double Duets with linked stories about bad-boy twin brothers Cole and Zack Bailey—and the women who catch 'em!

Duets Vol. #60

Look for an exciting Western theme in this volume! Silhouette Romance author Gayle Kaye makes her Duets debut with a fun, sassy story. Joining her is new author Anne Gracie who takes us to Montana and gorgeous sheriff J. T. Stone. Enjoy!

Be sure to pick up both Duets volumes today!

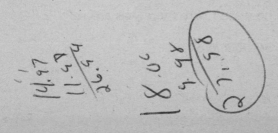

Kiss That Cowboy!

The lady wore a blush.

Candace had hurriedly buttoned her blouse, though she hadn't quite gotten the buttons in the right holes. Tanner thought there was something awfully touching about that.

"Come here and let me fix you up, sweetheart."

She followed his gaze to the front of her blouse. "I'm sure you'd just *unbutton* it, Tanner."

"You got that right, darlin'."

But Tanner suspected he'd better keep his hands off and maybe thank Dolly, the big horse who'd disrupted their fun in the barn to begin with, for returning the two of them to reality before anything more had happened.

"C'mon," he said, "let's give Dolly a few turns around the paddock to be sure she's over her malady," he suggested.

Tanner wasn't too sure he was over his malady, however. He had a definite case of the hots for Candy Porter.

And he wasn't sure there was a cure.

For more, turn to page 9

How the Sheriff Was Won

"Don't you dare touch me!"

A female arsonist? J.T. pulled out his flashlight, snapped it on and stared. It was the woman from the bus this morning. He frowned and reached forward to help her up off the floor.

"I'm warning you, buster. The sheriff of this town is a friend of mine, a very *close,* personal friend." She squinted, as if trying to gauge the effect of her speech.

J.T. paused. She was threatening him with *himself?*

She sounded about twelve years old. She looked about twelve, too, in those Road Runner print pajamas. One of her feet was bare, the other sported a fluffy slipper with the face of a dog.

Road Runner pajamas and fluffy slippers? What the hell was an arsonist doing in those?

"Okay, lady. Who are you and what are you doing in the Globe offices at this hour?"

"Who are *you* and what right do you have to ask me stupid questions?"

"Sheriff Stone at your service, ma'am."

Her jaw dropped.

"Why, Sheriff Stone, I'm Jassie McQuilty, the new owner of the Globe."

For more, turn to page 197

HARLEQUIN DUETS

ISBN 0-373-44126-6

KISS THAT COWBOY!
Copyright © 2001 by Gayle Kasper

HOW THE SHERIFF WAS WON
Copyright © 2001 by Anne Dunn

This edition published by arrangement with Harlequin Books S.A.

® and TM are trademarks of the publisher. Trademarks indicated with
® are registered in the United States Patent and Trademark Office, the
Canadian Trade Marks Office and in other countries.

Visit us at www.eHarlequin.com

Printed in U.S.A.

Kiss That Cowboy!

Gayle Kaye

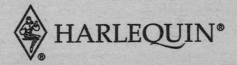

HARLEQUIN®

TORONTO • NEW YORK • LONDON
AMSTERDAM • PARIS • SYDNEY • HAMBURG
STOCKHOLM • ATHENS • TOKYO • MILAN • MADRID
PRAGUE • WARSAW • BUDAPEST • AUCKLAND

Dear Reader,

Ever wonder about the cowboy myth? Why this romantic figure has endured through the years? Whether he wears a white hat or a black hat he holds our appeal.

In *Kiss That Cowboy!* I sent my heroine, Candace Porter, off to Texas Hill Country to find out why. I gave her a problem or two—she's a sophisticated city girl from back East who doesn't believe the myth of the cowboy and sets out to debunk the fantasy. She's never met a cowboy, never attended a rodeo and is afraid of horses. She wears pink cowboy boots and pearls at her neck—and she's totally unprepared for her clash with the rugged, handsome, virile Texas cowboy, Tanner Carson. But can two polar opposites ever get things right?

I hope you enjoy their story and fall in love with Tanner Carson as I did.

Happy reading!

Gayle Kaye

Books by Gayle Kaye

SILHOUETTE ROMANCE

To Cathy Helvey and Jeff Langle—
thanks for sharing your beautiful
Texas Hill Country with me.

And to Mamie—
the newest member of our little family.
Welcome, sweetheart.

1

CANDACE PORTER slipped off her glasses, which made her look more studious than sexy, skewered up her usual plucky courage and stepped through the door of Gunslinger's. She needed a table where she could observe—and not stick out like the sore thumb that she was.

At the edge of the dance floor she spotted just the right vantage point—an eagle-eye view of the line of cowboys at the bar, nursing their long necks and hoping to get lucky.

The place throbbed with the strains of a country-and-western band playing at the front of the room. The walls shuddered from the beat, and the roof rose a good inch, maybe two. Her gaze scanned the broad shoulders and straining denim, the cowboy hats tipped at the required cocky angle.

Nothing.

Not one of the group elicited even a tiny flutter of her feminine heart—and she knew her project was going to be the success she'd envisioned. Her new article, an opinion piece for *Millennium Woman Magazine,* would soon prove her theory that cowboys were no sexier than the other males of the world. Texas testosterone was no more potent than any other.

She was certain *that* was just the fantasy of some women—and had no basis in fact. A few weeks observing the western male in his natural habitat and she'd have enough data to prove her point and write her article.

"What can I get you?"

Candace put her thoughts on hold and glanced up at the barmaid standing over her.

"A glass of white wine, please," she ordered, then gave an uneasy glance around. She wasn't in Connecticut now, sipping wine at a fancy cocktail party. This was hard-drinking territory—and she'd just branded herself an outsider. One quick glance at the barmaid's raised eyebrow confirmed it.

"This ain't the country club, sweetie, but I'll see what I can do."

So much for keeping a low profile.

She anchored a red-gold curl behind her ear, crossed one slim leg over the other and leaned back in her seat. She'd come here to observe the Texas cowboy, explode the myth about his sexual appeal. And Candace was good at what she did.

Her work was thorough—and no-nonsense.

She prided herself on that.

By the time her white wine had arrived and she'd taken a few sips, she began to relax. Again her gaze traveled to the group at the bar. Still nothing to stir her feminine juices or stimulate one fantasy—even a mild one.

The men had begun to pair off with women—all except the man at the end. He sat alone, a little apart from the others, his predatory gaze sweeping the room—no doubt for an available female.

Her heart skipped a beat, then thunked against her rib cage as that gaze came to an abrupt halt.

On her.

She tried to glance away, but her breath caught. Against all reason, a slow, erotic fantasy began to take shape in her head. She must have had one sip too many. Yes, that was it.

She shoved the glass away from her.

The room was warm, the noise level high, the crowd packed in tightly. But the solitary cowboy at the bar seemed unperturbed by any of it. He looked at ease in the place, one booted heel hooked on the rung of the bar stool, his body loose and lean and male confident. His face—what she could see of it beneath his black Stetson—was hard angles and planes, his eyes dark and probing, his lips full and…seductive. For one wild, crazy moment she wondered what they would feel like against her skin, flushed from want and need and sex.

She drew her gaze away from his mouth, her mind away from the unwanted fantasy. Their eyes met and held, then he winked.

Broadly.

Boldly.

At her.

She gave a small gasp and quickly turned away, praying he hadn't been able to read her wanton thoughts, fearing he had. With chin held high, she swung her attention toward the dance floor, hoping to find the subject matter there less distracting.

She needed to remain cool, detached, if she was going to make her article a success, prove her theory.

The line dancing ended, and the band began a slow, earthy number about long, hot nights and unrequited love.

"Care to dance?"

She didn't need to look up to know that the low, rumbly voice belonged to the man at the bar, her every nerve ending aware that he was standing there beside her. She sensed his hot, restless gaze, his lean, hard body.

She should no more follow him onto the dance floor than she should strip naked in the middle of the highway out front. A half-dozen excuses came to mind, but Candace couldn't find her voice. No matter how hard she tried, she couldn't articulate a word.

Just one dance, she decided with some sentient part of her brain—then she was outta here. The bar was too full of diversions, not the best place to begin, after all.

Tomorrow she'd try again.

Somewhere safer.

He led her onto the dance floor, his hand finding the small of her back, then he pulled her close. Her heart ricocheted in her chest. A rivulet of perspiration trickled between her breasts.

"Relax, darlin'," he drawled, "you're as stiff as a spine on a Texas cactus."

Easy for him to say. He wasn't being held by six tall feet of male hormone and hard muscle. "Uh, it's a little warm in here, that's all."

He drew back and gazed down at her. His eyes were dark—like blue denim, she realized. His jaw was square, his skin tanned, a man comfortable with hard work and rugged weather.

And easy women, no doubt.

It didn't take any stretch of her imagination to envision a full bevy of willing females hankering after him.

A slow smile spread across his sexy mouth and quirked at the edges. He raised one eyebrow invitingly. "We can step outside, take a look at the stars...."

Candace had no intention of looking at the stars or anything else with this man, not with the way the wine had gone to her head, impairing her senses, inciting her usually docile hormones. "On second thought, I—I'm fine," she lied.

He tipped her chin up. His heated gaze swept her face. "I'll agree with that, darlin'."

That low voice reverberated through her, and she missed a step. Her docile hormones took flight. She needed to get back some semblance of equanimity, aplomb, self-possession. "You probably say that to all the girls who come in here."

"Nope—only the pretty ones."

For a moment she thought she saw sincerity shining in his dark eyes, then decided it had to be a trick of the light. She wasn't into suddenly believing that men had an honesty streak a mile wide.

She knew they didn't.

"A line that usually gets you what you want?" she asked.

The corners of his mouth lifted in a grin. "Sometimes. Not always."

That slow, easy grin had its effect on her.

She should have stuck with something nonalcoholic to drink, considering the way this man could rattle her senses, thwart her good judgment.

"So, what brings you into a place like this?" he continued. "You don't look the type for a female on the prowl. Although—" he paused "—you *did* seem to be checking out every cowboy in the room."

Candace sucked in a breath. Had she been so obvious? She'd hoped to go unnoticed, blend into the woodwork. Heat raced up her cheeks. She hadn't come here to…connect with some cowboy—but to quietly, unobtrusively gather her facts, perceptions, impressions.

That, however, was not something she intended to share with this man.

"Sorry to disappoint you—but I wasn't looking for someone to take home." That, at least, was the truth. "Can you say the same?"

That slow, easy grin worked its way onto his mouth again, that thoroughly sensual, lusty mouth. "Are you offering?"

Her spine stiffened and her pride bristled. "Most certainly not," she answered primly.

Prim usually put a man off, discouraged his attention, dampened his ardor, but this man...

Just then the song ended—and if she knew what was good for her, so would her evening. She'd had her one dance with him. Her little project had hit a brick wall, at least for tonight. She needed to leave—and retrieve her sanity, which she seemed to have checked at the door.

"How about another dance?" he asked.

"Um—sorry. I really need to go."

His denim eyes held a hint of disappointment—or maybe she'd just imagined it. Tonight her perception was definitely off.

"Cinderella at the ball?" He fingered a curl that had fallen against her cheek. His touch was electric—too electric. "It's not midnight yet."

A dimple showed in his right cheek. She hadn't noticed it before—or maybe she'd been too busy noticing other parts of him. "Let's just say I need my beauty sleep."

"Darlin', you're more than all right in the looks department."

Texas men had a way of making a woman fall for their charm. She'd have to put that in her article.

As a warning.

She headed for her table, determined to retrieve her things and leave. His hand touched her back, guiding her through the crowd. Slow heat raced through her veins and tripped over her nerve endings. The next time she set out to prove her theory, she'd omit the dancing—especially with a man who couldn't help her project in the slightest.

"So tell me, where are you from?" he asked.

They'd reached her table. She picked up her purse and placed the thin strap over one shoulder. "Why do you think I'm *from* somewhere?"

He gave a wry smile and gestured at the half-empty glass on the table. "How about the white wine, for starters?"

Definitely not a drink for this bar. She should have ordered a light beer—although "light" probably wasn't an inconspicuous choice around this place, either.

Since he'd so neatly pegged her an outsider, she might as well confess. "Connecticut."

"That explains the accent."

He had the accent—that slow, sweep-over-you Texas drawl. She'd spent too many summers with her grandparents in Chicago to have a hint of her eastern accent remain.

"Texas is a long way from home," he continued. "What brings you down here?"

What could she tell him? That she'd come to prove her theory about the cowboy, explode his mystique, peel away his sexual armor, bring truth to the question, Do cowboys do it better?

No man took well to having his sexuality probed—certainly not this cowboy. Nor, Candace was sure, would the rest of his breed.

She raised her chin. "I'm here on vacation," she said. "Now, I really must go."

He looked as if he had more questions, a curiosity to satisfy—about her. "I'll walk you to your car."

"Not necessary—I've been doing it myself for years."

Before he could say more she headed for the door, leaving him standing there, watching after her.

Once she was outside she let out a breathy sigh. The man's musky, male scent still invaded her senses, the feel of his sheltering arms wrapped around her.

Okay, so maybe she'd found *one* cowboy with sex appeal.

Or maybe it was just the night—and one sip of wine too many.

Next time she'd try someplace else to explore her theory—like the *library*. She doubted the place would have a heavy concentration of single, good-looking Texas males, but it would definitely be safer.

TANNER CARSON watched the lady sashay out the door and resisted the urge to go after her. He'd have liked one more dance, one more gaze into her sultry green eyes. He'd seen a smoldering passion in them, a passion waiting to be awakened.

And damned if he wouldn't like to be the man who got the job.

But Tanner knew—only too well—a woman like that could be trouble. He'd had his one dance with her. Now it was time to forget her.

But her image was determined to die a slow death.

The subtle fragrance of her perfume still clung to the front of his shirt—something that reminded him of spring lilacs. Her body, so slender yet rounded in all the right places, was imprinted there, as well.

The moment he'd drawn her against him, his groin had tightened into a sweet ache, the likes of which he hadn't felt in a while.

A *long* while.

Her reddish-gold hair had tickled his nose as he'd held her close, her head coming to rest at the angle of his jaw. Her legs, as long and promising as a new colt's, were barely hidden by that sassy short skirt of hers.

The ache in his groin hadn't dissipated—and wouldn't—unless he dashed all thought of tonight and the woman he'd danced with.

He needed a drink. Not a beer, but a stiff shot of

bourbon, maybe two. With luck that would dull a few memory cells.

But after downing a double he found he wasn't in the mood for tying one on. Besides, he had too much work to do around the ranch for a hangover in the morning. He was still trying to make the place pay. He had two mares about ready to foal. And more miles of fence to repair than he wanted to think about.

Shoving his drink aside, he settled up his tab and headed for the door—but he didn't kid himself that he'd had enough whiskey to forget one redhead he was sure would linger in his thoughts way past morning.

"I CAN'T BELIEVE you went to that bar alone. I hate to hurt your feelings, Candace Porter, but you're a greenhorn city girl. And ripe pickin's for that horde of hardworkin', hard-playin' rowdies who hang out there."

Candace braced herself in the passenger seat as her friend Darcy Garrett scarcely avoided hitting yet another rut in the road. She had no idea Texas Hill Country could be so crisscrossed with back roads, but Darcy seemed to know them all. Her battered red truck fairly flew over them—leaving a trailing plume of dust behind as it went.

Candace had heard Darcy's rebuke already—and she doubted her friend would give up on it any time soon. Not until she was convinced Candace wouldn't do anything else foolish in the name of journalism.

Instead Darcy'd come up with a better idea, one that involved dragging Candace over these mean back roads while she tended to every ranch critter with an ailment for miles around.

But Candace had to admit it was a chance for this "greenhorn city girl" to meet the cowboy—up close and personal.

But five ranches—and a dozen or more cowboys—later, Candace was sorely tempted to let the fantasy of the western male live unchallenged.

She was hot, tired and dusty. The only thing that sounded good to her at the moment was a long soak in Darcy's quaint, claw-footed bathtub.

She and Darcy had been friends since college— but if the day didn't end soon that friendship could be in question.

The two had been roommates at Northwestern University—Darcy, her heart set on becoming a large-animal vet, and Candace working toward her journalism degree. She'd been full of dreams in those days, both of them had.

But Candace had lost a few of those dreams. Love, the kind between a man and a woman, with no broken promises…maybe children someday.

Inane notions, Candace now knew. She preferred to pour herself into her work. Work was safe. Work wouldn't leave her high and dry.

Lost.

"Just one more stop," Darcy said, pulling Candace out of her dogged thoughts. "The Silver Spur Ranch, just this side of Johnson City. The owner there has two mares about ready to foal. I want to reassure myself everything will go as planned when it's time for delivery."

Candace groaned. "Just tell me there are no more men for me to meet at this Silver Spur Ranch. I've seen enough for one day."

She rubbed her temples where a headache had begun to throb. So far she hadn't met a single cowboy who could raise her feminine libido past complacency.

Oh, a few had definitely been good-looking, with work-hard muscles, wide, capable shoulders—and an old-fashioned, tip-your-hat-to-a-lady kind of gallantry about them.

Candace supposed these attributes could make a woman's senses stand up and take notice, but she hadn't exactly been bowled over.

She had, however, taken careful notes, which she'd review later while ensconced comfortably on Darcy's back porch, sipping a tall glass of iced tea.

"Not so fast, Candace Porter, there's one more case in point I want you to meet. And I've saved the best until last."

Candace was sure that had an ominous ring to it—but she had no choice but to go along. Darcy's old truck had just hurtled through the entrance to the big Silver Spur Ranch. Rows of fences stretched into the distance, as if to keep in the prickly cacti that dotted the terrain. Live oaks vied for life among scruffy cedar trees.

About a half mile up the road the truck bounced to a stop in front of a sprawling ranch house. Darcy gave a quick sound of the horn, and a tall hunk of a cowboy sauntered out from the stables into the afternoon sunlight.

An all-too-familiar cowboy.

Candace gave a quick gasp.

If possible the man seemed even taller by day, his shoulders a mile wider, his body leaner, more rugged, more...virile.

"I thought he might have that effect on you," Darcy said, a definite chuckle punctuating her words.

Candace's unbidden response hadn't been for the reason her friend believed. She *knew* this cowboy— and she had no desire to see him again.

Candace shoved on her studious glasses in the faint hope he wouldn't recognize her, and shuffled her notes. "I think I'll stay in the truck and organize my work," she said, feigning an interest in the data she'd gathered.

"Oh, no, you don't, Candace Porter. You came here to observe the cowboy for that misguided article of yours—and this man is a prime specimen."

The cowboy advancing toward them was that— and more.

And Candace knew she wasn't going to get out of this showdown.

2

"WELL, I'll be damned."

Tanner gave vent to his surprise at seeing the woman sitting in Doc's passenger seat. The lady had tucked a pair of definitely bookish glasses onto her pert nose—but if she thought they would put a man off, she was wrong.

Dead wrong.

He could already feel the blood in his veins heat up like a hot campfire on a cool Texas evening. In fact, he hadn't cooled down much since last night. And he'd definitely had very little sleep.

"Hello, Doc," he said, his gaze riveted not on Darcy, but on the woman she'd brought with her.

"Uh, Tanner—I have someone I want you to meet." Darcy motioned her reluctant passenger from the truck and dragged her front and center. "Tanner Carson, this is my friend—Candace Porter."

Tanner forced back a smile that threatened to surface. "The lady and I have already met."

"*Met? How?*"

At Darcy's high squeak, he drew his gaze away and fixed it on the good doctor. Her mouth was opening and closing like a trout snapping at bait. He'd known Darcy Garrett for the past three years—ever since she'd bought out old Doc Sloan's vet practice over in Dripping Springs.

"Well...we haven't met *officially,* that is." He scrubbed his palms up and down his denimed thighs, then held his right hand out to Ms. Yankee from back East. Where had she said she was from? New York? No—Connecticut. Wherever the hell it was, it was a long way from here. "Nice to meet you, Candy."

She stiffened—the way he remembered she had in his arms last night. She also didn't accept his handshake—something that was right unneighborly down here in Texas.

"That's *Candace,*" she said. "Not Candy."

Yep—she was certainly unneighborly. Had too much starch and buckram to her. And those studious glasses... She looked like someone's maiden aunt—*except* for the rest of her.

Against his good sense, his gaze slid slowly up and down her frame.

He remembered the way those curves had felt against his hot body last night.

His jeans tightened like they'd shrunk a size or two—maybe three. Not the best thing to happen in the presence of a pair of ladies.

"Uh, nobody gets away with calling her Candy, I'm afraid," Darcy said. "She sets 'em straight real fast."

Tanner had been about to withdraw his hand when she deigned to meet his handshake.

"It's nice to formally meet you, Tanner Carson."

That voice—how had he forgotten? Its velvet could slide over a man and make him weak in the knees—though not in other places.

Definitely not in other places.

"If I might interrupt here—" Darcy cut in "—when did you two meet?"

"A gentleman never tells," Tanner quipped.

Candy, er, *Candace* shot him a hostile glance. "Last night. We shared a dance—*one* dance at Gunslinger's," she said, determined to set the record straight.

"At Gunslinger's?" Darcy's curiosity obviously wasn't relieved. "You and I have a few things to talk about, friend."

A faint blush crept onto Candace's cheeks—or maybe she'd been out in the sun too long. They probably didn't get a whole lot of sun time where she came from.

"When could I have told you? You've been too busy berating me for going there in the first place—a place where *rowdies* hang out, I believe you said."

Tanner let out a hearty laugh at that. "Rowdies, huh? That's a little mild, Darce."

"I didn't want to *frighten* her," she returned. "Now, if you two will excuse me, I have a pair of mares to see to." She lifted her black doctor's bag from the back of the truck. "How are they doing, Tanner?"

Tanner explained about his patients as the three of them ambled toward the stables—but he didn't lose sight of Candace for a moment.

She wasn't wearing a short skirt today, but faded jeans that fit her tighter than bark on a willow tree, revealing every line and curve of her long, slender legs. Those legs had been the focus of more than one fantasy last night as he'd punched his pillow and tried to sleep.

On her feet were a pair of cowboy boots—in pink leather.

Pink?

They had to be Connecticut's version of the Wild West. No self-respecting shop around these parts would sell such a thing.

Her soft-faded denim shirt was open a button or two at the neck, revealing smooth, creamy skin that would burn easily in this hot Texas sun. She wore her hair off her neck, in deference to the heat, and pinned haphazardly to the top of her head.

One tug of that hair clip would send those red-gold curls tumbling to her shoulders—and Tanner's fingers itched to try.

He caught her gaze, those clear green eyes wide as if she might have read his thoughts. Why did she keep such an expressive part of herself hidden behind a pair of horn-rims?

The blush on her cheeks deepened tantalizingly, then she glanced away—obviously embarrassed.

They'd reached the stables, and Tanner set about trying to corral one set of rambunctious—and definitely randy—hormones, while Darcy dragged her stethoscope from her black bag and turned her attention to his mares.

Tanner preferred to breathe in Candace's sweet scent, but she'd moved on, scouting out his stables, peering into empty stalls and—unless he missed his guess—keeping a tentative distance from his horses.

Tanner grinned. The woman was every inch a Yankee.

"My estimate is they're due in five or six days," Darcy said, peeling off her stethoscope and dropping it in her bag. "What do you think?"

He nodded. "That'd be my guess—give or take a day." It was the best he could do—the best anyone could do. This was not an exact science. And any man who said it was had sawdust for a brain.

He snagged a clipboard from the wall and gave her a rundown of each mare's pregnancy, his observations, his hunches. Darcy listened. Tanner knew she put a lot of stock in a man's hunches. She'd grown up around these parts—and was savvy enough to realize a vet didn't know everything.

The woman peering into empty stalls and trying to keep ten feet away from the nearest horse, on the other hand, was a different breed entirely.

CANDACE FELT like she'd been forgotten as the two turned a serious note. But she was content to watch—and listen.

She marveled at Tanner's innate knowledge, his care and concern for his pregnant horses—thrilling just a little too much to the timbre of his voice, the inflections that rippled through her nervous system, the occasional softness when he spoke of the mare he feared might have a difficult time of it.

She wondered if his voice carried that same soft tone when he spoke to a woman he cared about.

Did Tanner have some special woman in his life?

Candace banished that thought before it saw fruition. Tanner's life, personal or otherwise, was none of her business. She'd shared a dance—one dance—with the man in a Texas dance hall, nothing more.

Still, she knew she wouldn't be able to resist asking Darcy about it at the first opportunity.

She'd call it a research question.

Not that she'd include Tanner Carson in any of her findings. The man confused her—too much to allow him to color her data.

With Darcy occupied with Tanner, Candace made a brief foray through the stables, admiring his horses.

From a safe distance.

Horses frightened her—had ever since she'd been bitten by one very unsociable beast when she was eleven. But that was a shortcoming she preferred to keep from Darcy—and definitely from Tanner.

It would be a laughing matter in this part of the country, she was sure.

The smell of leather and linseed oil permeated the stables, and the scent of clean, fresh straw tickled her nostrils. This was Tanner's life, his passion.

She wondered what other passions the man might have.

Of course, that, too, was none of her business.

Dredging up a measure of courage she reached out a hand to pat one particularly docile-looking creature on the nose. She noticed the name above the stall door—Ginger. Perversely, Candace wondered if the animal had been named for an equally docile girlfriend of Tanner's—or for the horse's coloring, which was lovely.

Just then the animal whinnied, and Candace jerked at the sound.

"Careful—" Tanner caught her hand "—some mares can be temperamental when they're about ready to foal."

A jolt of excitement flashed through her at his touch—or maybe it was just fear of being bitten by livestock. Candace preferred to think it was the latter. She didn't want to react to Tanner Carson in any way.

He'd appeared at her side, startling her—or perhaps saving her from a cranky mare. "I—I was just petting her."

"Petting her?" A slow grin arrived on his face.

Apparently *pet* wasn't a ranching word.

He'd released her hand and now Candace didn't know what to do with it. Nervously she tried to tuck it in her pocket—but her tight jeans couldn't accommodate it.

Where was Darcy?

Candace wasn't sure why, but she felt she needed protection from this overwhelming cowboy.

"C'mon," he said, "we'll head for the house for something cool to drink. Darcy's just finishing up."

His house? Candace sucked in a breath, then chanced a peek around his broad shoulders for some sign of Darcy. Spotting her friend, she relaxed.

A tall glass of iced tea sounded so good about now.

CANDACE DIDN'T even try to pretend indifference when they reached the house. Though she shouldn't be, she was curious about Tanner Carson. And the way he lived gave at least some insight into his personality.

She glanced around, taking in everything with the same intensity she gave to her journalistic projects.

The old ranch home was rambling and comfortably rustic. The walls were cedar, with rough-hewn cedar beams reaching upward to a pitched ceiling.

There was a warmth to the wood that gave the place a feeling of permanence somehow, of endurance.

The colors were male favorites—browns, blues and tans. A wraparound sofa in tan leather stretched along two walls, the kind a person could sink into. She pictured Tanner relaxing on it at the end of the day—with a beer or a shot of good bourbon.

Or…maybe a woman.

She blinked to eradicate the image. Though she wasn't interested one whit in Tanner Carson, the thought jarred some female response in her—some *silly* female response.

Tearing her attention away from the main room, she turned it instead to the adjacent kitchen. Tanner seemed to fill it—with his height, those male-wide shoulders—as he searched the cabinets for suitable glasses for their cold drinks. He wiped off a water spot or two, clinked in plenty of ice cubes, then poured iced tea from a pitcher. Candace realized how thirsty she was.

"Here you go," he said, holding out the first glass to her. "There's nothing better on a hot day than a tall glass of Texas iced tea—unless, of course it's a tall cold beer."

His grin was boyish, yet something far more dangerous. There was very little innocence about Tanner Carson.

"The tea looks great," she said. "Thanks." His hand brushed hers, only slightly, as she accepted the glass—but the heat of his fingers felt like a caress.

Quickly she moved away, physically as well as emotionally.

Obviously the day's sun had charbroiled her brain.

There was no reason she should react this way to Tanner. If she knew what was good for her, she'd sidestep him *and* his wayward charm.

Darcy was on the phone in the kitchen, no doubt checking in with her answering service. Candace hoped there'd be no emergencies to send them off on another call—and away from that longed-for soak in Darcy's tub. They'd covered more miles today than she wanted to think about.

And encountered one more cowboy than Candace could handle.

She sauntered through the living room, trying to distract herself. On the mantel above the rustic fireplace she noticed a framed photo—a rangy cowboy clinging precariously to the back of some menacing-looking beast in front of a crowd of cheering onlookers.

''Ever been to a rodeo?''

The voice behind her was low, swamping her senses. She spun around at the sound, then wished she hadn't. She was face to broad chest with Tanner. One slow lift of her head brought her within kissing distance of his too-sensual mouth.

She took a step away—for safety and a little

peace of mind. But she found neither. Her heart was thudding so loudly she was sure it could be heard into the next county.

She shook her head. "No, I've never been to a rodeo. I suppose that's you in the photo?"

He grinned. "Nope—that's my brother. That particular bull got the best of me that day. I limped my way over to the closest bar and got drunk, as I remember."

She laughed softly—and Tanner realized he liked the sound, had been waiting for it all afternoon. Too bad it came at the expense of his humiliating defeat.

"The creature took me down the following year, too. That's when I got smart and left rodeoing to the intelligence-impaired."

"I'm glad," she said, then blushed hotly as if she hadn't meant to say the words aloud.

"Would you—I mean, we can take in one while you're here, if you like." He'd never been so nervous asking a woman for a date before. At least, he supposed that's what he was doing—asking her out.

A woman from New York—or wherever the hell she was from.

A woman who thrilled him just a little too much.

He didn't need to complicate his life. He had a ranch to run. He didn't need to get mixed up with some city girl. Past experience had taught him that—and he wasn't likely to forget it.

Still he seemed to be riding hell-bent for leather into trouble.

Or maybe he just had a set of incorrigible hormones.

"Sure, she'll go." Darcy took that moment to place herself in the middle of the conversation. "You can't come to Texas and not take in a rodeo."

"I'm quite capable of making my own plans, thank you," she told Darcy, then turned her pretty head to him. "I—I'll give it some thought and let you know."

She skirted around him, set her half-finished glass of iced tea on the bar that divided the kitchen and stood huffily by the door, an unspoken message to Darcy that she was ready to leave.

Tanner gave a slow grin. Her stance was prim and proper, but it belied the rest of her—her reddish-gold hair starting to tumble to her shoulders, those full, tantalizing lips daring him to kiss them, her small breasts more tempting than he wanted to think about.

Why did he have the feeling that falling for this woman could be far worse than any fall from a bull?

Darcy followed Candace toward the door, then gave him a backward glance. "You two can discuss the rodeo at the barbecue I'm throwing tomorrow night. Expect you at seven-thirty, Tanner."

Tanner knew he should offer his regrets, avoid the barbecue and the Yankee woman who could be an unwanted complication in his life, but he said nothing.

He wasn't all that sure he could stay away.

3

"WHAT BARBECUE are you talking about, Darcy Garrett? I haven't heard one word about this until now." Candace frowned over at her friend as the old truck bounced its way down the drive and off the Silver Spur.

Darcy gave a small smile. "Okay, I admit it. There was no barbecue until a moment ago. But look at it from the proper perspective, Candace. You'll be able to get enough material on the cowboy to write a book on the subject."

"I'm not writing a book. Just an article—from a feminist point of view."

With luck, one she'd get a chance to finish.

"Fine, no book. You'll have enough for your article, then—*ten* articles."

"I don't see how a barbecue is going to help."

Especially one with Tanner Carson present, she added silently.

He hadn't said he'd show up, but even if he didn't, she'd spend the entire evening *expecting* him to. She'd be on pins and needles—too nervous to gather one iota of material.

But she didn't want to admit that to Darcy.

Didn't want to admit to *herself* that the man affected her.

"The barbecue is a part of Texas tradition—and you need to explore a few diversions before you pronounce judgment on the cowboy, Candace Porter."

Her friend turned off Highway 281 onto 290, heading for Dripping Springs. The scenery went by in a blur—or perhaps Candace's mind merely operated on autopilot, too numb to take in the passing landscape. If only she could tune Darcy out, as well.

But she knew her friend was right.

If she was going to do this article, she wanted to do it well.

"You're right, of course, Darce. I just wished you hadn't seen fit to invite Tanner Carson to this...this bit of Texas tradition."

Darcy's smile went wide, superior. "Then you are interested in him. I knew it!" Her friend fairly crowed.

"I'm interested only in doing my work, nothing else," she returned hotly.

"That's exactly what's wrong with you, Candace. Work."

"What's wrong with work?"

"Nothing—as long as it's not a substitute for men, dating, a *life*."

"I have a life—and I happen to like it just the way it is—without a man in it."

Candace didn't need the complication. Not again.

Not after Steven. She hadn't forgotten how the man had jilted her, left her nearly standing at the altar.

The snake in the grass.

Darcy knew about her breakup with Steven, knew he'd thrown her over for a college coed in one of the classes he was teaching at the university, how he'd told her she was the only woman in the world for him, how she'd foolishly believed him.

"Candace, it may surprise you to know not all men are louses. Some are even...nice."

Candace wondered if she counted Tanner Carson in that group. "I'll take your word for it," she countered.

Candace tried to put it out of her mind as Dripping Springs came into view—and Darcy's mini-ranch on its outskirts. Candace loved the place. It was Darcy, defined who she was.

When Darce went off to the stables to check on her animals, Candace headed for the tub and a long, deserved soak. A while later she was firmly ensconced on the big back porch with a tall, cool glass of iced tea and her notes from the day spread around her.

In the distance the sun was setting in all its fiery glory. The air was fresh and free. Spring wildflowers grew in abundance, bluebonnets, Indian blanket, prairie paintbrush, all flourishing in the hard soil.

She begrudgingly had to admit there was a certain romance to the country, maybe even to the Texas cowboy.

Maybe.

At least her notes reflected a few…*favorable* points for the breed.

The cowboy represented the last frontier, the last place where men were men. Maybe it was the John Wayne image—tough, macho, earthy men who loved the land, lived off it, became one with it.

On the flip side, however, there was dust and sweat—and sometimes a smell from their boots that made it clear where they'd been stepping.

They drank hard and played even harder—in other words, they were totally absorbed in their land, their animals, and when they weren't, they were out for a good time.

One cowboy came to mind—Tanner Carson, with all his sex appeal. Quickly she shoved the image aside.

Tanner was a distraction Candace didn't need at the moment.

What she did need was an inspired plan of action—something that would jump-start her little project, tie her article up in one nice, neat little package—just the way she liked it.

But what?

How?

This project was testing her mettle, not that she had any intention of giving up on it. On the contrary, she'd redouble her efforts, immerse herself in her writing—and forget Tanner Carson.

If that were possible.

TANNER COULD smell the barbecue in the air as he parked his truck on the edge of Darcy's drive. From the number of pickups already there, the party promised to be a big one.

He wanted to think it had been the prospect of great ribs and cold beer that brought him here tonight—but he knew it was something else.

He'd come to prove to himself that one certain Yankee female didn't mean a thing to him, that he had his hormones well under control and his brains intact.

Candace Porter from back East didn't bother him a bit.

Besides, he wasn't likely to fall for a woman with a penchant for pink cowboy boots and a tendency to tiptoe her way through the stables as if she was afraid of...*stepping* in something.

The woman was a Yankee through and through—and Tanner had had his fill of Yankee women. After Marlene. Marlene had come here on a lark—a college dare, he'd later learned—to lasso herself one tough Texas cowboy and lead him to the altar.

Tanner wasn't a man to fall easily, but he'd been taken in by her femininity, her polish—polish that didn't count for spit around a working ranch, he realized later.

Six months into the marriage she'd hightailed it back to Philadelphia—and her easy life there.

If—and when—he settled on a woman she'd be

someone from these parts, someone who knew how hard life on the ranch could be, how solitary.

He sauntered over to the party crowd, greeting a few people he knew. People born and bred in Hill Country—like himself. The picnic table was heaped with great-smelling barbecue and coolers of cold beer alongside. The sounds of George Strait mellowed the night.

He spoke to Jack Wooten, his neighbor to the east, filled a plate with ribs and potato salad, snagged a beer, then lowered himself onto a bench to eat and watch the dancing.

The sight of her hit him with a major wallop.

Candy—er, Candace.

She was on the patio, dancing with Jim Hanks.

All-hands-and-no-regrets Jim Hanks.

A swift dart of jealousy arrowed into him. His fingers clenched around his plate, and resentment broke over him like floodwaters down an arroyo.

What did the woman think she was doing? He knew Hanks's reputation—though strangely it had never bothered him much until this moment.

The ribs lost their taste as he watched her smile at the man. Then he heard her soft laughter. It broke through the night, a golden sound.

Damn it, he wanted that smile, that gilded laughter, directed at him—not Hanks.

He stood up to dispose of his plate, finish off his beer and keep one wary eye on Hanks.

And Candy—Candace.

"Having a good time, Tanner?"

It was Darcy. He gave his hostess one quick glance, then directed his gaze back to the dancing. His reply was something noncommittal.

And gruff.

Her gaze followed his. "Oops! Sorry to bother you—I can see you're quite…occupied." She started to walk away, then stopped. "She does look pretty tonight, doesn't she?"

"Go to hell, Darce—and don't stop anywhere on the way."

Not the nicest thing he could have said to her, given that she'd put on this shindig, but he'd apologize later.

CANDACE WAS working the room—well, party. She'd put her newest plan into action. She intended to dance with every cowboy here tonight, rate his appeal, his charm, his sexiness, on a scale of one to ten.

She trusted her instincts on this, her reactions to the vibes they gave off—or didn't give off. She could always size up a situation, and find the right slant for an article.

At least she'd been able to with every other project she'd taken on.

This one, however, was different—and she wasn't sure why.

But she intended to follow it through to the end.

So far, she was on her fourth dancing partner, a wolf in sheep's clothing named Jim Hanks.

Her first dance had been with a rather sweet but definitely non-sexy cowboy who'd given off no vibes whatsoever. Not even a sex-starved woman who'd spent a year lost alone on a desert island would have found him intriguing, much less sexy.

But Candace had given him a kindly two.

For his sweetness.

From the number of men here tonight she'd have little chance to enjoy Darcy's party. By the time the barbecue drew to an end she should have enough data, enough impressions to begin her article.

By the time the week was out, she hoped to be on her way home—back to Connecticut.

"How 'bout another dance, baby?" Jim Hanks wanted to know when the song ended and a new one throbbed to life.

"No, thank you—I need to…circulate."

And check her body parts. The man had his hands on her in more places than a masseuse.

He'd not be flattered at the rating she'd given *him*.

In addition, he'd scuffed her pretty pink cowboy boots.

She turned to find her next subject. That was when she spotted Tanner. He stood a little apart from the others, aloof, solitary.

A loner.

Or was he?

She couldn't quite put one of her neat little labels on him. And she didn't think she wanted to try. She had work to do. More men to dance with. Evaluate.

And one of them was headed her way.

She smiled at the tall, fairly handsome subject matter.

This man, she decided, might rate a little higher than the others.

TANNER PACED and tried to listen while Will Barton from down near Blanco gave him the lowdown on the latest head of cattle he'd bought. But his gaze returned every few moments to check out the dancing.

And the woman he told himself he wasn't interested in.

Those silly pink stompers of hers were going to be worn out if she kept up all that dancing. And damned if he didn't feel like cutting in.

He spent a half minute more trying to talk himself out of it, then made an excuse to Barton and headed her way like some heat-seeking missile.

Those snug jeans of hers hugged her willowy long legs and tight derriere. She wore all that red-gold hair down, allowing it to tumble over her shoulders. He wanted to touch it, know if it was silky, springy, if it gave off fire.

She turned as he neared, as if she'd somehow sensed his presence. Or maybe she'd been keeping an eye on him, the same way he had her. Her gaze was soft and sultry as she fixed it on him, her lips parted slightly.

"Mind if I cut in?" It wasn't a question, but a need. And he didn't give Sam Parker, the man she'd been dancing with, a moment to refuse.

Or the lady.

The song was half over, and Tanner didn't want to miss a second more of holding her close, gazing into those green eyes of hers.

"One dance, Tanner," she said, her tone sassy.

Tanner liked sassy, at least on her. But he bet that impertinence could be tamed with a little work, a few kisses planted on those sweet red lips.

He fought the urge to taste them, the urge to steal her away and make heated love to her.

He drew her into his arms, and she came willingly. The slow country beat flowed around them. He planted his hands on her curved backside, and she looped hers around his neck. A delicious shiver shot through him as her fingers brushed against his hair curled over his shirt collar.

"Sorry to have to cut in on Parker," he said, "but I was afraid I was going to miss my turn. Or were you even intending to include me in this little dance-a-thon of yours?"

"This is hardly a dance-a-thon. I'm merely be-ing...sociable."

"Yeah, well, you'd better be careful just who you're sociable with. Some of these yahoos are a dangerous breed."

"Does that include you, Tanner?"

He liked the way his name rolled off her tongue. Somehow she made it sound...intimate. What he wouldn't give to hear her say it in a moment of passion.

"Anything's possible, darlin'."

"I'll keep that in mind."

The lady apparently didn't scare easy. She, no doubt, thought she could hold her own around these rough-and-ready cowboys, but Tanner wasn't so certain she could. Especially when the lot of them had a few beers under their belts.

He'd have to keep a careful eye out, make sure none of them got any wild ideas in their head.

And that went double for himself.

He caught her gaze scouring the sidelines. For her next dancing partner? Any one of the bunch was willing. More than willing. But Tanner wasn't about to relinquish his claim on her.

At least, not yet.

"No offense, darlin', but this is the second night I've caught you...man hunting."

That drew her attention to him. Her green eyes went wide, then she closed them with those silky long lashes—and he couldn't read them.

And damned if he didn't want to, *need* to.

"Is this some kind of female Yankee sport we Texans don't know about?"

He couldn't help remembering the little game Marlene had played. Find herself a cowboy and lead him to the altar. A lark. Tanner had learned a bitter lesson—one he wasn't likely to forget.

CANDACE DIDN'T want to let Tanner—or anyone— know what she was doing, why she was dancing with every cowboy here tonight. Darcy was the only one who knew about her little project.

And she'd been sworn to secrecy.

"I happen to like dancing," she answered him. "If that's a crime…" She gave him her best smile. Candace didn't like to lie—to anyone. But she knew a subject's behavior often changed when he was aware he was being scrutinized, thus altering her perceptions. And she couldn't risk that.

This project was important to her.

"So, you…like to dance?"

She gazed at him. "Yes."

"Well, then, I'm all yours for another whirl or two."

Candace swallowed hard. She'd walked into that one.

"What's the matter, Cinderella? Your dance card full?"

"No, uh, my feet are tired." That at least was the truth.

He held her at arm's length and studied her toes. "With those pink stompers, it's no wonder."

Candace glanced at her overly trendy boots, then at his well-worn, well-fitting, hand-tooled pair. "Are you suggesting I'm a fraud?"

He laughed, a hearty, rich sound that ebbed through her, into her very marrow. What was it about Tanner that affected her the way he did? The way he shouldn't?

He draped an arm around her shoulders and guided her away from the dancing. "Buy you a beer, Cinderella?"

His banter was light, his arm around her casual, almost comradely, but she was intensely aware of his closeness, his clean, outdoorsy scent. She didn't need to lose her equilibrium. "I'd prefer an iced tea."

She thought she was going to get a ribbing, but he didn't bat an eye over her choice of drink.

"One iced tea coming up."

The party sounds swirled around her, the music, the conversation, the laughter. Darcy was overseeing the barbecuing—the man in charge was her most recent infatuation, Todd Wellman.

It was pairing-off time, and Candace found herself with Tanner. Not a good sign. She should be busy observing the dynamics of the night. The effect of the cowboy on his woman was, after all, what she was here to scrutinize.

But with Tanner around, she could barely think.

At least not clearly.

He'd returned with her glass and his beer. And a little too much charisma for a moonlit night and her shaky emotions.

Would she have danced with him if he hadn't cut in?

She knew her answer. She wouldn't have gone within ten risky feet of the man. He was one cowboy who refused to fit into her neat accumulating data.

An aberration to her story slant.

"Thank you," she said when he handed her the glass.

She turned and sauntered away, out into the night, away from the party, needing to clear her thoughts, her mind. But she wasn't sure she could with Tanner so close.

"I've always heard the stars were so much brighter down here in Texas—and I have to admit, they are."

"A fact we're awfully proud of," he returned.

She swung around and smiled at him. There was a lot of pride in this man, his proud bearing, his male control. She also saw a wariness in him, a wariness about getting too involved.

At least with a woman like her.

Maybe she should include Tanner in her little litmus test, after all. For balance. So far her notes were showing more *negative* data than positive.

Tanner would definitely tip the scales into the latter.

But could she keep a clear head around him? Could she keep her material non-biased and impersonal? She feared she could not. At least not where Tanner was concerned.

"Tell me about yourself, Tanner Carson," she said.

She might be playing with fire, but she was curious about him.

He gave her a glance rife with that wariness she'd noted in him, and she realized he wasn't sure why she was asking.

Neither was she—unless it was to satisfy that curiosity of hers.

"There's not much to tell," he said. "I own the Silver Spur…but you know that. I raise cattle, breed horses—paints, mostly."

"That's what you *do*. What about your personal side?"

He narrowed his eyes that looked navy-blue in the moonlight. "You sure know how to cut to the chase, don't you, darlin'?"

Candace glanced at her scuffed pink boots— which at least were beginning to acquire a more broken-in look—and realized she'd slipped into her research mode.

She glanced up, more in tune with the casualness of the evening. "It's an—" she started to say an occupational hazard, but caught herself in time "—a bad habit of mine. I'm sorry. I really had no right to ask."

He studied her as if evaluating the truth of that. "No offense taken. It's just that I'm not sure there's anything all that interesting about my personal side.''

''You're all work and no play then?''

A smile teased at his lips. It was downright sexy—and would be right off the scale if she were rating him. ''I'm *not* all work, darlin','' he said. ''Especially when I see a woman who intrigues me.''

She knew she should draw her gaze away—or better yet, run. But he held her captive with only that sexy smile and the definite hint of want in his dark eyes.

She could break the spell—if she found her voice, if she found the strength to step back from his closeness. But her gaze remained locked with his in some test of sanity, some sense of the moment that would pass all too quickly—and this insanity would be lost.

He leaned closer, his gaze shifting to her lips. She could almost feel them swell—as if his mouth had already bruised them. Would his kiss be hot, passionate?

Or a gentle promise of something more to come.

She wanted to know.

Her gaze went to his lips as if anticipating the taste of them, their texture, their…want.

But he didn't kiss her. He let the moment pass, and disappointment, swift and sure, hit her like a lightning strike. She'd been so close. *He'd* been so close.

She'd wanted it.

He'd wanted it.

"I think you intrigue me a little too much, dar-lin'," he said, his voice low, regretful. "You could wreak havoc with my personal side—and I'm afraid to let that happen."

4

CANDACE went back to circulating.

She'd nearly forgotten her purpose for the night—to evaluate the Texas cowboy for her article, debunk the foolish myth. Only seeing Tanner again, falling—or nearly falling—into his lair had led her astray.

And that almost-kiss.

She hadn't wanted it to happen.

Who was she kidding? She'd practically begged for it.

Well, she had news for that big hunk of a cowboy. She didn't want *her* life complicated any more than he did his.

And men could do that, any man—not just Tanner Carson.

She was determined to ignore him the rest of the evening, and also Darcy, who—Candace knew—was entirely too curious about how everything was progressing, or not progressing, between her and Tanner.

If she knew what was good for her she'd keep her mind dutifully devoted to her plan of action for the remainder of the party.

At least the barbecue had provided her with the opportunity to observe the cowboy—and she was grateful.

Or at least she would be, if Tanner wasn't there to derail her thoughts.

Her gaze kept sliding back to him. Tanner had too much raw masculinity for her sensibilities. Still, she was convinced the man was a fluke, a throwback, an exception to the species.

The cowboy mystique existed only in the minds of a few foolish females.

And she aimed to prove it.

She just wished Tanner Carson would get out of her way so she could.

"If you want him, you'd better stake your claim fast, Candace." It was Darcy—and Candace knew she was referring to Tanner.

Her gaze crossed the patio in one quick moment. Too quick.

So much for pretending he didn't affect her. For some irrational reason, he did. And so did the three women sidling up to him as if he were theirs for the taking.

And Tanner—drat him—looked like he was enjoying it far too much.

She shrugged her indifference. "I'm not interested in staking a claim, Darce—and those women, well, they're welcome to him."

Her friend smiled. "Right. You don't have an interested bone in your body."

Her bones were fairly humming—but she didn't want to admit that to Darcy. Or even to herself. She'd always been levelheaded, her feet firmly planted in reality, and she'd never succumbed to a fantasy in her life.

At least not until Tanner.

The man seemed to bring out the worst in her.

She turned away from the scene unfolding across the patio. If Tanner took one—or all three—of those...sweeties home with him, Candace didn't care.

"Don't you have anything better to do than stand around trying to match me up with that cowboy?" she asked Darcy.

Her friend huffed in irritation. "Candace, you need a lot of work," she said, then sauntered off to join her other party guests.

Candace gave a sigh of relief and struggled to regain her composure, but before she could, she felt a tap on her left shoulder.

She spun around.

"Darce, I told you I'm not interested in Tan—"

It wasn't Darcy, but Tanner, who stood in front of her.

He crossed his arms over his very male chest. "Well, I'm certainly glad to hear that," he drawled. "Women are more trouble than a pack of mean coyotes."

"And men are no prize heifer, either," she retorted.

One dark eyebrow rose, and his lips twitched in silent amusement. *"Heifer?"*

"Yes."

The amusement went to a full-blown chuckle. "A heifer, darlin', is the female of the species."

"Oh." She blushed hotly. She knew that—or would have, if Tanner hadn't rattled her so much. "So, my analogy is a bit off."

"I'd say so. And since we've established that neither of us is interested in the other, how about a dance? Just to pass the evening, of course."

Candace nodded in the direction he'd come. "What happened to your group of…admirers?"

His smile was disarming. "Let's just say I'm attracted to pink cowboy boots."

She should walk away—now—but those pink boots he referred to suddenly seemed glued to the spot. No, not glued—one toe was tapping to the beat of the music.

She did want to dance.

And Tanner was the only man here who halfway interested her.

Or maybe she just wanted to prove to herself she could resist his charming personality.

"I'm not sure I'm up to another dance with you, Tanner."

"Sure, you are."

He led her into the midst of the dancing couples. The music was slow, dreamy, mellow. The night was winding down. He pulled her into his open arms, and she struggled to fend off the onslaught of emotions his touch set off in her.

The heat of his body surrounded her, sapping her strength, her good sense. She fit against him too well, the rhythm of the night and the music setting the pace. His scent was all male, his touch electric, and Candace sensed the danger in that, in her shaky reactions to him.

This did not bode well for her article.

Still, she couldn't resist staying there, swaying with him to the honeyed strains of the music, drinking in the essence of him.

Did the cowboy possess some sort of mythical charm, after all?

Or was it this particular cowboy—and her reaction to him?

She sensed a danger in wanting to know.

All too soon the song ended and Tanner released her. Candace shivered at the sudden loss of his male heat. Party sounds once again edged into her consciousness.

"How about taking in that rodeo with me on Saturday?" A smile flashed in his tanned face, and Candace's heart thudded like a berserk jackhammer. "I can swing by for you about one o'clock."

Candace knew nothing about rodeos—except that attending one with this man could be hazardous to her good sense. She was far too attracted to him—and she didn't want to be.

That could only mean trouble—of the kind she didn't need in her life.

"The rodeo this Saturday? I'm not sure I—"

"She'd love to go, Tanner."

Darcy had overheard her stumbling refusal and apparently saw the need to answer for her. Candace didn't like that. "Darce, why don't you butt out of my social life?"

"I'm just giving you a friendly shove in the right direction," she said. "Besides, you can't come to Texas and not take in a rodeo. It's a Texas tradition—like the barbecue. And remember, you came here to experience—"

Candace quickly cut her friend off before she spilled the beans about her article. "I'll go to the rodeo."

She glowered at Darcy, then offered a faint smile to Tanner.

What had she just gotten herself into?

DAMNED if the woman wasn't wearing those silly pink stompers again. Not exactly the attire for a wild and woolly rodeo. But Tanner doubted he'd be concentrating all that much on her footwear.

Not when he couldn't get his gaze off the shape of her in those skinny jeans. Or the way that pale blue shirt hugged her breasts. The shirt was open a button or two at the neck, and he thought of how much he'd like to plant a kiss there in the dewy hollow of her throat.

But Candy—er, Candace didn't seem anywhere near willing to let that happen. She was sitting all prim and prissy next to the passenger door of his pickup—as if Tanner had some sort of contagious disease.

Damned unsociable.

"Rattlesnake got your tongue?" he asked, not enjoying the distance that gulfed between them. He remembered the other night at the barbecue—and how she'd leaned into him during that slow, heated dance they'd shared.

Her head swiveled in his direction. "What?"

"You're awfully quiet," he explained.

"Sorry. I didn't mean to be. I suppose I should thank you for taking me today. You probably had plenty of work you needed to do on the ranch."

"Not so much that I don't have time to squire a pretty lady around."

She blushed at that—and Tanner enjoyed the glorious color in her cheeks, enjoyed even more that he could evoke that response in her.

But he knew he'd better rein in his hormones or he'd end up finding himself roped and hog-tied. And he had no intentions of letting that happen again.

Still, he'd promised the lady a good time.

And Tanner always kept his promise.

"I don't know how they do things where you come from, but down here in Texas a woman doesn't cozy up to a man's door handle."

She glanced down to take in her clinging-vine act with his passenger door, then gave him a tilted smile. "Where I come from a woman sits where she wants."

She did, however, scoot her shapely little bottom a tad closer to the center of her seat.

Tanner swallowed hard at the sexy wriggle and focused his eyes on the stretch of highway in front of him. Maybe he should just let her be prim and prissy, after all. There was safety in that.

But prissy, at least where Candace was concerned, turned him on. And he wasn't sure he could keep his hands to himself.

They reached the rodeo grounds, and Tanner found a place to park under the shade of a tree.

Shade.

"You're not wearing a hat," he said as he helped her from the pickup. "You're going to get that pretty little nose of yours sunburned."

"Don't worry—I'm wearing sunscreen."

"That's not good enough." He stopped at a stand and plunked down a few bills for a straw cowboy hat, then turned to her and settled it on her head. "There, that's more like it," he said and cinched the tie beneath her chin. "Damned if you don't look like a real Texan."

He gave a glance at her boots. "Well…almost."

She gave an impertinent sniff. "I think I'm here to see a rodeo—so lead the way, Tanner." She doubted anyone could measure up to Tanner's criteria. Not unless they'd been born and bred on Texas soil.

Maybe she should have stayed at Darcy's and immersed herself in her work. She wasn't all that sure a rodeo could be of much use to her article, anyway. If men wanted to risk their silly necks roping some unfriendly beast, why should she care?

She preferred other pursuits—taking in a play, the ballet, something with more substance than the hootin' and hollerin' she heard going on around her as Tanner led her to their seats high in the bleachers.

"This'll give us the best view—and we'll be away from all the dust," he told her.

Candace was glad of that.

She was allergic to dust.

And probably to the critters in the ring, as well.

"Oh, good," Tanner said, "we made it in time for the bull-riding event." He steeled his eyes on the arena in front of them and settled himself more comfortably on the bleacher seat, ready to take in the action.

Candace tried to do the same. She wished she blended in a little better with the crowd around her, certain she stood out like a neon sign.

A city girl.

She wasn't even sure if she was supposed to root for the menacing bull or the cowboy astride him.

Whichever, she'd be happy if she just didn't make a fool of herself before the day was out.

"The bull riding was what you competed in?" she asked Tanner, deciding she'd try her best to understand this macho sport—and just possibly the man she was with.

"Yeah—along with a few other events. I rode the rodeo circuit for a number of years. It wasn't the best pay, but I made enough to buy the Silver Spur."

There was pride in Tanner's voice. She couldn't help but admire the determination and strength it took to do something so dangerous.

Or was it just foolhardy?

"And the ranch was important enough to risk life and limb?" she asked.

"To me—yes."

She saw it in his eyes—his love of the land, the animals he raised, nurtured. It was what drove him, completed him. Candace had never known a man like him. He confused her—as well as kindled her admiration.

The sport was dangerous—and the thought of it sent a shiver through her. "I'm glad you don't compete anymore."

He gave her a long, slow look that sent a shiver of a different kind racing through her. "You worried about me, darlin'?"

Candace wasn't about to admit something like that. "I—I just meant, it has to be rough, skirmishing with one of those...creatures."

"Maybe, if you don't know what you're doing."

"And you always know what you're doing?"

"I try to."

TANNER WASN'T sure he did at this moment, though. Looking into the shimmery green eyes of this Yankee woman had all his emotions tied in a knot. He hadn't forgotten the last Yankee female who'd done that.

He needed to keep his wits about him.

Something that wasn't easy to do with Candace's sweet scent wafting around him. She was far too beguiling for his peace of mind. He had the feeling he'd be better off on the back of a mean-tempered bull than sitting here dangerously close to temptation.

"In this event the rider needs to stay on the bull for eight seconds," he explained, hoping he could distract himself with conversation.

"Eight seconds—that's a short ride."

"It's a *long* ride—when you're trying to hang on to the back of one of those brutes."

Candace watched as the chute opened and bull and rider spilled into the arena in a mad test of wills. The crowd went wild around them. Dust spiraled from the ring, and the cowboy hit the ground in an unceremonious heap.

She gave a small gasp. "Is he hurt?"

"Nope, just a little shaken up, that's all."

Tanner didn't want to tell her how it felt to take

a tumble like that. His battered bones still screamed some nights when he crawled into bed.

What, he wondered, would it be like to have a woman like Candace around to ease his pain? With her soft hands. And tender sympathy.

A dangerous thought, he reminded himself.

He focused instead on the announcer's glib patter. The next rider was ready in the chute, just waiting for the ring to clear, and Tanner let himself become caught in the action.

The chute opened with a clang, and the crowd was on its feet again, cheering boisterously.

All except...

Tanner glanced back to see Candace rooted to the bleacher seat. He leaned close to her. "You might be able to see more if you opened your eyes, darlin'."

"I can see enough."

Through her eyelids?

Tanner forgot about the rodeo. She'd had enough. He reached out a hand.

"C'mon," he told her. "Let's go get you something cold to drink. You're looking green around the gills."

And the color didn't go well with her boots.

THE RIDE BACK was embarrassing—and silent. Candace wished he'd go ahead and say it. She was a greenhorn city girl. She'd also made him miss the rodeo he'd wanted to see.

She took a fortifying sip of the cold drink he'd bought her on the way out of the rodeo, then glanced at his rugged profile. "So—go ahead and say it. I'm macaroni, a sapless pansy city girl. Or maybe you have a colorful *Texas* aspersion you'd like to slap on me."

He turned and gave her a slow grin. "Why should I say a word when you've done it so eloquently?"

She frowned and stared stonily ahead. Candace knew she'd never fit in Tanner's world, not if she stuck around till hell froze over.

The sooner she finished her article and got back to Connecticut, the better.

Just then Tanner slowed his pickup and pulled into a crowded parking lot. A red-and-blue neon sign proclaiming the best ribs in the state winked its message from above the door of a hole-in-the-wall restaurant.

"I thought we'd get a bite to eat," he said, wheeling into the nearest parking spot. "You're still looking a little peaked. Some food will fix you up."

A fast plane headed easterly would fix her up better, Candace thought. But then she'd have to add *quitter* to her growing list of shortcomings. And Candace wasn't a quitter. She'd finish this article—despite Tanner Carson.

"Sounds good to me," she answered, then slid from the truck before he could assist her.

The Texas male was nothing if not chivalrous— even when a self-sufficient independent woman like herself didn't need the courtesy.

Still, she had to admit that on occasion, it did feel nice to have a man treat her like a real lady.

And Tanner did that—even if he did think of her as some citified hapless moron.

Roadhouse Willie's was a small place, but it packed in the crowds. Tables were squeezed into every nook and cranny and every place in between.

Candace was met with a sea of cowboy hats and the assault of hickory-smoked barbecue. If the aroma was any recommendation for the taste of the ribs, the place lived up to its advertising.

Tanner spoke to a few people on his way in. All the while his hand was resting proprietarily on the flare of her hip—as if he wanted every man in the place to know she belonged to him. A man who could easily have any woman in the room.

Candace would be a liar if she said that didn't raise her feminine ego a few notches.

What, she wondered, would it be like to *belong* to Tanner Carson?

What was the matter with her? A few days in Texas and she was forgetting that a strong, independent woman didn't *belong* to any man. She was her own person.

That might be an idea for her next assignment. Could a woman belong to a man and still remain strong and independent?

Not a popular belief in this day of high feminism.

Tanner steered her to a secluded spot along the back wall, a booth for people who wanted to be alone.

Or were in love.

She slid into the scarred wooden booth. The music was loud, twangy and country. "You know many of these people?" she asked him.

"Some. Not well—just to speak to."

She'd suspected Tanner was a loner, that he played his cards close to the vest, not easily sharing the personal side of himself.

Something Candace could understand well.

It was safer not to open yourself up to hurt, betrayal. A small part of her longed for closeness— but she only had to think of Steven and the mistake she'd made in sharing herself with him to serve as a reminder not to get too close.

The barmaid arrived to take their order, and when she left, Tanner gave Candace a slow once-over. "Tell me about yourself," he said.

Candace wasn't sure what he meant—or if she wanted to divulge anything, at least of a personal nature.

"Such as...?"

"How long have you and Darcy been friends?"

She would have thought Darce would have told him that—but then, she wasn't certain Darcy and Tanner were close—except on a professional level.

"We've been friends since our college days,"

she told him. "Surprising since we had such different goals in life. Darcy wanted to work with animals, and I..."

"What did you want?"

She counted the number of holes in the pepper shaker. "I wanted to work for a magazine—and pursued a career in journalism."

"And did you do that—go to work for a magazine?"

"Yes."

She hoped he didn't ask her for details, because she didn't want to have to explain. Certainly not about why she was here, about her article.

Candace had the feeling he was about to ask more, but the waitress arrived with their food and she was saved by the proverbial bell.

"I'm famished," she breathed. "And this barbecue smells wonderful."

Tanner smiled. "If there's one thing we Texans do well, it's our barbecue."

Candace could imagine there were *many* things Tanner did well—and just the thought of them had her cheeks heating up.

She tucked her napkin into her lap and contemplated the plate of ribs in front of her, wondering how best to tackle them. One glance at Tanner told her the hands-on approach was de rigueur.

"You don't have to sneak up on 'em, darlin'. The cow's dead. Just dive in. Or are messy fingers not your style?"

He gave her a grin that said he was going to enjoy this neophyte trying to eat delicately. But Candace wasn't going to provide his entertainment.

She started with an end piece that looked promising, pulled it apart and gnawed the delicious meat as if she had ribs for every meal—plus snacks.

Tanner continued to watch her over his food, just waiting for her to show her city stripes.

"Mmm," she said. "These are good."

Candace had no idea something so difficult to eat could have such a delectable, sweet taste. It was heaven on earth.

When she reached for another piece he touched the corner of her mouth with the flat of his thumb. "Sauce," he said. "We wouldn't want you to be messy."

The brush of his thumb rocketed through her like a lightning bolt.

Candace tried to ignore it.

"I believe you have a little more color to your cheeks, darlin'. The food must have fixed you up."

She doubted the color on her face was from anything she ate. It was his electric touch.

Why did she react this way to him?

"I'm sorry about the rodeo," she said. "I hate that you missed it."

Tanner didn't mind in the least. He'd rather sit here at Roadhouse Willie's and watch that pert tongue of hers flick over her lips to savor the sauce.

"You didn't make me miss anything, darlin'."

Certainly not this show. He could go on watching her eat forever. He even had the feeling she might one day master the art of eating barbecue.

She licked her fingers one by one, and Tanner felt heat curl in his belly and his wayward anatomy grow hard.

Damned if he wouldn't like to crawl over that table right now and kiss the taste right off those sweet lips of hers.

"Are you sure I didn't make you miss anything?" she asked.

Only that kiss.

"At the rodeo? No—that was for you, darlin'."

"And I disappointed you."

"You didn't disappoint. Now eat up."

"I'm not sure I can. I'm stuffed."

"Then how about a doggie bag?"

"Yes."

Their waitress brought them the carryout container along with the check, and Tanner ushered Candace out through the crowded restaurant.

The sun had set, and evening had come. All too soon their day would end—and Tanner wasn't ready for it to. Before they reached the pickup, he drew her to a stop, tipped back his Stetson and planted a kiss on her surprised lips.

He could taste the barbecue sauce on them—and something far more delightful. He could taste Candace. Her arms looped around his neck, and she returned the kiss, hesitating a bit at first and then with feeling.

He felt the press of her small, pert breasts against him, her body soft in all the right places and fitting against the length of him with sweet perfection. His tongue demanded entrance, and her lips granted it, and the exquisiteness of the moment—of *her*—swamped his senses.

Before he wanted her to, she drew away, breaking the kiss—but not his want of her. That would be a long time passing—about three cold showers long.

"Darlin'—you sure know how to bring a man to his knees."

5

OVER THE NEXT few days Candace did her best to forget Tanner's kiss—that earthshaking, wild, erotic, plundering kiss.

It was all she'd been able to think about since the rodeo.

Today, however, she'd locked herself in Darcy's study with her laptop and the multitude of notes she'd gathered over the past week and a half. She was determined not to emerge until she'd finished at least a rough draft of her burgeoning article.

But she couldn't seem to keep her mind off Tanner and the feel of his mouth savoring hers.

She needed to get him out of her system before he set her journalistic endeavor flat on its ear.

And the best way to do that was work.

When the going got rough, the tough went to work—and that's what Candace intended to do.

She put on her glasses, picked up her notes and pulled out her determination.

What did she have so far?

In a positive vein, she'd noted that the Texas cowboy was tough, macho, earthy. He had shoulders broad enough to take on the world and a heart soft enough to nurture a new young colt—or a child.

Against her will, Tanner came to mind—and Candace felt a pluck of her heartstrings as she saw him in the role of protector and nurturer.

What would he be like with a child of his own? Or a woman he loved?

Maybe she'd better look at the negative, she decided.

And keep Tanner Carson out of her musings.

The negative... She shuffled a few notes, not needing to look far to find a few opposing insights.

Ah, yes. The Texas male, she'd noted, was still firmly entrenched in the Dark Ages.

Or earlier.

At least, he wasn't exactly on the side of feminism.

Women were the weaker sex—and in dire need of his direction and enlightenment. He had an ego larger than the state he came from. He was tough, raw, untamable, a man who'd no doubt sowed more wild oats than he fed to his livestock. A man as dangerous as an outlaw, who could steal a woman's heart as if it were his for the taking.

She groaned.

Tanner had once again worked his way into the picture.

She needed to separate her thoughts of him from her image of the cowboy. Or she'd end up in a conundrum she'd never be able to work through.

She tossed down her pen and paced the small office, fearing she was losing not only the battle, but the war, as well.

Tanner was confusing the issue.

Maybe she should have done an in-depth study of the staid pencil pusher instead. It might not be as interesting—but it certainly would have been easier.

Darcy's phone rang. Her friend, she knew, was on a house call and wouldn't be back for another hour. Candace reached for the phone and also the pad and pen Darce kept next to it for messages.

"Garrett's Veterinary Practice," she said. "May I take a message?"

"Candy, is that you?" Tanner's voice boomed over the line.

She started to correct him about the diminutive of her name, but there was something about his tone, something that told her this wasn't a casual call.

It wasn't a call for her at all.

"Yes—this is Candace. Darce is out, Tanner. Can I help you?"

"Help?" She thought she heard a strangled chuckle, but she could have been mistaken. "'Fraid not, darlin'. For this I need Darcy. One of my mares is in foal and she's having a rough time of it."

"Oh, Tanner." Candace swallowed a knot of worry that clogged her throat. "I'll try to reach

Darcy, but she had an emergency up near Lampas-sas.''

''Great.'' He ground out the word, and Candace felt the tension in him. He was concerned about his mare, and nothing else mattered. ''Yeah, get a message to her,'' he said. ''Tell her to get here as fast as she can.''

''I will, Tanner.''

Candace hung up and tried Darcy's pager number. She left a message for her, then raked a hand through her hair. She didn't have much hope of getting Tanner the help he needed as quickly as he needed it. But...

She could go herself.

And do what, she wondered, since Tanner found her about as useful as a burr under his saddle.

So maybe she wasn't worth her salt around a ranch. She was going anyway. She took a quick glance into the hall mirror to check her hair, then decided she needn't bother—Tanner was so absorbed with his pregnant horse he wouldn't notice if she'd dyed it purple.

With a slam of the door on her staid little rental car, she sped down Darcy's driveway, leaving a plume of dust in her wake. One thing she'd learned since coming here was that neighbor helped neighbor—and Candace was doing the neighborly thing.

Even though she wasn't *officially* Tanner's neighbor.

He'd sounded so worried, how could she leave him to tackle this delivery alone?

If nothing else, she could offer moral support.

Dusk was edging the sky by the time she arrived at the Silver Spur. She drew her rental car up beside Tanner's big truck and parked, then scooted out of the driver's seat.

She headed toward the stables, feeling her first pangs of trepidation. Horses frightened her, something she'd forgotten in her zeal to be Good Neighbor Sam to a man who made her heart beat faster than a Texas two-step.

Maybe coming here hadn't been such a good idea, after all.

She should leave—and hope Darce finished up quickly in Lampassas.

Yes, that's what she'd do.

Leave.

She turned to go, but just then a ruckus from the stables stopped her in her tracks. It was a high-pitched whinny from one of Tanner's horses.

And from the strident sound of pain buried in that whinny, she knew it had come from the mare in labor.

That realization made her want to hightail it out of there even faster. But, from somewhere down deep, she dredged up a shaky breath of courage and abandoned her plan for retreat.

Tanner needed her.

And how could she turn her back on someone in need?

She stiffened her spine and started toward the open stable door.

TANNER HEARD the approaching footsteps.

Thank goodness, Darcy had arrived.

With his entire attention focused on the mare in front of him, he shouted over his shoulder. "Doc, I need your help. She's in the throes of hard labor," he said as he held on to the foal's emerging feet and tried gently, or not so gently, to ease the little critter out. "If she doesn't deliver quick I could lose both of them."

Behind him he heard a feminine gasp, and something akin to desperation told him that wasn't the gasp of a practiced large-animal vet.

That was a gasp of one desirable but totally useless Yankee female.

"Hell and damnation." He cursed ripely over that selfsame shoulder. "Candy—I hope you have Darcy with you."

Candace swallowed a gulp of panic. She had no such person within helping range. But Tanner needed assistance, whatever kind of assistance that might be.

She'd assumed nature always took care of these things, but apparently not this time.

"No, Tanner—I don't have Darce with me. But I'm here." She wasn't sure she wanted a translation

of the grumbled expletive that fell from his lips.
She ought to just leave him to weather his emergency alone, but she knew she couldn't do that. "Is
there something I can do to help?"

He struggled with the animal in front of him and
didn't answer.

Maybe he hadn't heard her offer.

The horses in their stalls had set up quite a
clamor, whinnying deafeningly and stamping their
feet—er, hooves.

She tried again. "Tanner?"

She was sure she heard a disparagement about
Yankees and hapless city girls in equal displeasure,
but she stood her ground.

Finally he answered. "Okay—if you're so all-
fired determined to help, get the horses into the paddock out back. The mare's making them skittish."

Skittish? She'd sure hate to hear *upset*. "Is the
baby coming now?"

He gave a strangled sound. "Baby?"

"The...uh, little horse."

A blue northern of a curse ripped the air. "It's a
foal, and no, that's the problem—it's not coming.
I've got a breech delivery on my hands. Now, get
those animals out of here."

Tanner didn't know if she was doing as he asked
or not—he was too busy. The pregnant mare was
thrashing on her side in the clean straw he'd put
down for her, and time was short, unless he wanted
to lose both his mare and her foal.

He cooed softly to the mare, something he hoped was reassuring, when reassuring was far from what he was feeling. He just wished Darcy was here instead of—

"Shoo, shoo, horsy. Shoo."

"What the—" Tanner glanced around to find his horses milling mindlessly in the open stables. Behind them Candace was making little swishing sounds and hand gestures.

The whole scene might have been funny if he hadn't been busier than a one-armed man swatting flies.

He decided he'd better handle this one himself.

"Look, uh, darlin', I'll take care of the horses. Go to the house and boil up a kettle of water."

He made a swishing motion of his own to send her on her way.

He didn't need the hot water, but it would get her out of his hair for a while.

"Right, Tanner—hot water."

She tiptoed gingerly around the rump end of a horse and headed toward the ranch house.

Tanner endured a moment of guilt for sending her off on this fool's errand, but it was for her own good.

And his.

He took another moment to watch her cute little backside as she sashayed out, then herded the horses into the paddock with a well-delivered swat to their rumps.

They understood that better than "Shoo, horsy," he was certain.

CANDACE didn't want to miss the birth and feared she would as she impatiently waited for the water to boil on the big kitchen stove.

Tanner had been edgy. No, *cranky* was a better word. She'd come here to help him out, but she couldn't help it if the horses didn't want to follow her directions.

She had tried her best—but the man was an ingrate.

To him she was just a Yankee city girl. And nothing she could do would change that.

Finally the kettle on the stove began to boil. She turned off the heat, found a hot pad and lifted the water from the burner.

At least she knew how to boil water—something she was sure would surprise the man in the stables.

She hurried to Tanner, hefting the water he'd asked for. Not that she expected any gratitude for her effort. Tanner didn't seem to need anyone. He had life under control.

As she neared the birthing area, she saw that was true when it came to delivery skills, as well.

"Oh, Tanner," she said in awe as he eased the backward foal out as if it were a simple birth— though she suspected it had been far from that.

The man could be both tough and tender, she realized, and when he smiled at the foal as if he were its proud papa, she felt a tug on her heart-strings.

She set aside the hot water, ignoring whether it was needed, and edged toward Tanner to watch as the new mother nudged her little one to its feet.

Seeing that softness in Tanner's eyes, what woman could resist the cowboy?

Was this part of that elusive mystique?

The tough and tender cowboy, with skills that commanded a woman's appreciation—*and* turned her insides to mush?

TANNER SMILED AT the look of wonder on her face. Women couldn't resist babies, he decided—even the equine variety.

But somehow he was pleased to be sharing this moment with Candy. He'd come too close to losing both mare and foal—and he wanted to enjoy this feeling of victory over nature. It was part of ranching, part of life.

Not that he always trusted nature. *Or* life.

Both sometimes soured. Just when a man thought he could count on them.

Still, he wanted to savor the moment, enjoy it with Candace.

"Do you want to name the little colt since you helped by, uh, bringing the water?"

He felt like a heel about that now.

"Oh, the water—I'm sorry, Tanner. I didn't get it here in time."

"I didn't need it after all," he admitted, hiding a grin. "But thanks anyway. Now—how about that name for the new little arrival?"

"You mean it? I can name him?"

"I wouldn't have suggested it if I didn't."

He hadn't meant his voice to sound so gruff— but it wasn't easy for a man to let his feelings show.

And he supposed that's what he was doing with Candy.

She smiled wide, expectant—and Tanner felt a surge of desire hit him smack in his libido. *Keep cool, cowboy,* he warned himself. *This woman could take you down.*

He watched her face as she tried to think of a name, apparently considering and dismissing several.

He only hoped she didn't come up with something...Yankee.

Her forehead puckered in thought, and so did that kissable little mouth of hers. He remembered well the taste of it. Sweet as...*candy.*

"Stormy," she said, "for his difficult arrival into this world."

"Stormy." Tanner tried out the name, deciding it was a good fit. "I like it."

She smiled at that, and Tanner knew he'd never forget that smile. It would haunt him long after she'd gone back to Connecticut.

"Well, it seems you two have everything under control."

It was Darcy.

Tanner and Candace glanced up to see her approach, doctor bag in hand.

"I came as soon as I could, Tanner." She glanced at Candace and gave a wry grin. "But I see you had all the excellent help you needed."

Tanner knew she meant his city-slicker sidekick, but for reasons he didn't want to explain, he felt like defending her. "Hey, the lady earned her spurs tonight."

She hadn't been the expert he could have used, but she'd been gutsy enough to offer her help.

And he was appreciative.

Darcy glanced at Candace with new regard. "Well, I'll be hanged. Maybe we'll make a Texan out of you yet."

Candace blushed. "I'm not so sure of that, Darce."

CANDACE KNEW she'd never fit in here—at least not in Tanner's eyes—but she had to admit his faint praise of her had made her glow inside.

Darcy opened her doctor bag. "Since I'm here, why don't I have a look at the patients," she said and took a step toward the animals. "A difficult birth, was it, Tanner?"

"The foal was lying breech and impossible to turn," Tanner said, joining Darcy and leaving Candace to observe from a short distance away.

Candace had watched Tanner do magic tonight

and she had to admire his skill, his coolness under pressure.

Careful, girl, she told herself, *you could end up falling for this big cowboy.*

Not a good idea, she knew.

Still, she couldn't take her gaze off him, his wide shoulders that seemed capable of anything and everything, his muscled thighs as he stooped to help Darcy as she examined the new colt.

She'd seen the tenderness in him tonight—and ached to have a bit of that tenderness aimed at her, ached to be enveloped by those wide, capable shoulders, lean against his hard chest, have his denim-blue eyes spark with want and desire for her.

Just then Darcy's pager went off, interrupting Candace's thoughts.

"Another emergency?" she asked, when her friend had finished the call.

"'Fraid so," she said. "Sorry, Tanner—I'm going to have to leave. I'm needed over at Jim Monroe's place."

"Candace and I can manage from here," he assured her. "But thanks for coming—and for checking out the colt."

"Both are healthy, Tanner. You did a great job with a difficult delivery."

"Thanks."

When she'd left, Candace offered to fix something to eat. It was late. Dark had settled, and she was certain food had been the last thing on Tanner's mind.

He smiled. "Sounds great. I'll just finish up here and come in and help you."

"Take your time. I can handle rustling up grub."

"Grub?"

"You know, *dinner*."

"I know what *grub* is. I just didn't know it was part of a city girl's vocabulary."

"Hey, we Yankees have a *few* skills."

He grinned at that. "And I hope you show them to me, darlin'."

Candace swallowed hard. She'd walked right into that one. "I think I'd better go cook."

Before he could say more, she took off toward the house.

TANNER FINISHED in the stables. He'd returned the other horses from the paddock and fed and watered them. The new colt and his mother were doing well—and Tanner was ready for a delectable meal. He hadn't realized how hungry he was—and not just for food.

He wanted another taste of sweet Candace, and he hoped he could steal another kiss or two.

He smelled the smoke before he got to the house. It was wafting out the kitchen window, and behind it was a feminine pink hand waving in an effort to dissipate it.

Tanner groaned. Was this one of those Yankee skills she'd bragged to him about?

He hurried through the back door, greeted by more smoke and the stridency of the smoke alarm going off.

"I just burned the biscuits—but don't worry, I'll bake up some more."

Smoke roiled from the oven as she opened it and reached for the baking sheet—without oven mitts.

Tanner grabbed her hands and jerked her away from the smoke and the heat. "In case you hadn't noticed, that oven is hot."

He planted a kiss on both palms, just because he wanted to, then reached for the mitts and pulled out the charred lumps of biscuits.

She looked woebegone as he dumped the blackened disks into the sink to be fed to the garbage disposal when they'd cooled.

"I know how to bake," she said dismally.

"I'm sure you do."

"It's just that, well, I was trying to have everything just right."

He waved the smoke from between them, where it seemed determined to linger. "Hang the biscuits. I'll bet everything else is wonderful."

"O-o-omelettes," she said. "Oh, no, Tanner. I forgot them, too." She reached for the omelette pan on the stove.

The smell of scorched egg told him it was going to be slim pickings for dinner.

"They're not *too* bad," she pronounced, sliding them onto a waiting platter and shutting off the burner.

"I'm sure they'll be fine." Tanner glanced at them, hoping for the best, and in truth, they were only a little bit crusty.

On the bottom.

The top looked edible.

And she'd done a great job setting the table—though maybe she'd been expecting the queen.

She'd obviously rummaged around in his cabinets until she'd found plates that matched and weren't overly chipped, cups without coffee stains—and was that *his* silverware?

She must have polished it, because it gleamed.

And from somewhere she'd found cloth napkins. *Cloth.*

He always made do with paper towels.

He brought out a smile. "The…table looks lovely."

That made her cry.

"Ah, darlin'." He didn't like women to cry. He didn't know what to do with them.

He put his arms around her, but apparently that was the wrong thing to do. It only made her cry harder.

He'd never understand women.

She'd been scared to death of his horses but hadn't backed down from trying to shoo them out into the paddock. She'd tried to help with the foaling without fear of messing up her manicure. She'd burned supper without a tear. But when he gave her a compliment about the table, she'd opened up like Niagara Falls.

"Look," he said, "don't cry."

He kissed her eyelids, tasting the salt of her tears, the sweetness of who she was—and he knew he'd never wanted a woman as much as he did this one right now.

6

CANDACE MELTED into Tanner's kiss. Her heart beat a crazy tattoo, and her head had taken a permanent vacation. But his mouth felt so good on hers—untamed, unrestrained and unswerving.

She'd forgotten about the smoke and the burned biscuits. Forgotten that she'd been trying so hard to fix a nice dinner and show Tanner she wasn't some bungling dimwit. That she might not be good in the stables, but that at least she knew her way around a kitchen.

But instead she'd done everything wrong.

And then he'd kissed her.

Was kissing her.

And she didn't ever want him to stop.

His strong arms crushed her against his chest, making her feel helpless.

And wanted.

His tongue dueled softly with hers, and he let out a moan of pleasure she understood only too well. He was melting her bones and her inhibitions.

Her good sense had skittered away to where she'd never find it again.

Somewhere in the far reaches of her brain she

remembered the article she'd come here to write. But kissing Tanner had a way of blurring her purpose.

Not a good sign.

Finally she drew herself away from the delicious taste of him and dragged in a shaky breath. "I—I don't think this is a good idea, Tanner."

His tongue traced the shape of her mouth. "Definitely not."

He reached for her again, but this time good sense prevailed. "I think we'd better eat—"

"I'm ready."

"—dinner."

"Right," he said, disappointment evident in his tone. "The crusty omelettes."

She wasn't going to start crying again. Anyone could have a catastrophe in the kitchen. "I'll make some toast to go with them—they'll be fine."

TANNER RELEASED her reluctantly. She was so delectable, his head was still spinning. It would take other parts of him even longer to return to complacency. Food was the last thing on his mind at the moment.

He wanted Candace, though that was not the greatest idea he'd had in a while.

He didn't need to go getting himself involved in a romantic entanglement with a woman who could make his good sense evaporate faster than rain in a hot desert.

He had a ranch to run, and a ranch was a tough mistress, jealously requiring all his attention.

He backed away from Candace and stuffed his hands in his pockets to ensure he wouldn't reach for her again, the way he was sorely tempted to do. "Toast—you make the toast. I'll warm the omelettes and put them on the table."

He reached for a beer in the refrigerator, then thought again. With the table set for royalty, he'd better crack open a good bottle of wine to go with dinner.

He only hoped he remembered where his wineglasses had gotten to.

"SO, TELL ME, why do you hate being called Candy?"

Candace took another sip of her white wine. Their dinner hadn't been too bad. At least the omelettes hadn't tasted like burned charcoal. Afterward she and Tanner had done the dishes without getting in each other's way.

In fact, she had the feeling Tanner had tried hard to avoid touching her. But that was probably for the best. Just his nearness in the close confines of the kitchen had been torture enough.

And she hadn't forgotten his kiss—or its devastation to her senses.

They'd retreated to the living room, Candace careful to keep a discreet distance from him on the sofa. "Candy makes me sound all sweet and frothy, like—"

"Cotton candy?"

She frowned. "Or something with a nougat center."

TANNER DIDN'T know about the nougat center, but her kiss had been as sweet as warm honey and had whetted his appetite for more of her.

But he wasn't sure he could ever get enough of that sweetness.

"Maybe you're more like your nickname than you realize."

Her haughty glower told him to back off. A man picked his battles—but he liked a woman with a little fight in her.

And he had the feeling this woman perched on the corner of his sofa, prissier than a duchess, could give as good as she got.

"Tell me about your life back in Connecticut," he said.

She took a dainty sip of wine, then studied him over the rim. "What do you want to know?"

He thought he detected a certain wariness in her response. "Is there anyone waiting for you? Anyone...special?"

He hated the fact that he wanted to know, hated that she made him curious.

And vulnerable.

"If you're asking if there's a man in my life, the answer is no."

Tanner released the breath he hadn't realized he'd been holding. He shouldn't care whether she had one man or ten dancing attention on her. But the truth of the matter was, he did.

"Good," he said, not regretting the honesty in his statement.

She looked so damned right here in his living room, had looked so right sitting across from him at the dinner table, cooking in his kitchen. She'd even added her own quirky presence to the stables.

He stopped short of picturing her in his big four-poster bed, mussed from sleep and sated from love-making.

She was the kind of woman who could fit all too easily into a man's fantasies, *his* fantasy. But she didn't belong at the Silver Spur. He had learned that lesson with Marlene. And Candace was no different. A city girl who'd itch to escape to her ivory tower at the first sign of a little hard work.

Still, he had to admit Candace had pitched in to help him tonight. Or did he just want to think this woman might be different?

But old memories died hard.

And so did old wariness. Wariness kept a man from making mistakes. And Tanner didn't like making mistakes.

"What about you?" she asked. "Don't tell me there aren't a bevy of females in your life."

He gave a slow grin. He liked it that she was a little curious, too. About him.

"Make that a herd of females and you'd be right. In fact, at last count, they totaled thirty-eight. All of them from prime stock, too."

Her expressive green eyes widened, then narrowed at him as realization dawned. "I wasn't referring to the four-legged variety," she said.

"That's the only kind there is right now."

She studied him long and hard, as if deciding whether or not she could believe him—then her silky lashes lowered.

She toyed with a loose thread at the hem of her blouse.

"What about the women I saw you talking to at Darcy's barbecue?"

"Friends."

"Friends?"

He nodded. "The ranch doesn't leave a lot of time for the kind of romancin' a woman expects from a man."

"And what, in your opinion, does a woman expect?"

Tanner thought of Marlene. If he'd given her a slice of the moon, that female wouldn't have been happy. Maybe if he'd sold the ranch, given up his dream and gone back East with her, agreed to go to work for her daddy like she'd wanted...

Tanner hadn't needed a woman that bad.

Hadn't been about to let her stuff him into a suit,

strangle him with a tie and send him off to work in an office the size of a tin can.

He needed space around him, land, horses, cattle, the kind of things that meant something to a man, the kind of freedom he knew he couldn't live without.

"They want hearts and flowers, champagne nights on the town. Some want to make you into something you're not."

Those sultry green eyes roved his face, reading him—and he felt warm around the collar.

"Sounds like some female went barking up the wrong tree with you, Tanner."

He refused to duck her gaze. "Maybe."

"For your information, not all women are like that." She took a slow sip of wine. A drop beaded on her lower lip, and she licked it away with her tongue.

Tanner felt his heat rise and his body harden. "What do you expect from a man?" he asked, thinking he'd damn well give her anything she wanted at the moment.

She lowered her gaze. "Honesty."

Unless he'd missed his guess, she'd been hurt by someone, as well. Maybe that was the reason for the hesitation he read in her eyes, the hurt he saw when she thought no one was looking. "That's not so much to ask."

Her gaze shot up. "For most men it is."

"Most? Don't go categorizing us, Candy."

MAYBE SHE DID categorize, Candace thought. In a way, that was what had brought her to Texas in the first place. To sum up the cowboy, analyze his sex appeal—or lack thereof.

Not that Tanner had any lack.

That was part of the problem.

The man had so much of it, he shot holes the size of doughnuts in her little project. Tanner was the sexiest man she'd ever met.

She stood up and paced the floor, feeling the need to put distance between them.

"Wanna tell me about it, Candy?"

She spun around. "What?"

"Wanna tell me about the man who hurt you by his dishonesty?"

She let out a breath in relief. He wasn't talking about her article but about the man who'd hurt her. Steven. Her secret project was still safe.

If not foolproof.

She could still decide whether to try to salvage it or abandon it as a total failure.

She returned to the sofa and took another slow sip of wine, then glanced at Tanner. Those denim-blue eyes held want in them. Why did he have to be so handsome, so sexy?

So…desirable?

Maybe the wine was going to her head.

Oh, no, even without the wine, she had to admit Tanner was a sensual man. There was no getting around it.

"Maybe I shouldn't have said *most* men—just *some* men," she amended.

"*One* man. What did he do to you, Candy?"

She paused. "He stood me up. A week before we were to be married, he called off the wedding. I found out he'd been seeing someone, a student of his at the university where he taught. I felt…"

"Betrayed?"

"I'd been lied to." She shook off the mood as best she could. "I—I don't have a very high opinion of men."

She noted Tanner's expression. It was as if he could see the hurt and pain she felt, and she fought the urge to run into his arms and kiss him soundly.

But being kissed by a man with no more good intentions than the one who'd left her standing at the altar wasn't the way to go about restoring her faith in the opposite sex.

"The man was a fool to ever let you go," he said softly, then planted a chaste kiss on the tip of her nose.

His rarin'-to-go libido knew how much pain it caused him to keep it at that.

Candace was beautiful—and giving. And Tanner wanted to take everything she had to offer.

But that would make him no better than the guy she'd escaped from.

She smiled, and Tanner nearly lost his resolve. Instead, he finished his wine and set the glass on the coffee table in front of them.

Candace did the same, then glanced at her watch. "It's late," she said. "I really should go. I don't know the roads very well after dark."

It *was* late.

The sun had set hours ago.

Time had slipped away while he and Candace had talked.

"That's right," he said, "you don't know these roads, *especially* after dark. I'll take you back."

"No, it's too far. I can't let you do that. I'll be fine."

She stood to leave, but Tanner stopped her. "I don't want to be worrying about you. If you won't let me drive you, then stay here. Leave in the morning."

She gave him a wary glance, as if weighing the wisdom of being in close proximity with him a moment longer.

"Look," he said, "I won't touch you. I promise. And a cowboy's word is his bond."

Probably not something she'd believe after some yahoo had lied to her, but he meant it.

"Darcy's emergency was out past Kerrville," he added. "She might not be home for hours."

That seemed to convince her.

She gave a slow sigh.

"I promise to sleep on the sofa," he offered. "You can have the bed."

She shook her head at that. "Oh, no—if I agree to stay, I take the sofa."

CHIVALRY was not dead, but Candace wished it was. Tanner had insisted on giving her his bed—and it was causing her a sleepless night.

Fantasies of a naked Tanner sleeping between these sheets plagued her. *Her.* A woman who didn't believe in fantasies, who saw them as pure foolishness, a waste of good brainpower.

The old four-poster bed was big, with a soft dip in the center—where two bodies could roll together.

Tanner's scent lingered in the room like some taunting ghost.

She pictured his head on the pillow, his jaw unshaven and slack with sleep.

Oh, yes—the man might as well be in bed with her for all the rest she was getting.

As soon as the first fingers of daylight struck she intended to be up and out of here. She didn't trust herself to keep her hands from his cheek, from curling in the hair at his nape, her mouth from tasting the raw male desire she'd seen in his eyes tonight.

But Tanner had been true to his word. He'd left her alone, hadn't touched her, though just the thought of those big arms around her was inviting, kissing her awake in the middle of the night to make love to her, his hands caressing her skin, his tongue setting her body on fire.

More fantasies, fantasies that refused to be banished from her mind. This was crazy. *She* was crazy. That was it—all the hard work she'd done since Steven had dumped her was finally getting the best of her.

Maybe she should have made this trip a vacation instead of more hard work, probably the hardest of her blossoming career. Then maybe Tanner wouldn't affect her the way he did.

WHEN DAYLIGHT finally came, Candace slipped out of the big bed, stripped off the soft cotton T-shirt Tanner had loaned her to sleep in, complete with his scent on it, then slid into her clothes.

There was no sound in the house, and she quietly eased open the bedroom door.

Tanner was still asleep on the sofa. She hadn't had a lot of opportunities to watch naked men sleep, but she hadn't expected the experience to be so sensual.

Erotic.

Her heart thudded against her ribs at the sight of him, one arm flung over the side, the other resting on his bare chest. A small scrap of blanket hid the lower half of him, but only slightly.

His jaw was slack with sleep and deeply shadowed, his lips slightly parted. She remembered the feel of those lips on hers, a memory that had no doubt triggered last night's fantasies, as well as the one she was having right now.

She tried to ignore them and her racing hormones and took a few tentative steps across the hardwood floor.

Tanner continued to sleep.

And her fantasy continued to play.

She fumbled for her purse on the table, then headed toward the back door. She sneaked one last peek at him, then slipped hurriedly out the door.

A horse nickered softly in the stables. No other sound disturbed the early morning air. She tossed her purse into the rental car, then thought of the new colt.

How could she leave without checking on him?

The stable door creaked as she slid it open and stepped into the shadowed darkness inside. She heard the faint rustling of straw, a low whinny or two. The animals probably thought it was time for breakfast.

Did horses eat breakfast?

She left the stable door open so she could see to make her way inside. She was eager to find out how the little colt had made it through the night.

She also needed to give herself something else to fill her head besides fantasies of Tanner. The man had had her senses on full alert ever since she'd come here.

Maybe she'd have to leave and head to Connecticut before she got him out of her system.

Well, that was the plan, wasn't it?

She'd come to get her article, then she was outta here.

However, her article wasn't going well.

And that was all Tanner's fault.

She heaved a sigh, then headed for the mare's stall.

A pawing and stamping of hooves from the other horses frightened her—and she gave them a wide berth. She hadn't forgotten last night and how incompetent she'd been with them, how they'd foiled her every attempt to get them to move out to the paddock.

Making her look bad in front of Tanner.

Mother and baby had their ears pricked at her arrival. She wished she had a piece of apple or a raw carrot to offer them instead of just her presence.

The mare gave a soft whinny, and the colt, curious as a toddler, crept toward her for a closer look.

Candace petted—*patted*—his nose. "How are you this morning, little guy?" she asked, and was rewarded with a nuzzle against her hand.

Candace giggled at the feel of it.

"Getting braver, are we?"

At the sound of the deep male voice Candace whirled.

Tanner stood in the dim light.

Thankfully he was dressed—in boots, low-slung jeans and a shirt that looked hastily pulled on.

His shadowed jaw creased with a slow, heated smile, and Candace swallowed hard. Did the man have to look so appealing this early in the morning?

"I just wanted to see the new colt again before I left."

He hooked his thumbs in the pockets of his jeans.

"I didn't think you'd come to rustle the livestock—but I *was* hurt you didn't stay for breakfast."

"Breakfast?"

"Yeah—flapjacks. They're my specialty. And it's the least I can do since you fixed dinner last night."

Was this more Texas hospitality? If it was, she wasn't sure she'd survive being the recipient of it—not with a man who looked like Tanner.

"I'll have to take a rain check," she said. "I left a message for Darcy last night that I'd be home early." She knew she was already going to get the third degree from her friend when she got home. She didn't need to compound it by staying half the day, as well. "Besides, I'm sure you have lots of work to do."

TANNER DID, but he hated letting Candace go. He wasn't sure why exactly, but this city girl was getting to him—and he was letting it happen.

She looked so damned beautiful in the pale light of the stables, its glow brushing her face with shadows that couldn't hide the heated blush on her cheeks.

Her red-gold hair was in a delightful disarray—and Tanner regretted he hadn't been the one to muss it. The pillow had done that.

Her lips were dewy-sweet and inviting, taunting—and he couldn't take his eyes off them.

He should let her go—now—before he did something foolish like ravish her here in the straw.

"Fine," he growled, a little more gruffness to his voice than he'd intended. "A rain check then."

"It's a promise," she said, then bid the little colt a last goodbye with a pat on his nose.

Tanner followed her into the morning sunshine and opened her car door for her.

"Candace, I appreciate all you did last night, coming here, offering moral support, dinner—"

She shook her head. "I'm afraid I wasn't all that much help."

Her smile was hesitant, and Tanner wanted to kiss the edges of it. "I meant every word of what I said."

He closed the car door and told her to drive carefully, then watched as her car bounced its way down the rutted drive to the highway.

He only hoped he had enough work to do around here today to get Candace out of his system—but he wasn't very hopeful that would happen.

He had the work, that was certain, but forget about Candace?

That wasn't very likely.

"DON'T THINK you can sneak past me into the house, Candace Porter," Darcy called from the clinic as Candace tried to do just that.

Darcy was handfeeding one of the newborn calves that hadn't been thriving under its mother's care. "I...you just looked busy, that's all," Candace said, pausing outside the clinic door and realizing she wasn't going to get away with the simple, "Hi, I'm home" she'd hoped for.

"I'm not too busy to hear what happened between you and Tanner last night," she said as Candace finally acknowledged defeat and slumped onto a clinic chair.

"Well, you'll be disappointed then, because *nothing* happened."

"Right—and I'm the tooth fairy," Darce replied.

Candace stood up and paced the small clinic. "It's true just the same."

She gave her friend the briefest rundown of what happened once Darcy left them alone together—her disaster in the kitchen, why she stayed the night instead of attempting to drive home.

Darcy was glad about the latter, not surprised about the former, but still wanted to know everything in between.

"That's it," Candace said, "nothing else happened."

She didn't want to mention about Tanner kissing her or she'd never get away from Darcy's probing questions.

"So, did you sleep with him?"

Candace blushed. "No, I didn't sleep with him."

This had been a whole lot easier when they were in college, sharing a dorm room and swapping confidences.

Maybe it was because Tanner was so much more than the guys she'd dated in college. Even her feelings for Steven, she realized, hadn't reached into her and touched her soul the way Tanner seemed capable of doing.

And that she wasn't about to confess to Darcy.

"Oh, yes, I got to name the new colt," she announced. "Stormy. What do you think?"

Darcy glanced up from what she was doing and arched an eyebrow at her. "I think you're trying to divert my attention. Stormy's a fine name—but I want to hear more about you and Tanner."

"Well—you're fresh out of luck." Candace gave her nosy friend a smug smile and turned to head toward the house. As an afterthought she turned back. "I'll fix lunch—if you lay off grilling me about Tanner."

And maybe pigs sprout wings and fly, she thought with a grimace.

7

THE NEXT AFTERNOON Darcy announced they were going shopping in Austin. Darcy needed a date dress and insisted she couldn't decide on one without Candace's help.

Candace was only too happy to abandon her work in progress, which wasn't progressing at all, and indulge herself in this favorite feminine pastime.

Besides, the date the dress was for was Darcy's, not hers, and for that she was relieved.

Tanner did nothing but confuse her, and the more distance she put between them, the better.

She and Darcy set out, prepared to shop until they dropped.

"So, how hot is this big date you have Saturday night?" she asked Darcy when they'd finally collapsed into chairs at the trendy little restaurant in the shopping center.

Darcy gave a wide grin. "I have an idea—why don't you and Tanner go with us?"

Darcy was warming to the idea a little more than Candace found comfortable. "Tanner and I are not an item, nor are we likely to be," she returned.

Darce raised an eyebrow. "I wouldn't be so sure of that, Candace. I've seen the way the man looks at you—as if he'd like to eat you up."

Candace had her doubts about that, and she didn't need her friend encouraging a relationship that made no sense whatsoever. She and Tanner were as different as night and day, despite her physical attraction to him.

"I know you'd like to see us together, Darce, but it isn't going to happen. Besides, I don't think Tanner needs—or wants—anyone in his life."

Certainly not a woman from Connecticut, she thought.

Darcy toyed with a curly carrot strip on her plate. "He likes to give the impression that he doesn't *need* anyone," she said. "Maybe to keep the women at bay. There are more than a few around who'd love a chance with the man, believe me— but, so far, no one's been able to catch his eye for long."

Candace thought about that for a moment. Tanner was a loner, but she had an idea there was more to it than that.

"I get the feeling he's been hurt before," she said, taking a sip of her ice water and hoping Darcy was in the mood to fill in a few blanks where Tanner was concerned.

Maybe if she understood him...

Darcy nodded and leaned forward confidentially. "Tanner doesn't talk much about himself, so I don't know the whole story, but I do know he was married once. Her name was Marlene. And Tanner was very smitten. I don't know what went wrong between them—but one day she just pulled up stakes and moved back to Philadelphia.''

Maybe that accounted for what she'd seen in Tanner's eyes, his projected attitude of needing no one in his life. His wariness.

''They weren't married long,'' Darcy went on. ''Six months maybe. They were both very young, and somehow they didn't seem at all suited to each other.''

''So much for the opposites attract theory,'' Candace said, but she knew her friend had given her another dimension of the man she couldn't keep her mind off for longer than ten minutes at a time. Another reason she and Tanner would never work.

Candace didn't come from Tanner's world.

And never would be right for him.

But that was something she'd known all along. And Darcy had just confirmed it.

''So, tell me, how is the article coming along?''

Candace allowed Darcy to draw her out of her mood—before her friend read her thoughts, her musings about Tanner and his past.

She needed the change of subject—and her article would bring her back to her world, her reason for being here in the first place.

''My article, I'm afraid, is not going well,'' she answered. ''Maybe I should just call it quits and go back home to Connecticut, find a new project. I can't seem to pull this one out of the fire—and I'm not sure why exactly.''

"Well, I know why. That hunk of a cowboy has your senses in a turmoil. Tanner has that effect on women—and you, Candace, are no exception.''

Tanner again. The man seemed to dog her thoughts—as well as this conversation.

"Maybe you should admit defeat,'' her friend went on, "admit that the Texas cowboy is one sexy varmint.''

"I'm not so sure of that, Darce,'' she said. At least she wasn't ready to admit it. It made no sense that one segment of the male species could be all that different from another.

It stood to reason—and Candace liked to rely on facts, not fiction. And definitely not some foolish feminine myth.

Candace was a realist.

But her friend wasn't giving up the subject.

"I see you need a little more convincing, Candace Porter, but you'll tumble yet. That article of yours will soon be applesauce—if it isn't already.''

Candace didn't have a comeback for that. Her little project might very well end up applesauce, but if it did, it would be because of Tanner, because she couldn't seem to get him out of her mind.

Fortified by lunch, she and Darcy continued their trek through the mall in search of the perfect dress.

Finally, in the last shop they came to, her friend struck gold—or rather black silk.

It was just the dress for her date, sleek and slim, with a pretty neckline that would show off Darcy's peaches-and-cream complexion.

She also found a dress for Candace, and Candace had to admit she'd love to have it, though not for a date with Tanner, of course. But they didn't have it in her size.

It was shimmery emerald-green, which would make her eyes large and luminous, and against her non-frivolous nature she could picture herself dancing with Tanner in the moonlight, him kissing her shoulder the dress would leave bare.

When the saleswoman offered to order it in from another store, Candace was tempted. Would Tanner think she looked beautiful in it?

She didn't intend to have any chance to wear it with the man, though, she remembered—so she declined the offer.

Darcy was deflated. "I don't know what's wrong with you, Candace. Aren't you the least bit tempted to go out with Tanner Carson?"

Candace didn't want to admit how very right her friend was about that.

CANDACE HAD decided no more hesitating—and no more distractions of the cowboy variety. Darcy would be all involved with her date tonight—which would leave Candace free to work on her little project.

She'd always been able to plot the direction of her article, but not this time. Was there some crazy truth to the myth of the cowboy? Maybe she'd been in Texas too long—she was losing her objective.

Candace tapped her pen in a staccato beat, then tossed it down and picked up the phone. She needed to talk to her editor in New York.

The woman answered on the fifth ring.

Candace pictured her sitting at her cluttered desk, a thousand callbacks to make and a magazine to get out. Maybe this was a bad idea. Liz Talberg didn't have the time to baby a writer—even if Candace was one of her favorites.

"Darling, how are things out there in the wilds of cowboy land? Have you stepped in anything yet?"

Candace grinned. Liz didn't know how accurate she was. "I've been very careful," she told her editor. Maybe this was what she needed—a definite tug to her own time zone.

"Excuse me a tick, dear—Lenny just brought in my favorite latte. Remind me to give the boy a raise."

Candace waited as Liz thanked her male secretary, then sampled her drink. How long had it been since Candace had indulged in a latte?

Instead she'd been indulging in fantasies—of Tanner.

"How's the article coming?" her editor asked when she returned to the conversation. She gave a dramatic shudder. "Texas is just the end of the earth. You're such a brave heart to take on this project."

More like a fool, Candace thought. How could she tell Liz that one cowboy had her feminist protégée writer in his strong clutches?

"Darling?" Liz asked curiously. "Don't tell me you're having problems with these macho males."

"No, of course not," Candace heard herself say. She was right. She shouldn't have bothered Liz with this. Tanner was her problem. So were her fantasies. "I just…just thought I'd touch base with you."

"Oh, good—you had me worried for a minute. Now I've got to go, darling. You get back to work."

Candace sighed as she hung up the phone. How could she have told Liz the truth, that her project had hit a stone wall, that the cowboy might be an incorrigible brute, but that he had a tender streak a mile wide…and knew how to treat a lady.

She just needed more time to absorb how two such different instincts could exist in one person.

She glanced at the clock on Darcy's wall and realized her friend hadn't come in from the stables. She'd be late for her date if she didn't hurry—and tonight was important to her, Candace knew.

Maybe she should go in search of her.

She found Darcy with one of the horses in the paddock, one of Darcy's own.

"What's wrong?" she asked. "Did you forget Todd Wellman's picking you up in forty-five minutes?"

"Oh—no. I forgot to call him and cancel."

"Cancel?" Candace fairly shrieked. "Why?"

Darcy sighed. "It's Dolly. She's not over her case of the colic—and I'm afraid to leave her."

"But you really wanted to go tonight."

"I know."

Her friend looked desolate, and Candace knew she had to do something.

"Tell me what to do—and I'll watch Dolly for you." Candace couldn't believe what she'd just offered. But how hard could it be to baby-sit a horse?

Then she remembered Tanner's herd of critters and her night in his stables trying to get them to mind.

Darcy gave her a hopeful glance. "You'd do that? You'd watch Dolly?"

"Sure, what are friends for?" She swallowed and mentally berated herself for her hasty offer.

"Come on," Darcy said, "help me dress. I'll explain what to do while I get ready. And I'll keep my pager on tonight. You can beep me if Dolly gets worse."

Candace glanced at the dappled old horse. She looked so…big. Nothing like the tiny colt or the quiet mare doting on her little one.

She wished she didn't have the feeling she'd just gotten herself into more trouble than she could handle.

TANNER HAD ridden fences today, mended a weak spot along the south fence line, then driven part of his herd of cattle over there to tend to the grass that could stand being a little shorter—but he wasn't tired.

In fact, he was restless.

Not the go-into-town-and-belly-up-to-the-bar kind of restless. He wasn't in the mood for a drink. No, this was something more…indefinable.

He'd been plenty pleased with his life just the way it was for a long time now, solitude being something he enjoyed, but lately…

Maybe he just needed a good meal. He tried to work up an appetite for mashed potatoes and chicken-fried steak at his favorite restaurant.

But after a hot shower and a change of clothes, he found himself driving to Dripping Springs instead of stopping in somewhere for dinner.

He hadn't seen Candace in three days and didn't want to admit she was the reason he was heading his truck up Darcy's long driveway.

He alighted from the truck and started toward the house, then stopped and directed his steps toward the stables instead.

A faint light filtered through the partially open

door into the gathering dusk. Curious, he approached the stables and swung the door wider.

Tanner was certain his eyes were playing tricks on him.

He blinked, but the vision remained.

Candace.

She was crouched atop a stack of straw bales, eye to eye with one of Darcy's horses. Dolly. The grande dame of the herd, graying around the muzzle but as gentle as a lamb.

When he stepped through the door Candace glanced up. "Oh, Tanner—it's you. Help me. This…this beast is trying to bite."

She teetered on the top bale and nearly lost her balance as she tried to remain out of the horse's questing reach. Unsteady, she grabbed at a support beam and held on for dear life.

At least she wouldn't fall—which, as far as Tanner could see, was the only danger she was in.

The horse only wanted the carrot Candy had tucked into the pocket of her jeans. But he'd bet his next month's feed bill *she* didn't know that.

He stifled a chuckle he was certain she wouldn't appreciate. "She's trying to bite, huh?"

"Yes, I…I just came out here to check on her, and she tried to *attack*."

He bit back his amusement and leaned lazily against a stall door. "Attack?"

That was a strong word, even for Candace.

"Yes—why don't you quit repeating everything I say and *do* something?"

"And what exactly would you like me to do?"

"Make her go away." The horse nudged at her, and Candace let out a wounded yelp. "See, she's attacking."

Tanner couldn't hold back the laughter any longer. "I can see that, darlin'."

"Then *help* me."

"Darlin', she's not after you—she just wants that carrot peeking out of your pocket."

She glanced at the horse, then at him.

"Oh."

Color rose in her cheeks.

"Oh," she repeated, this time with a little more conviction.

Then with a fierce glower that said she dared him to laugh at her again, she withdrew the carrot and held it gingerly in front of the horse, careful to keep a cautious distance away.

Dolly snagged the tidbit and munched noisily, content to have finally gotten what she was after.

"It's safe now—you can come down."

Candace's green eyes still held a wariness. She studied the beast in front of her, then the distance to the floor and finally Tanner's open arms.

"I think I'll just stay here," she said.

"Suit yourself."

Why was the woman so afraid of him?

He turned away, but Candace called him back.

"Okay—help me down," she said, as if the thought of remaining there all night didn't appeal to her, after all.

Tanner obliged. He put out his hands and caught her around the hips, lifting her down. She slid along the length of him, their bodies touching enticingly.

"Thanks," she said, her voice a husky whisper.

Tanner had no voice. His breath had been stolen from his lungs at the feel of her against him. Her body branded him with its lush curves. The scent of her, so feminine, surrounded him, drowning his senses.

He should release her, but at the moment, he couldn't fathom ever letting her go.

CANDACE FELT the minute something changed between them. She'd been mortified, caught looking foolish in front of Tanner.

Again.

But how was she to know that big horse wasn't going to take a nip out of her?

Tanner had been amused. His irritating, sexy, *maddening* grin was something she wanted to wipe right off his handsome face. Then he'd helped her down—and her body had betrayed her.

She could no more deny she was affected by Tanner than she could fly.

And Tanner was affected, too.

Desire sizzled between them, and neither could pull away—not if their lives depended on it. She forgot Dolly, forgot about looking like a fool in Tanner's eyes, the city girl once again out of her element.

But *this* she understood.

This heat between them, the sparks that threatened to ignite and consume them both.

His lips, his full, sexy lips, were a hairbreadth away, his breath warm, silky, fanning against her—and her mouth went dry.

He gave a low, guttural groan that spoke to the turmoil within him. Candace had the same turmoil roiling in her.

"I've got to kiss you, darlin'. I hope that's okay with you because I have the hounds of hell chasing me—and I can't fight them off."

The hounds of hell sounded far worse than a bite from Dolly.

"It—it's okay." The words didn't sound like they were hers, but some inner impatient voice from within her.

His lips descended, brushed hers lightly, teasingly, heightening her need of him, fanning the flames that threatened to consume her.

She couldn't believe how good his mouth felt, how right that she was kissing him back. Her heart pounded, her pulses leaped and everything in her reached out for more of him.

His long, strong fingers tangled in her hair as he drew her closer, deepening the kiss, deepening the connection between them. She stood on tiptoe to get more of him.

He drew her harder against him. She could feel the press of his desire for her, knew he wanted her—and she wanted him. At least for the present—and hang the future.

Hang the fact that she could be—was—making a mistake.

But she didn't want to think of that now.

This—Tanner—felt so good she never wanted him to stop kissing her, holding her. She wanted him to love her—and she'd worry about the consequences tomorrow.

He touched her through the crisp fabric of her blouse, caressing one breast, kneading it with strong male fingers, teasing its nub to life.

His touch set off a sweet ache low in her belly, making her yearn for more, yearn for him, his touch. He teased the other breast, awakening more fireworks within her, more need.

"Candy." He breathed her nickname, and she felt less like correcting him than she ever had. Couldn't, not even if she could work up the ire.

He popped open the buttons of her blouse and lightly brushed a kiss over the fullness of each breast. His tongue flickered and laved and set her on fire—and if she didn't have him now, she thought she would die.

"Aach!" Candace let out a yelp as a cold nose

nudged her in the back where Tanner had drawn up her blouse. She was sure she felt...

Teeth.

Tanner let out a curse, then laughed as the horse broke up what was going on between them. "Dolly, your timing leaves a lot to be desired," he complained.

In the meantime, Candace had lurched forward until she was hiding behind Tanner for safety.

Her blouse was twisted and hanging partially open, and she struggled to right herself. "I don't have another carrot, so this time I know she attacked me."

"*She* doesn't know you don't have another carrot."

But Tanner saw the humor in what had happened, though he'd been plenty happy with the way things had been developing between Candace and him.

He'd been right ready for a tumble in the hay with her if she'd been willing—and from the way she'd been kissing him back a moment before, she'd been willing, all right.

Had it not been for Dolly's penchant for carrots...

"She sure has an appetite for a horse with a case of the colic," Candace said with a frown. "This is the last time I offer to baby-sit a sick animal."

"A case of the colic, huh?" Tanner studied the beast in front of him. "I'd say she's recovered nicely."

"You think so?" Candace looked relieved. A smile slid across her face—as if she could take credit for the cure.

"Wanna get another carrot and we'll pick up where we left off?" he asked her.

The lady wore a blush. She had hurriedly buttoned her blouse, though she hadn't quite gotten the buttons in the right buttonholes. There was something touching about that.

"Come here and let me fix you up, sweetheart."

She followed his gaze to the front of her blouse, then splayed a hand over her front. "I'm sure you'd just *unbutton* it, Tanner."

"You got that right, darlin'."

But Tanner suspected he'd better keep hands off and maybe give Dolly a big slurpy kiss for returning the two of them to reality before anything more had happened.

"C'mon," he said, "the best thing for a colicky beast is walking her. Let's give her a few turns around the paddock just to be sure she's over her malady."

Tanner wasn't too sure he was over his malady, however. He had a definite case of the hots for Candy Porter.

And he wasn't sure there was a cure.

8

TANNER in the moonlight was even harder to resist. His hair glistened blue-black in the night's glow, and his blue eyes turned to liquid silver.

Candace tried to keep her distance from him as he walked Dolly. Both man and beast made her nervous, wreaked havoc with her peace of mind.

As they finished the first lap around the paddock, Tanner turned to smile at her, that turn-her-insides-to-mush brand of smile she couldn't let herself fall prey to. "Wanna learn to ride a horse?" he asked.

"Now?"

His eyes danced merrily. "No, not now—tomorrow. My place. I have an old plug that just might be your speed."

Candace bristled. "An old plug? Well, thanks for the compliment."

"Now, don't go getting all testy on me, darlin'. I just meant he'd be a safe horse for a—"

"A know-nothing city girl?"

"Let's just say a…beginner."

Candace was certain that word hadn't been his first choice.

"Can't tomorrow. I'm learning to wrestle a cactus—and that sounds like a whole lot more fun."

She didn't need any more close contact with Tanner. She couldn't trust her feelings, her shaky emotions. Besides, she'd survived life this long without learning to ride. She could survive longer.

He gave her a crooked grin. "Very funny. If you don't want to learn, you could just say so. But a few riding lessons would get you over that fear of horses."

"I'm not afraid of horses, I just treat them with a healthy dose of...respect."

"Really?"

"Really."

She wished he didn't look so sure of himself, wished he didn't intrigue her as much as he did. She wanted to know more about him.

And not just to satisfy her journalistic hunger, either.

"I promise I'll get you up on a horse some day," he said as if prophesying her fate.

Or her doom.

She shook her head. "I'd prefer to keep my feet firmly planted on the ground, if it's all the same to you."

By the time they'd returned Dolly to her spot in the stables, Tanner had let up on his threat to treat her to the dubious joys of riding.

And for that, Candace was grateful.

She'd kept herself out of reach of Dolly's four

hooves and however many teeth the old gal still possessed. She hadn't forgotten how the beast had chased her to the top of those straw bales—nor would she anytime soon.

"I think Dolly's doing fine—with no lingering ill effects from the colic," Tanner proclaimed as he closed the door to her stall.

"Good."

Dolly was in for the night, and Candace was just glad she hadn't done anything to make the horse worse. Darcy had been able to go on her date, and Candace hadn't had to call her to come home early.

Tanner had ridden to her rescue.

Though she wasn't so sure that was a good thing.

"By the way," she asked, "what brought you to Darcy's tonight?"

Tanner let his gaze roam over her. She had a piece of straw sticking out of her hair. He reached out and plucked it loose. His fingers brushed one silken curl.

Just that touch made him want to delve his fingers into its richness, its fire.

Maybe it was time to be honest, he thought. "I just wanted to see you again."

Surprise registered in her green eyes, and a pleased smile curved her lips before she carefully schooled her reaction.

But it was too late.

He'd seen it, knew she was happy he'd come by. Though he doubted she'd be eager to admit it.

Maybe she sensed the same danger he did about this relationship. No woman had ever turned him on before like Candace Porter.

And never was there a woman more wrong for him.

"Would you like to come in for a beer—or an iced tea?"

He'd love a good cold beer, but he didn't need his willpower compromised by alcohol. Not tonight. It was shaky enough.

And all because of Candace.

"Maybe an iced tea," he said. "It's a warm night."

He followed her out of the stables and toward the back door of the house.

She seemed familiar with Darcy's kitchen, he noticed as she stirred around getting their drinks ready. She looked domestic—and so desirable.

Dangerous thinking, he decided.

He'd do well to keep reality front and center in his brain.

"When do you go back to Connecticut?"

There, that should remind him of their situation.

"Are you anxious to get rid of me, Tanner?"

He should be. She was danger just waiting for him. A major screw-up in his life. Or at least that was the way he should look at her.

"Texas is a free country."

She grinned. "Spoken like a dyed-in-the-wool

Texan. You consider this big state a country all its own.''

She'd said it with a hint of a grin—but there was an edge to her comment, as well.

Did she feel like a misfit, like she didn't belong here and never would?

Probably.

And he'd done his fair share of making her feel that way.

He felt a stab of remorse for that, for the teasing he'd inflicted on her. But he'd done it for self-preservation, so he wouldn't succumb to her charming little blunders—or the blush of embarrassment that marched across her cheeks.

''Okay—I admit it. We Texans are damned proud of our state. We have a kind of snobbery about it.''

''And what about outsiders?''

''What about them?''

''Where do they fit into the scheme of things?''

He welcomed outsiders—except for the Marlene type, outsiders who came and took, who descended like a plague of locusts, complete with their own agenda.

What had brought Candace here? he wondered.

That was a silly question. She was here on vacation. A little rest and relaxation. A visit with her old college chum, Darcy.

He was seeing trouble where it didn't exist.

''Okay,'' he said, ''I've been a bit rough on you,

but, darlin', you are a little out of your Connecticut
element—"

"Out here in your wild and woolly West?"

"Out here in our wild and woolly West. We
don't raise our little pinkie when we drink from our
bone china cups. In fact, we don't have bone china
cups."

"And you don't drink white wine in your Texas
honky-tonks—"

"Wearing pearls," he added to her statement.

Her hand fluttered to her neck and the delicate
beads there.

"But they do look right purty on you, ma'am,"
he drawled in an exaggerated Texas twang.

He was more interested in that satiny skin beneath the beads.

But that was an urge better not acted upon.

She grinned at him. "Do I stand out all that
much?"

She was the Eastern sophisticate, and she could
put on a haughty look that could singe a man's
hide—but maybe that was a deception. She had a
soft side to her that could wring a torrent of feelings
out of him, out of anyone.

She stood out, all right.

That arresting beauty, her smile, those smoldering green eyes, her elegant long legs—a man's gaze
wouldn't miss her in a crowd of beauty contestants.

"Let's just say you don't go unnoticed, darlin'."

Tanner finished his tea, ice cubes clinking, and

stood up. It was time to go, before he forgot his resolve to leave the lady alone.

The trip back, the night breeze blowing through the truck windows, ought to cool his socks off a bit. And other parts, as well.

"Thanks for the cold drink," he said. "And maybe you'd better stay out of the stables when Darcy isn't home."

That got her temperature rising.

"Don't worry—you won't have to rescue me again," she said.

He hesitated at the back door, weighing the pros and cons of kissing her once more. The overhead lighting glistened in her hair, turning it to golden fire. Her skin glowed with the heat of her embarrassment.

Or was it anger?

And her full lips held a pout he'd sure love to taste.

He gave a low groan. "Give Darcy my regards," he said, then headed outside before he ended up doing something foolish.

He heard her soft, "Good night, Tanner," as he stepped off the back porch and into the dark night.

CANDACE WATCHED him go, coughed at the stir of dust his truck kicked up, watched until his taillights passed the stables and disappeared from her view.

Her heart sank in her chest. She and Tanner always seemed to be at polar ends of a logjam. He belonged here in the wild, wild West. And she…

She belonged back home, away from this big brute of a cowboy.

DARCY BABBLED all the following day about her date with Todd Wellman, but that was fine with Candace.

When Darce was talking about her own love life, she was too busy to ask about Candace's. Not that Candace *had* a love life.

She didn't.

And wouldn't.

Life was simpler when a woman went through it solo. There was no chance for trouble, heartache. It would be a long time before Candace gave another man the opportunity to trample her heart.

She had finished helping Darcy dry the last of the dinner dishes when the phone rang. It was Tanner. He wanted to alert Darcy that his second mare, Ginger, was in labor, but all was going well this time.

He was certain he could handle it alone.

"Are you sure, Tanner?" Darcy said to him. "I can drive out…." She glanced at Candace, who had tucked on her bookish glasses and was studiously at work on her notes. "I mean, *we* can drive out. Candace is just sitting here not doing a thing."

Candace glowered at her. She didn't like Darce

offering her services. Especially where Tanner was concerned.

The man impaired her senses, and she needed to keep her distance.

Tanner assured Darce he had everything under control and promised to call if he needed her.

"Thanks, *friend*," Candace said with sarcasm when Darce had hung up.

"What did *I* do?" her friend asked with feigned innocence.

"You mean, besides trying to pair me up with Tanner? *Again*."

"Oh, that."

"Yes, *that*. As you can see I'm not sitting here doing nothing, I'm knee deep in work."

Darcy sighed. "Candace, when are you going to give up on that project and admit your theory doesn't hold water? I mean, if Tanner Carson is not just chock-full of sex appeal—"

"Tanner has nothing to do with my project."

"Well, he should. He's a cowboy—one of the Texas male species you have under your mental microscope, a very *sexy* Texas male, I might add."

Candace couldn't argue with that.

Tanner was the very reason her article didn't add up.

Maybe the other men she'd met weren't quite Tanner's caliber, but they, too, possessed a certain charm.

And that was the bane of her article.

Why her heart wasn't in what she was trying to write.

She'd come here to evaluate the Texas cowboy—but her mental microscope found something different than she'd expected. She'd be a liar if she said she didn't find Tanner Carson sexy.

Maybe it was time to admit the cowboy mystique was alive and well, blasting her little theory to smithereens.

But would her very feminist editor be impressed if Candace admitted that women were vincible after all, that the cowboy could reduce them to marshmallow fluff with just a smile and a tip of his hat?

Candace doubted it very much.

And what about the danger of researching such a theory?

Tanner was temptation with that sweep-over-you Texas drawl, his dangerous denim-blue eyes and a smile that could melt a woman's bones.

She shouldn't go within six miles of the man.

Tanner hadn't called back asking for Darcy's assistance, but Candace knew his situation hadn't been far from her friend's mind.

She'd been fidgeting nervously for the past twenty minutes. Standing by wasn't Darcy's style. She liked being in the thick of things. Each patient was her own personal concern.

"C'mon, Candace, let's take a quick run out to the ranch, see how Tanner's coming along with the mare," she said when Candace was certain the woman had worn her boots to a nub on the wood floor.

"Count me out," she replied, not certain if it was Darce making yet another attempt to put her and Tanner together in the same spot on the planet or if she just wanted company on the ride over.

Either way, Candace knew she'd better not go.

She hadn't forgotten the taste of Tanner's kisses—or her wanton reaction to him.

And she didn't trust her shaky emotions right now.

"Scaredy-cat," her friend taunted.

"Fear has nothing to do with it. I'm sure Tanner can handle everything without my help. Besides, if anything goes wrong, he'll have you there."

Darcy gathered her doctor bag, then hesitated at the back door. "Last chance to come along," she called.

Candace perched her glasses on the end of her nose and picked up her notes with deliberation. "I have plenty to keep me occupied," she said. "Give Tanner my regards."

When she heard the last sounds of Darcy's truck fade away into the night, she shoved her glasses to the top of her head and tried to tell herself she'd done the wise thing by not going along.

"TOLD YOU you should have come with me," Darcy said the next morning as she flipped the flapjacks for breakfast. "Tanner was *very* disappointed you hadn't come along."

Candace, seated at the kitchen table, took a slow sip of the strong black coffee she'd made. "I'm sure he survived quite well without my help," she returned.

She knew he didn't need her greenhorn incompetence to muddle the situation.

Darcy paused long enough in her breakfast preparations to fix her with a glower. "I don't think the man said two words all night that weren't about you," she went on, obviously not intending to give up her issue easily.

Candace took another slow sip of coffee. "That I'm sure is an exaggeration."

"Okay, don't believe me."

She flipped the pancakes off the griddle and onto a big white platter and set them in the center of the table.

"I won't."

But Candace wanted to believe every word her friend had said, though it was foolishness on her part. She couldn't afford to get besotted over the cowboy.

She forked a golden pancake onto her plate and slathered it with butter and strawberry preserves. She would weigh a ton by the time she got home. Darcy's cooking was definitely fattening her up.

"So, tell me about the new little colt," she said, hoping to stem the tide of Darcy's chatter.

"Mmm, he's precious," Darcy asserted. "He has coloring like his mother, a white blaze on his head and an inquisitive nature."

"It was an easy delivery then?"

Darcy took a swig of coffee. "It went like nature intended. Tanner's developing quite a herd of horses. He's determined to make the ranch a paying concern—and he'll do it, too."

Candace had no doubt that the man could do anything he set his mind to.

Even winning her over.

But she couldn't afford to feel anything about Tanner.

She and Tanner came from two different worlds.

Darcy's prattle about the new colt—and the new colt's owner—finally wound down, and she excused herself to get to work in the clinic.

And once she'd done the breakfast dishes, Candace went to do the same.

CANDACE couldn't get her mind off Tanner the rest of the afternoon. By late in the day her curiosity got the best of her and she headed to the Silver Spur.

She wanted to see the new little colt. At least, that's what she told herself. But the truth was, she wanted to see Tanner, too.

Had he really missed her not coming with Darcy last night?

A part of her wanted to know.

Needed to know.

She aimed her car up the long drive to the ranch house, then realized Tanner might not be around. He could have gone into town or be out mending fences somewhere on the land.

But Tanner was there.

At the sound of her car approaching he stepped out of the stables.

Despite her best intentions her breath caught in her throat and her heart did a back flip. He looked so tall and muscled, his skin bronzed from the sun, and a slightly wary smile tilted his lips.

She remembered the taste and feel of those lips, the feel of those big arms holding her, the sure and steady beat of his heart as he drew her against his chest.

A warm blush heated her cheeks.

"I—I came to see the new baby," she said, suddenly feeling awkward and unsure of herself.

"He's out in the paddock trying to get his wobbly legs to work. C'mon," he said.

If he believed that wasn't her sole purpose in coming here, he didn't let on, and Candace fell into an easy step beside him.

The new arrival was as cute as Darcy had claimed.

"Tanner, he's beautiful," she said.

He called the little fellow over to the fence, and he came with equal parts of wariness and curiosity. Tanner patted his nose.

"He's waiting for a name," he said, clearly giving Candace the honor.

It wasn't an honor she was sure she deserved. She hadn't even come by last night.

Because she'd wanted to keep her distance from Tanner.

But, in truth, she couldn't seem to stay away from him. She definitely couldn't keep her mind off him.

Candace feared she'd fallen, and fallen hard, for this big cowboy.

Now he was inviting her to name yet another colt of his—and in a way leave an imprint on the ranch, a part of herself. She tried to tell herself that was silly, it was just a name, but it was what she felt.

Tanner was waiting, and Candace struggled for an appropriate name for the little colt.

"How about Dark Beauty," she said.

"He is a little beauty, isn't he?" Tanner agreed.

Candace reached out and hesitantly patted the animal's nose.

"I think he likes his name," Tanner said when the little fellow nuzzled her hand, making her laugh giddily. "I was disappointed you didn't come out with Darcy last night," he said when Dark Beauty pranced on trembly legs to his mother.

"I was afraid I'd just be in the way."

She didn't want to admit the real reason, that Tanner set fire to her senses.

"For a Yankee city girl, you're okay," he said, slanting a smile at her.

She didn't like the reminder of the difference between them, but she did like being missed by him—even a little.

"Stay for supper," he said. "I'll do the cooking. And I'm not half bad."

Candace knew she should make an excuse that she had to get back to Darcy's, but in truth, she didn't want to leave. She wanted to stay here—with Tanner.

Besides, seeing a rough-and-tumble cowboy in a domestic role was an opportunity no Yankee city girl should miss.

"I'll stay," she said.

"Three-alarm chili is my specialty," Tanner said as he waved a large skillet at her.

"It sounds...hot."

"Hotter than a firecracker on the Fourth of July, which is the only way to make it," he announced.

Candace feared her insides would never be the same, but she wasn't going to admit to fear. He'd love another chance to point out what a muffin she was.

It didn't take long before Tanner had dinner simmering on the stove and corn bread baking in the oven. She had to concede that, so far, she was impressed by his talents in the kitchen.

He didn't go so far as wearing an apron, but he

had an adorable smudge of cornmeal on his strong, square chin that made him look delightfully domesticated.

"You'd make someone a good wife," she teased, which prompted him to chase her out of the kitchen wielding a wooden spoon.

Candace fell laughing onto the sofa with Tanner landing in a heap on top of her.

"I demand a kiss for that wisecrack," he said.

"Then put down your spoon, Martha Stewart," she gibed.

"Martha who?"

"Never mind," she said, realizing this macho male had never heard of the renowned maven of domesticity.

A moment later his very sexy mouth descended on hers.

She felt dutifully subdued—and found she was enjoying it very much. She was perfectly content to stay here forever, succumbing to this man's kisses.

Tanner knew what he'd been wanting the past few days—another taste of this woman's lips, the feel of her pressed against him, all softness and desire, sweetness and need.

Did he need her in his life? Was that where this was leading? Or was it just his hormones dragging him into dangerous territory?

Candace felt right here with him, he couldn't deny that. And he never thought there would be a woman who would. Certainly not a Yankee.

He warned himself to be careful, but his body wasn't listening. He delved his fingers into her thick hair and deepened the kiss.

She responded with equal ardor, her tongue meeting his, softly exploring the taste and feel of him. He was bewitched, bedeviled by her, and there was no hope for him.

The timer on the stove went off, an interruption he could have done without. He ignored it and dove in for another taste of her delight.

"I think your corn bread's done," she said between muffled kisses.

"Let it burn."

"Not a good idea," she said. "Remember the biscuits?"

"I like burned corn bread."

She giggled and pushed him off her. "I prefer mine without the singe."

"You drive a hard bargain, woman," he said. He picked up his wooden spoon and headed for the oven calling to him.

"Damned bad idea, dinner," he muttered to himself as he shut off the squealing timer and pulled open the oven door.

The savory smell of baked corn bread and the lure of his favorite three-alarm chili simmering on the stove came in a distant second to the woman he wanted to take to bed.

9

DINNER WAS GOOD. The man had a talent in the kitchen, it seemed—as well as other places. But Candace had to be careful not to end up on the sofa with him again.

Tanner's tempting kisses were able to make her forget that she had a life back home, an article she had to write.

An article that was fast losing its appeal.

Together they washed the dishes, continuing their dinner conversation, sometimes arguing, sometimes agreeing over various topics. Candace found she liked hearing Tanner's opinion on life, the environment, food, politics, ranching—even if she didn't always agree with him on every issue.

She'd never been able to talk with Steven the way she could with Tanner, to hang on his every word, to have him listen to *her* viewpoint.

Steven, she realized, was uninspiring and just plain dull.

It had begun to rain, and the sound of it on the tin roof made it seem cozy inside. Secure. She hadn't recalled ever taking the time to listen to the rain before—and she'd certainly never heard the sound of it on a tin roof.

Tonight Connecticut seemed a world away.

And far less appealing than being here with Tanner.

They'd dried the last dish and put it away in the cupboard when the rain kicked up into a full-blown storm. Lightning slashed across the dark sky. Thunder crashed at the windows. They heard the frightened whinny of the horses over the pandemonium.

"I need to go out and see to them," Tanner said, then snagged a slicker from a peg by the back door and slipped into the night before Candace could tell him to be careful.

The rain slashed down so hard that Tanner soon became a vague blur as he made his way to the stables. Hugging her arms to herself, Candace stepped away from the window and tried to distract herself from worry over Tanner and worry for the frightened new colts.

The storm raged like someone had angered the weather gods of Texas—and she could think of little else except Tanner and his safety.

She paced the kitchen floor, tried to sit on the sofa and calm herself, but the storm outside did little to quiet her nerves. She watched the back door, thinking with every sound that it was Tanner returning, but it wasn't.

Maybe she should go out and check on him. He

could have tripped over something in the dark, hit his head, be lying out there—

She knew she was being silly. Tanner was a capable man. He knew how to take care of himself. Still...

Worry finally won out.

Candace swung open the back door. The rain gusted in, and she had to struggle to pull the door closed behind her. A flash of lightning illuminated the stables, the path a running river.

Her pretty pink boots would never be the same again.

By the time she reached the stables, she was soaked to the skin. She slid the door open and stepped inside. The place smelled of horses and damp straw—but it was warm and safe and dry. She stood there dripping and trying to catch her breath.

"Candace, what are you doing out in this storm?"

She glanced up as Tanner strode toward her. "I was worried about y— Uh, I was worried about the colts."

At the moment, she was soaked through and through—and the vision was delightful. Her pink cotton blouse clung to her pretty curves like the peel on a peach.

And Tanner couldn't take his eyes off her.

Then she noticed where his gaze had gone and she crossed her arms in front of her. "Tanner, you are no gentleman."

He grinned, not in the least displeased by her assessment. "There's an old flannel shirt on a peg over there. You can put it on if you want," he said.

Chivalry was not dead in Tanner. A spark still lived, Candace thought. She fixed him with a narrowed glower and went to do just that.

She was chilled to the bone in the wet blouse, and dry flannel would definitely cut down on Tanner's...ogling.

The shirt smelled of the outdoors—and Tanner. She sniffed deeply of its scent, then slid out of the blouse and into the softness of the shirt.

"How are the colts?" she asked when she returned to where Tanner was trying to gentle them.

"The storm's abating, so I'm sure they'll be fine now," he said. "I'm sorry I dragged you out in this."

"You didn't. I came of my own accord."

She watched as Tanner stroked the animals, quieting them. She liked the gentle streak she saw in him. She liked the raw toughness, as well.

It was who Tanner was, what he was. Tough and tender—and that combination in a man made a woman weak in the knees. Herself included.

It was part of the cowboy mystique—and Candace had fallen victim to it.

Just standing here next to Tanner made her vulnerable. She could feel his body heat, the male scent of him. Her feminine awareness was heightened, on edge.

Was she falling in love with this big cowboy?

Her very nerves tingled. Her heart beat faster when he looked at her, touched her. And when he kissed her—

"C'mon," he said, "let's get back to the house before you catch your death of cold in this night air."

His hand found the small of her back. His touch was warm, tingly, possessive. Candace liked feeling possessed by this man.

The rain continued to fall in sheets, so they had to make a run for it, then fell laughing into each other's arms once they reached the security of the big kitchen.

Tanner's closeness sent a shiver through her.

"You're cold," he said, misinterpreting her reaction.

"No, I—I'm fine."

"You're not." He led her to the bathroom. "I want you out of those clothes now, woman," he told her.

Her eyes widened at that, and a smirk tilted her lips. "Do you say that to all the ladies?"

"Don't give me ideas, darlin'." He threw a white terry-cloth robe at her. "Take a hot bath and put this on. I'll dry your wet things."

He pulled the bathroom door closed, and Candace stood clutching the thick robe to her chest. Where had all her good sense gone? Tanner made her feel things she didn't want to feel, made her want what she shouldn't want.

Him.

And in a way she'd never wanted Steven, or any man, before.

Why?

She'd tried so hard to resist this cowboy, but he was forever on her mind. And trying to creep into her heart and soul.

With a sigh, she stripped off her clothes, ran the water in the big bathtub, then sank into its warm, enveloping depths.

TANNER HEARD the water running in the tub and tried not to picture Candace stripped to the buff.

Earlier, Tanner was certain she'd been about to say something else, like she was worried about *him*. A small smile curved his lips at the thought of this woman caring about his tough hide.

What, he wondered, would it be like to have Candace by his side, looking at him with want and need in those green eyes of hers? Heaven? Or would it be…hell?

Damn, but Candace had gotten to him, worked her way right past his defenses. He'd fallen for her that very first night at Gunslinger's, with her mincing city-girl ways, her sassy short skirt and her flirty smile.

He hadn't listened to the warning bells going off in his head; he'd paid no attention to past mistakes.

And now he was picturing her naked in his bathtub, her skin all rosy from the steam, her skin like silk.

Damn, he thought, he had to get a grip.

He was getting in over his head. With a woman who was here only on vacation. A woman who had a life, friends, a career back home.

In Connecticut.

Where things were a whole lot different than Texas.

Different from life on the Silver Spur.

Had he forgotten Marlene, how she'd hated the ranch once she'd been here awhile?

He hadn't.

But still, he wanted Candace, wanted her in a way he'd never wanted Marlene. With his soul. His very being.

Damn, but he had it bad.

Just then Candace came out of the bathroom, one hand holding the edges of his robe together, the other clutching her damp clothes.

Her skin glowed from the heat of her bath. She looked so young, so fresh, so innocent. Her damp hair curled into ringlets around her face and danced along her neck.

Tanner kicked his brain into gear, hoping a few neurons still worked. "Here, I'll take your clothes and dry them in the dryer," he said.

Maybe the activity would get his thoughts off Candace and onto something useful.

Their fingers brushed as he took the clothes from

her—and he saw the heat and awareness in her green eyes, an awareness that matched his own.

"They'll be dry in no time," he said.

He hoped. Then he'd send her home. To Darcy's. And eventually Connecticut.

And out of his life.

He set the timer on the dryer, then tried to settle his fraying nerves. He'd been alone with desirable women before. What was it about this small slip of one that had him unraveling now?

"Tanner?"

He spun around to see Candace holding two mugs of steaming coffee. "To warm us up," she said softly.

Just what he needed—warming up. He was already so hot with want for her, he couldn't think straight. "Thanks," he said gruffly and took the cup from her hand.

She smelled like soap, clean, fresh. He reached out and touched her cheek. Silk. She felt like silk. He brushed the rough pad of his thumb across her bottom lip, and her lips parted in a gasp.

"Candace…"

He didn't get to finish the sentence. He had to taste her. Her lips, her silky skin, all of her. He took the mug of coffee from her hand and set it on the countertop along with his, then drew her toward him.

His mouth found hers, tasting, exploring, demanding what she had to give. Just the brush of her lips had him spinning out of control.

"Woman, you're making me crazy," he said and heard her soft, feminine giggle.

Maybe to her it was funny.

To him it was...painful.

He tightened his hold on her and drew her hard against him, needing to feel her there, close, his.

All his.

Her body heat melded with his, and her soft fragrance teased at his senses. The robe she was wearing fell open in front, and her soft, full breasts were crushed against his chest. His hands itched to cup them, caress them.

"Candy, I want you so much," he said. "You'd better say no now—or later it'll be too late."

"I want you, too, Tanner." Her voice was low, husky.

Tanner gave a low groan and knew nothing could save him.

Mistake or not, he wanted this woman.

He stripped the robe from her shoulders and stood looking at her in the soft light. "You're beautiful," he said softly. "So perfect."

"And you, Tanner, are...dressed."

Her fingers went to his shirtfront, working to unsnap the pearl buttons.

"Let me help," he said.

Her touch was driving him wild. He wanted nothing between them. He wanted *her*. His shirt met her robe on the floor, then he picked her up and carried her to his bed.

The rain continued to pelt against the windows, the roof, but Tanner barely noticed. Candace occupied his every thought. She'd been on his mind too much lately. And after making love to her, he'd never get her out of his head.

But he'd worry about that later. Right now she felt so right, here with him. He settled her on the bed, then shucked off his boots and jeans and joined her there.

Her silky arms slid around his neck and she kissed him, a kiss that set him on fire.

"Oh, Candy, darlin'."

"Please, Tanner."

It was all the invitation he needed.

Candace melted under Tanner's touch. He was all beautiful brawn and muscle and raw sensuality. She knew now that she'd wanted him from the first night she'd seen him, when he'd held her in his arms on the dance floor.

But nothing in her fantasies had prepared her for this.

His mouth found her breast, and Candace thought she would die from the ecstasy of it. Her nipple hardened immediately, and her breast swelled with need. She leaned into him, wanting more, wanting the luscious feeling to go on forever—and then some.

Her fingers tangled in his hair as he abandoned

that breast and reached for the other, laving it with the roughness of his tongue, suckling it until she thought she'd go crazy.

"Tanner." She called his name, her voice low, guttural. Barely recognizable as hers.

"Yes, darlin'."

"Mmm…more." It was all she could say.

If this was a major mistake in her life, a step into more trouble than she'd bargained for, more pain than her relationship with Steven had caused, she didn't want to think of it now.

This…Tanner…felt too good.

His fingers found the heat at the juncture of her thighs, and Candace groaned at the pleasure she'd never felt before. Not like this, not with Tanner's tough and tender ability to slowly drive her into madness.

Because that was exactly what he was doing, slowly driving her into madness.

She ran her hands over his shoulders, down his chest, that hard-muscled, all-male chest, reveling in the feel of him. Tanner's body was beautiful, chiseled to a perfection that her fingers were only now discovering.

What would it be like to belong to this man? To have him love her every night? And twice in the morning?

She shouldn't want to know.

Tanner was a man for the night. And beyond that?

Candace couldn't let her thoughts go there. Tanner didn't need a woman in his life. Certainly not her. But that she would sort out tomorrow.

Right now, she wanted to feel, experience, *love* this man who'd turned her article—and her fantasies—on end.

He kissed her mouth, his tongue plunging, plundering, his fingers doing the same. Heat built in her, rising, rising. She reached for him and found him rock hard and ready for her. And the thought of it made her suck in a breath.

"Tell me what you like, Candy."

"You. This. Everything."

It was all she could say. She was drowning in feeling, sensations, her body eager, reaching, wanting, her brain stuporous.

Tanner was carrying her to new heights, an ecstasy that robbed her of breath, thought, everything but what she felt.

"Please, Tanner, now. Love me now."

"No, not yet, darlin'. I want you weak and crazy."

"I am, Tanner. I am."

He worked more magic on her. It seemed his mouth was everywhere on her, bringing every nerve ending to a ragged, feverish pitch she wasn't sure she could endure a moment longer.

"Now, Tanner, now."

TANNER couldn't hold back any longer. Candace's soft, feminine pleas tempted him beyond measure.

He wanted her ready, eager, and he wanted to give her every pleasure she cried out for.

He wanted this to be right, to be good for her. He already suspected what this would be for him. Fireworks like he'd never experienced before.

He fumbled in the nightstand for protection, cursing the time it took to slip it on. But he wanted Candace safe.

She was soft and feminine and tempting. Oh, so tempting. And when he sensed she was beyond ready, he slid into the heat of her.

He heard Candace gasp as he entered her. Her hips rose to meet him, to accept all of him. Pleasure, certain and swift, crescendoed through him, carrying him to heights he never thought possible, and he knew Candace felt the same as she writhed beneath him and cried out for release.

"Tanner." She called his name as completion came.

For both of them.

"Oh, darlin'."

Tanner could barely speak. He lay completed, sated, next to her. Her head rested on his arm, and her hair spilled across the pillow. She was beautiful. He trailed lazy fingers over her breast, not wanting to lose the touch of her, the silkiness.

She quivered slightly, and he leaned toward her and caught her mouth, kissing her slowly, savoring the taste of her.

He trailed his tongue lazily over her lower lip,

tracing the curve of it. Just that activity made him hot again, wanting her.

She responded in kind, and they were soon making love again. Slowly, leisurely. Tenderly. He'd never felt such strong emotion, such caring, before, this sense of wanting to please, give pleasure and feel it in return.

Her body was limp from their previous lovemaking, but she peaked to awareness with his touch. This time it was slow, delicious, but then he suspected every time with Candace would be something different, but always wonderful.

Afterward he cuddled her in his arms, neither wanting to lose contact with the other, and soon they were both asleep.

Tanner only hoped Candace wouldn't have regrets in the morning.

He hoped *he* wouldn't have regrets in the morning.

CANDACE AWOKE and stared at the lighted clock across the room. It was close to midnight. She hadn't told Darcy she'd be gone—at least not all night—and she'd be worried. Or maybe curious, *nosy,* would be a better word.

She hated to leave the warmth of Tanner's bed, the warmth of *Tanner,* but she had to go home. She scooted out from under his enfolding arm carefully, without waking him. They'd made love not once but twice. Wonderful, powerful, tender love. She struggled not to regret that.

She knew she'd fallen in love with the man, a man who wanted her physically, but certainly not forever, not in a till-death-do-us-part sort of way. And she'd have to live with that.

Somehow.

She made her way to the laundry room, withdrew her tumble-dried clothes from the dryer and slipped into them. She folded Tanner's robe, sniffed deeply of its scent, one last scent of Tanner, and laid it on top of the machine.

She reached for her purse, upended it in the dark kitchen, reached to stuff everything back into it, then stepped into the night.

This time she didn't take a moment to check on the new colts. Checking out Tanner's new colts seemed to be what got her into trouble in the first place.

Got her into loving a man who was a loner. A loner because a woman from back East had once broken his heart. He wasn't apt to trust another woman who would remind him only too much of that mistake, the pain of it.

No, Candace would have to tuck her memories of tonight, her memories of Tanner into some secret part of her heart, some part that wouldn't hurt every time she thought of it.

If there were such a place.

Tanner was the most beautiful man she'd ever

met, every woman's fantasy rolled up into one hunk of a man.

The cowboy mystique existed. It was real. Very real. And that knowledge would cause her pain for a long time to come, she was certain. Her article, if she wrote it, would be very different from the one she'd set out to write.

Candace got into her car and turned it toward Dripping Springs and away from the Silver Spur.

Tears clouded her eyes.

She loved Tanner Carson.

10

_____

CANDACE TACKLED her notes again.

She had promised the editor an article—and that's what she would deliver.

But it would be the *real* truth about the cowboy mystique, that it was alive and well—and could sneak up on a woman and catch her unawares.

She sorted through her notes while the bright morning sunlight poured through Darcy's study window. Her glasses were perched on the end of her nose, and a strong pot of coffee sat beside her.

But it seemed part of her notes were missing— her list of attributes favorable to the cowboy species. Along with a few candid observations about Tanner, as well.

She'd last had them in her purse.

Yes, that was where they were.

She remembered now.

She turned her large pouch of a handbag over and dumped out the contents. Wallet, cell phone, lipstick… She'd been looking for that lipstick.

Drop Dead Red.

She tucked it into the pocket of her jeans. She remembered how Tanner had said her lips looked sexy when she wore it. And Candace intended to buy five more tubes.

Maybe ten.

The notes were not there.

She tucked a few stray tissues inside her bag and plunked it beside her laptop on the desk.

Where could those notes have gone?

Then she remembered upsetting her purse on Tanner's kitchen floor before she'd left the ranch last night. Had they fallen out of her purse then?

And had Tanner found them?

That was a possibility she didn't even want to contemplate.

She scoured Darcy's study one more time for the missing notes, checked her briefcase, her car—and finally made one last futile search through her purse.

Nothing.

She knew there was only one possible place those notes could be—the ranch.

Candace was in big trouble.

She also wasn't looking forward to facing Tanner again after last night, after making love with him, love that had been wonderful, intimate…unforgettable.

But did Tanner feel the same way?

And how would he feel if he read her notes?

Candace had no choice but to go to the Silver Spur—and face Tanner in the bargain.

She stopped by the clinic to tell Darcy she had

an errand to do and would be back later. Fortunately Darcy was too busy with one of her four-footed patients to ask many questions, and Candace escaped without her friend's usual third degree.

By the time she reached the ranch, the sun was high overhead. It was turning out to be an unseasonably warm spring day—but that wasn't the reason Candace was feeling the heat.

It was the thought of seeing Tanner again, remembering his touch last night, the delicious feel of his body melding with hers, his passion, hers.

She sucked in a breath—and gathered up her courage.

TANNER SAW Candace's car coming up the drive in a plume of dust. He'd been disappointed when he woke up early this morning and had found her gone.

He hated it that she'd driven back to Dripping Springs late, over roads she didn't know very well. Anything could have happened to her.

Besides, he'd anticipated waking up in the morning and finding her there beside him, her head on his pillow, her body all warm and soft from last night's lovemaking.

He remembered how he'd felt in that empty bed, like something precious had slipped from his life. He'd felt a loss, a loneliness he'd never felt before—and certainly hadn't expected to feel.

Candace filled a void in his life he hadn't even known was there.

And then he'd found her notes—pages Candace had apparently dropped when she'd left, pages he was sure she hadn't left for him to read.

He'd found them on the kitchen floor and had started to fold them up, intending to return them to her later that day. But then his name had jumped out at him from one of the pages. And Tanner had read them.

He'd suspected Candace was a woman with an agenda.

Now he knew it.

CANDACE SAW TANNER the moment she drew to a stop in front of the stables. He stepped out of the shadows into the warm sunshine, and she remembered the first time she'd seen him do that, the day she'd come here with Darcy. It seemed so long ago now.

So much had happened.

So much had changed.

Namely her.

From the dark, wounded expression she saw on Tanner's face, she knew that he had found her notes.

And read them.

"Are these what you came for?" he asked, when she stepped out of her car. "Or do you want to sleep with me again, see how I rate for your little survey, whatever its purpose?"

"Sleep with you—"

Candace didn't understand for a moment what that had to do with her notes, then it hit her like a semi slamming into a butterfly.

Tanner thought she'd slept with him last night to evaluate his...performance.

And he couldn't be more wrong.

But from the anger she read in his face, the hurt, the pain, she doubted he'd believe her if she told him that.

"I don't expect you to believe this, but I made love with you last night for one reason only. I wanted to."

She wanted to add that she'd fallen in love with him, but something made her hold back. Maybe it was the closed, shuttered look in his eyes; maybe it was guilt. Guilt because she hadn't told him about her project, her article.

She hadn't been sizing Tanner up.

She hadn't wanted him to affect her article one way or the other. But the truth was, he had. Despite all her efforts.

But she didn't expect Tanner to buy that, not now, after the fact.

She hadn't been honest with him.

"The...the notes are for an article I'm doing for *Millennium Woman Magazine,* an article on cowboys in general, why they're appealing to women...."

Oh, Lordy—she was making this worse.

"I mean...why women have fantasies about..."

This wasn't working well at all. Why didn't she just shoot herself now and get it over with?

"I mean, I didn't believe that the cowboy could have any effect on women, and then I..."

She stopped again.

His right eyebrow had arched sharply. In disdain. Disdain for her. Disdain for what she'd done.

"I don't expect you to understand," she said lamely, futilely.

"Just believe you, believe I wasn't part of your little project, your in-depth analysis of—" he glanced at her notes "—*the cowboy species*. Does that say it, Candace Porter?"

She wanted to say yes, that was it in a nutshell, he wasn't part of her evaluation. But she couldn't find the words. Nor did he want to hear them, she was sure.

"I'm sorry, Candace. I thought somehow you were different, but I see you're not. Now, if you'll excuse me, I have work to do—and obviously you do, too."

He shoved the notes at her, turned sharply in the dust and headed to the stables, his shoulders straight and proud, his bearing unrelenting.

Candace felt tears course down her cheeks in rivers, but she didn't have the strength to wipe them away. She'd lost the man she'd fallen in love with. The man wanted nothing to do with her.

And all the tears in the world couldn't change that.

HARD, BRUTAL WORK was the best thing for Tanner. He'd spent the past two days driving fence posts into the hard earth on the new land he'd acquired.

He remembered how he'd started out, buying just enough land to make the Silver Spur a respectable venture. It had been all he could afford at the time.

He'd worked hard and done without to add to his holdings, buying up property adjacent to his ranch whenever it became available and he had the money.

Land was something tangible, something that didn't betray a man when he least expected it to. Unlike a woman, the ranch was something Tanner understood.

Today the sun was bright overhead—and hot enough he could work without a shirt. Despite a breeze, sweat dripped off him. He could use a good, cold drink, but he wouldn't allow himself that luxury.

He needed to keep his mind off Candace—and this was the best way he knew to do that. Work. At this rate he'd have the ranch in spit-and-polish shape in no time.

He drove in another fence post and called himself

ten kinds of a fool for getting himself hooked up with a woman like Candace.

Hadn't he learned his lesson with Marlene?

Did he have to have a ten-ton boulder dropped on him to see the light of truth? That's what it had felt like when he'd found Candace's notes.

A ten-ton boulder hitting him in the gut.

The woman had come here for one reason only, to get herself a story. That was why she'd been surveying all those cowboys at Gunslinger's, why she'd danced her sexy little legs off at Darcy's barbecue.

But apparently, from her notes, he'd been the only guy she'd slept with—all in the name of journalism. He was the only guy she chose to wound. The night they'd shared, their lovemaking, had been nothing but a sham, a cold, calculating sham.

He'd been a fool to think Candace was different—but she was a Yankee female. And he'd learned long ago how treacherous a Yankee female could be.

He remembered when he'd asked Candace what she expected from a man, and she'd answered, "Honesty." But she hadn't been honest with Tanner.

And damn, but that hurt.

Hurt like nothing he'd ever felt before.

Tanner slammed in another post, trying to forget the innocence of her smile, the softness of her body, the clean, sweet scent of her.

All of it had been designed to fool him—or make a fool of him. And Tanner allowed no one to do that, least of all a Yankee female.

He stood back and surveyed the long row of posts he'd put in, but he didn't get any glow of satisfaction from all the hard labor he'd done—the way he usually did with every bit of progress he made on the ranch.

He felt as lousy as he had the day he'd found Candace's notes.

The day he'd learned she'd betrayed him.

Tanner gathered his supplies. Maybe he'd drive into town and find himself a stiff drink.

And a willing woman.

One who didn't have Candace's sweet smile.

CANDACE didn't think she'd ever smile again. She'd lost Tanner—before she even had him. And she hurt worse than she ever thought possible.

Worse than she had with Steven's betrayal.

She'd been hurt because Steven hadn't been honest with her, and yet she hadn't been honest with Tanner. She should have told him about her little project.

But she hadn't.

And now it was too late.

But, more to the point, she shouldn't have fallen in love with him.

She and Tanner were as different as night and

day—yet when she was in his arms, it all felt so right.

Candace tore up her notes, deleted her misbegotten article from her laptop. She no longer wanted to do the story. It was too painful.

She'd do another article, one that had nothing to do with one hunk of a cowboy who could so easily break her heart. Her idea file was loaded with possibilities. Any one of them would do.

As long as it had nothing to do with Texas.

Or cowboys.

Tanner was right. She was a Yankee, completely out of her element. She never could have fit into Tanner's life. Nor did he want her there.

Candace wiped away the hot tears that refused to quit falling and dragged her suitcase out of the closet. There was no longer any reason for her to stay here and impose on Darcy's hospitality.

She had just started throwing her clothes into the suitcase when Darcy came into the room and demanded to know what she was doing, why she was packing her things.

"If those are tears I see in your eyes, I have the feeling this has something to do with Tanner Carson."

Candace sniffled, not wanting to go into it all with Darcy, not right now, not when she hurt so much, when she felt so wounded, so vulnerable.

"With that remark you could only mean that Tanner and I are wrong for each other—and I finally realized it. And you'd be right, Darce. Now, please, let me get packed up. I've stayed too long as it is.''

Darcy took up residence on the edge of the bed alongside Candace's suitcase. She looked more concerned than nosy—and that bothered Candace more than if her friend was just her overly curious self. Darce looked for all the world like someone had died.

Well, it wasn't someone, it was something.

Her relationship with Tanner.

And before the flame of it was little more than an ember. Then she remembered their night of love-making, and decided *ember* didn't quite fit.

Their union had been a conflagration.

But either way, it was a dead issue now.

Candace fought back more tears and tossed panties and bras into her suitcase, followed by nighties and shoes. Who cared if she did a neat job of packing or not?

Certainly not her, not when her life was shattering into pieces.

''Maybe you'd better tell me what's the matter,'' Darcy demanded, ''before you soak everything in that suitcase.''

''I told you what's wrong.'' Candace swiped at a tear. ''Tanner and I are wrong for each other— and I finally realized it. I should have known from the beginning.''

Darcy crossed her arms over her chest and

huffed. "Candace, you are not wrong for each other. Now, what happened? If he hurt you, I'll tan his hide until he won't be able to ride a horse again."

Candace sniffled and choked back an unamused laugh. That would be a sight to see—Darcy taking on the indomitable Tanner. She would lose that battle.

"No, Darce, he didn't hurt me. I'm afraid it's the other way around. I hurt him." She swiped at her nose. It was running like a dike that had sprung a leak.

"I think you'd better sit down and tell me about this. All of it," Darcy said. She shoved Candace's suitcase to the other side of the bed, then patted a spot beside her, but Candace stayed on her feet.

If she let down now, she'd dissolve into a puddle of tears.

"He…he thinks I slept with him because of the article."

"You slept with him?" Darcy looked delighted. "You slept with him?"

Maybe delighted was too mild. Darcy looked like there was going to be a wedding—soon.

"Darcy, he thinks it was because of the article."

"You slept with him." This time it wasn't a question, but a statement, a gleeful statement.

"Darce, you are *not* listening to me."

Her friend could be obtuse at times—and this was one of those times.

"Oh, I heard you—the article." She waved a hand through the air as if dismissing that small point. "Don't you worry, Candace. I'll talk to him, set him straight."

Candace looked aghast. "You will do no such thing, Darcy. Nothing. It's my problem—and I'll deal with it myself."

"How?"

"I don't know."

"Then you need me."

Like a turkey needed Thanksgiving, Candace thought.

"It's a moot point, anyway, because I'm leaving. Tomorrow. There's a flight out of here at two—and I've already booked a seat."

"Oh, no, you don't, Candace Porter. You have that man panting after you. Give Tanner time. When he sees you didn't put anything specific about him in your article... You didn't, did you?"

Candace shook her head. "That's not the point, Darce. I was dishonest with him. I should have told him why I was here. Instead, I told him I was on vacation. He thinks—well, it doesn't really matter now what he thinks. Or that he's wrong about it. It's over now."

Darcy wouldn't give up. "Tanner will come around—I know he will. He just needs time to cool off."

Candace sighed. "No, I don't think so. It's better this way, anyway. I don't belong here—and I never would. I'm a greenhorn city girl, just like you said.''

"I was wrong. I've been known to be wrong—on occasion.''

Candace smiled through her tears. Darcy must be desperate for her to stay if she admitted to that. But it didn't sway Candace.

She'd lost Tanner.

And she hurt inside knowing that.

Tanner was a man who could outrival any woman's fantasy. Certainly hers. He made her heart pound, her palms sweat. She shouldn't have allowed herself to fall in love with him, but she did.

And now she had to live with the ache in her heart.

DRINKING hadn't helped.

And Tanner hadn't wanted a woman.

None of them could have measured up to Candace, anyway.

Instead, he'd spent another sleepless night trying to forget Candace, the woman he couldn't banish from his thoughts during the day, the woman he couldn't banish from his dreams at night.

Tanner never had it so bad.

This morning, early, he'd ridden out, hoping that riding over his sweep of land would soothe him, quiet his needs, his want.

But instead of any release from his pain, his hurt, he'd found one of his horses caught in the barbed wire fencing, a nasty long gash on his foreleg from trying to free himself.

Tanner soothed the animal as best he could, clipped the tangled wire and freed the stallion. But the gash needed professional attention.

He wrapped the cut, fixed a makeshift halter and led him to the stables.

He'd have to call Darcy, he knew.

After stabling the animal, he headed for the house and dialed Darcy's number.

Candace answered the phone.

He felt his tongue tie up. A thousand fantasies flitted through his head at the soft, lilting sound of her voice. He remembered how she'd called out his name when he'd made love to her. Pain and want slammed into him with the velocity of a high-speed train.

"How are you, Candace?" he asked past the lump lodged somewhere in his throat.

"I—I'm fine, Tanner—thank you. Did you call to ask me that—or are you looking for Darcy?"

She sounded noticeably miffed. Well, he supposed he couldn't blame her for that. He hadn't spared her his anger, whether she'd deserved it or not.

Tanner supposed some of it was his damned male pride—but he didn't like what she had done. Or how she had done it. Still, he didn't like hearing the hurt in Candace's voice.

"I called for Darcy," he said, then muttered

something apologetic for coming down on her so hard, not that it changed his feelings any. It didn't. Candace had lied to him. And he valued trust and honesty as much as the next guy. Maybe more. "But yes, I care how you are."

Candace felt her heart slam into the pit of her stomach.

She didn't want any pity from this man, any concern whatsoever. "I—I'm just fine, Tanner," she said, fabricating. She had her pride, after all. "If you'll hold on, I'll get Darcy for you."

Darcy had just come in from doing her morning ranch chores and took the phone from Candace.

"Tanner," Candace mouthed to her friend, then disappeared to her room to finish her packing.

She was leaving in a few hours.

And from the devastation she'd felt at hearing Tanner's voice again, it wasn't a moment too soon.

A few minutes later Darcy stepped into the bedroom. "I'm taking a run out to the Silver Spur," she said. "One of Tanner's horses got into a fence, tore up his leg pretty bad. Why don't you ride out with me?" She gave Candace's suitcase on the bed a grimace. "I promise to have you back before it's time for you to leave for the airport."

"No, thanks, Darce. I still have packing to do."

"You've *been* packing. What's left to do will take you about five minutes," her friend challenged.

"Darce, just go. Please. And don't you say one word to Tanner about…anything."

"All right, I won't," she answered dejectedly. "But that doesn't mean I have to like it."

"I'm not asking you to like it—just keep quiet about Tanner and me."

Darcy left, and Candace slumped onto the bed, feeling the weight of loss on her shoulders. How would she ever be able to forget Tanner, a man who'd sauntered into her life with his dangerous charm and good looks—and enough sex appeal to ignite fantasies in women from the age of eighteen to eighty?

11

TANNER WATCHED as Darcy alighted from her truck, doctor bag in hand. He let his gaze linger a moment longer, curious whether she had her trusty sidekick in tow——but no charming redhead sat in the passenger seat.

He didn't want to admit his disappointment.

"She didn't come, Tanner."

Tanner spun around, but Darcy had started toward the stables, leaving him to trail along behind her. Was he that obvious?

Was he wearing his heart on his sleeve? For Candace?

"I have no idea what you're talking about, Darce."

"Well, I'm not going to explain it to you. In fact, I don't intend to talk to you. I'm here to treat your injured horse."

"That's fine with me."

He couldn't expect Darcy to be on his side in this. Candace was her best friend. Besides, women stuck together. Everybody knew that.

True to her word, Darcy tended to the stallion

and ignored Tanner. She spoke to the animal in soft tones as she worked on his foreleg.

The stallion responded to her soft voice, her adroit touch.

Tanner cleared his throat loudly to let her know he was still there—but she acted as if he'd left the planet.

"You know, Darce, this is between Candace and me. It's none of your business."

She didn't give a hint she'd even heard him, just continued to croon to the horse as she stitched up the jagged tear in his leg.

The doc could be hard-nosed when she wanted to be.

"If you're not going to talk to me, I guess you won't be telling me how much I owe you for your services," Tanner said when Doc had finished with the horse's leg and packed everything into her bag.

She stood up and gave Tanner a sharp shove in the chest. "I'll send you a bill."

She started toward her truck.

Tanner glanced at the neat wrapping job she'd done on his horse's foreleg, assured himself the animal was in fine fettle now—even if *he* wasn't—then followed her outside.

He supposed he was still hoping she would say something about Candace, that she was all right, that...

Hell, he didn't know what he wanted her to say.

Doc hopped into the cab of her truck. "I just

hope you realize what you're throwing away, cowboy," she said.

"Look, Darce—"

"She's leaving today, in case you're interested. Taking the two o'clock flight."

She started the engine, then took off, the truck spitting dust in his face.

Tanner hardly noticed.

Candace was leaving—today.

Well, what had he expected? That time would just stand still until he gave up being a jackass?

Now, where had that thought come from? He was in the right here. Wasn't he?

Somehow being *right* didn't feel all that satisfying.

It felt wrong.

But in time he'd forget her, the pain would ease—and maybe he wouldn't find himself so eager to get involved with another female.

Besides, what did he want with a woman in his life? A woman so different she drank white wine in a Texas honky-tonk and thought a pair of trendy pink boots was western wear?

She was even afraid of horses.

Well—he reconsidered that point. She might be afraid of horses, but she had pitched in and helped him that night his mare was in labor. She forgot about her fear.

To help him.

That took courage.

She'd even come out to the stables in a driving rainstorm because she'd been worried about him. Tanner had to admit Marlene wouldn't have done that.

He thought of Candace's smile, soft and sweet, a smile that made him feel as if he were the most wonderful man in the world.

He remembered the fire and want he'd read in her eyes the night they'd made love, the way she'd called his name in the heat of passion. A passion that couldn't have had anything to do with a story for a magazine. She couldn't have fooled him—her need had been too real.

As real as his.

He remembered the sound of her voice today when he'd put in that call to Darcy. He hadn't wanted Candace to answer. He'd wanted to forget her. But just hearing her say hello had been like a kick in the gut.

She'd acted like she didn't care two hoots about talking to him, but Tanner wasn't so sure. He'd heard her hesitation, the slight catch in her voice.

Hadn't he been as tongue-tied?

Was it possible she was hurting as much as he was?

Damn, women could be so confusing, they could get under a man's skin before he even realized it. And Candace had gotten under his.

Was he in love with her?

Whatever this hell was he was going through it sure felt like love. But how was a man to know?

He kicked a rock with the toe of his boot and sent it flying, hitting the side of the stables. He had more than his fair share of tough, male pride. He'd worn it like an armor ever since Marlene. Had wrapped it even tighter around him when he'd found those incriminating notes of Candace's.

Was he letting his tough Texas pride get in the way of loving the sweetest woman he'd ever known?

And what about Candace—did she love him?

Could she love him?

Damn, but Tanner had to know.

CANDACE RETURNED her rental car at the airport and headed for her gate. She'd taken too long saying goodbye to Darcy, promising they'd keep in better touch with each other—but Candace stopped short of saying she'd come back for a visit.

She knew she couldn't do that. It would be too painful, remembering...

She'd hoped against hope that Tanner would call her before she left, tell her he didn't want her to leave, tell her he loved her as much as she loved him.

But there had been no such call.

She'd come to Texas to explode the myth about the cowboy—and instead had found out that it was true. She'd gotten caught up in the romance not just of the cowboy, but of one cowboy in particular.

Tanner.

How long would she have to pay the price for that? She had the feeling it would be forever.

She shouldn't have let herself fall for him, shouldn't have let herself fall in love with him.

She'd always been so sensible, always looked before she leaped, but Tanner had caught her unawares. He'd blindsided her—and she was lost before she even realized it.

She arrived at the gate. They hadn't begun to board yet, so she found a place where she could sit and organize her thoughts. She was headed home.

She had a life there, friends, her career.

She'd get back in the groove soon. Perhaps not easily. But life would go on.

Without Tanner.

But her life would never be the same again.

She wouldn't forget Tanner—ever.

He'd claimed a large part of her heart—all of it. No man would ever match his stature, that wonderful combination of tough and tender that was so much of who he was, why she loved him, his voice, his smile, the way he touched her, as if she were the most important person in the world, the most important person in his life.

But she wasn't in his life.

Not now.

Not ever.

And that hurt so much she ached from the pain of it.

TANNER LEFT his truck parked in a no-parking zone at the airport. He didn't care if it got ticketed or towed. He just knew he had to get to Candace before her plane left.

Before she disappeared from his life.

And left him kicking himself for the rest of his days.

What would he do if he didn't have the brightness of her smile to warm him every day, make his life good and purposeful? What would he do if he didn't hear her soft laughter, make him realize he needed to laugh more, to laugh at himself?

What would he do if he didn't have her to share his bed at night, make wild, passionate love to him, make him realize that was what was important— love? Not fear. Not male pride. Not work to the exclusion of everything else.

He saw a vendor selling flowers as he made his way through the airport. That was what he needed—flowers. Women loved flowers.

He pulled out a big bill, snatched the largest bouquet he could find and told the vendor to keep the change.

Maybe the bouquet would soften her up a little, at least convince her he could be a romantic—if she'd give him enough time.

Hell—flowers weren't going to make her fall in

love with him. He had to convince her he could be different. He could be any man she wanted him to be.

If only she'd give him the chance.

He had to convince her he loved her more than he'd loved anyone before, more than he could love anyone—*ever*.

He reached the gate area and scanned the milling crowd, searching for Candace. Then he saw her, sitting a little apart from the others. She wasn't wearing her pink boots and denim jeans, but a severe blue suit that made her look like she was on her way to a board meeting.

Tanner missed those pink boots.

She toyed with the simple strand of pearls at her neck. Her red-gold hair touched her shoulders, tamed today instead of blowing free in the Texas breeze.

She was headed back to her world. Connecticut. Did he have the right to ask her to stay? Would *this* Candace want to stay? Want him? Want life on a ranch?

Tanner couldn't move. The flowers felt like cement in his hand.

She must have sensed him standing there because she glanced up then—and surprise registered in her green eyes.

Tanner had never been so nervous before. Would she tell him to get lost? *Should* he get lost? Leave her alone to go back to Connecticut? Tell her good-bye and to have a nice life?

Tanner knew he couldn't.

She noticed the flowers he clutched in his hand, and a look of confusion touched her pretty face.

"Tanner?"

Her voice was low and sultry. Sexy. The way he remembered it the night he made love to her.

Suddenly she was just Candace, not some woman in a prim blue suit. He tried to open his mouth to speak, but he didn't know what to say.

"You didn't have to come and see me off."

He swallowed with a dry throat. "I—I wanted to. I *had* to."

The look of confusion was back. He was handling this all wrong—but then, he hadn't had a lot of practice at proposing.

Proposing?

How was he ever going to get to that if he couldn't even spit out a simple hello?

"Are those for me?" she asked, indicating the flowers he had a death grip on.

"Yes." *Brilliant, Tanner. You're really wowing her.*

He stuck out the hand holding the bouquet. Their fingers brushed as she took it, and heat sizzled up his arm.

She smiled, and the smile lit up her face like the morning sunshine after a long, dark night. He had dreams about that smile.

And he loved it when it was directed at him.

"Can we go somewhere and talk?" he asked.

She glanced over her shoulder at the boarding gate. "My plane...they'll be boarding any moment now."

Great! He probably had a whole two minutes to convince her to stay and spend the rest of her life with him.

He glanced around.

No one was within hearing range.

"I—I came to tell you that I'm sorry. I couldn't let you leave without saying that."

She clutched the flowers to her chest and nodded. She didn't look at him—and he wanted her to. He wanted to see her pretty green eyes.

Then he saw a slow tear slip down her cheek. Why did women have to do that—cry? Didn't they know it unnerved a man? "Candy, I didn't mean to make you cry."

"You—you didn't."

Okay, she didn't want to admit to tears.

"Let's sit down," he said and drew her to an empty row of seats.

She perched on the edge of one seat as if she were a bird about to take flight.

"I wanted to tell you that I—I misjudged you and your motives the other night and I shouldn't have done that."

"It's okay, Tanner. I'm not going to do the article, anyway."

"You're not?"

She shook her head.

"Because of me?"

"Partly," she answered, "and partly because I realized I didn't know what I was writing about, I don't know a thing about cowboys."

"You know me."

"No, Tanner—I don't know you. I thought I did—but I hurt you—and I'd never have done that if I'd understood you."

Tanner swallowed hard. "Look, Candy, I jumped to all the wrong conclusions about you because of something that happened a long time ago. It had to do with the past, my past—and nothing to do with you. I realize that now."

"Look, Tanner, you don't have to explain."

"Yes, I do."

At least she was listening. She hadn't told him to take a flying leap off the back of a mean-tempered bull.

"I thought you were like Marlene. My ex-wife. She came to Texas to find herself a cowboy and she settled on me. I was young, very young, and I fell for her ploy. And when I found out the real truth, we were well into a bad marriage, and my male pride was sorely damaged. I thought you'd come here with an agenda, too, that you made love with me because—"

She put two fingers to his lips. "I know, Tanner—how it must have looked to you, but it wasn't like that. I'm not Marlene.''

The last was a whisper, but she was saying loud and clear what he should have realized all along. Candace wasn't Marlene. She was Candace.

And that was why he loved her.

''Don't leave, Candy,'' he pleaded.

That reminded her of her plane, and she glanced over her shoulder again at the gate. Tanner felt time slipping away all too quickly.

''My plane,'' she said. ''I—I have to.''

''Why? Why do you have to? Can't you stay and give us another try?''

''Us?''

''You and me. I guess what I'm trying to say, and not doing a very good job of it, is that I love you.''

''You—you love me?''

''Yes.''

''But, Tanner, you don't know me—not really.''

''I know enough—enough to know you're sweet and generous and kind, that you're afraid of horses, but that didn't keep you from coming to my assistance when I needed it. I know you make love with passion and feeling and…your whole heart. And I think if you really tried, you might be able to love me, too.''

''Oh, Tanner.'' Tears filled her eyes again. ''Tanner, I do love you. I realized it a long time ago, but—''

Tanner frowned. "But what? Whatever it is, we'll work it out. Together."

"It's not that easy, Tanner. I don't know anything about Texas or ranching or horses or—"

"That doesn't matter."

She shook her head. "It does. I'm not from here. I'm a fish out of water, a...Yankee city girl."

"And a beautiful one, too," he said. He reached up and wiped away a tear that was headed south.

She put a hand to her cheek. "I—I must look awful."

"You look wonderful."

"I hate to cry."

"That's good," he said. Now, if he could just get her to work on that. He knew one thing, he'd never hurt her. Not ever again.

If she'd just agree to stay.

"Candy, I want to marry you. I love you, and if you love me, we can work on everything else."

He made it sound so easy. Candace had a million and one reasons she couldn't marry Tanner—but right now none of them seemed all that important. Not when Tanner wore that beseeching look on his handsome face.

But what did she know about being a rancher's wife?

What did she know about being a wife, period?

Nothing.

"My job at the magazine," she said. "Tanner, I have to go back."

"We have magazines in Texas. Or maybe you could work from home—you know, send those articles in on one of those fax machines."

He looked so eager. He looked so sexy. She might be able to think straight if something else filled her mind besides letting him sweep her up in his arms, take her to his ranch and make wild, passionate love to her.

"In fact," he said, "I think you need to finish that article you started—the one about why women have fantasies about the cowboy."

With that male ego he was loving this, she decided. But she had to smile—and it made her think that possibly, just possibly, she could write that article.

And there *were* fax machines, as Tanner had said, if she decided to stay.

Stay.

And marry Tanner.

Her head was swimming, and she couldn't think clearly.

She loved Tanner, but could she be his wife, a rancher's wife?

They called her flight. The plane was boarding—but she needed time, time to think.

"Oh, Tanner…" She clutched her boarding pass.

"Marry me, Candace—say yes."

Her throat closed up. She glanced toward the boarding gate where passengers were disappearing through the door and onto the jetway, then back into the eyes of the man she wanted with all her heart.

"Tanner, I need time to think." She stood up. "Please, give me time."

She kissed him, a quick goodbye kiss, gathered her carryon bag and headed for the gate.

Tanner stood there, devastated. Time. She was leaving. He wasn't certain he trusted time. Time could bring her back to him. Time could serve as an enemy.

How could she leave?

He loved her. She loved him—she'd said so. He dragged a hand through his hair. He felt like life was being ripped from him.

She gave him a shaky smile and a little wave, then disappeared in the crowd of passengers and through the door onto the jetway.

He wanted to go after her, grab her and drag her back—but he didn't want Candace on those terms. He wanted her to want him.

It was the only way it could work.

Pain ripped at his gut. Desolation settled on his shoulders. How could he live without Candace?

He glanced around. The gate area was empty now, the crowd had boarded—and suddenly he knew he couldn't let her leave, after all.

He hurried toward the ticket counter and yanked out his wallet. "I need a seat on this flight," he demanded, and shoved his bank card at the agent.

The woman glanced at him in surprise. "I'm sorry, sir. The flight is leaving."

Tanner wasn't going to accept that. "I need a seat on that flight. Hold the flight."

"Tanner."

Tanner turned around.

Candace stood behind him, looking so beautiful, so gorgeous, so inviting, he thought his heart would burst.

She was smiling.

"I—I couldn't leave."

Tanner's heart stopped beating. He couldn't believe his good fortune. She wasn't leaving, after all. He tried to grasp that—and get his lungs to working again.

"Candy, are you sure?" He could barely say the words. His heart was in his throat.

"I'm very sure, Tanner."

Tanner pulled her into his arms tentatively, as if she might evaporate into thin air, as if she might change her mind and disappear down that jetway again.

And out of his life.

She came into his arms eagerly, willingly—and Tanner knew he'd never let her go.

"Candy, I love you. Marry me now. Soon. As soon as we can."

"Yes, Tanner. Yes. How can I say no to the only man I let call me Candy?"

Tanner grinned. "Candy, Candace—I just want to be able to call you *my wife*. Forever."

"And fire my every fantasy?" she asked.

"And fire your every fantasy," he promised.

He kissed her then, long and hard. Tanner had never felt anything so wonderful in his entire life, had never felt love like this before.

Candace melted into Tanner's kiss. Now she knew what it was like to belong to a man totally, completely, irrevocably—and she thought her heart would burst from the feeling.

"There are a million more kisses where that came from," he promised, his voice low and hot and seductive.

And Candace knew she couldn't wait to find out if that were true.

Epilogue

CANDACE LEANED against the wooden fence, one pink-booted foot resting on the bottom rung, and watched as Tanner taught their twin sons to ride the new pony he'd bought for them. She heard their excited squeals of delight and knew they were enjoying it.

Tanner had never been able to get Candace on a horse yet—but they'd had other matters to keep them busy. The boys were three now. A perfect time for her to give them a new baby sister.

She was carrying a girl, the sonogram had confirmed it last week, but she had known it before then.

She put a hand on her swollen abdomen, loving the feel of the baby kicking. She loved it when Tanner put his hand there to feel the new little life within her.

He was such a good father—just like she'd known he would be. He was that wonderful mix of tough and tender that never failed to excite her—and always would, she was sure.

In addition to being a wife and mother, she was the new senior editor of one of Austin's most popular magazines. Her life was full and happy and complete.

Tanner and the babies made it complete.

As if he knew she was thinking about them, he turned and glanced at her. She felt the warmth of his smile, and she smiled back.

The twins were oblivious to what was passing between their parents—they were having too much fun.

The boys would grow up to be like their father—loving the land, the ranch, horses. But their little girl would be all sugar and petticoats—at least Candace hoped.

Candace had learned she didn't have to be tough and ride well to catch her husband's eye. She could be who she was—an Eastern city slicker who didn't know which end of a horse was which.

Tanner loved her anyway.

Still, she was learning, learning to love the ranch as Tanner did, learning how to be a rancher's wife, to worry with him when a mare was in foal, worry when the droughts came, the fences were down and the cattle got out on the road.

But there was one thing she knew she never had to worry about—and that was Tanner's love.

He led the pony over to where Candace was standing.

"Hi, Mommy, see us ride," Joshua said, sitting tall in the saddle and acting proud.

"See me, too, Mommy," Jackson added, not to be outdone by his brother.

Tanner smiled at her, then leaned in close and planted a kiss on her waiting mouth. His kiss was hot and full of the promise of more to come.

How the
Sheriff
Was Won

Anne
Gracie

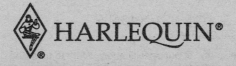

HARLEQUIN®

TORONTO • NEW YORK • LONDON
AMSTERDAM • PARIS • SYDNEY • HAMBURG
STOCKHOLM • ATHENS • TOKYO • MILAN • MADRID
PRAGUE • WARSAW • BUDAPEST • AUCKLAND

Dear Reader,

I write a regular newsletter for my local area.
Theoretically, other people can contribute to it, but
in reality I do the lot. The power is entirely in my
hands...and it gave me an idea.

Take a New York journalist and toss her into
small-town Montana to write, edit and publish
the local newspaper. Picture said journalist getting
a teensy bit carried away with lust when it came to
reporting on the activities of the reluctant object of
her desire—the totally gorgeous town sheriff.

When a girl gets total editorial power for the first
time in her life, and at the same time is beset by
total frustration in the man department, she can lose
her sense of perspective.... Headlines happen. And
people react.

And so a story was born.

I hope you enjoy my first Duets!

Anne Gracie

Books by Anne Gracie

HARLEQUIN HISTORICALS
557—GALLANT WAIF

To Shannon & Maryanne—
thanks, gals. Thanks also to Alison who makes
a career out of support and encouragement.
To Barbara S., official godmother to the sheriff,
and to Anne McAllister, who writes the best
Montana cowboy books in the world,
and who generously shared "her" Montana
with me—thank you.

1

Subject: Your love life
Date: Mon June 12 18:46:36
From: "Rita DeLorenzo" <Rita@dotmail.com>
To: <Jassie@dotmail.com>

Message: Jassie, honey, it's time you had a fling!
You take love way too seriously. It doesn't have
to be about happily ever after. It can be fun! After
what that rat Murdock did to you, you deserve
some fun for a change. So while you're out west,
do yourself a favor and have a fling. Plenty of
hunks in Montana, I hear. Go for it girl! love Rita.

JASSIE MCQUILTY—have a fling? As if! Jassie looked
up from her friend Rita's e-mail for the twentieth time.
She sighed. A fling was the last thing on her mind.

She looked out the window and sighed again. Miles
and miles of space. Big—really, really *big*—sky. Jagged
bluish-gray mountains brooded over the wide shallow
valley with its rippling fields of beige and gold, watching the interlopers arrive. Jassie felt like an intruder. She
didn't belong here. She felt like a settler on a wagon
train. Out of place. Vulnerable. Who knew what awaited
her in them there hills?

But she wasn't a settler and she wasn't in a wagon
train. She was on a bus. A bus heading for a dude ranch.
Not that she was going to a dude ranch, and she couldn't
honestly call this thing a bus, either. But, as she'd dis-

covered when she'd flown into Montana, public transportation was considered an eastern city fad.

A bus? To Bear Claw? No, ma'am. A train? Laughter, hastily stifled. *No, ma'am. A taxi? Yes, ma'am. But it'll cost you an arm and a leg. Rent a car? Yes indeed, ma'am, but not today. Today, all the cars are rented. If you like, ma'am you could ask Don Klein over there if he can give you a ride to Bear Claw. He runs a service for some of the dude ranches.*

Don, a cheery little Santa Claus gnome, was only too happy to give her a ride into Bear Claw. For eight dollars fifty. So here she was, crammed into an ancient, twenty-seater "bus" with a bunch of happy "dudes" bristling with chaps and spurs, fishing poles and children. Jassie's New York clothes and laptop computer fit right in. Not!

Jassie glanced down again at the e-mail. Have a fling? She'd never had a fling in her life! She was pretty good at breaking her heart, though. Twice now, she'd done it. Maybe Rita was right. She did take love too seriously.

She glanced out the window and closed her laptop. They were coming at last to a town. The sign read Welcome To Bear Claw, Montana. Population 800. Jassie blinked. Only eight hundred people? The sign was propped in the paws of a giant wood carved bear. If she had to meet bears here, Jassie decided, she preferred the wooden variety.

The bus turned off the highway and Jassie gloomily surveyed her new home. It was like something out of an old Western movie. She liked old Westerns. Watching them, that is. With a big bowl of buttery popcorn and a glass of white wine.

But to live in one?

A single wide main street. Perfect for turning wagons in. Jassie didn't have a wagon… But the street was lined with parked cars—cars? Pickups, she corrected herself—and stores. Jassie did like stores. Every girl needed a hobby, and shopping was hers.

These stores were of the rustic Western-style variety, with old-fashioned false-timber frontages. Frontages that had carved bears and elks and wagon pieces attached to them. And antlers—lots of antlers. Many of the stores had signs advertising their wares. Jassie read one: The Finest Fishing Flies In Montana. Special Discount Price. They *sold* flies here? Jassie shuddered. She killed flies with a spray can. Her new neighbors apparently shopped for them. Flies at bargain prices. Great.

The bus slowed as it approached the end of a line of dusty, timber-fronted stores where a splash of green bisected the road—a creek, the banks lined with huge, green, towering trees. Cottonwoods, she heard a dude explain chattily to her neighbor. And aspens and birch. Houses were scattered amongst the trees, nestled in the dappled shade.

No rippling fields of golden beige here, though the blue-gray mountains still brooded in the distance. Down at this end of town it was all green. Green, green, green! Her eyes lit on a splash of crimson. Rambling roses! She wasn't sure which was worse, the brooding mountains and wide-open spaces, or the rampant vegetation splashing itself around.

The bus wheezed to a halt in the shade of the trees. Through the open windows Jassie could hear an ominous sound—birds tweeting merrily. She sighed and tried to not think wistfully of good solid concrete, soaring towers of glass and stone, the friendly hum of traffic.

Green wasn't *that* bad a color to have to live with, she told herself firmly. She'd once lived in a green apartm— No, better not to think of that dump; she was supposed to be cheering herself up.

There were *lots* of positive things about green. It was supposed to be a very soothing color. Her friend Rita went on about it all the time. Jassie stared at a nearby bush for a minute or two. The bush sat there being green. Jassie didn't feel one bit soothed.

She sighed. She'd just have to get used to this place.

She was going to do time here—a whole long year. At least.

She glared at the rambling rose balefully. Roses belonged in florist shops or in vases, not sprawling in wild abandon. In public! She peered a little closer. The roses were rambling over an arch made of deer antlers! She tried to not think of where those antlers had come from.

The white-haired gnome of a bus driver turned and beamed at his passengers. "Welcome to Bear Claw, folks, where the mountains and the lakes and God's own beautiful scenery will make sure you never want to leave."

Never want to leave? Ha! A one-horse town bristling with antlers, where there were no taxis and everybody drove pickups, where mountains brooded sulkily over everything and everyone and stores sold insects at a discount? Yeah, right!

Twelve months at most and she'd be out of here with a fat check in her pocket and a plane ticket to a city, a big city—any big city. It didn't have to be New York where— No! She wasn't going to think about that.

"We'll stop here for an hour, folks," the grandfatherly little bus driver continued, "so you can have a look around, maybe buy a postcard or a cup of coffee or use the bathrooms in the restaurant here. At 3:00 p.m. sharp, we'll be heading out to the Rocky Canyon Dude Ranch. That's another forty minutes into the hills." The bus driver beamed again and Jassie couldn't help but smile back. The man's obvious good nature was infectious. And the town did look pretty, she told herself.

Yeah, like a chocolate box, her inner voice snickered. A twelve month sentence in a chocolate box.

In front of the restaurant where they were parked there was a huge bench sporting a carved wooden bear at each end. Each bear was flanked by a tub of smiling pansies and spilling pink-and-white geraniums. Jassie averted her eyes.

She tugged her bulky shoulder bag down from the

overhead rack and stowed her laptop inside it. Draping her jacket over her shoulder, she clapped Rita's gift onto her head and joined the small line of passengers slowly shuffling to the exit at the front of the bus, trying to think positively.

It was going to be just fine living in the middle of nowhere in a sea of wild greenery, Jassie told herself firmly as she moved forward. There were lots of things she liked that were green.

Mostly wearable or edible, whispered her inner voice. And none of them *grew!* Except for mold…

"Oops!" She ducked to avoid a collision between Rita's gift and the waving end of the fishing pole of the man behind her. Not for the first time, Jassie wished Rita had been less of an extravagant gift-giver.

Rita's Gift, as Jassie now thought of it, was not the typical small token people usually gave departing friends. It was, instead, a huge, handwoven, straw-and-wild grass sunhat liberally encrusted with yellow-and-purple "things," which Jassie suspected were meant to be flowers, and brightly colored lumpy objects—allegedly fruit.

Rita was a self-proclaimed straw artiste and Jassie had decided that the best place for her gift was out of sight and out of mind. On her head, in other words, where other poor unfortunates had to look at it, not her. She would have ditched the horrible thing at the first opportunity, except that Rita was her best friend and the hat had been a labor of love. A good person would never ditch a friend's labor of love.

Besides, Rita was bound to visit Jassie in Bear Claw and if she didn't see the hat, she'd smell a rat. And a rat-smelling Rita was not a pleasant sight to behold. So the hat stayed. On Jassie's head. Instead of in the trash can.

It took forever to get to the exit, as there were small children ahead of her. They carried bundles of belongings—bunnies and blankets—or rather, they dragged them along, dropping the odd toy as they went. Their parents tagged along after them, picking up. It all seemed very inefficient to Jassie's impatient eye.

"Welcome to Bear Claw, ma'am," the driver said from his seat as she reached the exit.

"Thank you." Jassie smiled and began to step down. As she did so the fishing pole carried by the passenger behind her collided with Rita's Gift, which slid forward over her eyes. Jassie reached up to straighten it, but her heavy shoulder bag swung forward and she lost her balance. She tripped over a pink bunny, missed the step completely and catapulted out into the road.

"Whoa there! Gotcha!"

Jassie was caught in an iron grip, and held there. Rita's Gift was squashed hard against her face; her nose felt as if it had been pushed up somewhere near her left ear; her shoulder ached from where it had been wrenched by the falling shoulder bag, her ankle was probably sprained if not broken, and Jassie was plastered against a big warm object that rumbled in her ear.

So why did she feel so good?

She wriggled a little. The hat shifted, the thing she thought was her nose turned out to be an escaped straw cherry and the rumbling in her ear turned into words.

"Are you all right, ma'am?"

It wasn't the bus driver. Such a deliciously deep rumbling sexy voice could not possibly come from the white-haired gnome that had brought her here. Besides, he was still on the bus. The huge warm object she was plastered against was definitely bigger, stronger and more masculine than anything she had been pressed up against in years.

The iron grip released her gently and Jassie slid down the length of a hard male body. It felt heavenly. She sighed and closed her eyes.

"Ah, shoot! I think she's fainted." The grip tightened again and Jassie obligingly encouraged her knees to buckle—they were tending that way anyhow. She was hauled up against that big warm body again and, joy of joys, he swept her into his arms. Scarlett O'Hara, she thought, eat your heart out.

Thump. "Ouch!" Jassie objected as she was set unceremoniously on a hard wooden surface. The bench with the bears, no doubt.

"The things some women wear!" The words rumbled in her ear. Without ceremony, he tossed Rita's artistic creation aside.

"Ow!" said Jassie as a purple flower caught in her hair.

"You're alive then," the deep voice growled sardonically. Jassie looked up, squinting into the bright sunlight at the dark silhouette of her rescuer bending over her.

"Hello, there," she murmured in her best breathy Marilyn Monroe voice.

"She's fine, Don." The silhouette turned to the driver, inadvertently blocking out the sun and making every inch of his face visible to Jassie's eager gaze.

Hard, sculpted planes and strong bones. Not a young face, but older in experience than he was in years, she decided—mid- to late-thirties, probably. And dark. Dark hair, brutally cropped to remove what Jassie could tell would be the most wonderful curls if they were allowed to grow. Dark crispy curls, the sort a girl could really sink her fingers into. Dark sweeping brows, and high cheekbones. Tanned skin with lines etched into it stretched tightly over them. Worry lines were around his eyes and furrowed his forehead—lines of pain, not laughter. Long deep grooves ran vertically down each cheek, bracketing his mouth. And oh, what a mouth! Straight, unsmiling, hard-lipped and scarred with the teensiest, sexiest scar that cut right through his thin upper lip. She couldn't see the color of his eyes, but she didn't need to see them to know that they would be dark, too, as was the rest of him. What a man! Not handsome, not beautiful. Just...magnificent.

Oh, let him not be married, Jassie prayed. She reached up and laid a hand on his sleeve. It was not ironed, she noted exultantly. Not that it was a mass of wrinkles or anything, in fact it looked quite neat and businesslike...except for that faint stippled texture, which, to the experienced eye, declared the shirt un-ironed. Folded neatly as it came out of the drier. In Jassie's book, an unironed shirt suggested an unmarried man. And an unmarried man was an available man.

"Thank you for catching me so cleverly," she said, giving him her best come-hither smile, which was a little hard to do given that the sun was back in her eyes and she couldn't see a thing. She was probably squinting like a demented Buddha.

He stepped back. "It was nothin', ma'am."

His eyes were green! The most intense, deep, heavenly green!

"Jassie McQuilty." Jassie sat up and held out her hand.

"Ma'am." He touched his hat, nodded and walked off. Jassie watched him leave, her mouth agape at his brusqueness, her eyes admiring the slow easy lope of his walk. He was tall, probably about six feet or so, and beautifully muscular—not a meaty kind of muscle, but the hard, ropy kind that spoke of vigorous outdoor work rather than gymnasiums.

And his eyes were green. Beautiful, fabulous deep, dark green. Green! Her new favorite color. It was an omen.

Rita's words chanted insidiously in her brain. *Have a fling...*

"Say, who was that masked man?" Jassie murmured dreamily.

"Hey what? 'Mask' did you say?" said the bus driver, Don, who was still hovering anxiously on the sidewalk.

"The Lone Ranger," she said, nodding in the tall, dark stranger's direction.

Don chuckled. "You mean, Sheriff Stone? Around this time every day he drops into Ma's Diner over there. He often meets up with the bus."

"Sheriff Stone…" Jassie sighed, then catching sight of the driver's very interested stare, she gathered her scrambled wits together and got to her feet.

"You sure you're okay, ma'am?" He hovered anxiously.

"I'm just fine, thanks to your sheriff," Jassie assured him. "I really must thank him properly once I get settled in. It could have been a very nasty fall."

She hesitated, knowing it would be a little unsubtle to ask, but unable to resist. "I must invite him and—Mrs. Stone?—over to dinner." She looked at the bus driver, waiting for him to confirm or deny the sheriff's married status.

Don grinned knowingly. "Planning on staying awhile, are you?"

His eyes twinkled. Jassie's eyes narrowed. He was deliberately withholding information. She'd forgotten she was in a small town. She might be a big-city person, but Jassie knew small-town habits. As a junior reporter she had once been sent out to the wilderness of New England to do some interviews. Small-town folks were exactly like big-city journalists—fresh news was like gold and no information ever came free. Don would tell her the sheriff's marital status just as soon as she told him who she was and why she was here.

"I'll be here long enough," she said. He didn't need to know of the one-year plan. If that got out, it would do her no good at all in a place like this. Anyway a year here in "The Sticks" was bound to be like ten years in any decent place, any big city.

"Working here?" he said in surprise.

She nodded. "*The Globe.*"

He frowned. "You a Realtor? I heard a rumor the paper might get sold now old Paddy Kelly's dead."

Jassie smiled. She could understand his concern. *The*

Globe was the town's only newspaper, a weekly journal that had been in print since the 1880s.

"No," she said. "I have every hope that *The Globe* will keep operating for a long time yet." A year, at least. After that, it would be up to the new owner.

The hook was baited. She closed her mouth and surveyed her surroundings in a leisurely fashion, then glanced back. Don was frowning. He cleared his throat and looked at her expectantly. He was clearly dying to know more. Jassie gave him a ball's-in-your-court sort of smile.

"Sheriff Stone ain't married," Don said at last. "I heard he was once, but…" He shrugged. "Didn't work out I guess."

"Does he have a girlfriend, anyone special? You know, in case I should invite her, too," Jassie asked casually. *He wasn't married!* My, but the big guy had really knocked her out. She had never responded so strongly—or so quickly—to a man in all her twenty-eight years. But she hadn't let it throw her; she would play it supercool, not look too eager.

"I didn't know there was anyone doin' any hiring for *The Globe*," countered Driver Don.

Rats! Obviously she hadn't given him enough information to warrant an answer to her question. Yet.

"There isn't," Jassie snapped impatiently. "I'm the new owner. Paddy Kelly was my great-uncle. I never knew him, but because I was the only journalist in the family he left *The Globe* to me in his will." She waited for Don to speak but he just peered at her inquisitively, like an old, white-haired sparrow waiting for his breakfast.

"Oh, all right." Jassie gave in. "I'm twenty-eight, single, never married and Paddy's brother was my grandfather on my mother's side. I was working in New York, but I wasn't happy there. I thought I'd make a change for the better and come to live and work here in beautiful Bear Claw, Montana. I'm going to keep *The*

Globe operating, run it myself.'' And if that didn't give the old vulture enough gossip to last him a month she'd eat her hat! Rita or no Rita.

Don grinned from ear to ear. He slapped his knee in delight. ''Well, I'll be! Old Paddy Kelly's great-niece, eh? Welcome to Bear Claw, girl. What you say your name was?''

''Jassie. Jassie McQuilty.''

He took Jassie's hand in a gnarled grip and shook it vigorously. ''Don Klein, Jassie. Pleased to meet you. Just wait till people hear about this. Old Paddy's great-niece! And you're going to run *The Globe* yourself! My Dora will be so pleased. She'll be wanting to meet you as soon as she can. Why don't you come over to supper tonight, Jassie?''

Jassie was overwhelmed by his warm welcome. She sure was a long way from the big city now. She smiled, ''Well, thanks, but can I take a rain check on that, Don? I'm pretty tired, and I'd like to take a look at *The Globe* and its premises straightaway. I'm sure I'll have a lot to do before I get to bed tonight.''

''Oh, sure, sure, anytime. Just come whenever you can. But don't make my Dora wait too long, you hear?'' He patted her shoulder. ''And if you need a hand with anything, you let me know, okay, Jassie?''

He turned to leave, but Jassie detained him with her hand. ''Aren't you forgetting something, Don?''

''What was that?''

She blushed self-consciously. ''Sheriff Stone?''

''Eh?''

''You were going to tell me about Sheriff Stone...and his...um, friends.''

Don shuffled his feet and looked a little uncomfortable. ''Well, it ain't good news I'm afraid, Jassie-girl.''

Jassie-girl. Jassie felt a lump in her throat. Her father used to call her that. She hadn't heard it for years.

Don hemmed and hawed, and finally spat it out.

"J.T.—that's Sheriff Stone—well, he ain't interested in women."

Jassie's jaw dropped. "You mean, he's gay?"

Don looked horrified. "No, no, no! Good Lord, no! Nothing like that! No, he likes *women* well enough, it's just...well...*women* he don't like."

Jassie frowned. "I don't get it, Don."

Don was turning an interesting shade of pink. "Well, he likes women...some women, that is, er..." He trailed off, looking miserable. "It's just, er, *good* women that the sheriff ain't interested in."

"Good women?" Jassie hadn't heard the term used quite like that for years. She kept a straight face.

"That's right. And mind you, enough good women in this county have tried, the Lord knows."

"And he isn't interested?"

"Nope."

"So how do you know he isn't gay?"

The rich pink color on Don's face deepened to brick-red. Presumably, Jassie thought, men of his age in Bear Claw didn't commonly discuss this sort of thing with young women. *Good women.* She bit back a giggle.

Don, now an impressive shade of puce, made a strangled sort of sound way back in his throat. "I believe he, um, you know...visits, er, a place in the city, you know," he muttered at last. "Meeting, er, women who, er, date lots of men, if you know what I mean."

"Lots of men?" Jassie's voice squeaked with indignation. Did Don mean what she thought he meant? "You...you don't mean hookers, do you, Don?" Wasting all that beautiful manly vigor on *hookers?* Over her dead body!

Don made another strangled noise and turned purple. "No, no, no! Not er, um...you know...hookers." He practically choked on the word. "Not at all. Close enough though...floozies!"

Floozies? Jassie stifled another giggle. "What do you mean?"

He took out a large yellow handkerchief and mopped his brow. "He goes to a certain bar—a bar that's frequented by a *certain sort of woman,* you know?"

"No."

Don looked harassed. "The sort of women that go there are the kind that's got no interest in marrying, if y'know what I mean." Don pursed his lips. "And some of 'em are older 'n him by years. Goin' up to the city, drinkin' and dancing and Lord knows what!" He shook his head disapprovingly. "Man like the sheriff oughta be settling down with a good woman, 'steada wasting his time on floozies."

Jassie almost snorted. Rita's words were singing louder and louder in her brain. Jassie was way too serious about men, she needed to lighten up and have a fling. Suddenly, Rita's words didn't seem so ridiculous. Rita had known her for years, after all. They'd been roommates in college. And since then, in various apartments in New York.

If Jassie *was* going to have a fling, Sheriff J. T. Stone sounded quite perfect to her. A man who didn't want to be tied down wouldn't want to tie *her* down. There was no way she was going to stay in this place a moment longer than she had to. Besides, she had her career to think of.

After Murdock's betrayals, she didn't trust herself with men. She was going to concentrate on something she could control herself—a career.

Sheriff Stone sounded—and certainly felt—as if he were the very man to help a girl to while away a year in The Sticks. Up to now, she'd ignored Rita's nagging about a fling. Jassie wasn't that sort of person. At least, she hadn't been...

Maybe she'd left the old Jassie behind her, the Jassie that took men too seriously, whose love life was a disaster. Yes, that was it. She was a new woman. In a new place.

Rita might be right. Jassie was condemned to a year

in the wilderness, so what better place and time to have her first fling? Her time had come...so to speak.

"I see," said Jassie thoughtfully.

Don heaved a sigh of relief and began to fade back to his normal, cheery, pink self.

"Well, Don," said Jassie, "I've got a lot to do. I'd better get over to *The Globe* office and see what shape Great-Uncle Paddy's legacy is in. It's getting late. Will I need a cab?"

"A cab? No cabs in Bear Claw, Jassie. Ain't you got a car, Jassie?"

Jassie ignored the question. Of course she didn't have a car. She was from New York! Why did he think she'd come on the bus? She picked Rita's Gift out of the dust, beat it a few times, sending more fruity straw lumps flying, then set it on her head. With Don hovering helpfully, she gathered up her shoulder bag and various belongings.

"Is there somewhere I can leave my other bags until tomorrow? They're a bit heavy to carry all at once and I don't know where I'm staying yet. Can you recommend a good hotel?"

Don shook his head. "No hotel in Bear Claw, either. There's a tour group staying at the Silver Dollar Motel, so that's all full up. And there's the cabins down by the creek, but it's mainly fishermen that stay there. There is another motel about fifteen minutes back along the highway, but if you ain't got a car..." He frowned. "Look, why don't I just drop your gear at *The Globe* office on my way home. I guess you'll be fixing to sleep over there until you get your own place sorted out."

"Sleep over? In the office?" Jassie was surprised. It would never have occurred to her to sleep in a newspaper office. Not on purpose.

"Oh, yeah, your uncle did it all the time. Had one of the rooms fixed up with a bed an' all. Even got one of them mini refrigerators in it, like in a motel. He liked, er, ice, your uncle Paddy." He winked.

"Don." Jassie beamed. "You're a real treasure. Thank you so much. Now, where do I find *The Globe?*"

He pointed. "Back up Main Street toward the highway, about three blocks along on the right. Redbrick building—you can't miss it."

"Right, thanks again." Jassie turned and trudged up the street.

WHAT THE HELL WAS THAT? Sheriff J. T. Stone paused and stared up at the empty building, his eyes narrowed in suspicion. One lonely streetlight flickered, making it hard to see if there had been movement or not. Shoot! At either end of Main Street the streetlights shone bright and clear. Only here, where he needed good light, the lamp had decided that now was the time for it to die.

He laid his half-eaten burger on the roof of the patrol car and stared up at the shadowy building, using his hands to shield his eyes from the irritating flickering. There! Movement! Someone was moving around in a place where he had no business to be, at a time when every self-respecting Bear Claw citizen was sound asleep. Moving around in a dark building on a dark night, what's more. Honest people turned lights on, they didn't creep around in the dark.

Good thing he'd remembered to grab something to eat before Ma's Diner finally closed for the night. If he hadn't, he wouldn't have spotted this.

His stomach rumbled. He picked up his burger, took a mammoth bite out of it, laid it down again and felt for his gun. Quickly he crossed the road and tried *The Globe*'s front entrance.

Locked. The thief, whoever he was, had either locked it behind him or got in another way. There was a back door, down the side alley. Moving as swiftly and silently as a mountain lion, J.T. slipped through the shadows and found the side entrance. It was unlocked. He entered, closing the door noiselessly behind him, and paused, listening.

Upstairs. There were noises coming from upstairs, someone moving around on the wooden floor above his head. Only one person, he was fairly sure, moving lightly, almost soundlessly. There might be others standing still, or waiting elsewhere.

He reached for his flashlight, then changed his mind; it would warn the intruder, or intruders, that he was coming. His eyes had adjusted to the gloom by now. He slid the gun from his holster and moved stealthily toward the stairs.

He felt his heart pounding and the adrenaline pumping through his blood vessels and grimaced wryly. This wasn't New York or Chicago, he told his body. He wasn't stalking vicious killers or armed and desperate drug-dealers here. This was Bear Claw. It was probably only some derelict or a couple of runaway kids.

He took a few deep, calming breaths. After so many years as a cop on city streets, his body reacted automatically to this sort of situation, to the dark, to the hunt, to the feel of a gun in his hand. But in fact, it had been months since he'd even touched his gun, apart from cleaning it. Bear Claw was that sort of place. Oh, it got a little wild at times, but the folks were generally law-abiding. His gun didn't feel as if it were an extension of his body anymore. And that was a good feeling.

Slowly, cautiously, he crept up the stairs, two at a time, to minimize the risk of creaks or squeaks. He reached the top and paused to listen. The sounds were coming from a room on his left. Old Paddy Kelly's office. He moved silently toward it. The door was ajar. Flattening himself against the wall, Stone peered in. His pulse rate picked up.

The room was almost completely dark, but not quite. He could see the shapes of some objects clearly enough—chairs, a desk, piles and piles of papers, an empty soda bottle, a coffeepot, all lit by a flickering orange glow. A very familiar glow.

Fire!

No thief or derelict or runaway kids here. He was dealing with arson! Of course. The business was run-down, the building shabby and neglected. He'd bet his bottom dollar the insurance was all paid up. He sniffed. No smell of gasoline. Clever. A slow, natural-seeming fire. Good. Not so dangerous to the surrounding buildings then. And easier for one man to put out. After he caught the arsonist.

A shadowy figure moved in front of the light thrown out by the fire. Slim build. Not too tall. Clad in some sort of loose shapeless pants and top, moving unhurriedly back and forth, carrying bundles of paper, feeding the fire, no doubt. There was enough paper in this building for a dozen fires. J.T. listened, every sense on full alert. There was no one else around, he was sure of it. Just one lone, not-very-big arsonist.

He put his gun away, took out his handcuffs, then slammed the door open and pounced.

"Oof!"

Sheriff Stone and the arsonist hit the floor.

"Aaarrgh!" It was a very high-pitched, rather feminine scream.

A female arsonist? J.T. squashed his surprise. Hell, they'd entered a new millennium and he was an equal opportunity lawman! Male arsonist or female arsonist, he'd treat them the same. He gingerly groped to find her arms.

"Ow!" A clenched female fist pounded into J.T.'s left eye.

"Oof!" A very knobby female knee gouged his right thigh, just missing the vital spot.

"Yeow!" A set of very female claws raked down his cheek.

Equal opportunity——hell!

They rolled around on the floor, J.T. grappling to catch the woman's wrists and get them into the cuffs, while she used every trick in the women's self-defense manual.

Finally he managed to catch the flailing wrists. He clamped them to the floor over her head and slipped the cuffs on her, subduing the lethal knees and kicking feet with the weight of his own body. She lay there under him, panting and furious, emitting little wiggles and squeaks that put him forcibly in mind of something else.

He felt his body respond.

So did she. She went very very still and tense.

"Relax, lady, I'm no rapist."

She was still tense and wary. He could feel her trembling.

"I don't want to hurt you," he said, "but I might do it by accident if you keep fighting me."

Slowly he raised his body away from hers, and sat back on his heels. He could see her faintly in the dim flickering light.

"Don't you dare touch me!" She wiggled backward, on the floor away from him.

J.T. pulled out his flashlight, snapped it on and stared. It wasn't the face of your typical arsonist. Tumbled dark brown curls gleamed in the light of his flashlight. High cheekbones, a small tip-tilted nose peppered with tiny freckles, a pointed chin and angrily pursed lips.

J.T. focused on those lips. As far as he could tell, she wore not a touch of lipstick. They were pink and soft and very tempting. Her skin, too, was free of makeup and he fought to overcome the impulse to touch it to see if it was as soft as it looked. He couldn't tell the exact color of her eyes, the bright light of the flashlight was making her squint, but he thought they might be dark blue or maybe brown. They were fringed with long dark lashes.

It was the woman from the bus this morning. The one with the hat. Her face was bleached white in the bright light. He frowned. Underneath the hostile front she was putting up, she looked scared. The thought made him uncomfortable, but he smothered it, telling himself that a frightened criminal would confess more easily than a cool one. It didn't make him feel much better. He didn't like terrorizing women. He reached forward to help her up.

She flinched and kicked out at him. "You lay one finger on me, buster, and I'm warning you. The sheriff of this town is a friend of mine, a very *close* personal friend of mine, if you know what I mean..." She paused, squinting blindly into the bright light, as if trying to gauge the effect of her speech on her unknown assailant.

J.T. paused in surprise. She was threatening him with *himself?*

"He's a...a very jealous man and if you lay one finger on me, he...he'll kill you! He's over six feet, you know." There was a slight quaver to her voice.

J.T. grinned. She sounded about twelve years old. *My dad's bigger than your dad.* He played the flashlight over her body and grinned even wider. She looked about twelve years old, too, in those Road Runner print pajamas. One of her feet was bare, the other sported a fluffy slipper with the face of a dog. Its mate lay on its side a few feet away. It must have been knocked off in the struggle. One doggy glass eye gazed at him reproachfully.

"He'll be furious! He'll kill you—really brutally—if you so much as lay a finger on me!" snapped the slipper's owner.

Some twelve-year-old. And she sure as hell hadn't felt twelve when he was lying on top of her...nor when he'd held her in his arms at the bus sto—

Road Runner pajamas and fluffy slippers? What the hell was an arsonist doing in Road Runner pajamas and fluffy dog slippers? And what the hell was he doing staring at a good-looking woman when there was a fire to put out? He turned, and saw the source of the orange glow that had alerted him to her game.

A potbellied stove.

Old Paddy Kelly's potbellied stove, to be precise.

With the door open to display the fire inside. Not a burn-down-the-building-and-claim-the-insurance sort of fire, but a cozy, crackling, pull-up-a-chair-and-have-a-coffee sort. There was even an old-fashioned coffeepot sitting on top of it and by the smell of it, there was coffee in it. Shoot! Why hadn't he smelled *that* when he was checking for the smell of gasoline?

An arsonist he could handle. A female arsonist he could handle, just as easily. But a female who wore blue Road Runner pajamas and fluffy dog slippers on the job? Committing arson in a potbellied stove? Who made coffee to refresh herself while she did so? And whose getaway vehicle was the dilapidated dude ranch bus? J.T. sighed. It was going to be a long night.

He shone the flashlight on her again, and she squinted angrily back at him, spitting defiance.

"Okay, lady. Who the hell are you and what are you doing in *The Globe* offices at this hour?" He wasn't going to mention the pajamas. He had a funny feeling about them. And he wasn't even going to think about the slippers.

"Who the hell are *you* and what right do you have to jump on me and tie me up and ask me stupid questions?" She was very belligerent.

J.T. sighed again. A really long night. He wasn't very good with women. Especially angry ones. He turned the flashlight on himself.

"Sheriff Stone at your service, ma'am." He grimaced ironically and turned the flashlight back to see her reaction.

Her jaw dropped for three seconds, then she straightened, tossed back her mop of gleaming curls and blinked up at him from under preposterously long lashes.

"Why, Sheriff Stone, I'm flattered at all this masculine attention," she purred, holding out her handcuffed wrists, "but I'm not nearly as dangerous as you think." Her lashes batted in the glow of the flashlight. "I'm the new owner of *The Globe*."

2

SHERIFF STONE CLOSED his eyes and appeared to be counting to ten. He set his flashlight on its end, so that the light reflected off the ceiling. It lit the room with a soft glow, augmenting the flickering firelight. He reached for his keys. "This is a commercial building, ma'am. And it's not usually a night where any employee of *The Globe* would work late." He hunkered down and unlocked Jassie's cuffs.

She rubbed her wrists, watching him from under her lashes. "I'm not an employee, Sheriff, I'm the owner. Paddy Kelly was my great-uncle. I'm Jassie McQuilty, remember? We met at the bus stop."

The sheriff stood. From her seat on the floor, Jassie admired the smooth, contained grace of the movement and the long, powerful length of him. Even the dull khaki uniform he wore couldn't quite disguise the gorgeous body beneath it. Jassie bent her legs as if to stand, then thought better of it. She held up her hands, quite plainly indicating she needed a hand—his hand. Her gym instructor back in New York would have had a fit. But Jassie wasn't thinking fitness, she was intent on proximity. The sheriff bent, took her hands in a strong, warm grip and pulled her effortlessly to her feet.

"Thank you, Sheriff," breathed Jassie. Marilyn Monroe's voice was back apparently, seeping out of her vocal chords again. It seemed to happen every time she'd been pressed against some part of him, even an innocuous part, such as his hands. Jassie glanced at the hands in question, now resting lightly at his waist, thumbs

hooked through a thick black belt. Did she say innocuous? No. Big, square, slightly battered hands such as
those could never be called innocuous.

Good grief, thought Jassie. She sure had it bad.
Swamped with lust over a man's *hands?*

"People who work on *The Globe* at night usually
switch the lights on. If you'd done that, ma'am, I
wouldn't have jumped you like I did."

Oh, Sheriff, you can jump me any time you want,
Jassie thought. At least she hoped she only thought it.
Marilyn might have whispered it when she wasn't looking. But it was too soon for invitations of that
sort...although...he did like floozies—Don had said so.

Jassie smiled what she hoped was a floozy sort of
smile. "If I'd known who was jumping me, Sheriff, I
might not have put up such a fight. I didn't hurt you,
did I?" She hurried forward and tried to scan his face
in the flickering firelight, belatedly recalling she had
scratched him.

He pulled back awkwardly. "No, ma'am. You didn't
hurt me at all. You did okay, though. It's important for
women to know how to defend themselves. You take a
course?"

Jassie nodded. "If you're a crime reporter and you
work in New York, a self-defense course is as necessary
as a tape recorder and a cell phone."

The sheriff frowned. "Crime reporter?"

Jassie nodded.

"In New York?" he continued. "What paper?"

Jassie named it.

He shook his head. "You weren't reporting crime
when I was a cop in New York." It wasn't a question.

It was time to change the subject, Jassie decided. She
was a crime reporter—or she would have been if that
hardheaded old mule, Jake Kransky, hadn't kept her doing gossip stories and stuff for the lifestyle pages, the
sexist swine!

"Actually, Sheriff, I did have the lights on earlier,

then something went hiss! Fizz! Phutt!'' Jassie's hands gestured extravagantly to make her point. "And then bang! It was dark.''

"Hiss, fizz *and* phutt, eh?'' His lips twitched. "Sounds serious.''

Jassie nodded. "Yes. The lights went out all over the building. I don't know where the fuse box is and in any case I wouldn't know how to go about fixing it. I'll call an electrician in the morning. Any recommendations?''

He gave her a dry look. "There's only one electrician in town. I'd recommend him.''

"Only one?'' Jassie was horrified.

"This isn't New York, you know.''

Jassie closed her eyes. "Don't I know it,'' she said feelingly.

"I think I know where the fuse box might be,'' he said unexpectedly. "I could have a look at it for you.''

Jassie shook her head decidedly. "No, thanks. It's an old building, so I'd feel happier getting it checked out by a professional.'' Belatedly remembering her new career as a femme fatale, she glanced up at him from beneath her eyelashes and batted them. "And besides, it's pretty cozy with just the firelight. More romantic, don't you think?''

"I'd better make sure the power is all switched off then,'' he said, apparently oblivious. "Wouldn't want to have an accident.'' He strode off into the dark.

Jassie hurried along behind him, attempting to see her way in the moving beam of his flashlight. It was a good excuse to keep close to him, she thought, and then spent the next few minutes trying to analyze just what exactly it was about this man that had tossed her, head over heels with lust, in a matter of minutes.

It wasn't at all typical. Jassie actually didn't date all that much. Not since Murdock. She would have dated even less if it wasn't for Rita's nagging. And even with Murdock, before they got together, it had taken her ages to decide if she liked him or not. And even then she got it wrong.

So how come she had thrown herself—admittedly accidentally—at the sheriff, and continued to throw herself at the man. Only this time, with deliberate, very definite intentions.

"Ooof!" The sheriff had stopped at the fuse box and Jassie, her mind elsewhere, bumped into his broad solid back. Her hands shot out, one on his back, one on his hip—purely to steady herself, of course. A faint tang of cologne clung to him, mingling muskily with the scent of man. Utterly delicious!

"Sorry," she mumbled, forcing her hands to let go of him. They seemed to have developed minds of their own.

"I'll just shut off these switches, ma'am. Would you mind holding the flashlight?" He handed it to her and opened the switch box. Something fizzed.

"Don't touch it, you might get electrocuted!" Jassie grabbed his arm anxiously.

"It's all right, ma'am, I know what I'm doing." He smiled down at her, if you could call that fleeting rearrangement of granite a smile.

Jassie clung tighter to his arm. "It sparked. I wouldn't want you to get hurt—"

"It was just a wire burning out. I do know a little about electricity, ma'am. See." He reached out and swiftly flicked a big switch. "The master switch," he said, then turned off all the others.

"Oh. Right," muttered Jassie, the image of a sizzling sheriff fading slowly from her mind.

"That's that, then. The power is off now, so there's no danger of a fire, or of anyone getting electrocuted. See to it first thing though, ma'am. This building is pretty old. I guess old Paddy put off getting anything done."

He took the flashlight from her unresisting hand and ushered Jassie through the dark building toward her uncle's office, guiding her through the dark with one large, sure hand resting on the small of her back. It was a touch as light as a feather, yet somehow it burned. Her body was so aware of him that every molecule and cell inside her realigned itself to focus on that single point of connection. Jassie could think of very little else.

When they arrived, she collapsed into a battered wooden swivel chair, her knees were so rubbery. "So how long have you been living in Bear Claw?" she asked brightly, ignoring her knees.

He shrugged. "A few years." He bent and began to stoke the fire. Jassie tried to not stare at the way the khaki fabric tightened over his thighs. Long, hard, muscular gorgeous thighs…mmm. But it wasn't polite to stare at a man—her mother had always said so.

Mom could be watching over her now. It was more than eight years since she and Jassie's dad had been killed in the car accident.

Jassie politely shifted her gaze…and felt herself melt a little more. That was a truly fantastic butt. She found herself shaping her hand in midair, to fit that exact, fabulous curve.

He moved it, turning to face her. Jassie waved her hand, chasing off an imaginary fly, and tried not to look as if she'd been caught with her hand in the cookie jar…or in this case, on the…

"You came here from New York?" she asked hurriedly.

"Yup."

The man was not exactly a fount of information. She was obviously going to have to extract every morsel of information from his lips. Jassie examined those lips in the firelight. Firm, chiseled, thinnish, and that delectable little scar that sliced though the top one…mmm… Getting morsels was going to be a lot of fun, she could tell. And besides, it was her duty as a journalist.

Could tongues itch? Hers certainly felt as though it were.

"Was New York where you got that cute little scar?"
She pointed. "The one on your mouth."

"No."

"How did—"

"I'd better be on my way, ma'am. I've got my rounds
to make."

Rats! She would have been happy to sit here all night
extracting morsel after morsel from him, and even if he
refused to speak at all, she could still stare, couldn't she?
Firelight on granite, her favorite look.

He continued, "I hope you're not going to make it a
habit, sleeping over on the premises. This building is a
commercial property, not a residential one."

Lust took a sudden back seat as Jassie realized the
sheriff was laying down the law. And she didn't like
anyone laying down the law to her—even if he was The
Law!

"I understand my great-uncle used to sleep here almost all the time."

Stone shot her a look. "Your great-uncle was different."

"In what way?"

He ignored the question. "Find yourself another place
to stay, ma'am—there are several places to rent in town.
I don't want to find you sleeping here again. Town regulations, understand?"

"We'll see about that," said Jassie mutinously. "If
Great-Uncle Paddy could live here, I don't see why I
can't."

He shrugged. "Regulations."

Jassie reined in her temper. She had every intention
of living in *The Globe* building. She'd check the town
bylaws first thing in the morning. In the meantime she
didn't want to get into an argument with the hunkiest
man she'd ever seen, not without verifying her facts
first. And right now, the only facts she was able to verify
were the ones staring her in the face—facts such as a
broad, strong chest, big warm hands, eyes of the sort of

green a girl could go swimming in…delicious, delectable facts.

If only she'd realized earlier who she'd been rolling around on the floor with, whose big firm body had been pressing down on hers… If she'd known who he was…she could have verified some other more pertinent facts. Jassie resolved to get him down on the floor with her again sometime soon. Only not such a dirty one.

The thought gave new meaning to the phrase "get down and dirty." Some of those dust bunnies were as big as… A sudden idea hit her.

"Oh, Sheriff, before you go, would you mind giving me a hand?" Why had no one ever told her there was a use for dust bunnies!

He hesitated, looking faintly suspicious.

"I'm just covered with dirt and dust from when you knocked me to the floor." A tiny hint of Scarlett O'Hara entered her voice. All those years of watching classic movies were paying off at last.

He looked a little guilty.

"Could you just brush me down?" She saw his eyes run over her. His lips thinned and she added, "Just in the places where I can't reach." She turned and presented him with her back, looking at him wide-eyed from over her shoulder. Scarlett spoke again. "Some of those big ole dust balls are as big as tumbleweeds, I do declare. But a lot harder to get rid of. I'd do it myself, only it hurts a bit when I try to twist around." Scarlett was overdoing it.

Stone looked awkward. "You'd probably do better to dust yourself down after I've left." He nodded at the pajamas. "Give 'em a good shake."

"Oh!" Jassie turned around. Her hands went up to the top button of the pajama top. "You mean take them right off?"

Slowly she unbuttoned the first button, then the second. The sheriff watched, apparently mesmerized. Jassie saw him swallow twice and hid a tiny grin. She had no intention of stripping in front of him—she was only a rookie at this. But he wasn't to know that. And it was kind of fun to tease this big, gorgeous play-it-by-the-rules sheriff. She'd never felt so safe with a man in her life. Or so rampantly attracted...

She stopped, her finger on the third button, and glanced warily around the big shadowy building. "I know you don't want to help me out here, Sheriff, and I know dustin' down people ain't exactly your job, but do you really think it's a good idea for me to get naked up here, just for a few ole dust balls? I mean, I know I'm safe with you here, but I'm not so sure about..." She let her voice trail off doubtfully. "Maybe it'd be best if I did it with you here to protect me—if you'd just turn your back..."

The sheriff muttered something under his breath that Jassie couldn't quite catch. Then he grabbed her by the shoulder, spun her around and started dusting her down energetically.

Jassie winced and wiggled. His hands were hard and wide and were brushing over her body with all the eroticism of a corn broom. She felt a bit like a carpet being swept—vertically. Not that it hurt or anything—ow!—well, not much. Only when a too enthusiastic hand connected with her butt. Which it did, several times.

Finally he turned her around and stepped back. Jassie stood there in a small cloud of dust, blinking and trying to not sneeze. Eyes narrowed in the haze, she noted a faint, masculine smirk.

O-ho! she thought. The man wasn't stupid. Good, she liked brains as well as beauty. So he was letting her understand he'd known exactly what she was up to. So what? Jassie thought. She was only going to be living in this dumb town a year at most, and she didn't want to waste any of it playing coy-and-subtle boy/girl games. It might have taken her twenty-eight years to reach this point, but she was a grown woman and he was a man. All man. She liked him and for once in her life she wasn't going to be shy about letting him know it.

Better blatant than latent.

"I'll be off now, ma'am." He picked up his hat and flashlight.

"Are you sure I can't offer you a drink, Sheriff?" she breathed. "There's coffee on the stove, fresh-made and hot. And I found a bottle of whiskey in one of Great-Uncle Paddy's files. Irish whiskey of course. Imported."

"No, thank you, ma'am. I don't drink on duty, not even Paddy Kelly's best Irish, and I had coffee a little while ago. I don't like to drink too much coffee at night." He strode toward the doorway.

"Well, can I tempt you with some Horlicks?" Jassie called. The sheriff froze in midstride. Jassie smothered a giggle, knowing full well what he must be thinking.

He turned, a faintly stunned, suspicious look on his face.

"*What* did you just say?"

Jassie picked up a glass jar with a blue label and waved it at him. "Horlicks," she said, as innocent as Shirley Temple. "It's a wonderful British drink with malt and all sorts of good healthy things in it. And it doesn't keep you awake like coffee."

She smiled. "A journalist friend working in London told me about it. She keeps me supplied. Strange name, I know, but it's really good, especially at bedtime." Jassie narrowed her eyes in what she hoped was a sultry bedroom look. It was difficult taking up a new career as a floozy on such short notice. Obviously there were some areas in which she still needed some practice.

She squinted, trying to gauge his reaction. It was hard to tell, what with her sexily narrowed bedroom eyes and the lack of proper light and all, but she was almost certain that the tips of his ears had turned dark pink. Was that his version of a blush? A manly sheriffy sort of blush? Had she embarrassed this big powerful hunk with a little jar of bedtime drink? Jassie was delighted.

Stone cleared his throat. "I haven't got time for any kind of drink, ma'am," he said. "I've got to go. You can sleep here tonight, but I'll be back tomorrow night to check on the building, make sure you're not here. Check yourself into the motel or see Don Klein about rooms to rent." He reached the top of the stairs and started to descend. "You'd better follow me down and lock the door behind me."

Jassie followed. As he stepped out into the night air, he turned. "Good night, ma'am. Sorry if I bruised you or anything. Now lock that door, you hear me?"

She saluted. "Yessir, Mr. Sheriff, sir. And thanks for everything you did for me. 'Night." She waggled her fingers in what she hoped was a seductive fashion and shut the door. She waited a moment.

"Lock it!" he growled from the other side.

Grinning, Jassie locked it.

THE WOMAN had been hitting on him! No doubt about it. J.T. walked back to his patrol car. She had definitely hit on him. So what? Women often did, but he handled it. No problems. He didn't quite know why this one should be causing his internal alarm to go off, but she sure as hell was.

How long had it been since that had happened? He wasn't sure. Not for a long time. Not since Sybille. His gut at the time had said she was too good to be true—and how right his gut had been! It wasn't his gut he'd listened to, though. It had been another part of his anatomy.

This time, he was going to listen to his gut.

Shoot! He'd been giving out keep-away vibes for years now. That was how he wanted it. How he liked it. And they worked, too. At least they had, up until this damned woman.

J.T. wasn't quite sure how he felt. Part of him was

annoyed. And part of him was flattered. He grimaced and adjusted the fit of his pants. And part of him was too damn interested for words.

But dammit! He might be equal opportunity when it came to some things, but when it came down to who did the chasing, he was an old-fashioned kind of guy. As a sheriff, it was his job to chase the bad guys, and as a man, he did the chasing when it came to women.

Not that he was planning to chase anyone. But if he did, he would choose who he chased.

And it wouldn't be a woman who set off alarm bells inside him!

You gotta build again, boy. You got no choice if you want to live in this world. You gotta build. The old man's voice rang in his head, as it occasionally did. Old Pop, the tall, spare, grizzled old Texas rancher who, twenty years ago, had found a twelve-year-old runaway boy hiding out in his barn. Old Pop, with wild white hair, gnarled hands and shrewd yet kindly blue eyes, who'd casually offered a shivering boy acceptance, his first hot meal in days and a place to stay. Which had become his first real home.

You gotta build again, boy.

J.T. shook his head. He had no plans to let a woman into his life again, old man nagging at him or not! Once you let a woman into your life she took over it completely, filling up every crack and cranny in a man's heart. And just when he thought he was set for life, she left, leaving him with nothing but the cracks and crannies—grown wider—through which the cold winds of loneliness and betrayal whistled.

Sybille had taught him that, shown him just how many cracks and crannies there were inside him. Given his childhood, he had more empty crannies than most. No, he'd given up chasing women years ago. He was used to the cold winds now. He was pretty content with his life, more or less. He had a good job and some friends, and he liked Montana. It suited him better than New York.

It wasn't so bad, living alone. And an occasional visit to Bozeman kept his libido under control. In Bozeman there were plenty of women who were as commitment shy as he was, divorced women, for the most part. And in the time since he'd moved to Montana he'd met several quiet-living women who were in no way interested in letting a man into their lives again, but who'd let him know, discreetly, that they weren't averse to letting a lonely sheriff park his boots under their beds once in a while.

So over the past five years, whenever his loneliness had got too strong for his peace of mind he drove to Bozeman. That usually kept things under control.

Or it had until a certain female reporter had arrived in town.

He recalled how she'd felt in his arms when he'd caught her hurtling out of the bus. She felt good. Smelled good, too. Damn good. He'd noticed that right away. And was on his guard from the start.

And she'd looked good, too, with that glossy dark hair and those big eyes—when she wasn't scrunching them up, that was. He considered those eyes. What color were they? The fact that he couldn't remember irritated him. Damn! If she was a suspect he would have remembered what color eyes she had.

She'd kept squinting at him. Maybe she needed glasses and was too vain to wear them. Maybe that's why he couldn't remember, he hadn't been able to see the color.

He frowned. What he did recall, in all too vivid detail, was the feeling of having her body pressed under his. And those little squeaks and wriggles she made at the time... He'd almost forgotten he was arresting an arsonist...

So what! So she had an appealing body.

It wasn't going to make any difference.

He was not going to get mixed up with any perky little New York reporter. He'd set his rules five years ago when he'd arrived in Bear Claw and he had no intention of changing them just because some city reporter felt like hitting on him.

She probably hit on any male who came near her. A habit, like Sybille's. Hit on a man, get him all tangled up, then betray him behind his back. Nope, he didn't need it. He was wise now. His life was just fine the way it was.

He hitched up his pants and winced slightly. Jassie. What sort of a name was that, anyway? Women always had to be just that little bit different. He snorted. Her folks had probably named her Jessie.

Road Runner pajamas! Who wore Road Runner pajamas, for chrissake? He could see her now, undoing those buttons, one at a time....

He was a Coyote man, himself.

And he didn't mean the fluffy dog slippers.

Stone reached his car. His half-eaten hamburger still lay on the roof. He picked it up. As a cop in New York he'd gotten used to eating plenty of meals cold and on the run. It didn't bother him at all anymore. Cold coffee, cold burgers, warm Coke—hot or cold, it was all just body fuel and J. T. Stone did not believe in catering to bodily whims. Food, exercise, sex, it was all the same. A need was a need and all the rest was fancy nonsense.

He lifted the ragged burger to his mouth, then hesitated and looked at it distastefully.

"Damned woman!" He slammed the fist with the burger down onto the car roof, then walked around his car and tossed the burger into a nearby trash can.

He wasn't hungry anymore.

Or at least, not for food.

"Let me get this straight—there's no actual regulation that says I can't sleep on the premises?"

"No, ma'am. Not so long as you got a permanent

address in town. The law says you can't live there, but as long as *The Globe* ain't your permanent place of abode, there ain't nothin' to stop you sleeping over occasionally, just like your uncle Paddy did.'' The helpful elderly clerk smiled at her with a dazzling display of unnaturally white and even teeth. Jassie had been trying to not look at them. The teeth had an unnerving tendency to shift when the rest of his mouth wasn't.

''That law hasn't been used in years. It was passed way back in the early 1900s, an attempt to get rid of an inconvenient editor, I believe.''

''Some things don't change, it seems,'' she murmured dryly.

''That editor was printing stories which were mighty inconvenient to some people and he took to sleeping in the office to protect the printing press, so they got that law passed to stop him.'' The clerk grinned, the teeth almost danced with glee. ''But it didn't stop him, no sir.''

''And it won't stop me, either,'' said Jassie briskly. She could sense a tale coming on and wanted to make her escape.

''We're all real pleased you've come to keep *The Globe* going,'' the clerk added, discreetly shoving his teeth back into position. ''So many of us were worried that Paddy's heir would sell it off to one of those big multi-whatsit-media doodads and we'd lose all our local news. *The Globe* is real important to this town, y'know. Bear Claw wouldn't be the same without it. It's been running over a hundred years—the paper I mean, not the town. The town's a bit older 'n the paper.''

Jassie nodded. He was not the first person to tell her so since she'd arrived in town and she was depressingly sure he wouldn't be the last.

''Why, Bear Claw was started way back in '84— that's 1884, Jassie. Old Ethan Globe—he's the founder of Bear Claw, y'know—well old Ethan couldn't read nor write, but that never stopped him from...'' Having captured himself an audience, the clerk enthusiastically started reciting the history of the town.

Jassie listened halfheartedly, swallowing yawns. If only she *could* sell *The Globe* to a multi-whatsit-media doodad, she would, like a shot! What did she care if it turned into one of those papers where the only local things in it were the front and back page stories? She'd be out of this one-horse, one-electrician town—like a shot—with a big fat check in her pocket.

But Great-Uncle Paddy's will stated she had to run the paper for at least a year before she could do what she wanted with it, so run it she would. And *then* it would be hello multi-whatsit-media doodad, goodbye Bear Claw!

But she wouldn't tell that to Fang here. She tuned in for a moment. He'd reached the early part of the twentieth century, but Jassie had no time to wait for World War I and the Great Depression. She had things to do, articles to write, electricians to hire, sheriffs to seduce.

"Well, thank you Mr., er, for all—"

"Broome, Miss Jassie. Benjamin Broome—call me Ben, everybody does. Don told me you came in yesterday on the bus. I was real pleased to hear it. Your greatuncle was a good buddy of mine, a real good buddy." He grinned, adjusted his teeth again, wiped his fingers on his shirtfront, then held out his hand to her.

Jassie shook it gingerly. "Pleased to meet you, Ben," she murmured. Had absolutely *everyone* in this town been bosom buddies with her uncle Paddy? It didn't seem natural.

"Your uncle used to love the story about the time when old Ethan Globe's son—not the one he had by the Indian woman, the one he had by th—"

"Look, Ben, I'm really sorry, but I haven't got time to listen to your stories now, fascinating as they are. There's an electrical problem at *The Globe* and I have to get it fixed before the building burns down."

"Oh, but wait till you hear about—"

Jassie laid a hand on his and said in her most charming, but determined, reporter's voice. "Another time, Ben. Maybe I'll put some of your stories in *The Globe*."

"Really?" Ben was obviously tickled pink—bright pink.

"Really," Jassie said, cursing herself for forgetting this was not New York. Given the lack of population to hide behind, there was no way out of it, she really would have to interview this old dude and write up his pioneer tales of old Ethan. "It was good of you to explain the regulations about sleeping over at *The Globe* offices. I'll see you soon, right, Ben?" She smiled brightly and edged toward the door.

"Yes, soon, for an interview. Right, Jassie," called Ben Broome, smiling. His teeth waggled in a friendly fashion as Jassie finally opened the door and escaped into the bright sunlight outside.

"Ooof!"

"Oh," exclaimed Jassie, cheering up as she realized who owned the gorgeous set of muscles she'd just collided with. "Good morning, Sheriff."

"I might have known it," he muttered, attempting to set her back on two steady feet. Jassie's muscles were not cooperating. They wanted to say hello to his muscles for a bit longer. She floundered in his arms for a moment while they battled it out. The sheriff's muscles won. He lifted her off the ground and set her down a good two feet away from him. Jassie stood firm on her own two feet, a tad breathless, but feeling delightfully invigorated. This sheriff was more stimulating than an aerobic workout any day.

"Known what?" she said. "That I'd be up bright and early to check out your story on the regulations about sleeping over at *The Globe?*" She smiled brilliantly up at him. It wasn't easy to combine a sexy I'm-all-yours-you-big-hunk smile with a don't-mess-with-a-reporter-Sheriff one, but Jassie felt she'd made a fair effort.

"Nope," said Sheriff Stone blandly, seeming not to

notice the challenge she'd thrown him. "Might have known that whoever came barreling out onto the sidewalk without even looking would have to be you."

"Oh."

"It seems to be your style, doesn't it, ma'am?"

Jassie felt her eyes narrowing—*not* the bedroom sort of narrow. "Are you saying I'm clumsy?"

He shrugged. "I don't need to say anything of the sort." His face crinkled into the pattern of creases, which Jassie was beginning to recognize as his version of a sardonic smile.

"What do you mean by that?"

He shrugged again and his lips twitched. "First you come hurtling out of a bus—would have landed in a heap on the road if I hadn't caught you. Then we end up rolling on a floor at *The Globe*—"

"That was your fault, not mi—"

"You crash into me at the fuse box—"

"But it was dark—"

"And then you come flying out of this door here, in full daylight, and crash into me again. Doesn't matter what anyone says, facts speak for themselves."

Jassie, fuming, frantically scanned her brain for a sufficiently withering acidic response. She was *not* clumsy. And facts did not always speak for themselves. Facts could be misused and twisted. She knew all about twisting facts. She was a journalist, for goodness' sake!

She was still scanning for the perfect response when he touched his hat in an amused, faintly satirical salute and murmured, "Morning, ma'am. Now you watch your step, y'hear?" in a soft parody of civic concern, and sauntered off down the street.

Was that a touch of Texas in his accent? She stared after him, noting once again that he moved with the slow leisurely grace of a big jungle cat. What an arrogant, infuriating, impossible…utterly sexy, divine man.

JASSIE SPENT the rest of the day organizing her new life. She called in on Don the bus driver and arranged to rent a room at a boardinghouse he recommended around the corner from *The Globe* building. The rent was incredibly low, for the room was little more than a storeroom. The landlady, Beryl, suggested she store all her non-essentials there and have her personal mail addressed to the boardinghouse. Both Beryl and Don were thrilled about her "breaking the law" and giggled like a pair of elderly delinquents as Jassie brought in her empty suitcases and put them in the spare room as evidence of occupation. She hung a few winter clothes in the closet and that was that. Enough to keep the sheriff and his silly bylaws happy, she mused as she made her way back to *The Globe*.

The electrician came, fixed the fuses and checked all the wiring. As it turned out, the wiring was in good shape, so it didn't cost Jassie an arm and a leg, for which she was grateful.

Throughout the afternoon the others who worked at *The Globe* drifted in, one by one, to meet her. "The Bear Claw grapevine is obviously very efficient," she noted to no one in particular as she set about exploring.

First she met Pearl Johnson, a large middle-aged red-head dressed in tight jeans and a flowered top, who announced through a haze of cigarette smoke, "I only come to clean once a week. I don't cook and I don't do nothin' else and I hope you ain't as messy as yer uncle."

Jassie assured Pearl she wasn't and hoped it wasn't a lie. How did she know how messy her uncle was? She hadn't even known she'd had a great-uncle until the lawyer had contacted her. She wished she had met him though, as she didn't have many relatives. She'd been an only child, and when her parents had been killed in the crash she'd lost track of the more distant relatives. Rita had become the sister she'd never had.

Jassie continued exploring the premises. It was a huge, rambling building with lots of wasted space. She hadn't been in half the rooms yet. That was another business opportunity, she thought; maybe she could clear out some rooms and rent them to other businesses. The whole downstairs area, for instance, would make a great art gallery or museum. From all accounts, Bear Claw got its fair share of the tourist trade. A gallery might be a real possibility...after she got the paper operating.

"Er, ma'am?" A long, lanky man stood there, observing her lugubriously. "You'd be Paddy Kelly's gal, then?"

Jassie agreed that she was. Not that she'd ever refer to herself as a gal.

"Jeff Bassett, ma'am. I come on Thursd'y. Bind up copies. Take th' paper out t' everyone. In m' truck." He gestured to a rattletrap truck, and said, "Distr'butor."

Jassie wasn't sure whether he meant his truck needed a new distributor or whether he was talking about distributing the paper but she nodded wisely and Jeff ambled off.

Jassie made her way to her uncle's office. It was time to go through his files.

Around three, a skinny kid named Tommy Stewart dropped in. He looked to Jassie's inexperienced eye to be about fourteen or fifteen years old. Obviously a delivery boy.

"And what's your interest in *The Globe*, Tommy?" Jassie asked brightly. She didn't know much about kids, but she knew she shouldn't be patronizing. Or make assumptions.

He glared at her. "Don't you know?"

"No." She smiled encouragingly.

"I useta come and do stuff with old Paddy every Tuesday and Wednesday afternoon after school."

Jassie frowned. "Do stuff?"

"Yeah."

"Er, what stuff did you do?"

He shrugged with adolescent vagueness. "The usual

sort of stuff, you know. So, ya want me to come back on Tuesday?''

Jassie didn't know, but found herself agreeing. She'd find out about the delivery system soon enough. It couldn't be all that difficult to run the paper, she told herself. After all, it seemed, from her reading of back issues the previous night *The Globe* had kept operating even while Uncle Paddy was dying. It was a very thin newspaper, and with a lot more advertising than copy, but it had kept operating. It was an encouraging sign.

"And can you tell me who else works here, Tommy?'' The journalists, photographers and printers, for instance. They were the only ones she hadn't met— the most important ones.

He frowned. "You seen old Mrs. Johnson?''

Jassie nodded.

"How 'bout Bassett, met him yet?''

"Yes.''

He shrugged. "Well, that's it.''

"What do you mean, that's it. Who writes the stories?''

"Old Paddy—well, he used to.''

"*All* the stories?''

Tommy nodded. "'Cept for the gossip column, old Dora Klein does that.''

"Oh.'' Jassie was stunned. *One* journalist to write virtually an *entire* paper? Even if it was not a very big one—and a weekly at that!—it was still a lot of work. "And the photos?''

"Old Paddy.''

Jassie was appalled. Her photography skills were pathetic. "Oh. Well, who was in charge of the printing?''

"Old Paddy, o'course. Who else?''

Jassie's jaw dropped. "You're kidding me! He was seventy-six, for heaven's sake! And you say he wrote the *whole* paper, took the photos *and* ran the printer.''

Tommy shrugged offhandedly. "With my help, o'course.''

"You mean, he did the typesetting and everything?" Tommy frowned. "What's typesetting?"

Jassie ran her hands though her hair and sighed. "Never mind." The boy obviously knew nothing. Uncle Paddy had probably let him do a bit of filing or something to keep him off the streets. Make that street.

SHE SPENT THE REST of the afternoon trying to work out how to get the printer working. If she was to get an issue out by next Thursday, she'd better learn to use it. There was no point in getting advertisers and writing copy if she couldn't print anything.

The printing press was set up downstairs in the very front of the building, right smack in the middle of the bay window, where the whole town could see it—and whoever was operating it. A thick red rope cordoned the area off. Some sort of primitive safety arrangement, she supposed.

It was an enormous ancient black-iron contraption, the sort of thing she'd seen in old Westerns, just before the brave newspaperman got shot for printing the truth about the corrupt sheriff. She wished she'd paid more attention to the machine instead of the handsome actors.

There were knobs and wheels and levers and plates and hundreds and hundreds of little backward letters. She fiddled and poked and fiddled some more, feeling more desperate and despondent by the minute. She'd never be able to get this horrible old monster working. There was no sign of a manual.

Every fifteen minutes or so, one of the townspeople ambled by and peered through the bay window. Some knocked on it and waved to her, others smiled and nodded encouragingly, others blushed when she caught them staring and hurried away. But nobody came in and said, "Hi, having trouble? Let me help you." Drat them!

She found some oil in a back room and oiled every movable joint she could find. It didn't seem to help. She turned wheels, twiddled knobs and pulled levers. The vile metal creature moved and groaned, but nothing productive seemed to happen.

The more the dratted thing refused to print, the more bad-tempered and determined Jassie grew. She had *not* left a good job in New York and come halfway across the country to live in The Sticks only to be beaten by a mindless machine! She was going to make it print a newspaper if it killed them both!

Evening fell. Jassie switched on the downstairs lights and soldiered on. She unscrewed screws and screwed them back. She wiped old oil off and squirted new oil on. She untwirled a pressing-down thingy and twirled it back up. She found printer's ink and applied it to what looked to be the appropriate places. She rolled sheets of paper through, and they came out black and smeary or white and wrinkled.

Her stomach rumbled. Jassie ignored it. She fished out dozens of little metallic letters and words and set them down in order, squinting to see whether they made sense or not. She was not skilled at reading in reverse. Too bad. As long as they printed words on paper, she'd manage. She rolled another sheet of paper through the contraption and eagerly peeled it off. Shapeless black smudges.

"Oh, damn and curse, you invention from hell!" she yelled. "I'm going to give you just one more chance to print a nice clean set of words—legible black on white—or I swear to you, you're going to be melted for scrap first thing in the morning!"

"That'd be a shame," said a voice from behind her. "Old Paddy was mighty proud of that printing press."

Jassie jumped six feet in the air in fright. She hit the floor again and whirled around.

3

"DAMMIT, SHERIFF! Will you stop sneaking up on me?" she snapped, before recalling that this was the object of her desire, and that snapping like a barracuda at one's potential lover was frowned on in most seduction manuals.

Too bad, she thought. She was tired and grumpy and this horrible old piece of scrap metal was quite possibly standing between her and her glowing future. And no matter how gorgeous they were, sheriffs should not sneak up on people who weren't criminals, and then stand there grinning at them.

She sighed and brushed the hair out of her eyes. "Can I help you, Sheriff?"

He shook his head, and his lips twitched. "I doubt it."

"Well then, if you've come to tell me off for staying here illegally, I have to tell you I rented a room at Beryl—"

Peaceably, he held up a broad strong palm. "I know, I know. I was just checking to see that everything's all right. Do you realize it's after midnight?"

Jassie glanced at her watch in surprise. It seemed only a short time since the sun went down. "Um, the time slipped away from me." As if on cue, her stomach rumbled loudly.

One eyebrow rose slightly. "I take it you haven't eaten."

Jassie shrugged to try to cover her embarrassment.

"Not yet. But now that you mention it, I might stop for the evening and go out and grab something."

His eyebrow lifted even more. "Go out? Now? You're planning to go out now? At midnight?"

"It's nothing new for me to eat at midnight—I did it all the time in New York," she said airily.

The crinkles came back. "Well, Ms. New York, whereabouts in Bear Claw did you suppose you would go to buy this after-midnight dinner?"

Jassie wrinkled her nose. "I gather from your tone that everything is closed."

He inclined his head in confirmation. "It is. All two restaurants. And not a single twenty-four hour store to be had."

"Then it won't hurt me to skip a meal," she said, trying to keep her tone light and unconcerned. A perfect end to a perfect day! Her first day in Bear Claw and everything had gone wrong. If she wasn't so mad she'd cry. She had drinks upstairs, but no food. Not even a cookie. Maybe it was time she sampled Great-Uncle Paddy's whiskey. Great! She was going to turn into a lush!

"So," said the sheriff, strolling around the perimeter of the red cord, "you've been working on the old printing press."

"Yep."

"Big job."

Jassie shrugged. "Somebody's got to do it."

"Got it working yet?"

"Not yet."

"You've been working on it all afternoon and evening, I noticed."

"That's right."

"And you still haven't got it going?"

"That's right," she said brightly through gritted teeth.

The sheriff tugged thoughtfully on his ear. It was a nice ear, Jassie noticed. Not too small, not too big. A just-right ear.

"I can't help wondering why you're putting all that effort into it."

Jassie stared at him. Was the man kidding?

"I mean," he continued, "I would have thought you'd have a lot more important things to do getting the next issue of the paper ready to go."

"And how do you imagine I'm going to print the paper without the printing press?" Mr. Know-it-all, she added silently.

"Don't you know how to use the computer? I'm surprised. I thought a hotshot New York crime reporter would know all about computers."

Jassie's jaw dropped. "Computer?" There was a short pause, which grew into a long one. It was broken only by the sound of Jassie inhaling through her nostrils and counting silently to ten. Twice.

Crinkles reappeared on the sheriff's face. They spread and deepened. "Uh, I gather you haven't found the computer yet."

"Not yet," Jassie said crisply. She was still breathing through her nose. And counting.

His lips twitched. "It's over there, in the room off to the left of the storeroom."

Jassie's brows rose. "Storeroom? I thought it was a junk room." She stalked over and flung open the storeroom door. Behind towering piles of junk there lurked another door. With dignity she made her way through the junk, opened the second door and switched on a light. There, in a large, neat, organized room, sat a computerized printing press. It wasn't more than a couple of years old, either. Jassie knew—she had used a similar model once on a small alternative paper in New York. She closed her eyes in mortification. The whole town had watched her climbing over that ancient black printing press all afternoon and evening. They must have thought she was crazy.

Stone spoke from behind her. "It's a pretty complicated thing, I gather—does everything from start to finish—but don't worry, young Tommy Stewart can show you how to use it." He glanced at her face. His lips twitched again, but he continued. "Old Paddy loved his new computer, but he couldn't use it without young Tommy's help. The kid did all the layout and...er whatever it was needed doing. Your uncle paid him regular rates, even though the kid's only fifteen."

"I *know* how to use it, thank you." Jassie breathed slowly through her nose again. In. Out. In. Out. It was said to be calming. It wasn't working. She wanted to scream. She bit her lip and inhaled deeply instead.

There was another long silence.

"You all right?"

"Yes, thank you," Jassie snapped, blinking her eyes rapidly to stop the frustration from turning to tears.

"Sure?"

"I'm quite sure, thank you." She bit off each word.

"I'd better go then."

"Fine. Goodbye. Thank you for dropping by," Jassie mumbled, her stomach rumbling loudly.

The sheriff hesitated. He opened his mouth, then shut it. He shrugged and turned to leave, then paused again and sighed. "I have doughnuts," he said in a defeated sort of way.

"I beg your pardon?"

"I've got a big bag of doughnuts in the car. Ma— she runs Ma's Diner across the road—made them for me just before she shut down for the night. She's famous for her doughnuts. They're still hot."

Hot doughnuts! Jassie finished her deep breathing with a gasp. What on earth was she doing? Shooting the messenger?

An hour ago she was wrestling with a horrible Jurassic printing press and hadn't a hope in Hades of getting a paper out next week. She was hungry and tired and frustrated and so mad she could spit. Now, thanks to him, she had a computer. She *could* do the paper. Sure she still had problems, but with a computer she could manage.

And he'd brought her doughnuts. He wasn't an interfering smart-ass who'd come to rub her nose in her stupidity—he was a doughnut-bearing hero! And the most gorgeous creature in the whole state of Montana.

She beamed beatifically at him. "You've got yourself a deal, Sheriff. You fetch those doughnuts and I'll zip upstairs and make some coffee."

Her tiredness forgotten, Jassie raced upstairs. She quickly washed her blackened hands in the tiny sink in the washroom, cursing yet again the lack of a mirror in the room. Adding the item to her mental shopping list, she ran a brush through her hair, dived into the room she was using as a bedroom, ripped off her filthy shirt and slipped into a soft, clingy, scoop-necked T-shirt in a blue that almost matched her eyes. She reached for her makeup bag, then dropped it, hearing the door downstairs shut. She didn't want to be caught primping.

By the time the sheriff had climbed the stairs, Jassie had the ancient coffeepot on the burner and was coolly setting mugs and plates out on the table.

"Want me to light your fire for you?" he said, dumping the paper sack of doughnuts on the table. "Wind's coming down from the north and there's a nip in the air tonight."

Oh, Sheriff, honey, you can light my fire any day. She felt herself softening, then caught an amused look on his face and straightened. What was it he'd asked? Oh, yes, the fire. Was it cold? She didn't feel cold, but that was him. She actually had been feeling a bit chilly downstairs when she was wrestling with that horrible old machine. How amazing. Back in New York she would be sweltering away in the summer heat and humidity. Here she was actually almost cold. A fire would be very romantic...a fire to snuggle around. And a big, strong, handsome, gorgeous sheriff to snuggle with... bliss!

Jassie opened her mouth to accept, then shut it. Great-Uncle Paddy obviously hadn't chosen his furniture with snuggling in mind. Half a dozen hard wooden chairs. Not exactly an invitation to snuggle. No, she'd reserve that for another date. Jassie added a deep soft sofa to her shopping list. Green, to match his eyes.

She smiled seductively. "I'll take a rain check on the fire, Sheriff. It's not that chilly. We can sit around the table."

He pulled out a chair and sat in one fluid, graceful action. Leaning back comfortably, he stretched out his long legs under the table and watched her as she arranged the powdered sugar doughnuts on a large plate. Jassie, her every blood cell aware of his gaze, made each movement as sensuous as she could. It was a little tricky, though, as the doughnuts were hot and the sugar tended to stick to her fingers. Irritated she headed for the sink to wash the sugar off. She opened the faucet then shut it as an idea hit.

Pouting like a starlet she turned, murmuring in a breathy, seductive voice, "Oh, darn, I've got sugar all over me," and proceeded to lick it slowly from her fingers.

With those gorgeous green eyes on her, it became, for Jassie, an erotic experience. She closed her eyes and licked each finger slowly, languidly, twirling her tongue around it in long sensual sweeps. As she did so, she imagined it was his tongue. She felt it dipping into the crevasses between her fingers and shivered with delight, picturing him exploring her. She cleaned her palm with small lapping motions and then took her whole sugar-coated thumb into her mouth and sucked. She was tasting him, laving him with tenderness, surrounding him with herself. By the time she'd finished she was on fire. Her knees were weak and she felt all gooey and delicious inside. Slowly she raised her eyes to meet his sultry gaze.

Jassie blinked. He wasn't there at all. He was standing

at the sink with his back to her, apparently checking the coffee. Dammit. What a waste! He must have missed her whole seduction routine. And it had been brilliant. She'd never done anything like it in her life. Not in front of a man. It was a real floozy-style thing to do, and he'd missed it. The dratted man was more interested in his dratted coffee than in watching Jassie McQuilty give Emmanuelle a lesson in eroticism. Rats!

She wiped her hands on a towel and sat down at the table. He took a few minutes fetching the coffeepot, fiddling with this and that, rattling around with spoons and whatever. Why it should take such a time to fetch a pot of coffee, Jassie couldn't imagine. For a thirsty man, he was sure wasting time.

Her irritation faded as she watched him. She loved the way his cropped-but-you-could-tell-it-was-curly hair hugged his skull. Her fingers itched to run through those crispy, would-be curls. And he had a lovely tanned strong neck. Jassie's arms would feel right at home twining around that neck. She sighed, her eyes running over the rest of him. Such a nice broad back. And lovely long hard legs and narrow hips. And such a great butt. She sighed again. All she had to do was look at him— even his back view—and she turned into a mushy puddle of lust.

And while *she* was putting on the erotic show of the centur—deca—well, all right, the erotic show of the week, *he*'d gotten up and made coffee.

Her stomach rumbled again and Jassie cringed, hoping he hadn't heard. A seductress's innards didn't rumble.

"Right, can't keep that stomach waiting any longer." He turned, coffeepot in hand.

Emmanuelle's rival blushed.

He poured. She added milk. He took his black with sugar—two spoonfuls. They ate the doughnuts slowly and in silence.

"Delicious doughnuts," said Jassie at last, hoping her burning face had faded at last.

"Yep, Ma's are the best."

"You go there often?" Rats! What a cliché.

"Most days. I like to keep an eye on her, see she's okay."

Jassie frowned. "When you say Ma, do you mean your mother?"

His face crinkled up and Jassie felt a surge of warmth. She did love it when he smiled, even if it wasn't what most people called a smile.

"No," he said. "But give her half a chance and she'd mother me, all right."

"Oh," said Jassie. It was like that, was it? This Ma person was chasing the sheriff. And she obviously didn't hesitate to stoop to low tactics, such as free doughnuts. Jassie didn't like the sound of her at all. A doughnut-wielding floozy. Men were so vulnerable when it came to their stomachs. And these were extremely good doughnuts. Jassie chewed one sourly.

"She'll probably try to mother you, too."

Jassie sniffed. Men were so naive. As if a doughnut-baking harpy would be interested in her. Unless it was to eliminate the opposition. She looked at her doughnut in sudden suspicion.

"She's got six grandkids, but that doesn't stop Ma from—"

"Six grandkids!" So she was *that* kind of Ma. Jassie cheered up instantly. "What a sweet old lady. I'm dying to meet her." Relieved, she unselfconsciously licked the sugar from her fingers. "These…" lick "…doughnuts…" lick, lick "…are absolutely…" lick "…delicious." Lick.

"Gotta go." The sheriff stood abruptly, sending his chair teetering. He slammed the chair upright on the floor, grabbed his hat and headed for the door, moving a little stiffly.

Surprised, Jassie scrambled after him. "Oh, do you

have to go so soon?'' Darn! Another cliché! She'd
planned for him to stay much longer. She'd been re-
hearsing conversations with him in her head all afternoon while she'd wrestled with the printer. Intelligent,
witty, sparkling conversations. Sultry, suggestive, seductive conversations. And then he'd fallen into her lap,
so to speak, leaving her wits too scrambled to use any
of them. Instead she'd dazzled him with clichés. And
stomach rumblings. Darn it.

She pelted down the stairs after him. He opened the
door.

''Thank you for bringing the delicious doughnuts.''
She practically panted the words.

''You're welcome,'' he muttered. ''Thanks for the
coffee. I can't stay, ma'am, I'm on duty.'' Outside the
streetlights lit a cool silent street. His silhouette was
etched against the lights.

Jassie laid a hand on his arm. ''I enjoyed your visit,
Sheriff. Drop in anytime.''

He turned and glanced down at her face. Jassie
swayed forward, her lips pouting in invitation. *Kiss me,
you big, handsome lug,* she urged silently.

He didn't move. She peered up at him. He was grinning. It took her a moment to realize it. But that network
of crinkles was unmistakable. She was inviting him to
kiss her and he was amused.

Drat the man! What was so funny about a good-night
kiss? Jassie pulled back, feeling insulted. Dozens—well,
several—of the men she knew back in New York would
have climbed tall buildings...or at least caught the ele-
vator, to be offered a midnight tête-à-tête and a good-
night kiss from Jassie. They wouldn't have grinned
themselves silly. They would have swept her into a
powerful embrace and planted one on her.

Only she didn't happen to want one of them. She
wanted him! She looked at him again. He was still grinning.

"'Night, Jassie," he said softly. "Lock the door after me."

"Good night, Sheriff Stone," she said stiffly, and closed the door after him. She listened for his footsteps. Nothing.

"Lock the door, I said."

She locked the door, feeling foolishly pleased at his insistence. He might not want to kiss her good-night, but he was still concerned about her safety. Yeah, said a nasty inner voice, he was a sheriff—it was his job.

Slowly she walked upstairs. She washed the dishes, replaying their conversation over and over in her head. *Delicious doughnuts. Do you go there often?* How depressingly blasé. No wonder the man wanted to get back to work. But she still didn't see what was so funny. Oh, well, maybe she'd work it out in the morning.

Slowly Jassie stripped off her jeans and shirt and climbed into her favorite pajamas. Pushing her feet into her fluffy dog slippers, she walked into the bathroom and cleaned her teeth. It was so irritating not having a mirror. She made another mental note to buy one the next day. She sat on her bed and slapped cleansing cream on her face. It was so frustrating. Why on earth didn't he want to kiss her? Okay, she knew she wasn't gorgeous, but she wasn't a hag, either. And she could have sworn the attraction she felt for him was mutual.

She massaged the cream into her skin feeling more and more aggrieved. It wouldn't have hurt him to kiss her. Just a friendly little good-night peck. Was that so much to ask? A neighborly gesture, that's all she wanted from him.

Neighborly shmeighborly! Who was she trying to kid? She wanted the whole thing—lips, tongue, teeth and all. And that was just for starters. A delicious shiver ran through her at the thought. Drat the man, he had her all fired up with nowhere to go. She snatched a tissue and began to wipe the cream from her face...and froze as the tissue came away black. She grabbed another and wiped her forehead. Black.

Horrified, Jassie rummaged in her makeup bag for her tiny hand mirror. She stared into it. Two blue eyes stared back at her from a big dirty smudge! She grabbed the jar of skin cleanser and peered into it. Nothing but immaculate cream. She wiped her finger down her nose and looked at it. Black.

Then realization dawned. *Printer's ink.*

Jassie groaned out loud. She was going to have to forget about this inheritance thing. She had to leave town immediately. Before she had to face the sheriff again, face that darn crinkly grin and try to live down the fact that she had tried to seduce the best-looking man in Montana—with her face covered in printer's ink!

LORD! What a narrow escape. J.T. hurled himself into his car, gunned the engine to life and roared away from the premises of *The Globe* like a criminal on the run.

If he wasn't careful he'd be in big trouble. Jassie McQuilty was starting to take up too damn much space in his head...and other parts of his body....

She sure as hell was after him, no mistake. That thing with the doughnuts, licking off the sugar. He groaned. And the way she looked at him, all soft, hot blue eyes and moist lips. Swinging that sassy little body around the room.

J.T. hated it when women threw themselves at him. And Jassie McQuilty certainly was throwing herself at him, there was no doubting that. The woman was about as subtle as a stampede. And if he had any sense he'd get out of her way, just as any sensible man would avoid a stampede.

That was the problem. If a woman was throwing herself at a man, the man—if he didn't want to catch her, that is—ought to get the hell out of the way. That way he'd stay safe. And free.

Only Jassie was a mite clumsy. Accident-prone was

the word for it. She was always crashing into things and bumping into people—him mostly. And if she hurled herself at a man, and that man stepped aside...well, she might hurt herself.

He might not be interested in the woman, but he didn't want her hurt.

The glow of streetlights faded far behind him. The roar of his engine cut through the night, the headlights slashed the darkness. He eased his foot off the accelerator.

Who was he kidding? Not interested? For a start, the fit of his pants called him a liar. And how many other men would have been so tempted by those pouting pink lips puckering up at the door, inky face and all.

J.T. chuckled. Lord, she'd looked a sight. Like a kid all dressed up for Halloween. Printer's ink from here to breakfast. He wondered how long it would take before she realized it. Would she be mad or embarrassed? Both, he decided, feisty lady that she was.

He grinned again, recalling the scene in the bay window. The whole afternoon, he hadn't been able to stay away. He'd come back again and again. Watching her get dirtier and dirtier and madder and madder, climbing all over that big old printer like a furious filthy elf. An elf in tight jeans. Jeans that fit just right, hugging her cute little fanny like a second skin. He groaned again.

He was *not* interested, dammit.

The warning signs were a mile high. Jassie McQuilty was the sort of woman who'd seep straight into his every crack and cranny. The sort of woman that prompted a man to think of building. Building a home, building a family.

But he'd already built himself a home, a perfectly good cabin out of town a ways. And he wasn't a family sort of man. He'd never had a family. Not a proper one. Not since Social Services had taken him away from his mom when he was a little kid, kicking and screaming and vowing to run back.... And he had. He'd run away and ridden a freight train—a nine-year-old hobo—just to get back to her.

But she hadn't wanted him. His mom had sent him back to the foster home.

And then he realized, if his mom didn't want to keep him, no one would. So he'd kept running. Until the old man found him. Old Pop. He'd offered a lost boy acceptance, then friendship, then love. And a philosophy to live by.

You gotta build, boy. Life knocks you down, you gotta build again.

Only once in his adult life had J.T. tried to build something—a family—with a woman. Sybille. His wife. She'd taught him just how agonizing trust could be. Since then he'd papered over the lonely cracks and crannies inside him and vowed never again. The cold, whistling winds didn't bother him so much, once he got used to them.

He was like an old alley cat now—too scarred and suspicious to change his ways. But he was content. He'd moved to Montana. It was easier being lonely in Montana, with those mountains, than it was being lonely in the crowds of New York. He had his cabin, his truck. He had a job he liked and was good at. And he liked the town of Bear Claw. No, he wasn't going to change. He didn't need a wife. He didn't need a family. He didn't need the heartache.

And when the need came clawing up at him to hold a woman through the night, well, he could always make the trip into the city....

The car shot through the darkness at top speed, tall shadowy trees looming into the headlights and disappearing indifferently.

Need clawed up at him.

He ignored it. He had a court appearance in the morning. He tried to picture the case, an incident with a drunk driver, in his mind.

Instead he saw soft pink lips in a dirty face, gleaming

dark hair, a lithe, small body in tight jeans, and a pointed pink tongue wrapped around sugary fingers. He groaned as the fit of his pants became even more uncomfortable.

Damn, damn, damn! He had to stay away from Jassie McQuilty. She was a cranny-filler, if ever there was one. He'd told himself that when she first arrived. From the moment she'd tumbled into his arms off the bus, he'd known she was dangerous. His body had leaped to attention as if an electric current had passed through him. And that night when he'd thought she was an arsonist… He still dreamed of that stupid wresting match, but in his dreams it ended with him peeling off those stupid Road Runner pajamas…

Yeah, right, stay away from Jassie McQuilty. The way he'd managed to stay away from her all afternoon. Driving past the bay window a dozen times in six hours, watching her every move. And dropping in to talk to her after his shift was over. And as for bringing her hot doughnuts…hot doughnuts were a famed repellent for hungry women. Not.

He felt like a rusty old nail declaring itself totally indifferent to the shiny new magnet in town…even as he slid helplessly toward it—her.

He groaned again, thinking of her small pink tongue cleaning off that sugar. One thing was for sure, he was never going to bring her doughnuts again. Not ever. No way. Absolutely not.

"I KNOW I SAID you could help out like before, Tommy, but I don't need your computer skills the way my uncle did. I can do it all myself." Jassie frowned in concern. "I can't afford to pay you for something I don't need you to do. If there was something else…" She thought of the hundreds of tasks that faced her before she could get the paper out. There was no way she could manage it alone, the way her uncle seemed to have done. "Isn't there anything else you could do for the paper?"

The boy slumped in his chair, dejected. He picked up a pencil and began to fiddle with it.

"It's the money, isn't it?" Jassie touched him gently on the shoulder.

He shrugged.

"What did you need it for?"

Tommy glanced at her quickly, then looked away. "To go on tour with the team."

"Team?" Jassie prompted.

"The basketball team. The under sixteens. We— they're going on tour to Australia this year. We—they'll tour all over and play against kids over there. And stay in their houses and stuff. It's all organized."

Jassie hadn't missed the corrections. "And you have to pay? But surely—"

"We gotta pay some of the costs. They got sponsors for most of it. But every kid hasta earn part of the fare. It's part of the deal. So we'll learn to be responsible." He pulled a face and snorted. "I been working for years. With Old Paddy. Only I gave the money to Mom. To help out." He looked down at his feet and muttered, "My dad took off when I was a little kid."

Jassie felt terrible. She wished she could just put him back on his old wage and leave it at that. It wasn't that much money. But she was going to have to take on staff to keep the paper going, and her money was pretty tight as it was. She couldn't afford to pay someone to do something she could do herself, it was that simple.

"What are the other kids doing?"

He shrugged and his foot started to bang on his chair. "Most of 'em do yard work and their folks pay 'em." There was a long silence, broken only by the rhythmic sounds of his sneakers banging on wood, then he added, "My mom can't afford that."

Jassie knew how it felt to have a dream and no money. "Tommy," she said, "what other sports do you play?" He gave her a weary, cynical look and she knew he was expecting her to offer some bright and meaningless comfort about enjoying some other game. "Just answer the question, Tommy."

He shrugged. "Baseball. Football. The usual."

"Do you go to all the local games?"

"Most of 'em."

"Then that's it!" Jassie beamed at him.

Tommy looked at her warily. "What's it?"

"You can be my sports reporter. You can go to all the games and write them up for *The Globe*."

"Me!" His voice squeaked with shock. "Write for *The Globe*. But I can't."

"Why not?"

"I'm terrible at English."

Jassie looked at him. "Then you'd better start getting better at it, Tommy, otherwise you won't be going to Australia, will you?"

"But—"

"Look," she said, "I hate sports. I know nothing about them and yet *The Globe* always has heaps of articles about the subject—I've looked. The section's a big part of the paper and obviously very popular. If you don't do it, I'll have to pay someone to do it, anyway. I can't possibly learn all the rules of all those silly games *and* run the paper." She took a long sip of coffee. "So, what do you say?"

Tommy swallowed convulsively. "W-what if I'm no good?"

"Then you'd better get good, fast. I'll give you a month's trial and if you don't shape up by then, I'll have to get someone else." It was tough, Jassie knew, but it was all she could offer him.

"The girls' games, too?"

"Of course the girls' games, too. What are you, some kind of sexist? Anyway, I bet you'll love having an excuse to watch them."

He grimaced unconvincingly. "And you'll pay…how much?"

Jassie grinned. This kid was going to go far. And she wasn't talking about Australia, either. She named a sum.

Tommy's eyes bulged. "But that's more than Old Paddy—"

"I don't exploit chil—" She cut herself off, not wanting to offend this boy with the man-size sense of responsibility. "I'm asking you to do more than Great-Uncle Paddy did. And believe me, you'll earn it."

Tommy took a deep breath. "Okay," he said. "I'll do it." He spat on his palm and held it out to her.

Jassie stared at him, appalled. "Ugh! That's disgusting! Go and wash your hands at once, Tommy Stewart."

"But we gotta shake on our deal."

She eyed the outstretched hand in horror. "I'd be very happy to shake on our deal, but if you think I'm going to touch that, you're crazy! What a filthy habit! Wherever did you pick up such a revolting notion?"

"Your great-uncle Paddy, that's where," Tommy said a little belligerently. "He said when two men make a deal—"

"Well, I'm not a man and neither—" She stopped and took a deep breath. "Look, old people often have peculiar ideas. And they're not always as hygienic as they should be."

"Are you saying old people—"

"I'm not saying anything about anyone," snapped Jassie, suddenly recalling the number of old people she'd seen in this town. And quite clearly, word got around. The last thing she needed was for half the population of Bear Claw to think she'd accused them of unsanitary habits and peculiar practices. She thought of the clerk with the teeth and shuddered. "Just go wash your hands, all right."

The front door crashed open. Tommy glanced curiously at the man in the doorway and hesitated. "I said, go wash, Tommy," Jassie said firmly. Tommy went.

Jassie turned to the newcomer, smiling. Her eyes fell

to the large paper sack clutched in his hands. "Why, hello there, Sheriff Stone," she purred. "What can I do for you?"

He swallowed, cleared his throat and thumped the paper sack onto the counter. Jassie opened it and peered in. Her smile broadened.

"Oh, how very sweet of you, Sheriff. I was starving. How did you guess?" She beamed up at him.

He cleared his throat. "Oh, well, Ma, you know. Made 'em fresh. Gave me too many. Had to give 'em to someone and, er, you were the closest," J.T. mumbled, feeling very, very stupid. He tried to avoid her eyes. They were damn well shining, dammit. And her hair gleamed and bounced like dark liquid silk. And her damned skin looked so smooth and soft that his damned palms itched to touch it, just to *know*. In fact, the woman positively glowed...

With health. Yeah, that was it. She was healthy. That's all. Nothing special about a healthy-looking woman....

She buried a dainty little nose in the paper sack and inhaled deeply, "Ahh, heavenly. But you're right, there sure are a lot here."

"Oh, well." He felt himself shrugging like an awkward adolescent. "You know how some women are. Ma's trying to fatten me up. Reckons I'm too skinny."

"Skinny? Rubbish." Jassie's eyes ran over him in a manner that was pure arousal. J.T. could feel the dark blue heat moving slowly over his chest, his shoulders and arms, his torso and lower.... "I like a man who looks a little lean...and a little hungry," she purred.

J.T. moved away hastily, hoping that doing so would disguise his instant response.

"I'll put coffee on," she said.

"Uh, no. Not for me, I'm working," he muttered quickly. It had been a stupid impulse to come here in the first place. He should have known how it would be—*did* know how it would be. Stupid.

"You sure you can't stay?" Her voice was like molasses, sweet and dark and full of promise.

He had to get out. Now. While he could. Before she ate a damned doughnut and started licking her damned fingers.

"I'm sure."

"Oh." She sagged with disappointment.

He watched dumbly as she pulled out a doughnut and bit into it. Sweet red jelly oozed out, all over her mouth. She licked it away. A spot remained on her upper lip, trembling like a tiny red jewel. J.T. stared, riveted. His throat felt thick. He swallowed.

She bit into the doughnut again. The tiny spot of jelly quivered on her upper lip. Her lips were dusted with sugar. So were her fingers. He swallowed again. His mouth felt dry.

"Gotta go," he said hoarsely. "On duty." He rushed out the door, leaped into the patrol car and burned rubber.

Jassie stared after him in confusion and frustration. If she didn't know better she'd have thought he'd been called to a major emergency—a riot or a gangster shootout. Except he hadn't. One minute he'd been leaning in her doorway, looking big and gorgeous and adorably sheepish, mumbling something about having too many doughnuts and the next he'd rushed from the place as if his tail were on fire.

"C'n I have a doughnut?" said a youthful voice behind her.

Jassie held out the bag. "Sure, Tommy, there's heaps. Come on upstairs and I'll put some coffee on—you can have milk," she added, before he had time to grimace. She darted a look at his hands. They looked clean and dry, but... "And then we can drink to our new agreement. It's the modern way to do business, okay?"

JASSIE'S NEXT FEW DAYS passed in a blur. She hustled on the advertising, carried out research and interviews and ordered supplies. She spent her nights writing stories and articles and doing layout. She'd gotten to know half the town in a whirlwind of activity. She had to rebuild *The Globe*'s circulation back to what it was before old Paddy died. The best way to make people buy a paper was to mention as many of them in it as possible, so she'd decided to run a regular interview column with a Bear Claw personality and an opinion survey on issues, local or otherwise.

She'd contacted Dora Klein to ask her to continue her gossip column, and to pump her for suggestions of whom Jassie should interview. Dora agreed, and invited Jassie to dinner on Thursday night. "After the paper comes out on Thursday, I know you'll be too tired to cook, so I thought—"

Hadn't the woman heard of takeout? Or frozen food?

"—you'll be plumb tuckered out, and in need of some good healthy home cooking."

Reluctantly Jassie agreed. She'd earmarked Thursday as a night to further her acquaintance with the sheriff—she'd discovered it was his night off. But, she supposed, business was business, and right now, getting on friendly terms with Dora Klein, the Ear of Bear Claw, was business.

And besides, she'd hardly even clapped eyes on the man since the day he'd brought her the second lot of doughnuts. He lived out of town, she'd discovered, in some cabin he'd built himself. Five or six miles out of town. A long way for a woman without a car.

Jassie sighed. She was going to have to spend more of her meager capital. New Yorkers could live from one year to the next without ever driving, but in Montana, a car was a necessity.

She returned to her perusal of a dusty leather-bound book that contained the earliest issues of *The Globe*. She'd found dozens of these old books, the history of Bear Claw preserved for the future by all the previous editors of *The Globe*. It was a wonderful legacy, for which Jassie was extremely grateful.

Checking her circulation statistics, she had discovered that quite a few copies went to the guest houses, holiday venues and dude ranches that surrounded the town. Apparently visitors found the old-world, small-town flavor of *The Globe* appealing.

So Jassie was searching through the earliest issues of the paper and reprinting any odd and interesting items in a column she was calling, "Snippets from Old Bear Claw."

She also decided, reluctantly, that she'd have to interview Ben Broome, and spent a few hours with the man and his teeth, recording story after story. It was surprisingly interesting—as long as she didn't watch the teeth and lose her concentration.

Another of her small victories was a deal with the man who ran the hunting supplies shop. He'd write a regular column, "Huntin' Shootin' Fishin'," in exchange for free advertising for his shop.

Photographs were her biggest problem in the end. Jassie could point a camera just fine, it was what came out that was the problem. She didn't know her way around a darkroom, either. She was able to use a number of old photos for some articles, but she was well aware there was no way that could go on for long.

She had just decided to advertise for a part-time photographer when young Tommy solved the problem. His friend Josh, another boy on the basketball team, was a camera buff. Jassie sent Josh out with a roll of film and, when he returned a few hours later, turned him loose in the darkroom. When he emerged, he had half a dozen shots she could use in her first issue, so she made a deal on the spot. And checked his hand before she shook it.

On Thursday the paper went out. Jeff Bassett bound up the paper in bundles according to his own delivery system and Jassie heaved a huge sigh of relief as she stood on the sidewalk and watched his truck drive away.

She reeled inside, exhausted. She was going to sleep for a week. She'd been up almost all night, getting the paper done.

She had no idea how an elderly man had done it, virtually alone. At this rate, she'd be an elderly woman by fall.

She staggered upstairs and fell onto the narrow single bed, fully dressed. The phone rang. And rang. And rang. Jassie sighed, opened her eyes and picked it up.

"Jassie, honey? It's Dora Klein again. My Don says you haven't got a car yet, so I've arranged for someone to give you a ride."

Rats! Jassie had forgotten all about the dinner invitation. She had no energy to sit through a dinner, not even with two sweet old things like Don and Dora. Not even if they offered her roast beef and mashed potatoes, her favorite meal. Jassie's mouth started watering. Roast beef, dark on the outside, moist and pink inside... creamy white potatoes swimming in luscious brown gravy... She'd be crazy to turn down a home-cooked meal.

But no, she was exhausted. She didn't have enough energy to eat at the Kleins' tonight. Roast beef or not. She opened her mouth to make an excuse.

"You hear me, Jassie, dear? I've arranged for someone to bring you."

"Oh, Dora, I'm terribly sorry, but I don't think—"

"It's the sheriff."

Jassie bit her tongue. "Outhch! Wath thid you thay, Thora? Who ith bringin me?"

"I've arranged for Sheriff Stone—J.T.—to pick you up at six-thirty. And he'll bring you home after, of course. That all right with you, Jassie?"

All right? The woman was an angel. A goddess. A saint.

"That'll be fine, Dora," she managed to say casually. "Quite convenient. I was wondering how I'd get there and back."

"Our sheriff's a fine-looking man, isn't he, Jassie?"

"Mmm, er, is he?" Jassie mumbled vaguely. "Oh, yes, I think I know the man you mean. Tall, with dark hair?"

Dora laughed knowingly. "Don told me all about how the two of you met. Very romantic."

"He was just my bus driver, Dora. I have no designs on Don," Jassie joked, determined to get the wretched woman—no, the angel's—mind on other things.

"Not on Don, no. But you fell right into J.T.'s arms, didn't you? That's what I call romantic."

Jassie felt herself blushing. Romantic? It was instant lust. "So six-thirty, then. Can I bring anything, Dora?"

"No, no, not a thing. Just yourself. And J.T."

"No problem. 'Bye, Dora. See you tonight." She sprang off the bed, suddenly energized. She had a million things to do—wash her hair, do her nails, get rid of the bags under her eyes, give herself a facial, find something to wear and—oh, good grief!—only ten hours to do it in.

What a great day! A day of firsts. Her first issue of *The Globe*—the first of many such issues.

And her first date with Sheriff Stone. The first—if she had her way—of many such dates....

4

DAMN! SHE LOOKED GORGEOUS, thought J.T. as Jassie opened the door for him. She was dressed in some sort of soft greeny-blue thing that swirled around her body, clinging to her…er, upper body…and floating out in a swirl around her legs. And she had great legs, he observed miserably. Long and slender, like a newborn filly's. Damn! Why on earth had he let Dora talk him into this?

"Evening, Sheriff," she murmured, eyeing him up and down in a way that made his collar feel suddenly way too tight. Not to mention other parts of his clothing.

"I do like your outfit," she said. "I hadn't realized how attractive some of this Western-style gear can look. I love the jacket. The stitching is great, not overdone, like some I've seen." She reached up and stroked his dark brown suede jacket.

He could smell her perfume, some kind he'd never smelled before. He hoped she couldn't see his nostrils flaring in response to the tantalizing scent of her.

"And these are cute." She fingered the silver end on his collar. He could almost feel the heat of her fingers as they brushed past his jaw. Steady, boy!

"And what do they call this thing again?" she said, scratching ever so lightly down the front of his shirt with one dainty fingernail.

"Er, a bolo," Stone croaked as a shudder rippled through him.

"It matches your belt buckle, doesn't it?" She glanced down at his belt and he suddenly felt much,

much too hot for the cool summer evening. And his pants were much, much too tight.

"We better go," he said hastily. "It's getting on. Don and Dora like to do things on time."

"I'll just fetch my wrap. In case it's chilly, you know. I'm not used to these Montana summer nights." She emerged with a soft cobwebby-lace thing with a fringe around it and handed it to him. He crushed it numbly in his hands. She turned her back. He could see the delicate line of her backbone disappearing down into the dark shadows beneath the dress. Her skin was finely textured, pale gold, with a sprinkling of tiny freckles across her shoulders.

Her dress was sleeveless, held up with two skinny little bits of nothing over her shoulders. One little tug and the whole dress would just slide down those smooth, golden shoulders and fall right off her. He stared, his mouth dry.

"Wrap me, Sheriff," she said softly, smiling at him over her shoulder.

He wanted to wrap her, all right, but not in this little piece of nothing. Dammit!

Clumsily, for his hands were tense, he draped the shawl across her bare skin and wrenched open the door to the street. "I'm parked down the street a ways," he said.

Jassie locked the door behind her. He'd been as close-mouthed as a clam so far. He hadn't even said she looked nice! Even her first date when she was thirteen had complimented her, and he'd been forced into it by his mother! She'd never get to first base with J. T. Stone if she couldn't relax him a bit.

She had to make another attempt to get the conversational ball rolling. Men and their cars was generally a surefire topic. "What do you drive, Sheriff?"

"The green Ford." He gestured up ahead.

"What?" exclaimed Jassie, coming to a halt. "Is *that* what you drive?" Somehow she hadn't expected Sheriff

Stone to drive a sleek, shiny, road-hugging, green Ford Mustang convertible, but she knew at a glance it was his. It so suited him, with his graceful, untamed, pantherish stride, to be driving a beautiful, untamed, pantherish car. The dead giveaway was the color. It matched his eyes. Exactly. Men were so vain, really, but she found it rather endearing in him. "It's great!"

Stone glanced at her oddly. "You think so?"

"Oh, I do," she eagerly assured him. "I just love it."

"You really do?" Stone looked both pleased and surprised.

Jassie, enjoying the sensation, hastened to wax lyrical. "Oh, absolutely. It's just perfect."

"Yeah, well, I don't know about perfect, but I reckon it has character, unlike most modern—"

"I mean, will you just look at that terrible old rust bucket beside it. I mean, some people have no pride, do—" Jassie halted in midstream. A silence pressed over her. A silence that grew and gathered like fog, swirling around her head, growing thicker and colder by the minute.

She glanced at the sheriff's face. It looked especially granitelike. Positively grave. That look of faint surprise and pleasure she'd seen a moment ago had vanished.

Jassie looked back at the shiny new car she'd been admiring. The dark green Ford Mustang convertible gleamed and smirked and purred. Her gaze reluctantly shifted to the battered, rusty old Ford pickup next to it. The rust bucket gazed back at her, one crooked headlamp seeming to wink at her. It was a nasty, know-it-all wink. A character-filled wink.

Jassie hurried on. "I mean, will you just look at that dreadful, vulgar, ostentatious Mustang. Some people have *no* modesty. Flashy, flashy, flashy! And what's worse, flash without substance. And, er, as for character, not so much as a whit, as my Irish grandmother used to say."

Thin-lipped, Stone opened the passenger door of his battered old pickup. The door was gray. The panel on one side of it was pink, the other side, black. The hood was pale, peeling green. "Get in," he snapped. "It may be old, but it's very reliable."

Gingerly, Jassie slid past him into Old Reliable and meekly buckled her seat belt. With a growl of the engine, they pulled away from the curb and headed out of town.

"Well," she said brightly as trees flashed past her. "This is nice, isn't it?"

There was a faint noise from the driver's seat. It might have been a snort, but Jassie didn't care to examine it in detail.

She persisted with cheery conversation. "Is it far to Don and Dora's?"

Silence.

"Sheriff? How far is it to Don and Dora's?"

"Three miles out of town."

"Oh, that won't take long, will it?" she said cheerfully. "Now, what should I call you?"

He glanced across at her. "Call me?"

"Well, yes, I can't go on calling you sheriff all night, can I? I mean, it's so formal. What's your name, Sheriff?" Of course she knew perfectly well people called him J.T., she just wanted to know what J.T. stood for.

"It's John," he finally replied. "John T. Stone, ma'am."

John *T.*, Jassie thought. John was nice, but the *T.* made all the difference. *Rio Bravo.* One of her all-time favorite Westerns. John Wayne as the sheriff, John T. Something-or-other, and Angie Dickinson in a long, tight dress, saying to him in a low, breathy voice, "Hello, *John T.*" She'd always loved that movie.

And now Jassie had her very own sheriff, her very own John T. Almost. "Hello, John *T.*," she said in a low, breathy, Angie Dickinson sort of voice.

He made that sound again. Jassie decided it was a hello sort of snort.

"So, what do you think we'll have for dinner, John T.?"

He nearly smiled then, Jassie was sure of it. "Lord only knows." He glanced across at her quizzically. "What are you expecting?"

"Oh, I don't know. The usual, I suppose."

"The usual?"

"Roast beef and mashed potatoes. Or maybe a barbecue. They're pretty big on barbecues out this way, aren't they? We don't have them so often in New York."

"You like barbecues?"

"Love 'em. A big, juicy steak, just oozing with juice. My idea of heaven on a plate. Although roast beef is my real favorite. Whatever. I don't even care if it's hamburger. I'm starving."

"Oh, I think I can guarantee it won't be hamburger." A network of crinkles had appeared. He was grinning again. Jassie was delighted to see it. He'd been a tad moody, but he'd gotten over it. Her persistence had paid off. She smiled happily back at him. He was such a gorgeous man.

The pickup pulled up outside a large log cabin-style house with big bay windows in front. Lights were on to welcome them.

The sheriff leaped out of the pickup and hurried around to her side. Jassie sighed. He was planning to open her door for her, as if she were some helpless hothouse flower. It was sexist. It was old-fashioned. It was wonderfully romantic. But she couldn't allow it. She was not a hothouse flower, she was an independent modern woman. She groped for the handle, then sighed again and waited for him to open her door.

Yes, it was sexist, it was old-fashioned, it was romantic. It was also absolutely necessary. The passenger door of Old Reliable didn't have an inside handle.

"Thank you, John T.," she murmured as she stepped to the ground.

"DORA AND ME are vegetarians," announced Don as he ushered Jassie to a seat. The table was set with a blue-checked cloth and folded red napkins. An arrangement of gourds was piled in the center. A glass jug, beaded with moisture, contained a dense-looking greenish substance. He picked it up and poured her a glass.

"Oh, yes?" murmured Jassie with a sinking heart. She accepted the glass with a bright smile. Essence of Pond Scum, unless she was mistaken. He should have warned her, dammit! She shot a quick look across at the sheriff. Drat the man, he was grinning again.

"We took it up six years ago. Up to then I was a big meat man. Did a lot of hunting. Well, this is the place for it, elk, deer. I did like my venison." Don chuckled reminiscently. "But terrible for the bowels, meat." He eyed her untouched glass.

"Oh?" said Jassie faintly. She raised the glass to her nose, sniffed tentatively and with the sheriff eyeing her in cynical amusement, took a sip. She smiled beatifically at him and put the glass down gently. Definitely pond scum.

"Take my word for it—"

"Oh, I do, Don," she assured him, hoping that would head him off at the pass, so to speak. But it didn't.

"Not many people realize it, but—you're a meat-eater, right, Jassie?—well, at this very minute your bowels is clogged with pounds and pounds of rotting dead animal."

"Ugh, er, oh, how...er, interesting."

"Yep, pounds and pounds. You're probably sittin' on it right now."

"Fascinating." Jassie kept her face quite blank.

Stone glanced at her and started choking in what Jassie considered to be a very rude way.

"Oh, Sheriff Stone, are you quite all right? Perhaps

you need a drink?'' she gushed solicitously, reaching
for the glass jug. If she had to drink Essence of Pond
Scum so did he. That would wipe the insufferable smile
off his face.

"No, no, no." Don interrupted. "J.T. can't drink
that."

"Why not?" said Jassie brightly, through gritted lips.

"Very delicate constitution, J.T. has."

Jassie eyed the delicate six-foot-something collection
of masculine bone and muscle. "Yes, I can see that."

Don nodded. "The poor fellow doesn't look it, but
there are so many foods he's allergic to."

"Oh, re-eeally."

"Yes, indeed. And spinach juice is one of them."

"Indeeeed?" Jassie narrowed her eyes. Not a bedroom sort of narrow. More a who's-a-big-fat-fink sort
of narrow.

"Yes, unfortunately. I'm only allowed my own specially prepared juice." Mr. Delicate Constitution pro-
duced a large flask and poured himself a glass of thick
red liquid. Jassie eyed it suspiciously. It looked like tomato juice to her.

"May I taste?" She reached out a hand.

"No, no." He snatched the glass out of reach. "It
has my special medication in it."

Jassie snorted. "Medication my foot!" she muttered
under her breath. The sheriff grinned, toasted her and
downed half a glass of what, unless Jassie was much
mistaken, was tomato juice—heavily spiked with vodka.

"Is your medication popular in Russia, by any
chance?" she inquired sweetly.

"I wouldn't know," he replied solemnly. "I've never
been to Russia." The sheriff turned back to their host.
"Now, Don, you were saying…"

Don looked puzzled.

"In Jassie's bowel…" prompted the Evil One. "I can
tell when a girl is fascinated. You tell her all about it,
Don, while I go see if Dora needs a hand." Grinning,

he left the room. Jassie glared after him in speechless indignation.

"Right. Well, Jassie, right now in your bowel is three or four pounds of dead animal. Three or four pounds! Just rotting away inside you. Squirming with little bugs and stuff. Incredible ain't it?"

"Incredible." Jassie glared some more at the closed kitchen door.

"What was the last meal you ate, Jassie-girl?"

"A BLT," she admitted reluctantly.

"Aha! Bacon. Ain't nothin' worse than dead pig for the bowel."

There was a hastily muffled snort from the kitchen door as Stone entered the room carrying a mound of gelatinous gray matter. It trembled ominously, but stayed on the plate. Jassie hoped it was some sort of plant food on its way to the compost. Stone set it gently in front of her on the table.

If he grinned any more, his face would turn into the Grand Canyon, she thought sourly.

Don continued. "Good thing you came to dinner when you did, Jassie-girl. My Dora will feed you up real good with plenty of roughage. That'll shift that old dead pig for you."

"Lovely." Jassie attempted to look delighted. "Roughage. My favorite." She ignored the minor choking noise from beside her.

"Greens, that's what you want."

Jassie nodded. Green was how she felt already. Why were so many health nuts obsessed with bowels?

"You ain't drinking, Jassie-girl. Don't you like Dora's spinach juice?"

"Oh, no, I love it." With a gallant smile she lifted the glass and downed the pond scum all in one hit. "Ah, simply delicious," she announced defiantly, glaring into a pair of green eyes. They were glinting wickedly with heinous amusement. How could she have thought his eyes were so beautiful? They exactly matched her spinach juice—pond-scum green.

"That's it, girl," said Don happily. "Give old Mr. Pig his marching orders."

Stone choked again and lifted a napkin to hide the laughter on his low-down rotten face. Instantly, Jassie leaped out of her chair and began to pound him on his back as hard as she could. Thump! Thump! Serve-you-right thump! You-rotten-swine thump! "Is something the matter, Sheriff?" she cooed with saccharine concern.

"Crumb," he spluttered, fending her off him with one strong hand.

"Crumb! You haven't eaten a thing," she snarled, thumping his back harder. "And I doubt if you ever will."

"Oh, yes," he gasped nobly. "I wouldn't dream of disappointing Dora. I'll eat everything I can."

Speechless with…dignity…Jassie sat again and proceeded to ignore him.

"So, Don, you used to hunt a lot?" Not that she was at all interested in hunting, but at least it was better than bowels. And pond scum. And Mr. Pig. She repressed a shudder.

"Yep, now all I do is fish." Don reached for the jug and poured her another glass of green ooze. "I looove to go fishing. Dora and me ain't total vegetarians—we do eat plenty of fish. You'll be eating one of my catches tonight."

"Oh, good," said Jassie, relieved. There was not a lot people could do to ruin fish. She wondered if it would be baked, fried or steamed. She preferred baked fish, herself. Or sushi.

"That's it you're looking at now." Don gestured to the grayish blobby substance quivering gently on its plate. "Dora's famous fish mousse."

"Oh." Jassie eyed the famous mousse grimly. "Er, lovely."

Sheriff Stone sighed tragically.

Instantly Jassie knew what was coming next. She glared her best glare at him. It bounced off him harmlessly. He met her gaze frankly, his eyes limpid green and totally without guile.

"Unfortunately," he said sorrowfully, "as Don knows, I'm also allergic to fish. I'll just have to make do with salad and perhaps a morsel of Dora's delicious home-baked bread." He sighed again and manfully downed the rest of his medicinal Bloody Mary.

Jassie glowered and prayed for him to choke. Properly.

He survived. The devil always looked after his own.

BY THE END OF THE EVENING Jassie was in a thoroughly foul temper. Don and Dora were absolute sweeties, which made it all the more necessary that she smile as she choked down the frightful food. She'd never eaten so much roughage in her life and never wanted to again. But she couldn't feel angry with them. They were flowing with the milk—the soy milk—of human kindness.

And it was crystal clear that the two little old cherubs knew she was interested in the sheriff and were doing their level best to matchmake. They'd made Jassie and J.T. squash into a tiny cozy sofa when there were easily half a dozen other available seats in the room. They'd turned the lights down low and put soft music on and left Jassie and the sheriff alone for long periods of time. And furious as she was with the big rat, she couldn't help but melt at the sensation of his muscular, jeans-clad leg pressing all the way along hers.

She couldn't hold that against Don and Dora. They were obviously on her side, making the assumption that Jassie was out to hook J.T. She was, but not with a gold ring. Just for a hot fling. Just for a year, until she went back to New York or wherever. But she couldn't possibly tell Don and Dora that.

The evening wore on until finally the sheriff stood, clearly ready to go. It was only ten o'clock, Jassie realized in surprise as she kissed Dora and Don and thanked them for the lovely meal. It had felt much longer.

As she and J.T. roared away into the night in Old Reliable, she prepared herself to deliver a tirade. The wretch had it coming. She still wanted a fling with him, but she was *not* going to let him get away with his low deceit in feigning allergy to frightful food! Particularly when it meant that *she* was given double quantities of the stuff.

It was just lucky she'd managed to shovel so much of it into her handbag when nobody was looking. It was ruined, of course, but never had a handbag made a worthier sacrifice.

She opened her mouth to start the tirade, then glanced out at the road in puzzlement. The truck was heading into the mountains. The trees were getting thicker, the moon, a cool, pale disk glowing against the last remnants of the late summer twilight, was rising over the mountains. "Where are we going? This isn't the way to town."

"Nope. I'm heading for Bozeman."

"Bozeman? But why? It's miles and miles away. Bozeman is over the pass. And it's after ten o'clock at night."

"Yup, us Montana folks don't keep early hours like you city people. Why, 10:00 p.m. ain't nothin' to us. We often stay up real late—heck, sometimes all the way to midnight!" he said facetiously, his accent thickening.

"But—"

"Aren't you hungry?" he said. "I sure am. There's a place in Bozeman makes great burgers."

There was a short silence while Jassie coped with swelling indignation. She felt angry enough to explode.

"Don and Dora are wonderful people," J.T. continued, "but Dora sure isn't any cook. It was bad enough before, but since they turned vegetarian, well...I couldn't eat a thing," said the man who'd shamelessly devoured half a loaf of wonderful crusty bread, nibbled on three pieces of lettuce, and washed the lot down with several "medicinal" Bloody Marys.

"Well, I'm sorry, but I was raised to have manners. When I'm offered food I at least try to eat it," she said prissily. "I don't make up lies about allergies. So I don't want to go all the way over to Bozeman for a hamburger, thank you very much. I'm full."

He shot an amused look at her. "*You're* not full," he said. "Your handbag's full. Full of fish mousse and roughage."

Jassie breathed slowly and calmly through her nose all the way to Bozeman.

THE HAMBURGER was utterly delicious. Big, thick, and dripping with juice and onions. Even the smell was to die for. And the fries were crisp and perfect.

They ate in silence, listening to the sound of the old-fashioned jukebox playing numbers from the fifties and sixties. Jassie sipped the last of her chocolate shake and tried very hard to remember why she'd been so cross with him. It was impossible. You couldn't be angry with a man who had just bought you the best hamburger in the world. And the best fries. And the second-best chocolate shake. She sat back in the red-leather booth and sighed in contentment. She was as full as her handbag, only much more happily.

She buried the handbag in a trash can in the ladies' room and muttered a few words over it while John T. paid for the burgers. Luckily there was nothing of value in it; her keys and wallet had been in the mousse-free outside zip compartment.

The trip back to Bear Claw began in a haze of contentment, but soon an atmosphere of growing awareness developed. One sort of hunger had been fed. Now another began to make itself felt.

It started with his thighs. They sat there, straining at the smooth denim of his jeans. Inviting her to touch.

Just to reach out and lay her hand on the warm, hard muscle, to feel their strength, their warmth, their power.

And his hands on the steering wheel, loosely draped, long-fingered and capable, exerting power with the lightest touch.

His profile appeared stark and forbidding in the flickering moonlight, all hard planes and sharp edges. He was frowning slightly and his lips slashed a thin line of tension. She could just see that tiny scar that cut through his upper lip. It surely did fascinate her. She wondered how it would feel pressed against her own lips, against her eyelids, against her breasts. Would she be able to feel the scar?

Jassie shifted restlessly in her seat and stared out at the trees flickering past in the darkness. She longed for the courage to unfasten her seat belt and slide along the bench seat of the pickup until she was touching him. A dozen times her hand went to the buckle of her seat belt. A dozen times she let it fall to the seat instead. It was probably not a good idea to jump a man's bones while he was driving on back country roads at high speed through the inky blackness of night. Even if his bones were the most beautiful bones she'd ever seen in her life.

She ought to be admiring the scenery, which was pretty impressive on such a clear night. The scenery outside the truck was pretty impressive, too, she told herself.

As they breasted the pass, heading toward Bear Claw, the long wide valley lay ahead of them, blanched with moonlight, dotted with dark trees, lined with huge, impassive mountains.

Very pretty.

Jassie drummed the hard seat softly with her fingers.

The cab of the pickup smelled very masculine. A faint smell of old leather and new. She could just scent the tang of his aftershave. Nice to think he'd shaved before their date. Not that it was a date as such. He hadn't asked her, hadn't shown the slightest bit of interest. Good old Dora had arranged it. She could forgive the woman anything for that. Even that fish atrocity.

He moved slightly, stretching his neck and flexing his shoulders as if he were feeling a bit stiff, or tense. Her hands itched to give him a soothing massage, to delve into that fabulous mass of masculine muscle to soothe and relax him. And then pounce.

Was he as aware of her as she was of him? He didn't seem to stare at her half as much as he'd caught her staring at him. Was he interested? Maybe... She'd caught him looking, too, once or twice. Once or twice. It didn't exactly amount to an ogle, did it? It was a disconcerting thought.

Her fingers drummed harder on the stiff seat. Would he even *want* to kiss her good-night?

Jassie frowned. His wishes shouldn't come into it. It was the polite thing to do. He'd taken her out, entertained himself watching her deal with the most disgusting food she'd ever been forced to eat—or to feed a hapless handbag. He'd driven her miles and miles through some wild unknown forest and over some enormous mountain pass, just to get a hamburger, and if he didn't want to give her a good-night kiss, then it was just too bad! It was time Sheriff John T. Stone learned what his duty was! Simple good manners demanded he kiss her good-night!

She glared at his stern, impenetrable profile and found herself softening instantly. He was such a hunk! And once she had him in her hot little hands, she'd teach him to enjoy his duty. And manners would maketh the man!

"What the—?" The pickup abruptly slowed to the side and came to a sudden halt. Jassie felt as though her seat belt would cut her in two. She glanced across at John T. as she struggled to unbuckle it.

"Are you okay?" he said in a low voice. He put his

hand out and touched her gently on the leg, his eyes running over her in concern.

The seat belt fell off her unnoticed as the warmth of his big, strong hand pulsed right through her. Jassie's heart rate, already zappy, suddenly upped its rhythm. "I'm fine," she answered, "but—"

"Sorry, it was unavoidable."

"Did we hit—I mean I didn't feel any—"

"No, that was the point." He smiled, and Jassie turned to mush, loving the way his eyes turned into slivers of green. Not that they had much color in the moonlight. They looked like shards of gleaming obsidian, sort of. She didn't really know what obsidian looked like—probably fabulous, if his moonlit eyes were anything to go by. She felt herself grinning mushily back at him. Like a loon. All thoughts of their near-accident forgotten.

"Um, why are we whispering?" she whispered after a moment.

He didn't reply, just gestured silently to the road. Her eyes followed. There, just inches from the front bumper, was a small deer, staring wide-eyed into the brilliant headlights. It was a very tiny deer, Jassie realized. Not much bigger than Bambi. J.T. gestured, and as Jassie's eyes adjusted, she saw Bambi's mother waiting anxiously in the shadows of the trees on the side of the road. She was taking tiny indecisive steps toward her baby, then backing away in fear of the big pickup and its human occupants. The fawn stood frozen, its long, delicate legs trembling, its eyes wide, staring dazedly.

"They were crossing the road, but the little one was mesmerized by the headlights. It froze," murmured J.T. He switched off the headlights and Jassie watched, entranced as the tiny deer slowly came to its senses and looked around. In the brilliant moonlight, she could see the fear jumping in ripples across its dappled velvety hide. A movement in the shadowy brush caused it to twitch, but it didn't move away. The mother deer came out onto the road, wary, obviously frightened, but concerned for her baby. Bambi didn't move. Slowly, hesitantly, the doe came closer and closer, her wide dark gaze flickering between the truck and its inhabitants and her frozen baby.

Jassie watched, holding her breath. This doe knew what a hunter was, but she came on regardless. Love for her baby made her risk all. It was a poignant moment. Jassie had a lump in her throat.

Finally the doe reached her fawn and gave it a firm shove with her muzzle. It blinked and then made a faint bleating sound. Of recognition or protest? wondered Jassie. The doe took a few steps away from the pickup, shoving the baby along, then something startled her and in a few bounds she'd reached the roadside. Bambi raced after her in dainty little leaps and in seconds, mother and baby had vanished into the darkness.

Jassie was breathless with wonder and emotion. She'd never been so close to a wild creature before. It was magical. And the heartbreaking anxiety of the mother for her frozen, frightened baby. Mother love.

"That…that was wonderful," she breathed at last, turning toward the sheriff. He looked oddly blurry.

J.T. looked at her. He sighed and hauled her across the seat, hard up into his arms. She blinked up at him and he groaned and brought his mouth down to hers.

His kiss was tender, Jassie thought in wonderment. So tender that it could steal a girl's heart right out of her body without her knowing—if the girl was the falling in love sort, that is. Luckily Jassie wasn't that sort. Not anymore. But ohh-h, she'd never been kissed as if she were so precious, so tender…

SHE TASTED OF tears…and wonder…and woman. Sweet, tart, sultry…with a faint onion aftertaste from the hamburger.

He closed his mind to the warning bells going off in every part of his self-defense system, and gave himself up to the wonder of her mouth. He cupped her head gently in one hand, feeling his fingers slip through the cool silk of her hair. His fingers had itched to feel it all evening. Such glossy curls, like corn silk of the night. He pulled back a little and gazed into her eyes. They were still drowning, but with passion now instead of tears. He kissed her eyelids and sipped the tears that trembled on her lashes. His mouth wandered over her cheekbone and down along the pure line of her jaw. Her skin was soft…so soft, with a city woman's pampering.

She felt soft all over. He wanted to explore every inch of her. Her hands were twining themselves around him, one hand thrusting sensuously through his own hair, and he felt himself butting against her like a cat enjoying a petting. Her other hand wrapped around his neck, pulling his head back down to her mouth…demanding…needing…enjoying.

A surge of masculine triumph swept through him as he realized his desire was returned. Tenderness gave way to urgency…

He kissed her again, hard and long, and then moved away to continue his slow exploration of her skin, but she stopped him, catching his lower lip gently between her small white teeth. She growled lightly, like a kitten deprived of its prey, as he tried to pull back, and the sound reverberated through him like wildfire and hot whiskey. He gave her what she demanded then, long, hot kisses…deep…searing…burning.

She returned each with equal measure. He was blown away by her passion. She writhed around him, clawing the shirt away from his body, nuzzling her breasts against his skin, running her hands over his chest, rubbing and stroking and all the time pushing herself against him, as if she were trying to climb right into his skin.

And damn if he didn't want her to succeed, want her to come right into him, to be as close as any two people could be. The blood was pounding in his ears. He was as hard as a rock and the need pounded through him, clawing at his control.

He shifted his body and lifted her so she was lying all the way along him, thigh to thigh, breast to chest, belly to belly. And so she could feel his need. He began to caress her the way she caressed him.

The flimsy little straps of her dress fell off her shoulders exactly the way he had fantasized about all evening. His hands and mouth followed them, smoothing, stroking the warm pale gold skin, so soft, so satiny under the rough texture of his palms. She almost purred in response and nipped gently and provocatively at his nipples, and he arched against her as need powered through his body like a crashing wave. And as he arched, his elbow hit the horn.

It was a loud horn. One he'd had specially installed. After all, if he had to use a horn, he wanted one people would really hear. They usually did, from quite a distance.

It was even more effective at close quarters, if Jassie's reaction was anything to go by. She leaped off his body as if a bolt of lightning had passed through her, smacking her head on the roof of the pickup. Her knees jerked up in a fight-or-flight response—or as near as you could get to it sprawled along a seat in the cab of a pickup—and one knee landed in a spot that instantly ensured he would be in no condition to either fight or flee.

She glanced around, wild-eyed and confused, as he let out a roar of agony. Almost as loud as the horn.

''What the—?''

She looked up at his face and down to where her knee rested. She scrambled off him, babbling apologies. Once the first white-hot agony had passed, he opened his door and pulled himself out, where he could deal with being unmanned out of the sight of a pair of distraught, guilty blue eyes. He swore long and hard under his breath, and forced himself to straighten up. He sucked deep gulps of cool fresh air into his lungs, willing the nausea and dizziness to pass.

After a few minutes he'd recovered enough to return to the car.

"I'm so sorr—" she began, as he slid in behind the wheel.

"Forget it," he muttered tersely.

"But I truly didn't mean—"

"It's okay, just forget it!" Stone started the engine and gunned it noisily to cover his embarrassment. And to prevent any more talk. He was furious. Mortified.

With himself, not her.

Behaving like a horny damned adolescent! Making out in the front seat of a pickup! He swore under his breath and mashed the truck into gear. Serves him right. What the hell did he think he was doing? Making out with a cracks-and-crannies woman! And after an evening under the gimlet eye of the biggest gossip and matchmaker in the county.

Hell! He knew better than that.

What on earth had he been thinking of? Dora had twisted his arm to go in the first place, and if he hadn't been so damn fond of the old lady, he would have told her no to start with. Or put himself on duty. Or arranged to be called out to an emergency. But Dora would have found out he'd lied and made his life hell.

He wasn't good with women. Even old ones. Especially when they looked all hurt and miserable. And Dora did the best lower-lip quiver he'd ever seen on an old lady, dammit.

Damned women!

Damned deer! He gave the truck more gas and they shot through the night like an arrow.

Damned stupid move to go to Bozeman for the hamburger. Couldn't blame that on anyone except himself. Bozeman turned the evening from one in which he was just giving her a ride to Dora and Don's, into something that perilously resembled a date.

But he'd felt she deserved something after all that horrible food. He'd never enjoyed himself more than when he'd realized she was quietly shoving that fish mousse into her handbag, right under everyone's nose. He'd nearly choked, trying to not laugh. And her face as she'd forced down glass after glass of that spinach juice, smiling heroically as she did. While he drank Bloody Marys. He should have warned her about Dora's cooking.

Yeah, it was guilt as much as anything that had prompted the hamburger trip. He owed her.

He liked her, too. That was the trouble. Liked her spirit, liked her style. And liked her body too damn much for his own comfort....

But it was the damned deer that had caused the problem. Hell, she'd looked so appealing, watching them with those big eyes, as if she'd never seen a deer before. And then she'd turned to him, tears glittering on her lashes. Well, what could he do? The woman needed kissing.

Any man would have done the same.

He frowned. He didn't like the sound of that at all. Damn! It was worse than he thought. He had to get himself away from this woman and her big blue eyes and her soft-as-dewdrops skin. As far away as possible. He wasn't going to see her again. He was a man who valued his skin. And his freedom. And his peace of mind. He and his cracks and crannies were just fine, thank you! No more Jassie McQuilty for him. No see, no touch, no kiss.

He was driving back to Bozeman the first moment he could arrange it. And not for a hamburger!

JASSIE HUNG ON to her seat belt surreptitiously as the pickup roared through the night. God help any poor little deer on the road now, she thought. Even if J.T. wanted to, he wouldn't be able to stop in time. She stole another glance at his face. Granite. She sighed. If only... She glanced at the horn. Stupid darned thing! She'd thought her heart was going to burst out of her chest when it went off. She slipped a quick look at the sheriff's pants and wondered whether he was still in pain. And whether she'd done any permanent damage. She cringed, recalling the moment when she'd seen exactly where her knee had landed.

Yes, she'd been planning to make contact with that part of his anatomy, but not quite in *that* way!

She sighed and felt him dart a quick glance at her before planting his foot a little harder on the gas.

He looked furious. And no wonder. How criminally clumsy could a girl get? And what quicker way to end the most promising fling she'd ever had. Well, the only one she'd ever had. Murdock had been a relationship. And before him there'd only been Phil in college. That was a relationship, too—at least she'd thought so at the time. Until Phil had dumped her for that ditsy sophomore...

Rita was right. Jassie did take love too seriously. No way was getting heartbroken going to become the pattern of her life. No more relationships. Just fleeting, happy, lighthearted flings.

Yeah, right. Like the one she was having at the moment.

She sighed again as the half-dozen streetlights of Bear Claw hove into view. So much for the first date. No man would ask a woman out again after she'd done *that* to him.

And he'd been very aroused at the time... She wondered if that would make it hurt more. It wasn't the sort of question she could ask, either.

With a start she realized he'd driven right past the boardinghouse where she supposedly lived. She glanced at his face. Still granite. No questions of any sort, she decided. She'd just have to wait to see where he was taking her.

The pickup pulled up outside *The Globe* office. Jas-

sie's misery lightened a little. At least he'd tacitly acknowledged where she lived. He switched off the engine
and walked around to let her out of the pickup. He
seemed to be walking normally again. She examined his
face under the streetlights. His color was good, too. Jassie felt a little better.

She got out and felt a whisper of movement as he
shut the door behind her. She walked toward the front
door of *The Globe* office and heard his footsteps follow
her. She fumbled with the keys for a minute or two and
then he reached past her and took them from her hand.
Jassie watched as he inserted her key into the door. She
hated it when men did that. As if she were too incompetent to open her own door. So why did she feel so
happy?

He kept doing all sorts of things she just knew were
sexist to the hilt…and yet she kind of liked it… Thank
heavens, she was only going to have a fling with him.
If it was a relationship, she'd have to cure him of this
protective nonsense. And she wasn't sure he was cur-
able. Not in this environment.

Then Jassie remembered. She wasn't going to have a
fling with him. She'd blown it. Nearly crippled him for
life.

Dolefully she turned. "Thank you for a lovely night
out, John T.," she said, noting miserably that his eyes
were flinty and his jaw was set. "I-it was lovely."

His brows rose sardonically and Jassie flushed
slightly. "Well, the part where we went into Bozeman
was. Such a pretty city. And thank you for the hamburger, too. It was delicious." Oh, God, she sounded
like a polite twelve-year-old. How feeble could a person
get? "I—I'm so sorr—"

He interrupted her brusquely. "'Night, ma'am."

So they were back to "ma'am" again. Formal. Polite.
No more John T., no more long thrilling rides through
the night, alone with him in the cab of his pickup, no
more kisses…the most magical kisses she'd ever had…

"I'm glad we didn't hit the little fawn," she said finally. "At least something good came of this."

The sheriff stared down at her, frowning. "'Night," he muttered again after a moment.

"'Night."

He opened her door and when she just stood there, he gently pushed her inside. He turned to go, then hesitated.

"Thanks again for the ride, John T.," she said softly.

He grunted, acknowledging her words, and walked away from her. He reached his pickup and opened the driver's door, then stopped. From her position in the open doorway she could see the frown on his face. It was even blacker and more intense than before. He put one foot inside the cab, hesitated again and turned his head to stare back at her.

"Ah, hell!" she heard him mutter.

He got out, slammed the door and marched purposefully toward her. From the look on his face he was about to commit murder. Jassie waited nervously, her mind blank. She took one tentative step toward him and then, as the fearsome look in his eyes became clearer, took several hasty steps back. He stormed through the open door, grabbed her by the arms and planted his mouth hard on hers. It was a fierce kiss, almost ferocious in its intensity, and her mouth and body molded to his as she gave herself up to it with total, ecstatic abandon.

His kiss was wild, untamed, burning with tumultuous, angry desire…and yet beyond the anger, beyond the savage desire, was need. And if the passion thrilled her, it was the need that seduced her, the faint, buried thread of desperate masculine need. Need for her…for Jassie McQuilty…

Finally he let her go, setting her back gently against the doorjamb. Her knees sagged slightly but she fought the sensation. He stared at her again, breathing heavily, and the black frown was back. Helpless, not knowing why he was frowning, but unable to do anything else, she smiled at him.

He sighed, audibly. "Ah, hell." He grabbed her, kissed her again—a hard, brief kiss—and shook his head. He kissed her once more, softly, lingering, as if to memorize her taste, her texture, then set her back, muttering, "And that's it. Right?"

Jassie blinked, bemused. *It?* What was *it? Right?* Everything was certainly right. Completely, wonderfully right. More than right. Perfect. Perfectly perfect.

He seemed to want her to say something, so she nodded and smiled dreamily at him again. It simply was not possible for her to say a word. She was totally, utterly blissed out.

Swearing, he stormed from the building. "Lock the dam—darned—door behind me, you hear?" She heard the truck door slam and the instant roar of an engine. Two seconds later the sound of the pickup had faded into the distance; the only sign of it, the faint scent of burning rubber.

Jassie floated over to the door. She found herself caressing the handle. What was she supposed to do with the door? Oh, yes, lock it. She locked it, caressed it one more time, then floated toward the stairs. She looked up. There were an awful lot of stairs. She sank down onto one instead and leaned against the rail, dazed and blissful.

He'd kissed her again. Wonderful... Twice. Double wonderful. He didn't care that she'd nearly crippled him. He'd kissed her... She found herself hugging a stair rail. Magical yummy kisses, too. Kisses made of fire and lightning and honey and thunder and whiskey...

She was having a fling. Almost. With the most gorgeous man in the world. Wonderful... She leaned her head back on the steps behind her. They were covered in grit. The stairs needed sweeping. Wonderful... She'd do it tomorrow. Right after she called John T. and invited him over for breakfast.

She rose and floated up the stairs to the bedroom. She would have to improve her cooking facilities if she was going to make him breakfast in the mornings. She arrived at the bedroom and looked at her bed, her narrow, single, iron-framed bed, and decided there were far more important things to spend her money on than kitchen equipment or cars. A big man needed a big bed...

Slowly she undressed, eyes closed, sliding the spaghetti straps slowly off her shoulders, just as he had done before.... Best not remember too much, she decided.

She climbed into her pajamas. Maybe it was time she bought a sexy nightgown, too. No, she hated nightgowns...maybe a teddy, she thought. A black lace teddy, with a low scooped front... Whatever, she probably wouldn't be wearing it for long, not if she had any say about it. And she was sure he'd be happy to cooperate.

She pulled the covers up and switched the light off, smiling dreamily. She should have invited him up. Even if it was their first date... It would have been a terrible fit—he was a big man, and this was a narrow bed—but, oh! what a way to be squashed. She shuddered deliciously and hugged the pillow to her.

She still didn't know how that enticing little scar on his upper lip felt pressed to her lips. Oh, her lips must know...but they couldn't remember. She hadn't been able to think at the time. Sleepily, Jassie vowed to remember to notice how the scar felt the next time he kissed her.

And there would be a next time. She knew it now. He'd forgiven her... He'd kiss her. Soon...maybe tomorrow...morning...and she'd remember to...concentrate....

5

Subject: My love life
Date: Fri June 23 7:46:36
From: <Jassie@dotmail.com>
To: "Rita DeLorenzo" <Rita@dotmail.com>

Message: Rita, you were absolutely right! I feel wonderful! Am on verge of stupendous fling... The most gorgeous man in Montana! Bliss! Send slinky black teddy. Urgent! love Jassie.

"MORNIN', JASSIE. Good paper yesterday."

"Oh, er, thanks, Mr. er..." Jassie stared after the old fellow who'd shot a compliment out of the side of his mouth and stumped on past her. She'd never clapped eyes on him before, she was sure. And yet he'd called her by name. A smile touched her lips. He liked the paper! Yeah!

She skipped a little as she continued her way down the street, heading for the bakery. She'd woken feeling blissfully happy. It was a gorgeous sunny day. She'd been kissed practically senseless the night before by the most beautiful man in the world. And she was going to have croissants for breakfast.

"Like the historical page, Jassie. Good idea that. Kids nowadays oughta know more about our past." A middle-aged woman beamed at her and hurried on, her arms full of groceries.

"Thank you so much, Ms...er, Mrs., um..." called Jassie after her. Another one who knew her name. Had someone put up a sign or something? Feeling buoyed by the unexpected praise, she walked on.

A woman darted out of a clothing store. She was wearing a calf-length purple skirt, a white-on-white embroidered cotton shirt and a high-cut embroidered jacket in black, white and purple. And silver-and-purple cowboy boots. "Hi, there, now you're Jassie. I'm Missy Baines, pleased to meet you, and I want to say I like the new look of *The Globe*. Very modern in some ways, but pleasingly traditional in others, in a modern sort of way, if you know what I mean, and I'm sure you do—" The woman paused for breath and Jassie opened her mouth to reply.

"—because, of course, you did it and I can see that you and I are going to get along just fine, aren't we?" She beamed at Jassie, nodding her head enthusiastically.

Jassie attempted to return the smile, wondering whether she'd ever get a word in.

"Now, as you'd know, I run a Western clothing business, you know the sort of thing, I'm sure, because I happen to know it's the rage in New York at the moment and we all know you're a New York gal, so of course you'd know—"

Jassie nodded carefully and slid a cautious look at her surroundings. Maybe she'd just met the madwoman of Bear Claw.

"—and it struck me when I was looking at your paper that you'd struck just exactly the right tone for my Western fashions—traditionally modern, if you know what I mean."

Jassie nodded. She didn't have a clue.

"So I've decided it's the perfect place to advertise my range, even though the circulation isn't large, but I can see it's going to grow, Jassie. Take my word for it, you're on a winning combination here. If you can keep it up and I'm sure you can."

Jassie blinked. Advertising? Circulation? These were

words she understood. And growth? In both? What a charming woman.

"And I'd also like you to give me an estimate on my brochures, because although I get them done out of town at the moment, of course I'd prefer to patronize a local business—as long as they can guarantee the quality. And a competitive price naturally." She thrust an embossed silver-and-lilac business card into Jassie's hand. "Call me for an appointment. Maybe you could do me an advertising feature, and possibly a mail order catalog, yes? As soon as you have time, I can see you're a busy woman, no time to talk, catch you later, bysie-bye." The woman waggled her fingers jauntily at Jassie and rushed back into her store.

"Bysie-bye," echoed Jassie dazedly. *Bysie-bye?* She looked down at her fingers. They were waggling jauntily, too. Hastily she thrust them into her jeans pocket before anyone saw her.

She examined the window of the shop, decorated with clothing and tasteful cacti and suddenly it all made sense. Western fashions, clearly modern, yet with a dreamy echo of the Old West. Long, romantic-looking skirts and dresses, embroidered and beaded shirts, jackets and vests. Men's suits that carried a dashing air of Rhett Butler and John Wayne. And Sheriff John T. Stone. And boots—cowboy boots, embroidered boots, carved boots, boots with silver decorations. She eyed a pair of red boots. They looked her size. They were really quite cute. John T. always wore boots.

No, she told herself. She was not going to deck herself out as a cowgirl to please a man. These Western fashions were very nice, but they were not her style. She was a New York gal—woman!

"That danged Matt Glover! He don't know beans about fishing," bellowed a voice about six inches from her ear.

Jassie jumped.

It was a wrinkle-faced old codger. "That trout bait

he told your readers to use is all wrong,'' he snapped, ''and so I've told him more 'n a hundred times, the stubborn cuss.''

''Er, is it?'' Jassie noticed he had a hearing aid. That explained the yelling.

''Sure it is,'' snapped the codger. ''If you want to catch trout in these here parts, you need—''

Jassie held up her hand firmly. She was on her way to have croissants for breakfast. She was *not* going to listen to talk of impaling living worms or beetles on hooks. Not on an empty stomach. ''I tell you what, sir, you just write me a letter explaining exactly how you think it ought to be done and I'll print it.''

''You will?'' The old fellow looked stunned.

''I will.''

''Danged if you ain't a chip off old Paddy Kelly's block after all, gal. I'll do that letter, dang me if I don't.'' And with that he dipped his cap at her and scuttled off.

Jassie didn't know a salmon from a trout, but she could recognize the commercial value of a feud. With any luck the old codger's letter would provoke a storm of heated fishing arguments. There was nothing like controversy to sell papers, even if it was only about flies or worms or other disgusting things. Disgusting things were fascinating to fishermen. And fishing was a big deal in Bear Claw.

Jassie felt like dancing. What a morning! What a day! Three compliments about the paper. A new advertising account. And a complaint. And all before breakfast. All she needed to make the morning perfect was coffee and croissants. And a big sexy sheriff to eat them with.

SHE'D HAD THE COFFEE and the croissants. But no sheriff.

Two out of three wasn't bad. It wasn't good, though. He hadn't answered his phone when she called. So she'd strolled around town after breakfast, just happening to pass the sheriff's office. She'd spotted what she thought was his patrol car, but when she'd popped in with a sack of croissants, the deputy informed her the sheriff had just stepped out. She'd left the croissants with the deputy.

It was a little disappointing, but the man did have a job to do.

She didn't see him the next day, either, but hey! Jassie wasn't the type to moon after a man. Especially a busy man, with an important job. Bear Claw might look like Sleepy Hollow, but it was probably a real cesspool of crime. He'd contact her when he could.

In the meantime, Jassie enjoyed the great feedback on her first issue of the paper. It was a dramatic contrast with her New York job. In New York no one ever reacted much to her work. Editors and subeditors either criticized or cut and otherwise seemed to think she should be grateful to have her writing printed. Occasionally a colleague would make a comment, but never, never had so many readers gone out of their way to contact her to let her know what they thought.

And to Jassie's delight, praise definitely outweighed criticism. It was especially heartwarming because she'd had to work so hard to get the first issue out, and so many aspects of the job were unfamiliar to her, layout and advertising, especially.

So it was wonderful to go out to do the marketing or to post a letter and find complete strangers smiling at her and saying, ''Hi, there, Jassie,'' followed by a comment on the paper.

After a few days it seemed the only person in the whole of Bear Claw who hadn't told her their opinion of the new *Globe* was Sheriff John T. Stone.

She was a little disappointed, but it wasn't as if she was worried or anything. He was interested, he'd be back. She shivered pleasurably, reliving the kisses over again for the zillionth time. And if he thought she hadn't noticed that interesting bulge in his pants, well... Jassie's mom hadn't raised her only child to be stupid. He was interested, all right, he was just...busy.

Meanwhile the thought of that interesting bulge was just driving her crazy.

She picked up the phone and called him at work again. "Sorry, Miss McQuilty, ma'am," said the deputy. "Sheriff Stone has just—"

"Stepped out of the office," Jassie finished for him. It was getting just a tad annoying.

ISSUE NUMBER THREE was due out tomorrow. She'd been happy with Issue Number Two, the previous weeks. It had contained a Western-fashion advertising feature and a letter from the codger, among other things. The sports news had looked good, as had the photographs. Circulation had increased slightly.

Issue Number Three was looking even better—the best one yet—a Fourth of July special. Thank heavens, Great-Uncle Paddy had been a hoarder. She'd dug out a heap of old photos from the town's history, especially Fourth of July ones, and she was sure it would be a popular feature. And to go with the old photos she'd had Ben Broome write some of his stories about the town's past. Which meant that Jassie hadn't had to interview him and his teeth.

The fishing column had grown to a fishing page and a Western-fashion column had begun. Advertising had slowly but surely increased. Which meant revenue had, too.

Jassie stared at the computer screen. The layout was almost complete, just one or two tiny things to fix. But the editor's mind was not on the paper. She should have been on a high. She'd achieved so much in a mere two weeks.

Two weeks. Ha!

It was also two weeks since she'd eaten at Don and Dora's. Two weeks since he'd driven her through the mountains for a late-night hamburger.

Two weeks since the most sizzling, devastating, mind-and-body-blowing good-night kiss she'd ever experienced. Kisses, not just one.

Kisses that had nothing to do with manners and everything to do with blistering, boiling, scorching, white-hot lust.

Kisses that had turned her bones to honey and her brain to mush.

Kisses that had left her aching and hollow and wanting.

Kisses that still left her tossing and turning, sweating and writhing, waking up in the morning in a tangle of twisted sheets. In a brand-new bed she'd bought, just under two weeks ago.

And how long since she had clapped eyes on the cause of all this blissful, frustrating unrest?

Two weeks! The big, cowardly rat!

Jassie's temper had been slowly coming to simmering point over the past few days. She paced the room, muttering to herself. She knew darn well why he wasn't answering her messages, why he'd apparently stepped out whenever she was in his vicinity, why she hadn't set eyes on him in two weeks.

It was what she and Rita referred to as F.O.C.

It made her furious. She'd never experienced such…electricity…magic…chemistry…whatever! She wanted him more than she'd ever dreamed it was possible to want a man. And she knew right through to her bone marrow that he was just as interested in her as she was in him. But because of F.O.C., he was avoiding her.

F.O.C, the dreaded genetic disorder that attached itself to the Y chromosome. The feral gene that crippled practically every man in the western world.

F.O.C.: Fear Of Commitment.

And that was why Jassie was so darned cross. It was completely unjust of him to label her like that. She *wasn't* trying to tie him down to a fifty-year commitment. Just fifty weeks—less, if he preferred. All she wanted was a small fling, a teensy-weensy one. A fling-ette. Just a little touch of romance amid the mountains and the wilderness. To get her through a year in The Sticks.

But how on earth could she get the gorgeous great lunkhead to realize her intentions when he avoided her for all he was worth?

She glared at the headline story. A crime had been committed in Bear Claw that week, a foiled shoplifting; the desperate criminal, a thirteen-year-old boy. When John T. had seen her coming to interview him at the scene, he'd shoved the boy into his patrol car and driven off. When Jassie'd followed him to the sheriff's office, he'd sent his deputy out to give the interview. The big chicken! Him and his F.O.C.!

She'd just have to convince him he was wrong. And she was sure it wouldn't take much to convince him a fling with her was the very thing he needed.

There were all sorts of good reasons to have a fling, besides the fact that he was driving her crazy with lust. He wasn't the marrying type and neither was she. But plenty of local women wanted him. And they *were* marrying types.

A fling with Jassie could save all those poor innocent women from heartbreak, which was good for the welfare of the community.

And there were other reasons, now that she thought about it. It was unhealthy, saving up his…um, urges until he had time to go all the way to the next county. He had a difficult, stressful job. Everyone knew cops had it tough, she thought, ignoring the fact that the toughest thing she'd seen him do was issue a parking ticket to the mayor's bossy wife. He needed to relax more often, not to have to drive over several mountains to visit floozies.

If the man wanted flooziosity, well, Jassie was pretty darn sure she could floozy with the best of them. A little floozying sounded like fun, as long as she did it just with him and didn't have to make a career out of it. She had no intention of that.

She glared at the tattered map of Montana stuck on the wall. All that driving must be costing him a fortune in gas. Not to mention the damage to the environment. And Jassie loved trees, and bushes, and...um, and animals and clean air and all that stuff. Well, no she didn't—although she had liked that little deer—but in any case she was a responsible person. And responsible people cared about the environment.

If Jassie could help save the environment by having a fling with Sheriff Stone, then it was her bound duty to do so. Ask not what your country can do for you...and all that.

Only what do you do when the dratted man is so determined to avoid you? When there is no opportunity to tell him you don't want a ring—just a fling?

She glared at the computer screen in front of her. A boring, boring front page. Jassie paused, suddenly thoughtful. She looked at the lead article. The headline was pathetic. With a flick, she deleted it and stared at the empty space, frowning. After a second's hesitation, she rapidly typed in a new headline. She then rewrote a couple of lines in the article and grinned as she read it. It was great.

She frowned. No, she couldn't. She deleted it. Then put it back. Her grin grew. She took a final look at the headline and laughed out loud. Yep, that was it. She set the press to print and laughed again as she watched it go into action.

What was that thing about Mohammed and the mountain?

"WHAT THE HELL IS THIS?" Sheriff John T. Stone slammed a copy of *The Globe* down on the front counter and glared across it at Jassie.

Her mountain had arrived, looking uncannily like a volcano in training.

And about time, too!

Jassie looked carefully at the paper. "It's a copy of *The Globe,* John T." She smiled helpfully, enjoying the way a tiny muscle in his cheek kept flickering. He was so beautiful when he was angry. His thick dark brows swooped in a fierce dramatic arc. Green eyes sparked like kryptonite. His lips were pressed tight and thin and the teensy scar that sliced through his upper lip looked pale and interesting...very interesting indeed. Jassie licked her own lips in an attempt to head off incipient drooling. Drooling was not a good look.

"I damned well *know* what it is, Miss McQuilty, I want to know what it *means!*"

Jassie frowned thoughtfully and fanned his flames a little more. "Um, it means...you like my paper enough to buy a copy?" She beamed proudly at him.

"No..." he growled.

"You don't mean to say you *stole* it, John T.?" Jassie widened her eyes in shock. "I don't think that's a good example to set, do y—"

"I didn't damn well steal it. I paid for the damned rag, though I can't think why!" Her mountain was becoming a volcano. A magnificent rumbling volcano.

"Honesty is the best policy, I always say," said Jassie sweetly. "A sheriff does have a position to maintain, after all."

"I'm talking about *this!*" He stabbed one long strong finger on the headline on the front page. It was a lovely finger, thought Jassie. She reached out and laid her own finger over it, trailing it gently down over his until she touched the paper. And him.

He stared at her a moment, then snatched his finger back as if it were on fire.

"This?" Jassie asked.

He nodded brusquely.

She read the headline out loud. "'Sheriff Foils Robbery.'" She frowned in what she hoped was pretty confusion. "I don't understand, John T., did I make a mistake? You did foil the robbery, didn't you? I was sure—"

"It wasn't a robbery! It was a thirteen-year-old boy shoplifting, for chrissake."

"Shoplifting is robbery," said Jassie piously. "And I'm sure that boy learned his lesson. And you'll note, I haven't blighted his future by spreading his name all over the paper. He still has a chance to make something of his life, thanks to you." She beamed worshipfully at him and thought about batting her eyelashes.

"It's not that—I know you didn't mention the boy's name—it's me!" he growled, avoiding her gaze.

"You?" she cooed.

"What you said about me, dammit."

"Why, John T., whatever do you mean?" purred Jassie McQuilty, Southern Belle.

"That! And that!" He plunked his finger down on the opening paragraph, then snatched it back as Jassie's hand came toward it.

Bear Claw's own brave sheriff, the handsome, virile John T. Stone, foiled a daring robbery attempt...

"*Handsome,* John T.? You have a problem with that? Haven't you looked in the mirror lately?" The tips of his ears were turning that adorable brick-red color, she noted.

"I'm not...it's, er...I'm not—"

"But you are, John T. You are," she said softly, sounding like Bette Davis in *Whatever Happened To Baby Jane.* The tips of his ears went even darker.

"That sort of comment in a paper is quite uncalled—"

"Oh, but I don't agree, John T. I have lots of female readers and they like to know these things."

"But most of your readers live around here and they know—"

"How handsome you are? You're right, but I still thi—"

"Dammit, don't put words in my mouth. They all know what I look like, and it isn't—" He stopped. Seeing she was about to contradict him again, he took a deep breath and said in a dignified voice, "Whatever you think I look like, it is not relevant to the story. And neither is, er, the other word you used."

"*Virile*, John T.? Why not?"

"It's n—I'm n—"

"Not *virile?*" Jassie allowed her mouth to gape in what she hoped was a stunned yet not unattractive expression. "You're surely not trying to tell me you aren't virile, John T.? I don't believe it."

He slammed his fist down on the counter, making everything on it jump. Jassie did, too but she managed to hide it. He was so wonderfully impressive when he was riled.

"Look, my virility or otherwise is *none* of your business. You know nothing about it. And you had no business putting it in the paper—it has nothing to do with your damned newspaper, anyway. Now, Miss McQuilty, you damn well leave out comments like that in future, you hear me, or—"

"I hear you, John T.," Jassie said contritely.

He opened his mouth to continue the argument, then stopped, realizing she'd accepted his position.

"So you see my point?"

"I do, John T. And I'm sorry you're upset."

"Humph! Good, then. All right. That's better." He looked at her a moment, and she felt the heat of his gaze pass over her lips. He turned to leave.

"Oh, John T.?"

He turned back.

"Can I offer you a cup of coffee? There's some fresh made."

He hesitated.

"We could get a few things straight about editorial policy and the sheriff's office."

He started to nod, then Jassie added, "There are sugar cookies to go with the coffee."

"No!" he exclaimed, appalled. He recovered himself. "I mean, no thank you, Miss McQuilty. I, er, I have an appointment. Sorry." And he strode hurriedly from the room.

Jassie watched him leave with narrowed eyes. He'd reacted as if the offer of sugar cookies had been an invitation to torture. But the man had a sweet tooth, she was sure of that—all those doughnuts. So why had he rushed out of here as if there had been a pack of wolves after him?

What on earth was he so scared of? Tooth decay?

JASSIE CONTEMPLATED the next issue of *The Globe* thoughtfully. She shouldn't, she knew. But he deserved it. He was still avoiding her. He hadn't been near her in a week. Not since he'd laid down the law to her about how she'd described him.

She'd seen him across the street once or twice and the looks he'd given her had been hot enough to sear a steak. And she wasn't talking angry hot. She felt weak-kneed just thinking about it. And frustrated.

She'd made it as clear as she possibly could that she was interested in a bit of light dalliance. Or heavy dalliance, for that matter. Whatever he fancied. And a few more of those brain-scrambling kisses he did so well. All right, a lot more of them. But the ball had been rotting in his court for more than a week. Almost three weeks if she wanted to get technical. But she didn't want to get technical, she wanted to get physical, dammit!

Jassie looked at the fresh, crisp new issue of *The Globe* in front of her. Out back, Jeff Bassett, Tommy and Josh were loading up bound bundles of the paper

ready for distribution the next morning. It was very satisfying to note the piles were bigger than ever.

She smoothed her hand over the lower left-hand corner of the paper and smiled a tiny smile. Desperate times
called for desperate measures. And she was quite desperately in lust...

She glanced at her watch. It was getting late. In about
half an hour Tommy would drop a complimentary copy
of the paper in at the sheriff's office. And five minutes
after that...

Plenty of time for her to shower and change. She
wanted to look good for him. And to make sure she was
clean. It would be a long time before she forgot the
printing ink debacle. There were mirrors in practically
every room of *The Globe* building now.

THERE WAS AN ABRUPT HUSH as John T. Stone entered
Ma's Diner at his usual early morning hour. Showing
no awareness of it, he closed the door behind him.

"Mornin', J.T. Lovely day."

"Mornin', Newt. Mornin', all." J.T. nodded to the
elderly man at the other end of Ma's counter. His nod
took in the other dozen or so customers in the diner.
They were mostly regulars, mostly old-timers, but he
didn't usually see so many of them here when he
dropped in each morning for breakfast.

Wondering what was up, he slid onto his customary
stool and waited for Ma to pour him his coffee.

"Seen this week's paper yet, Sheriff?" someone
called out to him.

The sheriff turned to a couple in a booth near the
window.

"Mornin', Mrs. Goetz, Bill. No, not yet."

Mr. and Mrs. Goetz looked at each other and smiled.
The smiles made him a little uneasy, which was peculiar, since he'd known the Goetzes since he arrived in
Bear Claw and he'd always liked them. They were nice,
decent, friendly folk.

He smiled and turned back to the counter, noticing that virtually every occupant of the diner was looking at him while pretending to do something else. And every one of them wore a faint smile. A suspicious prickle ran down his spine. He sipped his coffee. Ma brought out a plate of bacon, eggs and hash browns and laid it in front of him.

The bacon looked crisp and perfect, the eggs over easy, just as he liked them, the potatoes golden brown and crunchy 'round the edges. Wisps of fragrant steam floated upward, flirting with his nostrils.

J.T. glared moodily at his breakfast. Up until the past week or two he'd always had doughnuts and coffee for breakfast. These days he didn't have the strength to face a doughnut. Not on an empty stomach. And especially not after a restless night's sleep. Doughnuts had lost their innocence.

"Interestin' paper this week," said someone behind him.

"Interestin' last week, too," said another one.

There was a short expectant silence. J.T. hunched over his breakfast, ignoring the talk. That damned silly shoplifting article. Hadn't they forgotten about it yet?

"Interestin' gal runnin' the paper." There was a murmur of agreement and a couple of muffled chortles.

"Pretty li'l thing. Ain't married, so I heard."

"Yet," said someone. The word echoed around the room.

"She sure has livened things up around here since she came. Every week just gets interestinger and interestinger," said one old-timer, snickering as he stirred sugar into his coffee.

"I wonder if she's going to stay here in Bear Claw. It's a big change for her after New York City," said Mrs. Goetz. "Lots of city folk change their minds after one of our winters. It's hard for a lone woman."

"Hard is exactly the word, from what I can make out," a man behind him muttered just loud enough for his companion and the sheriff to hear. The snickers increased.

J.T. chomped doggedly through his breakfast, his face like granite. It was bad enough that the woman interfered with his sleep at night. Did she have to ruin his morning, too? He'd had visions of her nibbling on doughnuts and sugar cookies all night, and of him helping her get rid of all those pesky little sugar grains that fell all over her when she ate them, especially the ones that stuck—

"Young Jassie seems to like it here, all right," said Mrs. Goetz. "I reckon she'll stay...if there's a reason to stay."

"If you ask me, that li'l gal sure likes somethin' here in Bear Claw."

"Hank, didn't your mama never tell you it weren't nice to call a person a 'thing'? It's politer to say some*one* not some*thing*. More accurate, too."

J.T. heard several distinct guffaws over the chuckles that greeted that statement. He glanced around the diner. A dozen stares slipped sideways. The smiles had become grins. Which their owners were doing their best to hide.

He glanced at Ma, who was leaning on the counter, arms folded across her large bosom, watching him. She wasn't hiding anything. She looked like the proverbial cat that ate the canary.

Keeping his expression impassive, J.T. finished the last of his breakfast in a few gulps. He downed his coffee and stood, pushing money across the counter. "Thanks, Ma. Mornin', all."

He could feel every eye on him as he walked to the door and pulled it open. The diner was unnaturally quiet. He could almost taste the disappointment on the breeze.

"Oh, Ma," he said.

The hush intensified.

"Open the windows. You need some fresh air in here."

As he closed the door, he heard laughter break behind him. And then a man's voice said, "Yep, he's antsy, all right. Twenty bucks says that li'l gal hooks him."

A voice answered, "I'll take it. Sheriff's been hunted by dang near every female in town and he's still single, ain't he?"

A chorus of arguments, bets and counterbets followed before he heard a woman say, "Who'll give me odds on a spring wedding?"

Et tu, Ma?

He forced himself to not hurry to his office where he knew the latest issue of *The Globe* would be waiting for him. It was fairly darn obvious she'd written something else about him. Something that was causing a great deal of amusement to half the town, if the population of Ma's was any indication.

If she'd called him virile again, he'd...he'd—well, he'd do something, he just didn't know what. But he'd think of something, that's for sure. And the first thing he'd do is get rid of those damned Road Runner pajamas. And make sure there wasn't a doughnut in the house.

He flung open the door of his office. There was no sign of his deputy. The newspaper was sitting dead-center of his desk. He snatched it up and scanned the front page. A small article in the lower left-hand corner leaped out at him.

Sheriff Rejects Virility Claim

The editor of *The Globe* wishes to apologize for the story in last week's issue that described the sheriff of Bear Claw, Mr. John T. Stone, as "virile." After consulting with the sheriff, *The Globe* editor, Ms. Jassie McQuilty, agrees to withdraw her statement unconditionally. She apologizes to the sheriff for any embarrassment she may have caused him and assures *The Globe* readers that before

printing any such future claim about the sheriff, she
will investigate it personally and in depth.

*Investigate...personally...and in depth? Future
claim...?* Surely she didn't mean... In disbelief J.T. re-
read the notice, then closed his eyes.

Hell! No wonder the folks in the diner had been all
but falling off their stools with laughter. Jassie had virtually promised to investigate his virility. *Personally!
And in depth!*

He slammed the paper down and stood, sending his
chair crashing against the wall behind him. Well, Ms.
Jassie McQuilty was going to get her first chance to
investigate his damn virility right now—up close. While
he throttled her.

6

THE DOOR CRASHED OPEN. Jassie jumped, even though she'd been waiting since last night for this moment. Keeping her back to the door, she ran her hands nervously through her hair and took a deep breath.

Boots crunched purposefully across the wooden floor toward her. "I want a word with you, Miss McQuilty."

Jassie turned to face her visitor. Vesuvius in person, she noted. Molten lava seethed under his skin. Delicious.

She allowed a surprised smile to dawn over her face. "Why, good morning, John T. So nice of you to drop in to visit me. How are you this beautiful morning? I must say, you're looking very well, very handso— Oops! I'm not allowed to call you that, am I."

Vesuvius ignored her dazzling smile, rumbled loudly and smashed a crumpled paper onto the counter with a clenched fist. A strong, virile-looking clenched fist. "What the hell did you think you were doing?"

Jassie glanced across the room. Tommy and his friend Josh were watching the whole scene avidly. "Will you excuse me for just one moment please, John T.?" She walked over to the boys and spoke to them in a quiet voice. Tommy nodded. Josh shrugged agreeably. The watching volcano simmered and smoldered.

Jassie returned to the counter and said, "Whatever it is you want to talk about sounds important. We'll talk in my office, John T." Without waiting for his reply, she sailed off toward the stairs.

Frustrated, J.T. snatched the paper and stormed after

her. His temper mounted and spread to other parts of his body as he climbed the narrow stairs behind her. Damn woman. What the hell was she wearing those damn tight jeans for? What sort of clothes were they for a newspaper editor to wear? Didn't the woman know about power dressing? And long, loose, concealing jackets. He stumbled, not watching where he was going, unable to take his eyes off the rhythmic sway of her hips and the enticing curves encased in soft, faded denim.

She entered a room marked Office and sat. He looked around for a place to sit. Damned silly office for a newspaper editor to have, he thought. No desk, no chairs, no files. Just a low coffee table, a rug, a big terra-cotta urn with a bunch of dead sticks coming out if it, and a big green sofa. It was probably all the rage with New York editors. Damn ridiculous in Montana, he thought. What the hell was the point of a sofa in a newspaper office? Old Paddy Kelly would be rolling over in his grave.

"Have a seat, John T., please do. I'll get a crick in my neck if I have to keep looking up at you much longer." She patted the seat invitingly.

He glared at her, sat at the far end of the sofa then slapped the paper onto the coffee table in front of her. "What's the meaning of this?"

Jassie slowly swiveled the paper around and perused it carefully. "Which part didn't you understand, John T.?"

"This!" He plunked his finger smack in the middle of the article, then, as she moved her hand toward it, snatched it back.

Jassie read the paragraph out loud and then looked up. "Do you mean my apology, John T.?"

"Apology!" He snorted.

Jassie frowned. She read it out loud. "'*The Globe* editor, Ms. Jassie McQuilty, agrees to withdraw her statement unconditionally. She apologizes to the sheriff for any embarrassment she may have caused him.' It's a very clear apology, John T. You don't get many news-paper editors doing that. What's the problem?'' She looked at him in concern and slid along the sofa toward him a little.

John T. Stone felt ready to explode.

'''Sheriff rejects virility claim.' What sort of a thing is that to say?''

''But you yourself did so, in this very building, not one week ago. You pointed out—very forcefully—and I quote—'' she made little curly marks in the air with her fingers ''—'you know nothing about my virility or otherwise and you had no business putting it in the pa-per.''' She closed her air quotes and continued. ''And you were right, of course. One should always check one's facts.''

''Check—''

''So I felt I had to withdraw the statement and apol-ogize. And I did.''

''You call that—'' He stopped and took a deep breath. ''That was not an apology, it—''

''It most certainly was!''

''It was a challenge.''

''A challenge, John T.?'' she said softly, sliding a little closer.

''You questioned my...my...'' He couldn't say the word virility, not with her looking at him that way, her mouth all pink and soft and moist. ''And in public!''

''Questioned your 'virility'? It's not a swearword, John T. It's okay to say it in front of a lady. But I most certainly did not question it. I wouldn't *dream* of ques-tioning it.''

''But you—''

''Your virility is most beautifully obvious to me, John T.''

He glanced down at his pants in horror, but it was okay. There was no virility happening down there. Yet.

''But in the paper you said—''

''No, John T., *I* said you were handsome and virile,

if you recall, but then, when *you* objected so strenuously, I felt obligated to withdraw the statement. And to apologize. Publicly.'' She slipped a little closer and laid a soft, contrite hand on his thigh. "I thought that was what you wanted."

"Y— No, er, dammit! Look. You don't get it. I don't want my virility, or otherwise, mentioned in the damned paper at all. Don't you realize what people are saying?"

"Oh, no, John T., they wouldn't be so cruel. And I do understand—now. I'm so sorry, but you see, when I first mentioned it in the paper, it never even occurred to me you might have a problem in, er, that area." Her fingers stroked his thigh soothingly.

He glared at her, appalled. "I damn well don't."

"Good," she purred, and slipped into his arms.

How the hell did that happen? he wondered dazedly as his arms closed hard around her and he hauled her across his lap. Her mouth was warm, sweet and spicy and he plunged into it like a man dying of thirst dives into an oasis.

He'd come here to throttle her. His hands slipped up her body and encircled her throat. Gently he tipped her jaw up to improve his access to her mouth and slipped the other hand into the silky curls at her nape. God, she tasted good…. He'd throttle her later…much later—

"Hey, Miss Jassie?" The knocking increased.

"Oh, good grief, it's Tommy with the coffee."

Reluctantly J.T. loosened his hold on her. He closed his eyes. He ought to be grateful for the interruption, as they'd been heading straight for the point of no return. But gratitude was not the dominant emotion he was feeling.

She slipped out of his arms, looking adorably mussed, and started straightening her clothes. He watched, wishing it was the other way around and she was wriggling out of them instead of wriggling in. She looked at him and grinned. "Hey, John T., button up, baby, we got company, remember?"

He glanced down and with a start, hastily started to button buttons and zip zippers. How the hell had that happened? They surely couldn't have gone so far in such a short time.

He fastened the last button just as Jassie opened the door to let Tommy in. He was carrying a pot of coffee and a paper bag on a tray. And wearing a smirk.

J.T. ignored the smirk. He looked at that paper bag. It was a Ma's paper bag. A familiar warm cinnamon scent wafted from it.

Tommy put the tray down, then left the room, closing the door firmly behind him.

Jassie, smiling like a dratted siren, reached for the bag. And in that moment J.T. knew he'd been heading straight for the rocks. At full speed.

"Sorry, Jassie, this has been a mistake," he said slowly. "I never meant it to go this far. I…I apologize." He strode out of the room at full stride.

Jassie stared at the door he'd just closed behind him. A *mistake?* He *apologized?* For what? For driving her out of her mind with desire and leaving her high and…well, that analogy didn't work, she conceded ruefully. She was neither high nor dry.

And in fact, she felt unaccountably low. Flings were not supposed to be like this…were they?

J.T. GLOWERED at the blinking light on his answering machine. He knew damn well who it would be. The woman had destroyed his peace of mind. He wanted her too damn much. And he knew what that meant. Danger.

He was going to have to deal with Jassie McQuilty. Much more of her and he'd crack wide-open, his every cranny exposed and vulnerable to the freezing winds. And then what would become of him? He had a comfortable solid life. It was organized just the way he was used to. He didn't need this. And he knew the solution. It was how he'd dealt with every other woman, since

Sybille, who'd got close enough to hurt. Reject her before she could do it to him.

But he didn't want to hurt her in the process....

And the old man kept nagging in his head. *Life knocks you down, you gotta build again. Ain't no choice for us, boy. You build again or you quit. And you don't look like no quitter to me, son.*

Old Pop didn't know everything. He'd had a family, a good life. A wife who'd loved him and stayed with him for forty years until she died.

JASSIE STARED at the phone. Should she call him—again? And listen to him make some feeble excuse—again.

What if he said, "Sorry, I'm not interested"?

She could deal with a man telling her that. It was no problem actually. She was a sophisticated adult. She'd merely accept it and continue on in her usual adult, cool, calm, civilized New York manner.

Jassie looked at the phone. She would give him one last chance. She dialed. J.T. answered. Jassie came straight to the point. "Is there any point in me asking you to dinner again?"

Silence.

"I'm not a child, John T. If you're not interested, you only have to say so."

There was a short pause. "I'm not interested," he said.

Liar! Liar! Pants on fire! screeched the sophisticated adult. "I see," said Jassie out loud. "Well at least we know where we stand."

"I'm sorry, Ja—ma'am," he said in a gravelly voice. "It's just...well, relationships and me, they don't mix. I wouldn't want to mislead you."

Mislead. Ha! She wasn't the one who was being misled here. She wasn't the one with the permanent, um, awkwardly fitting pants. She wasn't the one who kept hauling her into his arms and kissing her mindless. Not interested. It was disgraceful that a lawman should have so little respect for the truth.

"I guess I should have realized sooner," she said. "Those kisses were pretty boring, weren't they?"

There was a short pause. A pause that seemed to seep into the phone line and stare down its nose at her. A cold, slightly stunned, disbelieving sort of pause.

"Boring?"

Jassie grinned. Somebody sounded offended. Good! That made two of them. "Yep. Nice enough, but a teensy bit dull, didn't you think? Still, any port in a storm, eh, John T.?"

"Humph! If you say so."

"I do."

"Um, Miss McQuilty—"

"Oh, Sheriff?" Jassie interrupted sweetly.

"Yes?"

"That's *Ms.* McQuilty, not Miss, okay? Bysie-bye." She put down the phone gently. Then picked it up and slammed it down again.

It rang a few seconds later. Disdainfully she picked it up.

"Jassie—?"

"Yes," she said coolly.

"Look, I didn't mean to upset you—"

"Upset? I'm not ups—"

"Look, it's not you. It's m— Oh hell, you might as well know, people are laying bets on us, dammit."

"Bets?"

"Yeah, they're betting on us. Pretty near every damn person in this whole damn town is backing either you or me in the wedd—um, well, you can see my professional position, can't you? It's a problem and it's got to stop. Right now."

"I see," said Jassie coldly. "And *this* is the reason you have scuttled out the back door of the jail every time I've dropped in to get an interview."

"I did not scuttle! I, er, had an urgent appointment."

"Three urgent appointments on three separate occasions?"

"Er, yes."

"More urgent than an interview with the local newspaper editor?"

"Yes."

"And yet you have no crime stories to report to *The Globe?*"

"Er, no, I'm happy to say. Preventative action," he mumbled.

"Very well then, Sheriff, thank you for the interview."

"What int—"

"We've been talking, haven't we?"

"Yes, but—"

"Consider it an interview," she said crisply and hung up.

She glared at the computer screen and resized the lead story about a singing dog called Zane. Wretched man. In a lather because he thought she was trying to trap him into marriage. What an ego! She didn't want his name or a silly ring—just his body.

Marriage. Ha! No way did she want to spend the rest of her life in Sticksville. She was a big-city gal—person—to the core and she was having a fling, or trying to!

And, if he'd only cared to ask, he'd discover the very *last* thing she wanted was a permanent relationship. If she'd had any illusions left after Phil, her first lover, in college, then four years with Murdock had managed to crush them.

Flings were another matter. You couldn't get hurt in flings. You could get mad, furious, frustrated and downright explosive with lust. Obviously. But you couldn't get hurt.

You knew the score with a fling. It lasted until it burned out. You went into it *knowing* that it would end sooner or later.

Relationships. You went into them expecting them to go on forever in a misty haze of bliss. And when you least expected it, when you were happiest and at your most relaxed and vulnerable, you found they had ended.

She shuddered, recalling how everyone on the paper knew about Murdock's affairs, had known about them for years. Everyone except Jassie. She cringed. That was the old Jassie. The dumb, naive, trusting Jassie. The new Jassie was building her career.

She didn't want a relationship. She wanted a hot fling. With Sheriff John T. Stone. For a year at most. Just until she sold *The Globe*.

And then she was outta here. No baggage. No regrets.

People betting on them indeed—what a feeble excuse. Who cared what other people thought? How small-town, small-minded could you get? No, it wasn't a few little bets that got him all hot and bothered. It was F.O.C.

But she didn't want C. She picked up the phone and slammed it down again. Her fluffy dog slippers looked at her with big sad eyes. She kicked them across the room. Ha! She'd set him straight on that, if she ever set eyes on the big rat again, that is. Jassie fumed. How did you tell a man that he was being stupidly paranoid and that you only wanted his body temporarily?

That was usually the man's line.

Furiously she relegated the singing dog story to page three and began to type.

Bear Claw Hit By Gambling Fever, Claims Sheriff

The town of Bear Claw has been hit by an outbreak of gambling, claims Sheriff John T. Stone. According to Sheriff Stone, the gambling epidemic seemed to leave almost no one in the town unaffected. ''It's a problem and it's got to stop. Right now,'' he said.

That would show him. The whole town betting on them, indeed. As if! How many people did he call the whole town? Three? Four? Jassie grinned. How embarrassed would he be that she'd taken his paltry excuse as literal truth? Explain that away, Mr. F.O.C.

JASSIE DROVE her new used car carefully through the dusk. She was following a shiny dark green pickup. The truck slowed down and Jassie did, too, watching it like a hawk. She slowed as she saw the brakelights glow in the dusk and kept well back. They were a long way from town now.

The pickup turned off to the right, just as her tip had warned her. The unknown driver was moving fast. He was confident. Reckless.

Jassie gave a little, Ha! of triumph. Little did the pickup occupants know, Jassie McQuilty of *The Globe* was on to them.

She reached the turnoff, a bumpy, dirt road heading up into the mountains, which loomed, wild and rugged in the gathering gloom. She hoped her poor little car would cope, the vehicle up ahead was made for terrain like this. There was still enough light—almost—to see where she was going. But it was clouding up ahead, thick and dark.

She glanced at the camera on the seat behind her. Young Josh had fit it with a zoom lens and what he called near-enough to infrared film. Of course, he and Tommy had clamored to come when she got the anonymous tip about the hunters, but Jassie wasn't about to endanger a couple of innocent kids. Danger was her job.

Her pulse was racing. She'd never stalked hunters before. It would be a real scoop if she managed to catch them in the act. From what her informant had said, the occupants of the pickup belonged to some sort of paganistic men's hunting club and one of their rituals was to dance naked in the dusk before going hunting.

The things some people did to achieve male bonding!

Jassie thought. Men should *never* dance naked, in her opinion. They weren't built for it. Certain appendages couldn't keep up. They tagged along, looking silly.

Whatever the pagans did, however, Jassie McQuilty, intrepid reporter, was going to catch it all on film. It was the sort of story that might even make the big papers sit up and take notice. Jassie could do with the income as well as the kudos. She wished she had a digital movie camera—television would pay even more—but she didn't, so she'd just have to do the best she could. At least she had a zoom lens.

What this story could do for her career...hunters, ritual, nakedness, bouncing appendages... A story such as this could widen her options after she'd sold *The Globe*. She could go anywhere, maybe even a post overseas. Paris maybe, or—

Crunch! Her car came to an abrupt halt, causing Jassie to ram hard against the steering wheel. The engine wheezed once then subsided into silence. She spent a moment catching her breath before she worked out what must have happened. She'd run into a rock or a log on the track. She tried to restart the car, but apart from a labored whoom-whoomphing sound from under the hood, there was no action.

Cursing under her breath, she got out and inspected the damage. It was difficult to see anything, the clouds were making everything so gloomy, but it was clear that she'd veered a little off the track. More than a little, actually. The track was a good ten feet to the left. It had turned a corner to avoid a rocky outcrop, whereas Jassie had driven straight ahead and become more closely acquainted with Montana rocks than she wished to be.

She looked around her, feeling suddenly exposed and vulnerable. There were wild animals in the country. Bears. And wolves—she'd heard they were releasing them back into the wild. And bears. Elk. Bears. Maybe even mountain lions. And bears. She reached into her car and grabbed her purse. She kept a can of Mace in it. Did Mace work on bears? She hoped so.

It seemed incredibly silent. And though it was only evening, dark was falling. She hadn't known how dark night could be until she'd come to Montana. In the city it never got dark, it just got less light. And noise surrounded you constantly like a cocoon, assuring you that you were never alone. Even if you were.

Here Jassie darn well knew she was alone. The silence was deafening, like being smothered. And there was something wrong about it. She listened carefully, trying to work out what had changed. Then she realized. There was no noise at all, not even the sound of a pickup ahead. They must have stopped not too far away. She could still get her story. Slinging the camera around her neck and her purse over her shoulder, Jassie prepared to stalk the stalkers.

Keeping to the track she walked cautiously forward, straining her eyes and ears for signs of life—human or otherwise.

"Aaaaooooooo!"

Jassie nearly jumped out of her skin. She whirled around, but could see nothing.

"Aaaaooooooo!" It came again. Was it the hunters? Had they spotted her? Were they naked already? It sounded as if they were baying at the moo—

Oh. Jassie told her heartbeat to slow down again. Baying at the moon was exactly what it was. She'd seen a hundred Westerns, for goodness' sake! She ought to know what a coyote sounded like! Or was it a wolf? Whatever...

She slipped her hand inside her purse, tightened her grasp on the can of Mace, and resumed her stalking. Her walk dwindled to a creep, a stealthy I'm-gonna-get-a-scoop creep, not an I'm-scared-'cause-it's-dark-and-weird-out-here sort of creep. At least that's what she told herself. Jassie McQuilty, fearless reporter.

At last, just as her feet had started to emphasize their

dislike of inching across long distances over stony ground, she saw the shadowy shape of the green pickup silhouetted on the crest of a hill. She froze, listening for the sound of human activity. Nothing.

She tiptoed up to the pickup and peered inside. Nothing much, just the few bits and pieces people normally had in a truck. Nothing sinister, as far as she could see. Although there was a heavy, metal, padlocked box bolted to the bed of the pickup. Maybe it contained guns. Although they'd probably have taken them out now to shoot some poor defenseless deer.

Hastily she jotted down the license plate number, just in case. A cold wind started to blow and she shivered, wishing she'd worn a warmer jacket.

According to her source, the hunters performed their peculiar dance in a natural valley that formed a rough circle. A small waterfall, called Crystal Drop Falls, would help her to locate the spot. To the left of her, the view stretched for miles in undulating peaks and ridges. Behind her rose hills and crags, but to the right, the land dropped away into a small valley seemingly surrounded by a circle of hills. She craned her head, listening. A faint sound of falling water. Yes!

Stealthily she crept forward along the faint, narrow track that led down into the valley. There was a great rock in the center of it, as the informant had said, and that's where she'd find them. Jassie inched forward. It was very difficult to see because of the dark clouds rolling above her, but from time to time, there was a gap and light broke faintly through.

It was in one of these moments that she saw the rock. It was huge and jagged, thrusting aggressively up out of the ground. A perfect, indecently phallic symbol for macho weirdos to dance around.

The waterfall was on the other side of the valley. Even in the dull gloom of the evening, she could see the froth of white and crystal. The valley was beautiful, apart from the rude rock. It was pure sacrilege for hunters to corrupt such a lovely peaceful place.

There was no sign of naked weirdos yet. They were probably disrobing behind a bush somewhere. She looked around for a good place to take photos from. She soon found an area near a small clump of bushes not far from the phallic rock. If she crawled under there, the bushes would be dense enough to hide her and yet she'd be really close to the action. Perfect. All she had to do was cross the clearing.

Her heart was thumping loudly in her chest, almost echoing in the preternatural silence. Her mouth was dry and her nerves were ready to leap from her skin. At last a particularly dense mound of cloud passed over and the darkness thickened around her. Jassie closed her eyes, muttered a quick prayer under her breath and stepped out into the open. With her eyes and ears practically swiveling like antennae, she hurried toward the clump of bushes.

Suddenly a hand shot out and grabbed her by the ankle.

"Aaarrgh!" she screamed.

Whump! Her feet were jerked out from under her, her back and butt making instant contact with the hardest piece of ground she'd ever met. The breath left her body in a whoosh. She opened her mouth to try to gasp for air and felt a large hand close over it.

"Shut it!" a voice whispered in her ear.

Jassie frantically shook her head and pulled her mouth away from the hand. Her lungs burned. She simply couldn't breathe. She gasped uselessly and the hand clapped over her mouth again.

"Don't make a sound!" he hissed.

Frantically she pummeled on her captor's chest. She kicked and scratched. No way was she going to dance naked with him!

He swore and the hand left her mouth to restrain her flailing fists and feet. Jassie gasped for the third time and cold pure air rushed into her lungs. She sucked in big gulps of it until her breathing was finally back to normal.

Once she no longer had to gasp for oxygen, a different kind of panic set in. She was pinned under a bush in the middle of nowhere with a Neolithic pagan spread-eagled on top of her. Possibly a naked pagan. Yeeaaccchh!

There was only one way to find out. Gingerly she tried to move her head. And felt a sleeve brush her cheek. Relief flooded her. The pagan was wearing a jacket. Hopefully he still had his pants on, too.

She took a deep breath and prepared to reason with him.

"I said, keep quiet," the voice growled. A nasty whispering growl.

Jassie opened her mouth to argue, but her words were blocked by a hard, warm mouth. A pagan's mouth. Yeeaaccchh! She tried to recoil, but the back of her head was pressed against the ground and there was nowhere to go. She felt a scream building up inside her as his tongue glided over hers.

In a very familiar and delicious way.

Jassie put the scream on hold and concentrated on the tongue playing a dark duet with hers. Yum-mmm.

The pagan was her very own John T.

She threw herself into the duet.

After a time he lifted his mouth off hers. "What the devil are you doing here?" he whispered fiercely.

"What are *you* doing here?" she retorted, also in a whisper.

"Don't play cute with me, Jassie. What are you doing following me around? I told you, I'm not interested—"

Jassie was furious. "Following *you?* What sort of masculine assumption is that? What an ego! Careful you don't trip over it, Sheriff. Following you? Ha! The reason I'm here has *nothing* to do with you."

She could tell by the pause that followed that he didn't believe her.

"Look, whatever your reason, I want you out of here. I'm here on business," he whispered hoarsely.

"So am I."

"Dammit, woman, this is serious!" he hissed.

"I'm serious, too," Jassie hissed back. "I'm a journalist and I want this story, John T. Don't think you can stop me." She glared at his silhouette.

"What story is that?"

"You know darn well what story, John T. Don't play cute with me. I'm after those pagans, too. It'll make a fantastic scoop."

There was a short pause. "Pagans?"

"Yeah, don't try to pretend, John T. I know all about them."

"What do you know?"

Jassie thumped him on his shoulder with a fist. "Stop it. I want pictures of those hunters dancing and you're not making me leave until I get them."

"Dancing hunters?" he said after a moment.

"Ooh!" Jassie growled with frustration. "Look, I know all about it, the nakedness, the dancing around that disgusting phallic rock, the hunting... All right? And I want pictures. And you're not going to stop me."

There was a long silence. Broken after a few moments by a muffled snort. It sounded as if he was choking. Jassie reached out through the dark and laid a hand on him. His shoulders were heaving and jerking spasmodically. She clenched a fist and thumped him.

"It's not funny, drat you!"

The choking sounds increased and she thumped him again.

"Stop laughing. What on earth is so funny?"

"Hunters...? Dancing naked before the hunt?" Another snort of laughter rumbled up from the depths of his chest. "Jassie, sweetheart, someone's been pulling your leg. There's nothing like that going on around here.''

"How do you know?'' He'd called her sweetheart!

"I just do, that's all. I keep an eye on most things around here and believe me, if there were any hunters dancing naked I'd know about it. It's too darned cold up here for naked dancing, for a start.''

It was pretty cold, at that, Jassie thought.

"I got a tip,'' she said stubbornly.

"Who from?''

"I...he didn't say.''

He chuckled again. "I'll bet. No, sweetheart, it was a prank, I'm sorry to say.''

"But I followed them here. They were driving without lights. How suspicious is that?'' she said triumphantly.

She felt him shrug. "I drove without lights,'' he said. "So did you, I suppose, or I would have noticed you sooner. But I didn't see anyone. What sort of car was it?''

"A dark green pickup.''

There was a short pause. "A dark green pickup?'' His voice had that choking quality to it again. "You followed a suspicious-looking dark green pickup without lights?''

"That's right, Sheriff. And you missed them.''

"That pickup...I don't suppose you got the license plate?''

"Of course. I'm a professional newspaperwoman, after all.''

"Was it—?'' He rattled off a number.

Jassie peered at her notebook. "That's it. So you do know about them. Are they criminals?''

He was choking again. "Sorry to disappoint you, Ms. Professional Newspaperwoman, but that's my suspicious-looking pickup you followed.''

"That wasn't your pickup,'' she said scornfully.

"Yours is old and…and rusty and painted half a dozen different colors."

"My truck was painted yesterday. I picked it up this afternoon. It's now a beautiful shiny dark green. Looks pretty sharp, don't you think?" He chuckled some more.

Sharp? Sharp! Sharp wasn't the word. To think she'd been creeping around, scared half out of her wits, and all the time it was him, the big rat! And he obviously thought it the most hilarious thing he'd heard in years. Those chuckles were getting to be pretty darn irritating. All she could think of to do was to thump him again, so she did.

"Ow! Will you stop doing that?" he rumbled mildly in between the chuckles. He reached out and grabbed her with one solid arm and pulled her against him. Her arms were clamped to her sides and she was clamped to the sheriff. It wasn't such a bad arrangement, thought Jassie. The ground was hard and rocky and the night was cold and blustery, his body was big and warm and if she had to be clamped anywhere…

His mouth sought hers and all thoughts of argument immediately dissolved into bliss.

"So what are you doing here?" she said after a time.

"Endangered wildlife smugglers," he said.

"'Endangered wildlife smugglers'?" Jassie was stunned.

"Helicopter collection. Landing in this clearing."

"How do you know?"

"Tip."

"Anonymous?"

She felt him nod. "That's why I didn't call in support. Don't know how reliable the information is."

"But they said it was tonight?"

He nodded again. His warm breath fanned her skin.

Jassie frowned. "Don't you think that's a pretty big coincidence?" she said after a time. "I mean, we both get an anonymous tip on the same day and we both get told something big is going to happen right here, out of all the millions of deserted places in Montana—in this clearing.''

He stiffened. ''Your source specified *this* clearing? I thought you were just following me.''

''No, they mentioned this clearing and that disgusting rock.''

''Shoot! Me, too.'' He suddenly let go of her. Jassie felt the draft seep in between them as he moved.

''What are you doing?''

''I'm going to check out the rock. There's something fishy going on. I don't reckon there's another soul between us and Canada right now.''

Jassie scrambled after him, feeling her hair catch in the branches of the bush.

The rock rose out of the ground, bold and arrogant. Something pale glimmered on it in the moonlight. Some cryptic design, she thought. Jassie and J.T. peered at it closely. It was almost impossible to make out in the dark. The clouds swirled overhead. J.T. suddenly swore, long and hard.

''What?''

''That damned betting!'' he growled. ''Shoot! I should've thought of the betting. You and that damned paper of yours. You and that damned headline.''

''What are you talking about?''

''It was a trick to get us out here, curse it. To throw us together.'' He swore some more.

Jassie still could not see what had so upset him. She peered harder at the rock, and suddenly saw the white-painted letters. Very freshly painted letters.

JMcQ 4 JTS.

In a heart.

With an arrow.

And underneath, the sign Lovers' Rock.

And the word, *enjoy!*

7

"YOU MEAN TO SAY there are no naked pagan hunters and no wildlife smugglers? It was all just an elaborate hoax?" Jassie was furious. All her dreams of fame, fortune and fabulous headlines crashed around her. "For a *bet?*"

"Come on, that storm's going to break soon. I'll give you a ride back to your car." J.T. took her arm and began to hustle her up the hill.

"I broke it."

He looked at her in concern. "Broke what?"

"My car. I hit a rock."

"Oh. In that case I'll take you home. We can get someone out here tomorrow to see to your car. Just hurry. I don't like the look of that storm." He hustled her fast over rocks and dips, holding her arm in a firm, supportive grip.

They reached the crest and paused to catch their breath a moment.

"That was—" Jassie was interrupted by a distant scream of brakes, followed by a crash. "What the—"

"That came from the main road above us. An accident, by the sound of it," he said. "Quick! Into the truck." J.T. wrenched open the passenger door and thrust her inside. In seconds they were bouncing at breakneck speed along the rough track.

They reached the main road which twisted up into the mountains, and the sheriff accelerated even more. Dark shadowed stands of pine swooped up at them from out of the darkness, hung suspended in the headlights and then dropped away. A jagged cliff of rock rushed toward them out of the night then slid away as they roared around a corner. The road hovered on the edge of the mountain, an endless black abyss gaping six inches from the wheels. Jassie gripped her seat belt and closed her eyes, ready to sail off into infinity like Thelma and Louise.

She couldn't watch the road. She couldn't look away. In desperation she fixed her gaze on the man behind the wheel. His strong beautiful profile was faintly visible in the light from the dash. She stared at his long, blunt fingers holding the wheel lightly, handling it with such confidence, such certainty. The only thing that gave the slightest indication of the danger they were in was the intensity of his concentration, but she wasn't going to think about it. She needed some distraction. She stared at his mouth. It was a beautiful distraction.

"Where did you get that little scar on your lip?" she asked.

He gave her a brief, startled glance, then his mouth quirked as some memory came to him. "Kicked in the face by a mule when I was a kid. Split my mouth wide-open."

"A mule! You lived on a farm then? In Montana?"

"A ranch. In Texas. For a while."

Aha. She'd thought there was a touch of Texas in that accent of his. "So your family was in ranching?"

"Nope." He hesitated and then said, "My ma ditched me when I was a kid. So I was fostered out." He shrugged. "I went a bit wild there for a time. None of the foster homes worked out."

Jassie was horrified. She'd lost her parents when she was only nineteen, but she had nothing but happy memories of them. "Your mother ditched you?"

He shrugged again. "Yeah, it was pretty tough at the time, but I guess I can understand it better now. She wasn't much more than a kid herself when she had me, and then she teamed up with this guy." He shrugged.

"I guess, looking back, she thought I'd be better off with a family than with a guy who hated kids."

Jassie gazed at him, awestruck. To be able to forgive, like that... A lump came into her throat. He glanced across at her and his mouth softened. "Old Pop taught me that there's no use beatin' up over what can't be changed. He owned that ornery mule I told you about."

"Was he the rancher?"

"That's him. Found me hiding out in his barn when I was around twelve. I'd run away again from some place. He took me in, fixed it with the authorities to let me stay." There was satisfaction in his voice, a warmth that told Jassie that living with Old Pop had suited young J.T.

"How long did you stay with Old Pop?"

"Till I turned eighteen."

Jassie frowned. "And then he kicked you out?"

"Nope. He died. And his relatives sold the ranch."

Rain came, first in large heavy single drops, then in a dense gray sheet. Visibility dropped and he moderated his speed slightly, though nowhere near the speed Jassie felt comfortable with.

Oddly enough, while the rain made the driving more dangerous, Jassie felt almost secure. With drops pelting hard against the windows of the cab of the pickup, it felt almost cozy. The two of them against the world. Though not, she hoped, like Thelma and Louise.

She glanced out the side window and swallowed a shriek. They were skirting a black crevasse. She whirled back, fixed her gaze on his beautiful chiseled mouth and blurted out the first question that came to her mind. She was making conversation. She was *not* panicking.

"So what did you do after you left the ranch?"

"Oh, plenty of things. Drifted around a bit, did a stint in the army, became a cop in Chicago, then moved to New York and worked as a cop there." He was silent a moment, then added, "Then I got shot."

Jassie wondered where he had been wounded, but asked, "Is that why you left New York?"

There was a short pause. "No."

"So why did you leave New York?"

He hesitated. "A woman."

"Woman?"

His lips thinned. "A wife. It didn't work out." He shrugged, his mouth grim, his gaze on the road ahead. "The city, it taints people. Out here everything's cleaner."

Jassie was dying to know more. Who did he mean was tainted? "What was her name?"

"Sybille." He bit off the name.

"So what went wrong?" Jassie asked after a minute.

There was a short silence and for a moment she thought he wasn't going to answer, but then he shrugged awkwardly and said, "She took off with my partner when I was in hospital because of the shooting."

"What? You were hurt. And she left while you were still *in hospital?*" Jassie was shocked. She couldn't imagine anyone wanting to leave John T., but to leave him when he'd been hurt…

"Yeah. It was the opportunity they'd been waiting for. I found out later they'd been having an affair for months."

There was a short silence, broken only by the swish of the wipers and the roar of the engine. The headlights picked up a cliff of jagged rock. Jassie barely noticed it, she was so absorbed in what he had just revealed. It was more horrific than any old rock.

"Had you been married long?"

"Long enough." He negotiated a sharp hairpin turn, glanced across at her and added, "Four years."

Four years. Jassie thought about that. It was a significant length of time. She'd been with Murdock for four years. Four years was enough time to be sure of a relationship, to be thinking about babies. At least, Jassie had started thinking about babies. Murdock had thought about other women.

And John T.'s wife had run off with his partner. His partner...

Jassie hesitated. She'd heard that cops took their partnerships pretty seriously, especially in big cities, where their work was dangerous. A cop was supposed to be able to trust his partner with his life. "You say she went off with your partner. Had you been partners long?"

His smile was cold. "Yeah. I thought he was my best friend."

"Oh." Jassie was appalled. At least Murdock had never slept with Rita. Rita probably would have punched him out for even suggesting it. "You must have been terribly hurt."

"No, it was just a flesh wound," he said enigmatically. "Ah, there it is." He jammed on his brakes and pulled off the road.

Jassie would have missed it. There was no sign of an accident to her inexperienced eyes. The sheriff took a flashlight to the edge of the road. The rain had eased to a steady drizzle. Jassie got out and peered down into the gloom, gasping as his flashlight illuminated a path through torn and devastated vegetation.

It was a bus, a modified old schoolbus, she thought, hand-painted with bright New Age symbols. It lay on its side, bent like a banana around a rocky outcrop. The powerful flashlight picked up several signs of movement and Jassie thought she could hear voices.

Stone pulled out a cellular phone and punched in 9-1-1. She watched as he issued a crisp explanation of the accident and their location. He ripped open the big metal box in the bed of his truck, grabbed a first aid kit and shoved it into Jassie's unresisting hands, then pulled out a couple of hazard lights, which he turned on and set on the road. Finally he hooked a large coil of rope over his shoulder, picked up a spade, several burlap sacks and a folded tarpaulin. He glanced at her frozen face and smiled. "Ready?"

Helplessly she nodded back. She could no more resist that smile than fly.

"Good girl." He cupped her cheek briefly with a rough, cold palm. "Lucky we went chasing red herrings, after all." His hands full of gear, he plunged surefooted down the steep, grassy slope. Jassie followed.

'Yi-iikes!'' she yelled as her feet slipped from beneath her. "Yeow!" She passed him on the slope. On her behind.

"Whoa! Gotcha." He stopped her headlong slide, grabbing her jacket from behind. He picked her up and grinned. "Okay?"

She inclined her head in a dignified manner. She was covered in mud.

He grinned again and planted a quick kiss on her cold lips and Jassie immediately warmed. "Maybe we better go together." He picked up the stuff he had dropped, waited until she took his arm, and continued down the slope. Wet, a little sore and extremely muddy, she clung to his arm in a death grip, slipping and sliding on the soaked ground.

The vehicle looked worse than it actually was. It was some kind of alternative tour bus with only a few passengers who, miraculously, had all emerged uninjured, though a little dazed and in shock. J.T. rigged up the tarpaulin, stringing it between trees, to provide shelter from the rain. The passengers, dressed in an assortment of brightly colored clothes, soon sat quietly, huddled underneath.

"Is everyone all right?" she asked anxiously.

He nodded briefly. "The bus driver's trapped. We'll have to wait for the ambulance to get him out. He thinks his leg might be broken, but otherwise he's fine. He's amazingly calm about the whole thing."

He glanced down at her and gently smoothed a lock of sodden hair away from her eyes, absently, as if unaware of his actions. Jassie suddenly didn't feel so cold or wet or muddy. She moved closer to him, taking comfort in his big warm body. Wet as he was, he radiated warmth.

His gaze moved to where the half-dozen passengers sat in silence under the tarpaulin, a bright splash of color in the muted gloom. He frowned, looking puzzled. "They're very quiet."

"They're contemplating the great cycle of life," explained Jassie. "Searching for their inner oneness. One of them explained it to me."

Paramedics and a rescue team arrived and the area was soon bustling with competent people. The passengers were taken to the town to be checked over. Someone had brought a flask of hot coffee and Jassie took a cup down to J.T. The pines around the bus were lit eerily by the portable lights set up by the emergency team. The men worked quickly and competently.

Jassie handed John T. the coffee, but didn't stay to watch. She moved around to the back end of the bus. It gave a little shelter from the rain and the wind. She was drenched to the bone and frozen and exhausted and she still had a story to write. She decided to return to the pickup, where there was a pen and paper in her bag, and she could start making notes. She should take some photos, too.

"Mommy?"

Jassie froze. The frail little voice seemed to come from the black depths of the bus.

The noise of the wind died for a bare second. "Mommy, can I stop hiding now?" The voice was high and faint and scared.

Jassie stared at the crumpled bus. There was a child trapped in there. Oh, God!

"I'm here, sweetie. Don't worry. We'll get you out. Are you hurt?" She waited for the child's answer, praying silently.

"No, but it's dark in here and I can't get out."

Jassie heaved a sigh of relief. She raced around to the other side of the bus and grabbed J.T.'s arm. "There's a child trapped in there! A little girl, I think."

"Where?"

Jassie pointed. "Around the other side. I was heading to the truck when out of the darkness came this scared little voice calling for Mommy."

"Did it sound like she was hurt?" a rescue paramedic asked.

"More frightened than hurt, I think," Jassie said.

"Right." They turned back to their task.

"Wait! Aren't you going to get her out?"

The sheriff spoke gently. "Jassie, we've almost got this guy freed. We'll get to your little girl as soon as we can."

"But…but what if she's injured, too?"

He shrugged, his eyes dark with compassion, his jaw set. "You said she was more frightened than hurt."

Jassie stared at him, horrified. "But that was just a guess. What if I'm wrong? She could be hurt." She could not believe that anyone could make a life-and-death decision based on something she had said so unthinkingly.

He cupped a cold wet hand around her cheek. "We'll get to her as soon as we can, Jassie. She'll be okay. Not one passenger was seriously hurt. The little girl might be scared, but she's dry and safe for the moment. Why don't you go wait in the pickup? It's warmer there. And dry."

Jassie wrapped wet arms around her cold body. "I'm fine," she said. "Don't worry about me, John T."

"Atta girl." He planted a quick kiss on her lips and turned back to help the rescue team. He was trained in this work. He was needed. So was she. Jassie closed her eyes, feeling the rain on her eyelids. Oh, Lord! What was she to do? She couldn't go back to the pickup while that little girl waited. She went back to where she'd heard the voice.

"Mommy?"

"Mommy's busy, honey, she can't come right now," called Jassie. All the passengers had been taken away. "Are you all right? Does anything hurt?"

"I don't wanna play hide anymore. My leg is sore. I want my mommy."

"Is your leg hurting real bad or just a bit bad?" Jassie persisted in a calm voice. There was a short silence, Jassie held her breath.

Then the little voice came. "Um, bad-bad enough for a Band-Aid, maybe. Have you got Band-Aids?"

"Sure we have, honey."

"Maybe I can have two Band-Aids? Awwight?"

Jassie let out a sigh of relief. If the child was angling for more bandages, she probably wasn't too badly hurt.

"Sure you can, honey. We've got plenty of Band-Aids out here and in a little while you'll be out."

"Where's Mommy?"

"She's taking a ride in an amb—a car, honey. You'll see her soon, don't worry."

One of the first women taken away in the ambulance had had a concussion and kept fading in and out of unconsciousness. She must be the little girl's mother, Jassie thought. That would explain why she hadn't come looking for her daughter.

Silence fell, broken only by the sounds of the wind and rain and the sounds of men rescuing the driver from the bus. Jassie looked longingly toward the pickup. The rain was freezing and she couldn't stop shivering. She couldn't get the child out. She couldn't do anything to help…

In the pickup she could be out of the wind and rain. There was the flask with some leftover hot coffee. And if she could get hold of someone's cell phone she could phone a story in to the big papers…a story that would gain her nearly as much recognition as the mythical hunters. And money, which heaven knew she needed…

But she couldn't leave this frightened little girl alone

in the dark and the cold. She lay on the ground, and wriggled as close as she could to where she figured the child was, wincing as she landed in another patch of mud. She peered into dense blackness. "Hey, there, sweetie. It's me again, Jassie. What's your name?"

There was a pause. "A'e you a stranger? I'm not s'posed to tell my name to strangers."

Jassie couldn't help but smile. The rain beat down on her as she called back, "No, honey, I'm not a stranger. I'm Jassie and I'm going to stay here and visit with you until the nice men come and get you out. So what's your name, honey?"

"Dawn Sky Peacedove McKenzie."

"Oh. Well, I'm very pleased to meet you, Dawn Sky Peacedove McKenzie. That's a pretty special name you've got there. Can I call you Dawn?"

"I s'pose so, but my mommy a'ways calls me Dawn Sky. I want her. Why isn't she here?" Dawn Sky's voice wavered tremulously.

"Oh, don't worry, sweetie, it's going to be all right. I'm not going to leave you." Jassie felt desperate. "Look, I've got some candy for you here—a whole chocolate bar. Here, can you see my hand?" Jassie wriggled as far as she could under the wreckage and thrust the chocolate bar into the dark.

After a moment she felt the girl take it from her. There was a faint sound of paper tearing and in a second the shreds of paper were thrust back into Jassie's hand. Jassie swallowed on a laughing sob as she realized what the little girl had done. She was trapped under a wrecked bus on a mountainside in a storm in the middle of the night, but drop litter? No way! Jassie thrust the candy wrappers back into her pocket, then pushed her hand back toward Dawn Sky. Instantly a cold little hand closed around hers. Gripping tightly as if to a lifeline.

Jassie's eyes, already wet from the rain, filled. "That's it, sweetie, hold my hand and you won't feel so lonesome." Jassie blinked, trying desperately to think of some distraction. What did you talk to kids about— animals, that was it. They were all crazy about animals. "Have you got any pets, Dawn Sky?"

Dawn Sky stopped chewing and thought for a moment. "No. Have you?"

"No." Some conversational opener that turned out to be.

"I'm cold."

"Yes, me, too, Dawn Sky. But you be a good brave girl and hang on and pretty soon we'll have you out of that nasty old place."

"That's right, honey," said a deep voice close to Jassie's knee, "we're all working as fast as we can to get you out of there."

Jassie turned her head and blinked through the rain at John T., who'd hunkered down beside her. He smelled wet but warm, and she found his presence comforting.

He raised his voice. "Hi, there, in the bus. Is there a pretty little girl called Dawn Sky in there?"

"Yes, I'm here," called a quavery little voice. The cold little hand tightened around Jassie's.

"That's good, sweetheart. This is the sheriff here and I've just talked to your mommy. She's fine, honey, but she wants Ms. Jassie here to look after you for a while, okay."

"'Kay."

"Whereabouts in the bus are you, honey?" Stone called.

"Under the seat. I was playing hide with my teddy bear."

"Good girl. That was a smart place to be. You just stay put, sweetheart, and since you're such a good girl, Ms. Jassie here will tell you a wonderful story."

"Are you nuts, John T., I don't know any kids' stories," she hissed.

He grinned at her and patted her on the shoulder. "Hey, Ms. Professional Newspaperwoman, make it up—that's your job, isn't it?'' He grinned again and added in a low voice, ''You're doing a great job, sweetheart. Just keep the little one occupied until we can get her out. The driver's almost free. It won't be long.''

He raised his voice and called, ''Ms. Jassie's going to tell you a story now, Dawn Sky, and when she's finished, I'm going to come and get you out of there and get you someplace warm and dry with your mommy.''

Jassie stared at him in panic, but she'd never had any resistance to that smile of his—in or out of the rain. Or even in the pitch-black night. She might not be able to see it, but she could hear it in his voice and feel it wrapping itself around her. He'd called her sweetheart for the third time tonight. And with one warm masculine finger gently stroking the nape of her cold wet neck, she felt ready for anything. ''Hey, Dawn Sky, do you know the story about…um, the little baby deer,'' she began. ''He was called—''

''Can the baby deer be a girl?''

''Sure, Dawn Sky, she was a girl, now I come to think of it. Well, this baby deer was called Bam—er, what do you think her name was, Dawn Sky?

''Phyllis,'' said Dawn Sky with great certainty.

''Phyllis, absolutely right. Well, Phyllis, the baby deer, went out for a walk one day—''

''Where was her mommy?''

''Oh. Um, Phyllis's mommy was, um, doing the ironing— Er, deer have to iron their antlers, you know…ah, the velvet on them,'' added Jassie desperately, hearing a chuckle behind her. She felt warmth cover her as the sheriff tucked his jacket around her. She looked up at him to argue that he'd freeze now, without his jacket, but his silhouette just shook his head, nodded toward Dawn Sky and Jassie and hurried away.

Warmed by his jacket, his smile and the memory of his hand caressing her nape, she continued the story of

Phyllis the baby deer, while in the darkness a cold little hand clutched hers with desperate childish tenacity.

"COME ON, SWEETHEART, time to get you home," murmured J.T. Nodding tiredly, Jassie tried to stand. The rescue had taken a long time, but Dawn Sky was safely out of the wreck—miraculously unhurt except for fright and cold. She'd gone straight into Jassie's arms when she'd been freed and hadn't left Jassie's embrace until she'd finally fallen into an exhausted sleep. At that point Jassie was almost asleep herself. John T. had gently pried the little girl out of Jassie's arms and carried her to an ambulance. By the time she woke, she'd be with her mother.

Despite the relief to her cramped muscles, Jassie felt strangely bereft when Dawn Sky had been taken from her. She had never held a child before and she was amazed at how emotional she felt, seeing the little girl being taken away. Dawn Sky would wake up in the same room as her mommy, she told herself. Jassie was just a temporary substitute.

But she still felt bereft.

"Here." John T. held out a hand and Jassie took it. Effortlessly he pulled her to her feet and when she stumbled, he caught her against his big hard body. His clothes were as wet and clammy as hers, but he radiated heat and Jassie leaned into him, savoring the warmth and his nearness. She was so tired and cold, she could barely think.

J.T. smiled faintly as he looked down at her. She was filthy, her face and body smeared with dirt from lying on the ground, her hair hanging in lank wet clumps around her face. Her nose was red, her eyes matched and yet she'd never looked so appealing to him. He had it bad, he acknowledged. "I'd carry you if I could, honey, but I'm beat," he said ruefully.

Jassie mumbled something against his chest that sounded like, "I c'n walk by m'self, th'nk you," and reeled off in the direction of the ravine, walking like a zombie. He caught her and, supporting her with his arm, steered her toward his pickup.

He maneuvered her into the passenger seat and fastened her seat belt, fending off her hands as she muttered, "I c'n do it. 'M not helpl'ss, y'know." And then, instead of dealing with the seat belt, she reached for his shirt buttons and tried to unfasten them.

She fell asleep almost the moment the hot air of the pickup heater hit her.

They reached his cabin in a bare half hour. There was no way he was going to leave her alone tonight, not after what she'd been through. All those hours lying on stony, wet ground, making up stories to stop a little girl from panicking. He glanced across at her pale, dirty, rain-streaked features and smiled. Not to mention the staking out of a wild pack of naked dancing hunters...

She'd been out in the cold and rain for hours. She could wake up with a fever. She needed someone to keep an eye on her. And he'd elected himself for the job.

When they reached his cabin he couldn't wake her properly so he carried her inside and laid her on his sofa.

"Jassie. Jassie, honey, wake up," he said.

She didn't stir.

J.T. looked at his sopping-wet guest. There was no choice, he had to get her out of those clothes. And he wasn't sure he was strong enough to cope with the job tonight, his resistance to her was low enough already.

He shook her by the shoulder. "Jassie, come on, wake up," he said again, more loudly. "We've got to get those wet clothes off you."

"Grmmumphlmt," she replied. But she was shivering.

With a heartfelt sigh, he began to unfasten her clothing, trying to not look too much. He removed his jacket, which she'd been wearing, and pulled off her own thin

jacket and cotton knit pullover. Her wet blouse was almost see-through. He took a deep breath and averted his
eyes....

Not the most clever move. Undoing a woman's
blouse without looking was much more hazardous than
looking, he discovered quickly. His hands kept bumping
into...things. Soft, delightful things. He groaned. He
was a police officer, dammit. He had seen plenty of
naked females and he was assisting a woman in distress,
professionally and impartially, as befitted an officer of
the law. Yeah, right.

He forced himself to look, and closed his eyes. Call
that minuscule, provocative scrap of damp lace a bra?
With shaking hands he reached for the front fastening
and, trying to not look or touch, pulled it gently off her.

He quickly removed her shoes and socks and unzipped her jeans. Hooking his fingers into her briefs, as
well, he stripped them off her long, cold, wet legs. And
so she was naked.

As he stood there, mustering his control, trying to not
stare at the source of all his recent fantasies, naked, pink
and damp on his sofa, Sheriff John T. Stone realized he
had committed a major tactical error. He should have
carried her into the bathroom first and stripped her under
the shower. Now he was going to have to carry her—
naked—in his arms. And he didn't know if his profes-
sionalism was up to it.

"Come on, honey," he said helplessly. "Into the
bathroom. You gotta take a shower. A nice hot shower
to warm you up." He reached out a hand to shake her
again...and hesitated, realizing that if he shook her, certain...things would jiggle, and if they did, he couldn't
answer for the consequences.

Swearing, he swept her into his arms and, trying to
not notice how good she felt there—how right—he carried her into the bathroom and put her down in the
shower. Her knees instantly sagged and he realized he
couldn't let go of her. Swearing, he maneuvered himself

out of his own wet clothes and, naked, stepped into the shower with her, holding her against his chest. Ah, well, he supported water conservation, didn't he?

Hot water poured over them, streaming down their bodies in a tide of warmth and comfort. He thought about soaping them both down, and then decided against it. Despite the intense cold when he was wet, despite the heat of the shower, despite his best professional efforts at being impartial and disinterested, he was already wildly and painfully aroused. If he had to soap her beautiful soft skin he would probably explode on the spot. It was har—difficult enough just having to hold her close while the hot water thawed them out.

And those little squeaks and murmurs of pleasure she was making! Not to mention the way she kept trying to snuggle into him. And as for what her hands kept trying to do! No guardian of the law should have to endure such exquisite torment in the exercising of his duty.

Not that it was entirely duty, he wryly acknowledged as he smoothed a washcloth over her face. When he first made love to Jassie McQuilty—and he'd finally acknowledged that he would—he wanted her to be wide-awake and able to recall every moment. Well, almost every moment... He smiled. When he did make love to Jassie McQuilty he planned to drive her right out of her senses—with pleasure... It would be his pleasure to do so.

But first he had to get her dried off and into bed and off his conscience as an officer of the law. Tonight he was on duty and she was a citizen of Bear Claw, caught up in a disaster. But tomorrow—tomorrow was his day off and he'd be free to seduce her. One plain ordinary citizen to another. She wriggled in his grasp like warm slippery satin and he groaned. There was nothing plain and ordinary about this woman!

And she wanted him.

She'd made it as clear as...as clear as the Crystal Drop Waterfall that she wanted him. He knew it—hell the whole town knew it! So why fight her? Why fight himself? Let nature take its course.

There would be problems, but he would deal with them. So what if he hadn't succeeded in keeping anyone all his life? He'd never felt so lonely in his life as after the old man died. Until he'd discovered just how much more lonely life could be in a city of millions, when the partner he'd once trusted and the wife he'd once loved hurt him so deeply.

You gotta build, boy. You got no choice if you want to live in this world. You build.

And then the old man would look at him through eyes that had lived nearly seventy years, through fire and drought and tornado and snowstorm, eyes of a faraway blue embedded in a mass of lines and crinkles. Eyes that had experienced pain and grief and cruelty, and yet they had remained kind and had looked on an angry young runaway with acceptance. *Life knocks you down, you gotta build again. Ain't no choice for us, man or boy. You build again or you quit living.*

When he'd left New York he hadn't owned more than a car and his clothes. Sybille had taken everything. Yet now he'd built his own home and it was full of his own things. It was a home in the way the apartment in New York had never been. He'd lived in Bear Claw more than five years now. He was happy here, aside from the loneliness, and even that was bearable here. Bear Claw was the kind of place he could see himself growing old in.

A man could build again in Montana. It was something about the air, and the mountains.

Maybe now he was ready to let someone—a woman—into his life again. And not just any woman. One special woman. And Jassie McQuilty was special, all right. Never in his life had he felt anything remotely resemble the way she made him feel. And he craved it.

So what if he'd spent his life staying out of women's silken traps? Jassie McQuilty didn't look or feel like a

trap to him. Or if she was, then he wanted to be trapped.
If she wanted him—and it sure looked as if she did—
he was going to let her into his heart, cracks and crannies and all, dammit. He was going to let her in if he died trying.

All he had to do was make it through the night.

He turned off the faucet, wrapped her in a couple of towels and sat her on a chair next to the electric heater. Quickly he dried himself and then her. He would have put her in pajamas, but he didn't own any, so he found a cotton T-shirt and pulled it over her.

It was almost decent, apart from the way the soft fabric clung to her curves, and reached halfway down her thighs.

He had no hair dryer, either, so he toweled her dark curls dry, enjoying the way the silky dark mass slid through his hands and curled damply around his fingers. No! He refused to think about dark curls...

He lifted her again and carried her into his bedroom. His cabin was large and comfortable, but there was no guest room. The sofa was also large and comfortable, but what if she broke out in a fever? He wouldn't know about it until it was too late, maybe. He slipped her into his bed and stood there looking down at her, feeling very satisfied, despite his frustration. She fit perfectly in his bed. She looked exactly right in it, as he'd always imagined she would.

And since he was going to let her keep him, she'd be in this bed of his for years to come.

John T. Stone slipped into bed, beside her, and curled his big body around hers. She sighed and murmured something, a contented unintelligible sound, and snuggled into his warmth. Causing his ache to intensify. Pleasurably...almost.

He buried his face in her barely damp hair and inhaled deeply. Yes, he was going to let her keep him. He nudged a curl aside and gently tasted the tender skin at the nape of her neck. She tasted of peaches and rainwater and warm, sweet woman. His arms tightened around her and his body adjusted to fit hers.

Grimly he readjusted it. He was going to be able to hold her like this through the night for the rest of his days. In the meantime, there was the torment of tonight.

JASSIE WOKE the next morning to a feeling of wondrous comfort. She lay with her eyes closed, feeling warm and relaxed and too good to be bothered about getting up. Sleepily she tried to recall what she was supposed to do that day, and smiled. In New York it had taken a squalling alarm to drag her from the depths of slumber, and the instant she'd opened her eyes a thousand things came clamoring into her consciousness. There was never enough time in New York. Peculiar, she was working just as hard here in Bear Claw—she just felt more relaxed and in control.

She yawned hugely and stretched, then froze as her body came into contact with—with something. Something warm.

Eyes squeezed shut, like a kid pretending she was still asleep so nothing bad could happen, Jassie cautiously felt behind her. Her cringing fingers came lightly into contact with warm flesh…and a faint sprinkling of hair. Not enough hair to be a cat. Darn! A human body. A distinctly masculine-feeling body, she thought, jumping almost a foot as her blindly questing hand came into contact with something that was unmistakably masculine and from the feel of it, wide-awake and sitting up, raring to go!

She was clothed, thank goodness—if you could call wearing nothing but a stranger's T-shirt clothed. Especially when it was hiked up around her waist. The rest of her felt more naked by the minute.

Who the heck was in this bed with her? And whose bed was it, anyway? Oh, Lord! Friends had described this moment to her in a dozen ways, but Jassie had never done it before—waking up in a strange bed, in a rising panic, not knowing where she was. And more important, with whom.

It took all her courage to turn to face the unknown. She did it in slow motion, slithering as silently as she could, trying to not disturb the bed and the unknown man in it.

Incipient panic turned to relief as she opened her scrunched-up eyes and beheld...her sheriff. Sound asleep. Immediately the events of the previous night came rolling back into her consciousness—the fruitless hunt for the hunters, the bus crash and the long, slow rescue. The last thing she recalled was seeing little Dawn Sky carried away to the ambulance, fast asleep, her small face pale and dirt-streaked.

Jassie thought about the little girl, about how she'd felt when Dawn Sky came out of the bus and into her arms. Since Murdock, she'd put all thought about having kids aside. But now she knew she wanted them. Quite desperately.

She looked at the man beside her. John T. had brought her home last night to his own bed, the big sweet darling. She smiled, feeling vaguely triumphant. Her fling with John T. must have started last night at long last.

She smiled at his sleeping face, savoring the leisure to examine it, to stare as much as she wanted without him staring back, sending her into a flutter with those disturbing twinkling eyes. Some men looked boyish asleep. Not John T. His face was too strong-featured and lived-in for that. But he looked so much more relaxed and open in sleep. And perhaps a little sad.

The only thing boyish about him was his hair, which was poking every which way. If it hadn't been so short, it would have borne a good resemblance to a broom, she thought, smiling. He'd made the effort to dry her hair for her, but neglected to do the same for himself....

Oh, Lord! It all came back to her then. How he'd carried her inside. She vaguely remembered trying to seduce him, helping him undo his buttons. She certainly remembered him stripping her and how he'd carried her into the shower and held her against him while hot water sluiced over them both. She recalled the blissful pleasure of him drying her hair, the tender awkwardness of a man unused to such a task. She remembered him pulling the T-shirt down over her body and then carrying her to his bed.

And then...nothing.

He'd put her to bed like a child and then gone to sleep himself. Unmoved. Unaroused. Unseduced.

She'd been naked in the shower with the man, for heaven's sake!

But...nothing. He hadn't touched her, hadn't done a thing that could be construed as sexual. He might have been taking care of little Dawn Sky for all the awareness he'd shown her. He'd washed her and dressed her and put her to bed like a baby.

Jassie squirmed in humiliation as the truth finally dawned on her. She'd been pursuing this man for weeks in the most open, blatant, unsubtle way, utterly convinced he wanted her as much as she wanted him. He hadn't exactly encouraged her, though, had actually even tried to avoid her. And had she taken the hint? No. The man had done everything that a decent, kindhearted man could do to tell a woman he wasn't interested in her. Jassie squirmed in mortal embarrassment. He'd even said it in actual words. *I'm not interested.*

But did she take any notice? Oh, no, Jassie McQuilty, famous manhunter—not!—knew better. Blinded by lust she'd convinced herself he was just shy, that under that strong, silent man stuff he was attracted to her. She thought he just needed a little encouragement, that if she just persisted he would get the message. She'd told herself it was commitment he'd feared. She'd told herself all sorts of stupid things.

But the truth was, *he hadn't wanted her.*

He'd had her naked and willing in his bed and he hadn't wanted her.

Here he was, sound asleep and dreaming—if that flagpole under the bedclothes was anything to go by—of some floozy in the next county. While Jassie McQuilty, ready, willing, and almost naked had lain right beside him in his bed all night. Untouched.

Jassie groaned silently. She'd made a complete and total fool of herself in front of the whole town of Bear Claw. They were even laying bets on the outcome of her pursuit. That's how big a fool she'd made of herself—and him—she told herself savagely. She'd done much worse to him. She'd embarrassed a decent man in front of a whole town, a town he'd live the rest of his life in, while she…she planned to get out after a year.

No wonder he'd been trying to avoid her.

It was a wonder he didn't hate her.

He probably did.

Jassie had never felt so ashamed or miserable in her life. She took one last, wistful glance at the man asleep beside her, then slipped from the bed and crept out of the room. She reached for the phone, then put it down again.

There were no taxis in Bear Claw. It was going to be a long walk home.

8

WHAT SORT OF WOMAN pursues a man—blatantly—in front of a whole town, and then lets him undress her and shower with her and take her to bed. And then falls promptly asleep?

John T. Stone glared at his empty office, feeling distinctly annoyed. *The Globe* was due out the next day and he'd sent his deputy up to fetch an early copy. He paced around the office and glared out the window for the twentieth time.

And what sort of woman snuggles up to a man all cozy and sweet and then, when she's had him aching and aroused all night in her bed—well his bed, to be technical—slips away before the dawn? Before he could do anything. Leaving him still aching and aroused and damnably unsatisfied.

What sort of woman?

A tease, that's who! Worse than a tease, actually.

And what sort of woman spends weeks trailing a man's every movement, popping out of the woodwork every ten minutes, with hot doughnuts and seductive pink lips ready? Getting a man all hot and bothered and making the sight of even the most innocent sugar cookie the source of a hot, torrid fantasy? He'd had the ingredients for doughnuts in his cupboard for weeks. Not to mention several frozen packets. And then, she slips out before breakfast.

What sort of a woman does that to a man?

And what sort of woman then refuses to answer her phone? Or her door? The sort of woman who hides in her office when a man comes calling and sends a pimply faced teenager out to tell him she's busy. Jassie McQuilty, that's who!

Well, he'd had enough. He wasn't going to stand for it anymore, dammit. He'd decided to settle down. Decided to commit. And what does the dratted woman do? Run.

He was going to give her one more chance to decide to keep him. And if she didn't, then he was going to start playing dirty.

What the devil was Norbett doing? It didn't take that long to get to *The Globe* office and back, dammit.

He'd been surprised when the bus crash edition of *The Globe* had hit the street. Not because it was a brilliant story—which it was—but because there'd been no mention of how a certain courageous woman had spent most of the night lying on the freezing wet ground keeping a little girl's fear at bay. And that was the only criticism he could make of it.

But he'd thought it a little odd, given her previous reports, that she hadn't even so much as mentioned him except to say, "The rescue operation was carried out under the supervision of the sheriff of Bear Claw." There had been no mention of his name, let alone his looks, virile or otherwise.

Not that he *wanted* there to be. In fact, it should have been a relief. Instead, he'd been more than a little uneasy. Especially given the way she'd run out on him before dawn. And the way she hadn't returned his calls.

He'd told himself a hundred—a thousand—times that she was just a tease. But he still couldn't make himself believe it.

Something had changed that night. When he'd taken her to bed she'd been sleepy and loving and amorous, but too physically exhausted to act. He'd held her through the night tenderly, gently, not taking advantage of her state to ease his needs, as he'd known he could have. But he'd wanted her to be as much of a participant in their lovemaking as he was. Somehow, something had changed during the night.

If he didn't know better he'd have thought she was a virgin, getting cold feet. But she wasn't—she'd let it slip once that she'd lived with some man in New York. He shook his head. The man must have been an idiot to have a woman like Jassie and let her go....

He half wished she was a virgin because if she was running scared, maybe he'd know how to handle this.

But he had no idea.

And even though it had been just a week or so, he missed her like crazy. He missed her turning up wherever he went, turning the most routine job into an adventure. It felt weird going into Ma's and having no one slip onto the stool next to him five minutes later saying, "Hello, John T.," in that sexy little way of hers. He missed reading *The Globe* and finding damn-fool headlines about himself. He missed the fights they had afterward. And he sure as hell missed those...discussions they'd had on the green sofa. He couldn't get the taste of those...discussions out of his mouth. Or the memory of her, all pink and soft and damp and sleepy in his arms.

So why the hell was she avoiding him?

He hadn't even *seen* her since the night he'd put her into his bed. It was almost as if Jassie McQuilty was no longer in town.

Except he knew she was. Every night he made his rounds, he checked the light in her building where he knew she slept. She'd had a big new bed carried in weeks ago... And it was har—difficult not to think of her in it, Stone thought. He tilted his chair back on two legs, his hands hooked behind his head, and relaxed, imagining Jassie lying curled up in the middle of the big new bed. Maybe in those blue Road Runner pajamas. Or in one of his T-shirts. Or in nothing at all...

His chair teetered suddenly and his fantasy came to an abrupt end as his arms flailed out frantically in his attempt to regain his balance. His chair secure again, he looked around. Where the devil was that slow-moving deputy of his?

Up to now, he'd been forcing himself to wait for Jassie to come to him. He'd figured she liked to take the initiative and that it was probably good for him to learn new ways. Okay, so he'd never liked women chasing him before. A man could get into a rut if he didn't take notice that the world was changing around him. If she wanted to hunt him, it was okay by him.

He was giving her one more chance to put something about him in the paper, he didn't care how ridiculous. She did her communicating through the paper, so he'd give her a chance to do so.

And if not, he was going to forget this New-Age-man nonsense and do what his instincts had been clamoring at him to do the whole time.

J.T. picked up some paperwork and glared at it. Parking fines. He tossed them into a file. He'd given out a record number of parking fines lately...it was a reason to be on the street. But he hadn't spotted her once.

"Er, Sheriff?" Norbett poked his head around the door and hesitantly held out a newspaper.

"Took you long enough!" J.T. snapped, irritated by his deputy's tentative manner. He snatched the paper. "Anything interesting in it?"

"Er, gotta go. Parking tickets to write," muttered Norbett in a strangled voice. He rushed out the door.

J.T. stared after him. Parking tickets? At eight o'clock at night? He'd have to talk to his deputy, he decided. He'd been acting jumpy and peculiar for the past couple of weeks.

J.T. glanced at the paper. "What the—!" He glared at the front-page headline.

Stirring Sermon By Visiting Preacher!

Traveling preacher, the Very Reverend Ebadiah Jones, scourged, moved and cleansed churchgoers

last Sunday with a stirring sermon on the evils of
lust.

"Many people are finding joy and serenity in
the haven of celibacy," Reverend Jones assured his
small but enthusiastic audience...

J.T. scrunched up the paper and hurled it across the
room in outrage. The evils of lust, indeed. There was
nothing evil about what he felt for Jassie McQuilty,
dammit. And as for finding joy and serenity in the haven
of celibacy—he snorted in disgust—he for one could
testify on that subject. He hadn't slept properly in
weeks.

The haven of celibacy! It was a damned torture cham-
ber, not a haven.

And this damned article of Jassie's was more than
flesh and blood could stand.

He slammed his fist onto the desk. How dare she start
something and not wait around to finish it. He stood,
ignoring the chair that crashed to the floor behind him.
He'd had enough of being a modern, sensitive, New-
Age guy. The old ways were the best ways. Letting
women do the chasing. He snorted. Men were the natural hunters.

He'd had a gutful of the joy and serenity of celibacy.
He was going out to hunt down Ms. Jassie McQuilty—
starting now.

And *then* he was going to let her into his cracks and
crannies.

"BUT, JASSIE, HONEY, you just can't miss it!" Dora
Klein looked horrified. She clutched Jassie's arm ur-
gently. "Miss the Bear Claw Annual Founding Day Picnic. It's your first. You've just got to come to the town
picnic. Why 'most everyone will be there. My Don is
even driving the bus so anyone who wants to drink can
get a ride home safely. You've just got to come,
honey."

Jassie shook her head reluctantly. "I'm sorry, Dora. I can't. I've got, er, I've got to design those new brochures for Missy Baines's Western Fashion Boutique."

"But you can't work on a Sund—"

"I've got Rita, my artist friend, helping me, over the Internet, and that's the only day—"

"Oh, the Internet," said Dora vaguely. She sighed and looked at Jassie with big sad eyes. "It's a shame, though, with two such important people as you and the sheriff missing it."

Jassie frowned. "What do you mean?"

Dora heaved another sigh. "Well, neither you nor the sheriff can make it. I have to say I'm disappointed, Jassie, very disappointed."

Jassie watched in horror as Dora's lower lip started to tremble, just a little at first, and then more, until it was quivering uncontrollably. Jassie was aghast. This sweet old lady was going to burst into tears—right here in the main street—simply because Jassie wasn't coming to the picnic.

"Oh, Dora, please." She patted Dora's shoulder helplessly. "I mean— Oh, please don't cry."

Lower lip trembling piteously, Dora groped in her large raffia purse for a handkerchief.

"Oh, if it means that much to you, I'll come then!" Jassie gave in.

Dora looked at her, hope dawning in her tragic eyes. "You really mean it, Jassie? You'll come to the picnic?"

"Yes." Jassie nodded. She'd thought the sheriff was going, so she'd planned to not be within ten miles of the picnic. But since Dora said he wasn't coming, she was safe. "I have to run now, Dora," she said, "but I'll see you on Sunday."

"Don will pick you up after church. At noon, okay?" Dora called after her.

"Fine."

Dora watched Jassie go. She stuffed her dry handkerchief back into the raffia purse, marched purposefully across the street and turned down a narrow laneway.

"How did it go?"

Dora sniffed. "I don't like telling lies."

"But you did, didn't you? She's coming?"

Dora nodded, then shrieked genteelly as she was picked up bodily and whirled around. "Put me down at once this instant, John Stone or I'll...I'll..."

J. T. put her down. Then he picked her up again and kissed her on the cheek. "The most irresistible quivering lower lip in town."

"Oh, get away with you!" Dora pushed him away, blushing and bridling like a young girl. "I didn't do it for you. I did it to teach my Don a lesson."

"A lesson?"

"Yes." Dora nodded piously. "On the perils of gambling."

J.T.'s mouth dropped. "You mean...?" Even nice old Don had been betting on him and Jassie. He wasn't surprised that Dora was so angry with Don. This betting thing was sure getting out of hand. He'd be glad to see an end to it.

Dora sniffed disapprovingly. "He actually bet on you—that Jassie wouldn't succeed."

J.T. shook his head sympathetically. "So, you figure if Don loses his bet, it'll teach him that gambling is a sin, eh?"

Dora glared up at him. "No, it'll teach him that I'm right," she snapped. "*I* bet on Jassie."

"OH, ISN'T THAT NICE, he made it after all," said Dora placidly, passing Jassie a piece of green cardboardy stuff with a slice of tomato on it.

He? Jassie looked up from buttering bread and noticed that almost every eye in her immediate vicinity was on her. Gleaming with expectation. "He, who?" She looked around and it was as if the Red Sea had

parted before her. And instead of a bunch of angry
Egyptians there was a tall masculine figure carrying a...

"What you got in the basket, Sheriff?" a voice
called.

J.T. ignored the question. He strode forward, scanning the crowd. It was a picnic, wasn't it? So he carried
a picnic basket. What was in it was none of anyone's
business. And besides— Aha! There she was. His prey.
He tightened his hold on the basket and strode forward.

Jassie almost died of horror. She couldn't mistake
those broad shoulders. Nor that slow pantherish stride,
which was striding, she suddenly realized, in her direction. Through the parted waters of the picnicking
crowd.

Hastily she scrambled to her feet, and as casually as
possible—given she had a hundred or so people inter-
estedly observing—she hurried in the opposite direction,
heading for a dense thicket of bush on the edge of the
picnic field.

Sheriff Stone lengthened his stride.

The watching crowd heaved a collective sigh as Jassie, looking as though she were competing in an Olym-
pic-class walking race, disappeared into the woods, followed closely by the tall figure of the sheriff.

"Wonder what he's got in that basket?" some soul
inquired. But no one answered, they were busy specu-
lating on how much money they were about to win. Or
lose.

Jassie glanced behind her. Oh, heavens, he was gain-
ing on her. Still determined to not be caught fleeing
from him, she broke into an odd kind of walking trot,
then started to jog, as if she'd suddenly decided to get
fit. He continued to close in on her. Giving up all pre-
tense, Jassie ran. So did he.

She ran up small hills and darted behind rocky out-
crops. She clambered over rocks and plunged into thick
clusters of vegetation. Twigs caught in her hair, in her

clothing and long grass whipped against the bared skin of her shins.

And all the time Sheriff Stone gained on her effortlessly, like Puss-in-Boots in his seven league boots.

"What—" puff "—do you think—" puff, puff "—you're following me for, Sheriff?" she called, and raced down a slope.

He didn't reply, just came on like the Terminator. She caught a glimpse of his face and her pulse leaped with fright. He looked absolutely furious.

"Can't a girl—" puff "—get some privacy—" puff "—without being followed?" Puff. She clung to a large pine tree, gasping for breath, while she looked frantically around for a place to hide. She could hear him, just seconds behind her. She set off for a clump of rocks. "Why can't you just leav— Aaargh!" She tripped on a gnarled and twisted root poking above the ground and came down hard on a bed of pine needles.

"Ooof!" she gasped as a big masculine body came down over her in true caveman style, pinning her firmly to the ground.

"Are you hurt?" he growled, running his hands over her body.

"No, no thanks to—" Jassie stopped, catching sight of his face. "I'm fine," she muttered, and looked away from him, trying to not savor the feeling of his body pressing hers into the soft piney carpet. She could smell the scent of him, mingling with the smell of earth and crushed pine needles. Her heart was racing and her breath came in quick pants. So did his. It was very...evocative.

He glared down at her, one hand cupping the back of her head, the other still running over her body as if checking for broken bones. "Did you have to take to your heels in front of the whole damn town?"

Jassie closed her eyes as the full import of her actions came home to her. She'd humiliated him once again—in public. Oh, God, he probably wanted to murder her.

He could bury her body in these pine needles. They were thick enough.

"I'm sorry. I didn't think," she muttered.

"That's right. You often don't."

There was a short pause, broken by the sounds of their heavy breathing and, in the distance, the chirrup of calling birds. It was now or never, thought Jassie. It was time she said her piece.

She'd been planning to say it for weeks now, but kept chickening out. But her time had come. She took a deep breath, stared past his left ear at a nearby rock, and said quietly, "I'm sorry about all the things I've done to you. I'm sorry about the things I said about you in the paper. I-it was unforgivable."

He paused for a moment. She could feel the faint warmth of his breath on her averted cheek. "Why did you do it?" he said.

The million-dollar question. And she couldn't avoid it. Jassie swallowed. "I—I was attracted to you. I'm sorry." She wasn't courageous enough to look at his face, to see…what? Fury…mockery…pity…

"You mean, you were chasing me? In front of the whole town?"

Well of course I was, you great idiot! she screamed silently. *Do I have to spell it out in words a mile high? Do you have to humiliate me totally and completely?* "Yes," she mumbled, staring at a rock.

"So," he continued, as if he were addressing a courtroom, "you admit you're attracted to me and this attraction was so strong it led you to chase me in front of the entire town of Bear Claw. It didn't matter to you that people would notice, or even that people were laying bets on the outcome?"

It sounded appalling when he put it like that. Jassie squirmed inside. "No," she whispered in a tiny voice. "I'm very sorry."

"Right," he said in a completely different tone. Holding her firmly against him, he suddenly flipped over and

Jassie found herself lying on top of him. He continued. "Now that we've got that straight, you'd better do something about it."

"Do?" Jassie mumbled. "About what?"

"About me." He grinned wickedly and stretched, making Jassie aware of their extremely intimate position. She hurried to climb off him, but two steel-like arms snapped around her and she couldn't budge.

"I said, what are you going to do?" he repeated.

"What are you talking about?" Jassie pushed at his chest. "I don't understand!"

"You've been chasing me, right?"

Jassie nodded. "And I said I'm sorr—"

"Well, now you've caught me, what are you going to do about it?"

"Caught you?" Jassie pushed hard at the iron muscles holding her firmly on top of him. "What do you mean, I've caught you? It was you who chased me—over hill and dale, over rock and…and—whatever, and then you jumped on me like—" She stopped struggling and stared at him in confusion. "What…"

He grinned and hooked a hand gently around her neck. The expression in his eyes took her breath away. "You caught me, Jassie McQuilty," he said softly. "Weeks ago, if the truth be told. And I'm completely and utterly helpless." His hand tightened.

"Helpless," she murmured as her mouth was lowered slowly onto his. "Some kind of helpless."

It was her last coherent thought for some time. The world faded away and all she could do was feel. Feel his mouth as it explored hers, feel his pleasure and excitement as he tasted her, and feel her own reactions spinning out of control as they never had before in her life—except in his arms.

She lay on top of him, savoring the slow, masterful motions of his lips and tongue, the slow erotic caress of his big warm hands over her body as he pulled her closer, fitting her curves to the angles and planes of his.

His hands slid around the curve of her bottom and caressed and molded her. They slid down her legs and smoothed and stroked them, slipping up under the loose shorts to stroke the tender skin hidden beneath them.

She plunged her fingers into his wonderful crispy hair and returned his kisses, blindly, passionately, deliriously. She felt his hands pushing up her blouse, sliding caressingly over the planes of her back and she arched her body to give him room to pull the blouse off over her head.

He stared up at her, stared at her breasts barely hidden by a lacy bra. She looked down at him, at the buttons on his shirt and frantically started pulling at them.

"Easy, love, easy. One at a time," he murmured, and she wrestled with buttons as he lifted his head and nuzzled at the lace, nipping gently at the hard little nubbins that had risen to meet him and were butting against their confinement. Jassie gasped at the sensation and all ability to deal with buttons seemed to seep away. She plucked helplessly at his shirt, her eyes closed in ecstasy as he teased first one lace-covered nipple, then another. Smiling he slipped his hand around behind her and unfastened the clasp. Jassie watched as the bra slowly slid down her arms and landed on his chest.

She stared at it a moment, tossed it aside absentmindedly and returned to the battle of the buttons, her concentration ebbing and flowing like the tide as he brushed back and forth over her tender breasts with his knuckles. He lifted his head and took one engorged pink nipple in his mouth and she almost screamed in pleasure and ripped open his shirt. So that's why his buttons didn't work, she realized vaguely. They were snap fasteners.

His skin was so beautiful, warm and smooth, like stone-washed silk, and he seemed to purr like a big golden lion as she ran her hands over each muscle and stroked each plane. She arched uncontrollably as he tasted her breasts again and again, and scratched lightly around his own small male nipples, circling them and grazing them in a slow tantalizing rhythm that matched the one he was creating in her own body.

She felt his hands sliding under the waistband of her shorts. He unzipped them and pulled them down her legs in a slow, sensuous glide. She dealt quickly with the fastening of his pants. Thank goodness for snap fasteners and zippers! She might never have gotten this far with a button fly...

And then they were skin to skin, as they had been once before. Only this time the moisture on their skin was generated by the heat passing between them. She licked his skin, tasting salt and sweat and man—her man. She reached for him and her hand closed around him and began to caress him. And she was wet and aching and frantic and empty and more than ready and he was hard and throbbing and she wanted him—now! She wanted him and she began to grope and fondle and struggle into position.

"Slow down, love," he murmured, and gently removed her hand.

"I want you, John T., now...please..."

He smiled and kissed her on the mouth again, and as they kissed she felt him lift her and position her over his rigidity and then she felt herself slide over him. Taking him deeper into her than she'd ever taken any man in her life. And then he rolled, very carefully and began to move inside her and...oh-hhh...

Sensations crashed over her as the power of his body pumped through her and built to a slow frantic crescendo, higher and higher, until she felt stretched to the brink...poised to shatter...hovering on the edge of...

And then she climaxed, in waves and waves of glorious intensity. And he came with her, and together they shuddered and merged and clung tight as the storm swept through them and dashed them into oblivion.

JASSIE LAY SPRAWLED on top of him, boneless and dreamy and saturated with pleasure. Her face was

tucked into the curve of his jaw and she was enjoying
the faint prickle of his whiskers against her cheek and
the beat of his heart against hers.... She never wanted
to move from here in her life. Sun trickled through the
branches overhead and lay dappled on the fragrant
brown carpet of leaves. A breeze stirred the grasses
languidly, sending a whisper of coolness over her skin.
But Jassie was warm, right through to her bones. She'd
never felt so good. He was holding her, one arm protective and supporting, the other moving in slow, sensual strokes over her skin, making her feel...beautiful.
Cherished. Beloved.

It was funny, she thought. She'd always imagined
the first time they came together would be frantic, but
this...

The sun sifted through the branches of the trees,
slowly and lazily, catching glittering motes of dust as
they drifted around. She felt like that, all drifty and
warm and filled with sunlight, securely anchored to the
lovely warm man beneath her.

She rubbed her cheek against him, loving the sensuous rasp of his whiskers against her smooth skin. His
arms tightened and she snuggled lower on his body,
feeling incredibly content. She smiled as she felt her
ear being kissed and sighed with pleasure. She felt far
too content to move a single muscle, every single fiber
in her body was completely and utterly satiated.

There was a chittering in the treetops overhead and
a tiny showering of leaves. Jassie watched as they
floated languidly to the ground, flickering in and out
of the sunbeams and eventually coming to rest beside
a basket. The basket was lying on its side a few feet
away from her.

Jassie smiled. What a man. Chasing her through the
woods, over hill and dale, over rock and precipice, and
all the time carrying his picnic basket. She smiled and
planted a tiny kiss on his chest. She liked a man who
was tenacious. He'd certainly been tenacious about

chasing her. She smiled again as she recalled his words, *You've caught me.... I'm in your power—have been for weeks...* So-oo sweet.

She lay there, savoring the feeling of being draped completely on top of him. Her eyes returned to the basket. He must have brought something special to the picnic...maybe fried chicken...or ham...potato salad... fresh rolls perhaps...

Previously satiated fibers suddenly began to stir within Jassie, declaring themselves in need of attention, specifically nourishment. It suddenly occurred to her that, apart from that frightful green cardboardy thing that Dora had made her eat earlier, she hadn't eaten all day. Her fibers had been pretty darn busy, too, and were now clamoring for food.

"Um, John T.?"

"Hmm?" he murmured, continuing to stroke her.

She sighed. He really was a lovely stroker. But Jassie could be stroked and fed, surely. The two activities were not mutually exclusive.

"What's in the basket?"

"The bask—?" His voice changed. "Oh, the basket."

She lifted her head and looked at him. He looked faintly sheepish and completely wicked. He grinned. "You want to know what's in the basket, eh?"

She nodded. The man was purely irresistible.

He sat up with a surge of energy and she found herself sitting across his lap. She blushed, feeling naked and exposed, but she forgot that when he kissed her again. With one arm hooked firmly and possessively around her, he reached out and dragged the basket closer.

Jassie craned forward as he flipped open the lid. She was dying to know what was in it. She hadn't been able to get the thought of fried chicken and potato salad out of her mind. She was starving.

He pulled out a crumpled, greasy-looking paper bag

and a flask of what Jassie hoped might be hot coffee. Her face fell. Was that all? She supposed there might be some chicken pieces in the bag. Fried chicken would make grease stains and men probably didn't know about plastic wrap. She glanced at him hopefully. His gorgeous green eyes glinted devilishly and she realized it didn't matter all that much what was in the bag. As long as it was cold fried chicken.

He handed her the bag. and she pulled it open and looked inside. Her mouth fell open, slack with disappointment.

"Doughnuts?" She couldn't believe it. "You brought doughnuts to a picnic? And that's all?" Then she realized she was sounding ungrateful. "Oh, well, I'm sure they'll be fine. It's just…I prefer them hot."

He chuckled and she felt herself turning to mush at the sound. "It's okay," he murmured in a throaty growl. "I'm sure we'll find some way to warm them up."

"Warm them up?" She glanced around the piney woods, half expecting to see a microwave pop up somewhere. But there was no microwave in sight. Not even an electric socket. She turned back to him. He had pulled one of the doughnuts out of the sack and was holding it in a very…unusual way… Jassie's mouth dropped open again.

"Allow me to demonstrate," he murmured, bringing it toward her. His eyes were smiling in pure wicked devilry and Jassie felt herself melting all over again…

"YOU KNOW, you've become a danger to the community," John T. murmured after a while. He blew in her ear to wake her up. The golden afternoon sunlight was starting to fade and he wanted to get her home to bed. His home. His bed.

Jassie stirred. "Hmm?" she replied intelligently.

J.T. grinned and pulled her into a slightly more upright position. "Yup, a real danger to the community, all right."

"Whah? Who says?" she muttered, trying to snuggle down again.

He blew in her ear and she batted at it sleepily. "Danger," he murmured. "Just as much as a wild bear...or a wolf."

"Huh, what!" Jassie sat up with a jerk. "Danger?" Her head swiveled frantically and she clutched at him. "Bears and wolves? Where?"

He chuckled and passed her her shirt. "No bears, no wolves. Not yet anyway. I reckon we've been making so much noise that most wild animals would be scared off."

Jassie blushed furiously. It hadn't been "we" who'd been making all the noise. But she was sure she hadn't been loud enough to scare off animals. And even if it had been, it wasn't very nice of him to say so.

She glared down her nose at him in what she hoped was a dignified reproof as she allowed him to stuff her arms into the sleeves of her shirt. "In that case, what did you mean, danger. There can't be much more dangerous than a bear or a wolf—" She clutched him suddenly. "Oh, heavens! You don't mean there's a mountain lion, do you?" She glanced fearfully around her. Montana was really untamed.

He chuckled. "No cats, either, I reckon. They've got real good ears... Mind you they can be curious." He was teasing her, she realized. Scaring the wits out of her while he did up her buttons.

He continued, "What I said was, you've become a danger to the community."

She pushed his hands away from the buttons. "I can do that. What do you mean, I'm a danger to the community? I'm not. I'm a—"

He silenced her with a kiss. "You're a danger to my peace of mind." He kissed her again. "And I'm the sheriff and it's my job to protect the commun—"

Jassie smiled. "Oh-hh, are you now? Well, if you're the sheriff, where's your star, hmm?" She grabbed him by the shirt and started to undo the snaps. "Where is it, eh? Show us your star, Mr. Sheriff..."

He laughed and pushed her hands aside.

"Hey, I'm not finished with you, lawman," she growled and, pulling him closer, kissed him.

J.T. LAY IN THE REMNANTS of the afternoon glow, sometime later, his emotions in turmoil. He felt like a traveler who, having wandered the whole of his life, had suddenly found himself at the place he wanted to call home. He felt his pulse start to pound. He'd never expected to come to this, ever again. But this time it felt so right, so good. This time he could depend on his feelings.

He sat up and refastened his shirt. "C'mon, Jassie, honey. It's getting dark and we better get back. Here." He passed her clothes over and she started to struggle into them.

"Gonna take me into protective custody, hey, Mr. Sheriff?" she teased, zipping up her shorts with a wiggle and a wink.

J.T. looked at her, his heart full. She looked so beautiful, her hair all mussed with bits of grass and pine needles sticking out of it, her soft, soft skin all flushed and a little abraded from where his bristles had scratched her. She was radiant, wriggling into her clothes, teasing him, laughing. No one had ever looked at him with such a look of pure happiness and love.

Not ever. Not for John T. Stone. But *she* did. She was brimming over with it. There was no way she could hide it. He could feel her seeping into his cracks and crannies. And, oh, it was a good feeling.

His face was oddly stiff as he fought to contain his feelings. He felt his throat working. He had to do it. Had to say it now, while he had the courage. "Protective custody? Yep, I reckon I am."

Jassie poked her tongue out at him. "So, how long you reckon my sentence will be, lawman?"

John T. Stone took a deep breath. He forced the

words out, feeling them scrape against his throat. "I reckon the only thing that's going to satisfy me is a life sentence."

Jassie froze. She felt as if she'd suddenly flipped into a parallel universe. One minute she'd been joking and teasing and the birds were singing and everything was fun and light and blissful. And the next minute it seemed as though his joke about a life sentence was a matter of life and death.

She looked into his face and felt as if a cold hand had gripped her insides. He was deadly serious. His eyes were somber and the expression in them took her breath away.

Jassie took an involuntary step backward. This was way too intense.

"I'm asking you to marry me, Jassie."

Jassie was stunned. "But...but I'd only planned on a fling, John T.," she blurted. "I—I'm planning to leave Bear Claw in a year."

"Leaving? A year?"

Jassie nodded slowly. "I have to run *The Globe* for a year before I own it outright. I can't sell it until then..."

He straightened and stared at her as if he'd never really seen her before. "You're selling *The Globe?*"

She nodded.

"And you're heading back to the Big Apple?"

She nodded again, feeling absolutely dreadful.

There was a long silence. All Jassie could hear was the whispering of the wind in the pines. A wind that had grown suddenly cooler. She shivered and protectively wrapped her arms around herself. His eyes followed the movement, blankly, like chips of dead green ice. The sun disappeared.

Finally he spoke. "So...I was just a...a stud to keep you...satisfied until you went back to your real life." He didn't wait for her response, just bent down over the picnic basket and started to pack the flask into it.

Jassie watched, shaking, biting her lip, unable to say anything. It *had* been what she'd planned originally. But it sounded so...somehow...dirty...when he said it. She felt sick. She wanted to go to him, to reassure him, to say it wasn't like that...

But it was. She'd picked him out for a hot fling the moment she'd fallen out of the bus and landed in his arms.

He picked up the bag with one last remaining doughnut inside it and looked at it. His mouth twisted painfully and he stood and hurled the bag as far and as hard as he could into the woods. They both watched it disappear, but Jassie didn't see it land. Tears blurred her vision.

"Come on, lady," he said bitterly. "Picnic day is over." He started to walk back in the direction they had come, then he paused and looked over his shoulder at her. The look pierced her with its painful corrosiveness. "And so—in case you're wondering—are we." He strode off through the woods.

BY THE TIME they got back to the picnic area there were only a few people remaining. Don and Dora were long gone. Jassie's heart sank, realizing she was going to have to ask the sheriff for a ride home. She hesitated. Maybe she could get a ride with someone else.

"Find any orange blossom in the woods, Jassie?" someone called out. He was hastily shushed by his wife.

The sheriff didn't pause. He strode though the scattered remains of the picnic, heading directly for his dark green pickup. Eyes watched his progress speculatively. Avidly.

Jassie shriveled with shame. She'd forgotten the betting. She could almost hear the talk. Had they? Hadn't they? It was unbearable. She hurried after him. She couldn't ask anyone else for a ride—she couldn't bear to talk to them, to know what they were thinking.

Orange blossom! Of course they were thinking in

terms of weddings. And so was he. This was a small town. People didn't have flings—well, they did, but not openly, the way Jassie had been acting. God, what a fool she'd been. No, she was much worse than a fool. She was criminally stupid, cruel, thoughtless and selfish.

She'd never forget the desperate pain she'd seen in his eyes the moment before he'd clammed up and become all cold and businesslike.

Oh, God, she'd never wanted to hurt him. She loved him too much to ever want to hurt him, loved him too much to ever see him—

Jassie came to an abrupt halt.

She loved him?

He was the most beautiful, wonderful man she'd ever known, but was that love? Would she still think he was beautiful if he went bald and lost his teeth and got fat? Jassie thought about it and discovered the answer was yes. Amazing.

She stood stock-still, testing out this radical new notion in her mind. *She loved him?* She considered it. If it was love, it wasn't like anything she'd ever experienced in her life. She hadn't felt so wonderful with anyone else—ever. Or been so miserable in her life. Not even when she'd found out about Murdock. Murdock? Murdock was a flea bite compared to John T.

John T....she would rather cut off her arms than put him through another moment of the hurt she'd glimpsed in his eyes back there...

She loved Sheriff John T. Stone!

"You staying or going?" John T. stopped and called to her. "Doesn't matter which to me."

Jassie blinked and stared at him blankly. She loved him. *Of course* she did. How could she think a person who'd barely even flirted in her life before could turn around like that and embark on a red-hot fling—in public, no less.

She hadn't been starting a fling. She'd fallen madly, deeply, desperately head over heels in love.

"Okay, suit yourself." He climbed into the pickup and roared off. Jassie stood and watched him, dumb-founded.

Marriage? Marriage she could handle. Marriage—if she was honest with herself—was what she'd always craved. A man to love who'd love her back. Forever. And marriage to John T. was her idea of heaven. She thought of waking up every morning for the rest of her life to see that slow, teasing smile.

A tear trickled down one cheek. Oh, yes, she wanted to marry him. So much so, she hadn't let herself even consider the possibility.

But a lifetime living in The Sticks?

She sat among the remnants of the town picnic and considered the past few months in Bear Claw. Small-town life was not as boring as she'd imagined. There was crime, sort of, to report, and there was certainly plenty of intrigue, gossip, politics and economic wheel-ing and dealing—on a slightly smaller scale than New York, true, but every bit as important and newsworthy to the locals. And they read every word she wrote and responded to it.

Now that was a career.

What did she really have waiting for her in New York? More lifestyle fluff and arguments with narrow-minded editors like Jake Kransky, no doubt. Here, as owner, editor, reporter and printer, she could please herself.

And she was doing good things here in Bear Claw. No one could claim the world was a better place be-cause Jassie McQuilty had discovered the latest pasta bar for New Yorkers to flock to. But here in Bear Claw, she was fostering the careers of two promising young people, Tommy and Josh. And over time she could continue that. She liked working with young people.

The paper was going to be a success. And she'd expanded the business, printing Missy Baines's West-ern fashion brochures as well as all sorts of other things.

People had said the new *Globe* was bringing new energy to the town. In New York, she had been able to change or to influence nothing. Here she contributed to the life of the town. She didn't need to go back to New York to have a career she could be proud of. She had the best of all possible careers right here in Bear Claw. And the best of all possible men.

"Hey, Jassie, you want a ride with us?" It was Ben Broome. His teeth were smiling, but Ben looked concerned and sympathetic.

"No, Ben, she's coming with Randy and me," called Missy Baines. She was standing beside a shiny green Mustang convertible. A blond man sat in the driver's seat. "Don and Dora asked me to take care of her...in case, you know. They would have waited, but the bus, you know. People had to go."

Jassie's eyes blurred with tears. She had friends in Bear Claw, better friends than most of the people she knew in the city, apart from Rita. They hadn't waited here just to pry and gossip, they'd stayed to look after her, in case she blew it. Which she had.

Jassie thanked Missy and her escort, Randy, and climbed into the back seat of Randy's Mustang convertible. It was a very luxurious car, she thought miserably. She preferred trucks now.

She watched Ben Broome drive away, half a dozen kids hanging off the back of his truck. His grandkids, Jassie realized. Bear Claw would be a fantastic place to bring up kids....

Children... The bus crash had taught Jassie how much she wanted kids of her own. She recalled the feeling of holding little Dawn Sky in her arms, the bittersweet joy of those skinny little arms winding themselves around her neck. The feeling of being needed, the joy of offering comfort and love. John T. loved children, too, she could tell by the way he'd dealt with Dawn Sky.

A vision popped into her head of John T. holding a

child in his arms, a little girl with green eyes and a mop of dark curls. Or a sturdy-limbed little boy filthy from playing in the mud, smiling through the dirt with crystal-green mischief...

She was shaking, Jassie realized. Shaking because she wanted it so much.

Oh, God, why had she ever thought she wanted to leave? She had all the ingredients for a wonderful life right here in Bear Claw...and the most important ingredient was love.

She'd been offered love not an hour ago, after an afternoon of the purest, most heavenly bliss Jassie had ever experienced in her life. Or even dreamed of.

The love of the most wonderful, beautiful man in the world.

He'd offered it to her with naked, needy eyes, a commitment to love and to protect her for the rest of her life. And need and desire had just poured from him, the need for Jassie McQuilty in his life. Desire for Jassie McQuilty.

And what had Jassie McQuilty done with the most precious gift she had ever received in her life?

Tossed it away. Clumsily. Brutally. Trampling on his tender feelings like a great idiotic ox. Hurting, most grievously, the one man in the world who loved her. Whom she loved with all her heart.

And now, having destroyed her chance of seeing almost every dream she'd ever had come true, how was she to go on?

She allowed Missy and Randy to drive her home. In the shiny green Mustang convertible. In silence. With tears pouring down her face.

9

TIMES WERE TOUGH for men like him, J.T. thought resentfully. Basically he was the primitive type. He wanted to ride into town, toss her over his saddle and ride out again. And then show her where she belonged. And with whom.

But that was the old-fashioned way. The sexist way. He sighed. It was hell being a feminist.

If he wasn't, he might have done just that. Not the horse, maybe. He wasn't a good enough rider to manage a horse and a struggling female, as well. He'd toss her gently into the pickup and take her back to his cabin. And there he'd set about convincing her to— Ah, shoot. Kidnapping. False imprisonment. He was becoming a creep as well as a bad feminist. Frustration did terrible things to a man.

"Delivery for you, Sheriff."

J.T. looked up from contemplating his paperwork. It was Tommy Stewart. "Yes, Tommy," he said wearily. He couldn't seem to be interested in much of anything these days.

"It's a special edition of *The Globe*. Miss Jassie says for your eyes only," Tommy added in an aggrieved tone. He handed over a large sealed envelope, his eyes alive with curiosity.

J.T. took it gingerly. He didn't know what he thought about this new development. Why the hell did the woman do all her communicating through the damned newspaper! He supposed she was going to blast him for his assumption. He'd done a lot of thinking since the picnic and he'd come to the conclusion he was as much at fault as she was—almost. He'd rushed her, made assumptions that she felt the same way about him as he did about her...

He realized Tommy was still standing there watching curiously. "Thanks, Tommy."

Tommy didn't move.

"You can go now," said J.T. firmly.

Dragging his feet, Tommy went.

Cautiously, as if it was a letter bomb, J.T. opened the big envelope. In it was a single-page issue of *The Globe*, folded in two. The front cover was blank, except for the name. It was marked "Special Edition" and where the normal paper had its circulation statistics, it read, "Circulation—1." At least the whole world wasn't going to read whatever she thought of him this time. He took a deep breath and opened the paper to the center spread. A lump came into his throat.

Except for one long article down the middle, every inch of the double-page spread, from top margin to bottom, from one side to the other, was covered with advertisements. But they were not like any advertisement he'd ever seen before.

Every one of the ads said, "Jassie McQuilty Loves John T. Stone" in every possible print, typeface and design. Some were covered in hearts, others wreathed in flowers. In some the words were stark and bold, in others, subtly placed in a romantic design. They represented hours and hours of painstaking work.

His eyes blurred as he read them. Finally he forced himself to look at the big, central article. The headline was big and bold.

Jassie McQuilty Was Wrong

He read on...

This is a story about a city girl who came to the country for just a year. She came, telling herself she could handle anything—even a year in what she disparagingly referred to as ''The Sticks.''

His mouth felt dry and his heart was pounding. He continued...

She told herself she was cynical and sophisticated enough to have a fling. Not that she'd ever had one before, but that's what she thought she wanted. She even thought she'd found the perfect man to have a fling with.

And he was the perfect man...

But not for a fling.

The perfect man... He pulled out a handkerchief and blew his nose. Then kept reading...

She found gold and thought it was the dross she'd always known in the city. She was too stupid to realize she could never go back to live in the city, because you can't live in the city—or anywhere else—without a heart...

And Jassie McQuilty's heart will stay forever in Bear Claw—or wherever John T. Stone lives. Because her heart will forever belong to him. Whether he wants it anymore or not.

Jassie McQuilty has never met a man as fine and decent and honorable as Sheriff John T. Stone.

Nor a man as beautiful.

Nor a more wonderful, sensitive, utterly bliss-making lover.

Beautiful? Bliss-making? J.T. closed his eyes for a long moment, until the shaking stopped, then forced himself to keep on reading...

She regrets more than she's ever regretted anything in her life that she caused him hurt.

Jassie McQuilty apologizes with all her heart to John T. Stone.

She wants to tell him, and the world, that she loves him and will love him for the rest of her life. But she is a miserable coward and cannot bear to face rejection in his eyes—if there is rejection.

She begs his forgiveness.

And waits in desperate hope...

At the bottom of the article was written by hand, *I love you so much, John T. Please forgive me.* And it was signed with a dozen kisses.

"Uh, Sheriff?"

J.T. looked up from the paper impatiently. "What is it, Norbett?" He felt the deputy staring at him and dashed his hand over his eyes. "Damned dust in my eyes. You need to get this place cleaned up!"

Norbett glanced around the immaculate office and shrugged. "Okay, but—" he scratched his head, puzzled "—there's this, well they said it was an emergency, but the note says it's attention Sheriff Stone and...it's kinda weird..." He shook his head. "Anyway, it came in a minute or two ago and I don't quite kn—"

J.T. frowned. "Emergency? What emergency?"

Norbett scratched his head again and stared at the piece of paper in his hand. "It's from *The Globe* office—"

J.T. leaped to his feet. "*The Globe!*" He snatched the note from his deputy and scanned it anxiously. Then he straightened and carefully tucked the small paper into his breast pocket. "I'll deal with this," he said. He saw Norbett's eyes stray curiously to his desk and he hastily swept the special edition of *The Globe* into a drawer and locked it. "Evidence," he muttered. "Right, better get to this emergency."

Norbett stared. "You reckon it's worth checking out, then?"

John T. Stone smiled. "Definitely," he said softly, and reached for his hat.

Norbett scratched his head. "I dunno. What sort of break-in is it when the only thing that's stolen is doughnuts? And the note didn't say nothing about chasin' thieves, it says bring more doughnuts."

"That's right, Norbett," said the sheriff, "so I'd better fetch them right away. The note did say it was an emergency, didn't it? And you...you clean this office!"

THE DOOR to *The Globe* office was unlocked, but there was no one around. J.T. hefted the bag of hot doughnuts to his other hand and carefully locked the door behind him. He headed for the stairs.

She was in the room with the big green sofa, as he thought—hoped—she would be.

Holding the bag behind him, he pushed open the door and they stared at each other in silence. Her eyes were red, he noticed. As was the tip of her nose. Her hair was a mess and she was wearing those damn silly pajamas and those ridiculous slippers.

But her heart was in her eyes.

And she had never looked more beautiful to him.

"You didn't bring doughnuts," she said tragically.

Silently he brought his hand out from behind and showed her the package.

Some of the rigidity went out of her. "Are you going to let me have one?" she said hesitantly.

He shrugged and tossed the bag onto the coffee table.

"Forgive me, John T.?" she whispered, her eyes huge with entreaty.

"Depends," he said.

There was a long pause.

"On what?" she breathed.

"Do you want to build with me?"

"Build with you, John?" Jassie looked confused. "You mean, as in—"

"I mean as in us getting married. Building a family. And staying together for the next forty or fifty years."

She stared at him for a long, long moment. J.T. thought he'd explode if she didn't say something soon. She'd gone pale— Oh, hell. She wasn't—

"Oh, John T.!" Jassie shot out of the sofa and hurled herself at him. "Oh, yes, yes, yes! A thousand times, yes. I never thought you'd ask me again. I thought I'd really blown it before and that you'd never forgive me. Oh, John T., I love you so much." She feverishly began to plant little kisses all over him, wherever she could reach.

And John T. Stone just stood there, stock-still and let her.

She was going to build with him.

She was going to build with him!

He let out a whoop of joy and lifted her clear off her feet to plant the biggest, hottest kiss ever on her eager mouth.

Jassie McQuilty was going to build with him. And he was going to build with her. Forever.

"Oh, Jassie, honey, I love you so much, you'll never kn—" But her face was wet with tears and he couldn't go on, he was too choked up himself. So he just held on to her and let her cry and kiss him. And she held on to him and let him kiss her and pretend not to cry.

And after a while she led him into her other room to show him the big new bed she'd bought.

"I'm going to…" he muttered after a while.

"What? What was that, John T.?"

"I'm going to trust you with my crannies," he mumbled.

Jassie blinked, then smiled blissfully. "And you're welcome to my crannies, too, my darling. You do such lovely things with them."

J.T. stared at her a moment, then a slow grin crossed his face. "That isn't quite what I meant, love, but I'll take you up on the offer anyway." He lowered his mouth toward a very appealing cranny...

And afterward, they held on to each other all night. The way they planned to for the next forty or fifty years....

THE SUN POURED IN over the wooden floor of Jassie's upstairs room at *The Globe.* She smiled, enjoying the warmth, and the way the light glinted on the dark crispy curls of the man who lay beside her. He was sound asleep, but his mouth curled in a catlike expression of satisfaction. A big, contented, mountain lion's satisfaction. She and J.T. had had a blissful night. And she'd experienced what had to be the most decidedly blissful early morning awakening of her life...

She probably looked like the cat that ate the canary herself, she reflected, unable to stop smiling. She snuggled into the pale green sheets and curled against her man. And felt something bumping her. She explored a little with her hand. Another flagpole in the bed? Already? The man was insatiable. But then, so was she... She smiled and feigned sleep.

"Mornin', beautiful," he murmured in her ear. "Got anything planned for the next couple hours or so?"

"Mmm, actually, yes. I'm planning something..."

"What sort of something?" He nibbled at her bare shoulder and moved on, leaving a trail of pleasure behind him.

"A headline, actually," she said, arching into him. "I might be marrying you, John T., but I've still got my career to think of..." She found the flagpole and caressed it lightly. "My career as editor of *The Globe.* And it's only, um, four days to the next edition."

J.T. smiled. She was planning some big sentimental announcement about their wedding, he could tell. White lace and orange blossom, something borrowed, something blue—all that stuff. The romantic trappings were mighty important to women, he knew.

Him, he didn't care. As long as they stayed together, building, for the rest of his life, he didn't care if they got married by mail order, down a mine, or in the middle of a wheat field, as long as they got married and stayed married. But women were more romantic than men. "So what's this headline you're considering," he murmured indulgently.

Jassie grinned and gave the flagpole a friendly little pat. "I thought, 'Sheriff Proves Virility Question—*The Globe* Editor More Than Satisfied.'"

J.T. sat up like a shot. "You wouldn't dare!"

Giggling, she lay back against the pillows. "You planning on interfering with the freedom of the press, John T.? That's mighty unconstitutional of you. And you a lawman!"

He fixed her with a glare, then smiled as an idea came to him. "Go right ahead, honey, put whatever headline you want to. I don't mind." He grinned evilly, his eyes lit with the fiendish gleam she loved so much and trusted so little.

"What are you planning?" she said suspiciously.

His grin widened and he pulled her against him. "I wouldn't dream of interfering with the freedom of the press…" He settled her down in delightful proximity to the flagpole. "But if you print another headline about my virility—" he gave a little movement that left her gasping "—or otherwise…well, I suppose I'll have to take control of our social life."

Jassie scowled. "So, what's the big deal about that?"

"No big deal." He picked up one of her fluffy dog slippers that lay on the sheets and smoothed the hair out of its big sad eyes. "Just dinner with Don and Dora. Every week. For the next forty or fifty years…"

There was a long silence. Broken only by the sound of someone breathing through her nose.

"I knew you were a rat the moment I saw you," she said finally.

"No, you didn't. You thought I was the most gorgeous thing you'd ever seen in your life. You told me so last night, remember?''

She thumped him with her pillow. ''Smugness is very unattractive in a man.'' She pulled on a T-shirt.

''Who says?'' He pulled it off her.

''Me. I said so.'' She threw the T-shirt onto the floor.

He snorted. And pulled her close for a long sweet kiss. She cooperated with her usual enthusiasm, and then said, ''I'm the editor, buster.''

''So?'' he said, arranging the editor's limbs in a position more to his liking.

''Don't you know anything? The editor *always* has the final say!''

''Yeah righhhht,'' murmured J.T.

''Oh-hh, yes, it certainly is,'' gasped the editor blissfully. ''Absolutely…perfectly…wonderfully…right.''

''JOHN T.?''

''Yes, darlin'.''

''About those dinners with Don and Dora.''

''Uh-uh?''

''It's going to be terribly expensive, isn't it?'' Jassie murmured.

''What do you mean, expensive? Dora would be doing the cooking. I didn't mean a restaurant deal.''

''No, but how many handbags are you going to have to buy me if we have a weekly dinner with Don and Dora? Can you really afford it? Hmm?''

Subject: Your love life
Date: Fri August 4 10:00:20
From: <Jassie@dotmail.com>
To: ''Rita DeLorenzo'' <Rita@dotmail.com>

Message: Rita, about what you wrote me in June, you were wrong and you were right.

You said I take love way too seriously—wrong! Love is the most important thing in the world.

You also said there were plenty of hunks in Montana—right! And I've got the hunkiest of all.

Come and see what I'm talking about. You never know, you might find a Montana hunk for yourself. And P.S., bring a bridesmaid's dress.

I am sooooo happy!

love Jassie.

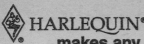

If you enjoyed what you just read,
then we've got an offer you can't resist!

Take 2 bestselling love stories FREE!

Plus get a FREE surprise gift!

Clip this page and mail it to Harlequin Reader Service®

IN U.S.A.
3010 Walden Ave.
P.O. Box 1867
Buffalo, N.Y. 14240-1867

IN CANADA
P.O. Box 609
Fort Erie, Ontario
L2A 5X3

YES! Please send me 2 free Harlequin Duets™ novels and my free surprise gift. After receiving them, if I don't wish to receive anymore, I can return the shipping statement marked cancel. If I don't cancel, I will receive 2 brand-new novels every month, before they're available in stores! In the U.S.A., bill me at the bargain price of $5.14 plus 50¢ shipping & handling per book and applicable sales tax, if any*. In Canada, bill me at the bargain price of $6.14 plus 50¢ shipping & handling per book and applicable taxes**. That's the complete price—what a great deal! I understand that accepting the 2 free books and gift places me under no obligation ever to buy any books. I can always return a shipment and cancel at any time. Even if I never buy another book from Harlequin, the 2 free books and gift are mine to keep forever.

111 HEN DC7P
311 HEN DC7Q

Name	(PLEASE PRINT)	
Address	Apt.#	
City	State/Prov.	Zip/Postal Code

* Terms and prices subject to change without notice. Sales tax applicable in N.Y.
** Canadian residents will be charged applicable provincial taxes and GST.
  All orders subject to approval. Offer limited to one per household and not valid to current Harlequin Duets™ subscribers.
  ® and ™ are registered trademarks of Harlequin Enterprises Limited.

DUETS01

*Harlequin truly does
make any time special....
This year we are celebrating
weddings in style!*

A
Walk
Down
the Aisle
WEDDING CELEBRATION

To help us celebrate, we want you to tell us how wearing the Harlequin wedding gown will make your wedding day special. As the grand prize, Harlequin will offer one lucky bride the chance to **"Walk Down the Aisle" in the Harlequin wedding gown!**

There's more...

For her honeymoon, she and her groom will spend five nights at the **Hyatt Regency Maui.** As part of this five-night honeymoon at the hotel renowned for its romantic attractions, the couple will enjoy a candlelit dinner for two in Swan Court, a sunset sail on the hotel's catamaran, and duet spa treatments.

A HYATT RESORT AND SPA

MAUI
the Magic Isles™
Maui • Molokai • Lanai

To enter, please write, in, 250 words or less, how wearing the Harlequin wedding gown will make your wedding day special. The entry will be judged based on its emotionally compelling nature, its originality and creativity, and its sincerity. This contest is open to Canadian and U.S. residents only and to those who are 18 years of age and older. There is no purchase necessary to enter. Void where prohibited. See further contest rules attached. Please send your entry to:

Walk Down the Aisle Contest

In Canada	In U.S.A.
P.O. Box 637	P.O. Box 9076
Fort Erie, Ontario	3010 Walden Ave.
L2A 5X3	Buffalo, NY 14269-9076

You can also enter by visiting www.eHarlequin.com
Win the Harlequin wedding gown and the vacation of a lifetime!
The deadline for entries is October 1, 2001.

HARLEQUIN®
Makes any time special ®

PHWDACONT1

HARLEQUIN WALK DOWN THE AISLE TO MAUI CONTEST 1197
OFFICIAL RULES
NO PURCHASE NECESSARY TO ENTER

1. To enter, follow directions published in the offer to which you are responding. Contest begins April 2, 2001, and ends on October 1, 2001. Method of entry may vary. Mailed entries must be postmarked by October 1, 2001, and received by October 8, 2001.

2. Contest entry may be, at times, presented via the Internet, but will be restricted solely to residents of certain geographic areas that are disclosed on the Web site. To enter via the Internet, if permissible, access the Harlequin Web site (www.eHarlequin.com) and follow the directions displayed online. Online entries must be received by 11:59 p.m. E.S.T. on October 1, 2001.

   In lieu of submitting an entry online, enter by mail by hand-printing (or typing) on an 8½" x 11" plain piece of paper, your name, address (including zip code), Contest number/name and in 250 words or fewer, why winning a Harlequin wedding dress would make your wedding day special. Mail via first-class mail to: Harlequin Walk Down the Aisle Contest 1197, (in the U.S.) P.O. Box 9076, 3010 Walden Avenue, Buffalo, NY 14269-9076, (in Canada) P.O. Box 637, Fort Erie, Ontario L2A 5X3, Canada.

   Limit one entry per person, household address and e-mail address. Online and/or mailed entries received from persons residing in geographic areas in which Internet entry is not permissible will be disqualified.

3. Contests will be judged by a panel of members of the Harlequin editorial, marketing and public relations staff based on the following criteria:

   - Originality and Creativity—50%
   - Emotionally Compelling—25%
   - Sincerity—25%

   In the event of a tie, duplicate prizes will be awarded. Decisions of the judges are final.

4. All entries become the property of Torstar Corp. and will not be returned. No responsibility is assumed for lost, late, illegible, incomplete, inaccurate, nondelivered or misdirected mail or misdirected e-mail, for technical, hardware or software failures of any kind, lost or unavailable network connections, or failed, incomplete, garbled or delayed computer transmission or any human error which may occur in the receipt or processing of the entries in this Contest.

5. Contest open only to residents of the U.S. (except Puerto Rico) and Canada, who are 18 years of age or older, and is void wherever prohibited by law; all applicable laws and regulations apply. Any litigation within the Province of Quebec respecting the conduct or organization of a publicity contest may be submitted to the Régie des alcools, des courses et des jeux for a ruling. Any litigation respecting the awarding of a prize may be submitted to the Régie des alcools, des courses et des jeux only for the purpose of helping the parties reach a settlement. Employees and immediate family members of Torstar Corp. and D. L. Blair, Inc., their affiliates, subsidiaries and all other agencies, entities and persons connected with the use, marketing or conduct of this Contest are not eligible to enter. Taxes on prizes are the sole responsibility of winners. Acceptance of any prize offered constitutes permission to use winner's name, photograph or other likeness for the purposes of advertising, trade and promotion on behalf of Torstar Corp., its affiliates and subsidiaries without further compensation to the winner, unless prohibited by law.

6. Winners will be determined no later than November 15, 2001, and will be notified by mail. Winners will be required to sign and return an Affidavit of Eligibility form within 15 days after winner notification. Noncompliance within that time period may result in disqualification and an alternative winner may be selected. Winners of trip must execute a Release of Liability prior to ticketing and must possess required travel documents (e.g. passport, photo ID) where applicable. Trip must be completed by November 2002. No substitution of prize permitted by winner. Torstar Corp. and D. L. Blair, Inc., their parents, affiliates, and subsidiaries are not responsible for errors in printing or electronic presentation of Contest, entries and/or game pieces. In the event of printing or other errors which may result in unintended prize values or duplication of prizes, all affected game pieces or entries shall be null and void. If for any reason the Internet portion of the Contest is not capable of running as planned, including infection by computer virus, bugs, tampering, unauthorized intervention, fraud, technical failures, or any other causes beyond the control of Torstar Corp. which corrupt or affect the administration, secrecy, fairness, integrity or proper conduct of the Contest, Torstar Corp. reserves the right, at its sole discretion, to disqualify any individual who tampers with the entry process and to cancel, terminate, modify or suspend the Contest or the Internet portion thereof. In the event of a dispute regarding an online entry, the entry will be deemed submitted by the authorized holder of the e-mail account submitted at the time of entry. Authorized account holder is defined as the natural person who is assigned to an e-mail address by an Internet access provider, online service provider or other organization that is responsible for arranging e-mail address for the domain associated with the submitted e-mail address. **Purchase or acceptance of a product offer does not improve your chances of winning.**

7. Prizes: (1) Grand Prize—A Harlequin wedding dress (approximate retail value: $3,500) and a 5-night/6-day honeymoon trip to Maui, HI, including round-trip air transportation provided by Maui Visitors Bureau from Los Angeles International Airport (winner is responsible for transportation to and from Los Angeles International Airport) and a Harlequin Romance Package, including hotel accomodations (double occupancy) at the Hyatt Regency Maui Resort and Spa, dinner for (2) two at Swan Court, a sunset sail on Kiele V and a spa treatment for the winner (approximate retail value: $4,000); (5) Five runner-up prizes of a $1000 gift certificate to selected retail outlets to be determined by Sponsor (retail value $1000 ea.). Prizes consist of only those items listed as part of the prize. Limit one prize per person. All prizes are valued in U.S. currency.

8. For a list of winners (available after December 17, 2001) send a self-addressed, stamped envelope to: Harlequin Walk Down the Aisle Contest 1197 Winners, P.O. Box 4200 Blair, NE 68009-4200 or you may access the www.eHarlequin.com Web site through January 15, 2002.

Contest sponsored by Torstar Corp., P.O. Box 9042, Buffalo, NY 14269-9042, U.S.A.

PHWDACONT2